The Fibonacci Confessions

About the Author

Graham Wade, writer and musician, living on the East Yorkshire coast, studied English at Cambridge University and is a Fellow of Trinity College of Music, London. He has published over twenty books among them his critically acclaimed biographical studies of the great Spanish composer, Joaquín Rodrigo, the classical guitarists, Andrés Segovia and Julian Bream, and the Greek pianist, Gina Bachauer, as well as works on musical history, and several slim volumes of poems.

In 2002 he was awarded the Schotts Gold Medal for his contribution to Rodrigo studies. He has written for many newspapers and periodicals including *The Times, The Independent,* and *The Guardian.* He is an Advisory Editor and contributor to both the British and American *New Grove Dictionary of Music* and the General Editor of a very successful series of paperbacks on music for a leading publisher in the USA.

The Fibonacci Confessions, the author's first published novel, presents the intimately personal letters of Leonardo Pisano (also known as Fibonacci), mathematician, scholar and traveller, looking back over a lifetime at the follies of youth, travels in North Africa, Egypt, and Syria, the disasters of various amorous affairs, and his endless pursuit of 'the numbers' in a quest which leads to both glorious and tragic consequences.

The Fibonacci Confessions

GRAHAM WADE

THE CHOIR PRESS

THE FIBONACCI CONFESSIONS

First published in Great Britain, ISBN 978-1-901148-09-1,
by GRM Publications 2010

This edition published in 2017
by THE CHOIR PRESS
132 Bristol Road, Gloucester GL1 5SR

ISBN   978-1-910864-83-8

Cover design by Chandler Design Associates Ltd

Set in 11 on 15pt Minion

for Beth

Contents

Historical Note

Leonardo Pisano (*c.* 1170–*c.* 1240), universally referred to as Fibonacci, was the son of Guilielmo Bonacci, a customs official representing the Republic of Pisa working in the Mediterranean port of Bugia (nowadays called Bejaia), Algeria.

The main details we have of Fibonacci's life are contained in his treatise, *Liber Abaci* (first published 1202):

As my father was a public official away from our homeland in the Bugia customs house established for the Pisan merchants who frequently gathered there, he had me in my youth brought to him to be in the study of mathematics and to be taught for some days.

There from a marvellous instruction in the art of the nine Indian figures, the introduction and knowledge of the art pleased me so much above all else, and I learnt from them, whoever was learned in it, from nearby Egypt, Syria, Greece, Sicily and Provence, and their various methods, to which locations of business I travelled considerably afterwards for much study and I learnt from the assembled disputations.

(*Fibonacci's 'Liber Abaci', A translation into Modern English of Leonardo Pisano's Book of Calculation,* L.E. SIGLER, SPRINGER-VERLAG NEW YORK INC., 2002.)

Many scholars, philosophers, artists, writers, kings and emperors, of the Middle Ages, have left a significant amount of biographical evidence. But with Fibonacci there is a tantalising void which this novel takes the opportunity to explore.

Fibonacci achieved immortal fame through his sequence derived from the following problem:

> *A certain man had one pair of rabbits together in a certain enclosed place, and wishes to know how many are created from the pair in one year when it is the nature of them in a single month to bear another pair and in the second month those born to bear also.*

Though this exposition takes up less than a page in Fibonacci's *Liber Abaci's* six hundred pages, these few words have captured the world's imagination ever since.

The Fibonacci Confessions are mainly concerned with how another of his great works, *The Book of Squares,* might have been inspired and created. Fibonacci, telling his own tragic story, keeps few secrets hidden as he passionately pursues his destiny in a medieval world where there are many hazards and few rewards.

GRAHAM WADE
FEBRUARY, 2010

Acknowledgements

The author acknowledges his debt to:

Laurence Sigler, editions of *Fibonacci's Liber Abaci,*
Leonardo Pisano's Book of Calculation (New York: Springer, 2003) and
Leonardo Pisano Fibonacci, The Book of Squares.
(Orlando, Florida: Academic Press, 1987).

Thomas Curtis Van Cleves, *The Emperor Frederick II of Hohenstaufen*
(Oxford: Clarendon Press, 1972).

Michael Chamberlain, *Knowledge and Social Practice in
Medieval Damascus, 1190–1350* (Cambridge University Press, 1994).

Marie Fadel & Schami Rafik, *Damascus, Taste of a City*
(London: Haus Publishing, 2002).

Odile Redon, Françoise Sabban, & Silvano Serventi,
The Medieval Kitchen (University of Chicago Press, 1991).

Maxine Rodinson, A.J. Arberry & Charles Perry,
Medieval Arab Cookery (Totnes: Prospect Books, 2006).

Statue of Leonardo Fibonacci in Camposanto, Pisa

Prefatio & First Letter

*Concerning the repulsive Master John of Palermo
and his wondrous wife, Beatrice.*

Aestuans intrinsecus ira vehementi,
In amaritudine loquor meae menti.
Factus de materia levis elementi,
Folio sum similis de quo ludunt venti.

THE ARCHPOET (*c.* 1130–67)

(Inwardly seething with angry indignation,
To my own heart I speak in sheer frustration.
As an element insubstantial in creation,
I am a leaf subjected to the wind's flirtation.)

Sire, My Admired Master Michael Theodorus,
Doctor of Philosophy to His Glorious Majesty Frederick II,
Holy Roman Emperor.

In reply to your request, I, Leonardo Pisano, mathematician, write to my esteemed friend in whose wisdom I have found good counsel and consolation.

You enquired after *The Book of Squares*, now in the library of His Majesty, how this book came to be written, and other matters.

I am at last pleased to answer and confess all, even concerning the loss of my beloved wife.

I

Having been introduced by Master Dominick to His Celestial Majesty, my Lord Frederick II, Emperor of the Holy Roman Empire, whom should I happen to encounter but that devious hypocrite, Master John of Palermo?

Of course, I knew Master John was little more than an intermediary between His Majesty and such as myself, a lowly scholar, flattered to receive even the least of favours from the finest patron of all the courts of Europe.

I had however hoped for further privileges, invitations to banquets and public occasions, intimacies with practitioners of the arts, diplomats or politicians, even courtesans. But the dreadful Master John, in his tactless manner, conferred few introductions or largesse, unless it suited his purposes.

Instead he handed out an excess of burdens, not least that I had to suffer his condescension and closeness of foul breath.

Among other things, I had to endure the company of his distasteful presence when summoned to dine at his dwelling. For Master John's table manners were not pleasant to behold or hear. Through misfortune with his teeth, some discoloured, Master John made sibilant noises as he masticated. Saliva spurted forth when he spoke. It was inadvisable to be seated too close as he spattered on about this and that.

Even so, there could be no complaints about his banquets, crammed with those lovely dishes accessible to one held in esteem by any number of wealthy sycophants.

As for his choice of wine, well, I can but shiver in envy for this was an ocean of possibilities. Sweet wines of Greece vied with *malvasia* from Liguria, and a cup of Tuscan *trebbiano*, as translucent as a golden fountain, could joust, cheek by jowl, with pink *clairet* from Bordeaux or Burgundy.

To remain sober on these occasions was unwise, especially in view of my loathing of Master John and the contempt which familiarity intensified. By diving into a sea of alcohol, all things became tolerably confused and his conversation more like the burbling of streams or a distant buzzing of bees.

In terms of his cuisine, abundance seduced eyes, nose and mouth with goodness. Following newly picked seasonal fruits, one progressed to pumpkin soup so finely prepared that compliments flew forth almost before the main confrontation had begun.

Ah, but wait for the centrepiece, whether spit-roasted hare, parsley-studded lamb (divinely sauced), or trout in aspic with herbs. Already bursting at the seams, our digestive scruples would be overcome by the *entremets,* Italian blancmange in Tuscan mode or apple jelly candies.

Such dining was topped off by marzipan tart and spice wine sweetened with honey. Then to the drawing room for the *boute-hors* with wine, coriander seed and ginger root to harmonise breath and settle the overwrought stomach.

There was little need to reply to Master John's discourse for indeed he hardly noticed any lack of attention from guests while his wispy beard wagged like a dog's tail or an artist's brush as he intoned thus:

"And as I told him, I knew that he was wrong...and that his position in the court established he was inferior to me...but I, as ever, offered no condescension to him nor awareness of my superior station in life...but only to advise him his ideas were out of favour..."

And so it proceeded, through the hours of hospitality. While he talked and belched and exuded moisture from his twisted mouth, and paraded absurd notions, I contented myself with murmurs concerning his wisdom and amusement at his wit (though he had no sense of humour as I perceived it), while foraging through the horizons of his menus.

Those to whom I have narrated these stories have asked what other inducements encouraged my attendance at his table when it was obvious I despised him.

The main spur was preferment. Master John was the conduit between myself and those who might appreciate my talents. If such a Rubicon could be crossed, let it be bridged by a false face and assumed smiles.

I can assure you that Master John seemed at first to have some affection for me. But this was well hidden under his constant boasting about how he had trounced an impudent courtier or double-crossed some knave of aristocratic birth and small wits.

But another inducement drew me to his house. Master John, of the teeth, the beard, and the ugly mouth, was married to an extraordinary wife, years younger than himself, the sweetest of all angels in my estimation.

While her husband talked, Beatrice the beautiful was smiling, her dark eyes chancing to look now and then towards her poor infatuated Leonardo (the most ardent of her worshippers), the whiteness of her neck and shoulders purer than a swan's feathers, her hands as expressive as those of the Madonna in the chapel.

The circumstances of their marriage were unfathomable. To look at her was to gaze on sublime art, fashioned by ancestry and nurture, her voice soft as plucked harps, her lips pursed like a spring rose.

Master John, talking more quickly as the meal proceeded, took no apparent heed of my glances at her face, her dress, her form, her eyes. Within I kindled the basest thoughts but to little avail.

Good Beatrice was pious, in the thrall of the church, frequently shriven, absolved by the lightest penances a prelate could devise.

By the length of their marriage one presumed she was barren or he was impotent for there were no children. But her bloom remained, a perennial flower blossoming among weeds, untouched, unravished, unattainable.

Against such perfection a man might vow celibacy rather than be married to another, aching perpetually for Beatrice, the wild horses of the heart stampeded by the very thought of her.

II

You know of course, dear Theodorus, of the mathematical problem first laid at my door by that rogue of Palermo, Master John.

It seemed at first a bauble that he brought me. Yet out of such a trifle I ventured to create answers which took an infinity of precious hours to calculate.

I had already endured enough time on this earth to reach an age when vital elements begin to fail and early winter progresses apace with many bad signs. The gross sum of that amount of revolving seasons is now considered by practitioners of medicine to be a reasonable accumulation of years in these days of rare longevity.

From the vantage point of having let a batch of precious summers and miserable winters slip through my veins in contemplation of mathematical riddles, I wonder if I could not have spent my energies in more fruitful pursuits, perhaps reflecting on matters of Divinity, the salvation of souls, or contemplation of mortality.

But I am no fit man to challenge destiny. A withered branch, a fading flower, a season in decline, describe me how you will, for any reproach to my failing flesh and pale appearance can no longer touch my tired spirit.

III

Master John's question was insidiously simple. I took the bait like a fish waiting to be hoisted from the water and cooked in the inferno.

He proposed a problem which he said had 'occurred' to him in a dream. I doubt whether such a thought could have 'occurred' to a mind weaned in the sordid heat of Palermo but rather came from some other far superior intellect.

But Master John, being the Emperor's representative, issued such a request as a command from on high. And I did believe that a solution to this problem might echo my name through those forthcoming centuries when all who now draw breath will be shrouded in the silent dusty dark.

Yes, I hoped my numbers would continue to reverberate in the human mind like the phases of the moon or the workings of an uneasy conscience.

Conscience and mathematics are, after all, but companions who journey in a similar direction, though to different destinations. What is conscience but a search for logic and truth, establishing what is right and in good order? My God, how conscience has troubled me these recent months in a thousand torments.

I am no stranger to that voice in the night, when the footfall of a passer-by arouses fear. Or before dawn, when the throat dries, the pulse pounds like a fist, and past sins swim to the half-asleep brain and induce a fever no touch can heal. Then light trickles through the curtains and dreams yield to the waking nightmare of the day.

In such manner I am troubled by the numbers. The litany of figures and symbols haunts me to exhaustion. Suddenly, the formula comes right, the problem is solved, the sculpture assumes shape. Until the next time.

But to revert to Master John. The question which had 'occurred' to him by night (in his bed, doubtless close to the fair Beatrice, oh brutal thought, as he lays hands and mouth upon her white skin and in the moonlight his forked beard falls upon her silver breasts), was this:

Find a square number from which, when five is added or subtracted, always arises a square number.

"His Majesty has read a portion of your book on numbers," he puffed, "and commented on it to several of his philosophers, astrologers, and men of thought, but chiefly to myself. And after coming for my advice, His Majesty has requested that I should formulate a proposition to tax your learning and enhance the court. From that point, as in a dream, the problem has manifested itself and on behalf of His Majesty, I present you with it as a gift."

Caught like a dove in a gilded trap by the remark pertaining to His Majesty, I blushed scarlet to the roots of my hair, which did not escape his eyes entombed in the pallid flesh of his face. Against such a fact, that His Celestial Majesty, the Holy Roman Emperor, had even glanced at the pages of my early scribblings, let alone shared his thoughts with his advisers, made me determined to do justice to the burden now loaded on my back.

Most of my life I had engaged in practical calculations to do with commerce, as well as those intricately diverse arithmetical puzzles which delight scholars.

But now, in ambition and vanity, I became drawn to solving the mysteries of the square roots, to the detriment of all else.

Before proceeding, beloved friend, to the twisted paths of temptation which enveloped my life, I digress to the early years so that you may understand those frailties which caused the town to know my shame and ruffians to pursue me with stones and sticks, while their dogs barked in the street mocking my fall.

But more of that anon, as I confess freely, not to any priest (for I am long past that), but to you in these letters.

That all things may become known and many secrets revealed.

Second Letter

Concerning childhood, Guilielmo,
and the unfortunate death of a swan.

...Ce fu au tens qu'arbre foillissent,
Que glai et bois et pré verdissent,
Et cil oisel en lor latin
Chantent doucement au matin
Et toute rien de joie aflamme...

CHRÉTIEN DE TROYES (*fl.* 1160–90)

(It was the time when trees burst into leaf,
 With iris, woods, fields, glorious beyond belief,
 And each bird in its own tongue
 Sweetly greets the morning with a song,
 And everything is on fire with joy...)

I

*Sire, My Admired Master Theodorus, Philosopher at the
Court of His Glorious Majesty, the Holy Roman Emperor,
Frederick II.*

To regress into the forest of childhood may be the place to gather the fruits and berries of understanding. But here we depart from the numbers, for memory is weak and full of fables.

As we imagine the past through the shadows of the long years, and as a candle flickers against a wall, so its shapes and ghosts depart in arbitrary order far from the certainty of logic and the written page.

Yet what has been inscribed on the inner heart remains equally durable, but ever more difficult to read from a distance with accuracy and truth.

To harvest the memories of early days is like a picking of flowers from a spring hillside, though in the plucking there may be taken a few weeds also, even thorns, briars, and brambles. Holding a rose on its branch (the better to bury the nose in its shell-like cavity and inhale its fragrance), may prick the fingers by chance and draw forth blood. That tiny hurting wound will last longer on the skin than the blossom's aroma. It is much the same with the perilous act of looking back, pain and pleasure being recalled in disproportionate degrees.

First must come the facts and circumstances of early days. As the centre of the universe is the earth, so is the point round which our childhood should revolve, that dear mother who gave birth to us, the origin of our mortal being, source of warmth, sense and breath.

But of my true mother I have no remembrance, for she departed this life shortly after I was born, leaving me to the care of young nurse or old nurse, the suckling wench, the wet sow, the paid stranger. As a consequence I loved many women, gazing into their changing eyes, feeling their embraces, each different from another, their hands soft with love or harsh from scrubbing and labour.

Ours was a fickle love, founded, yes, on affection for the tiny scrap of boy, but unmoulded by natural bonding of flesh to flesh, of born son to birth mother, of native lineage.

As I discovered when I rose to awareness, my father was well provided for, having inherited money and chattels from my mother's will. As a public servant among taxes and customs, he found diverse ways of increasing what might have proved a less than sufficient income. But his absences during my early years gave me a peculiar dependence on whatever matron supervised my infantile condition.

In the household in Pisa were several women, each selected by my father on the testimony of trusted acquaintances and for other features which at that time I knew not of.

Even at a young age, their differences were obvious, some full of smiles and frequent embraces, others chiding shortcomings, scolding for things not understood, punishing for misdemeanours of which I was innocent. I was a child playing a game with rules not yet fathomed, ever complicated by more catches, snares, frowns, harsh voices, and castigation with no apparent causality.

Here I came up against arrest without reason, courts with no appeal, sentences without a crime. But as the hours revolved so did the sentries change till once again I was in the care of angels who extolled goodness, ignored that which was less good, and all was harmony and peace.

I perceived rank and degree, the pecking order of old hens over younger chickens. Often I was flung into the care of the punishers when one of my dear saints was present. I saw then on her sad face, as in a mirror reflected, the pain inflicted on my body but she was powerless to intercede.

However, the aftermath was always sweet, as with the absence of the dragon, the virgin of compassion took me into her arms, and I sobbed happily against her, wetting the front of her dress with open mouth and tears, while she cooed dove-like into the soft well of my ear.

Thus adoration for some clashed with detestation for those of the birch. My tormentors sensed rebellion in my heart while those who lifted me from sorrow were rewarded with love as from an eternal spring. Never receiving retribution without resentment, I accepted affection as treasure they could not spend too freely.

Early on, I knew those who had suffered hurt in their youth, and continued to wound, in addition to others in whose souls the fires of love burn. For in women, such things are possible but scarcely ever in men, whose upbringing too often encompasses chastisement.

But more of the unfortunate ways of men anon, as it is hardly likely that any generation of boys will be spared the anguish of the rod or their teacher's fury.

꿎꿎 II 됆됆

Beyond the twilight months of those first experiences of our earthly being, when, with such difficulty, we learn the arts of cleanliness, speech, and movement, come the moments of primeval memory to which we hold fast whatever follows. After that happy time of the animal passions of the young, we pass through those foothills of study from which the eventual man is formed.

My father was eager I should enter the arena of knowledge at the earliest possible age. Though, as I have said, he was often far away with occasional returns to Pisa, he made excellent provision in both carers and tutors.

Our confessor, Father Josephus, attended daily to summon me from foolish play, persuading my thoughts towards other matters. He was a compassionate man whose duty was to initiate me into penmanship, literacy, and Latin grammar. Thus, I discovered how to wield the quill, the shaping and inscription of letters, formation of words, and the language of the beloved Romans, from whose speech emerged the mother tongues of the civilised parts of our continent.

Such discourse was a kind of game, as the priest teased out joyful participation, rewarding progress with praise and tardiness with jesting rebuke. As if to tempt a fledgling eagle into the air, so Father Josephus ignited a child's small fire of intellect by his kindling.

He made his visitation before noon, when the brain is at its most receptive. Already he had been active for hours, rising for meditation, walking in the garden with his book of prayer, before a light meal of bread, fruit and milk, followed by further devotions.

Next he visited the aged and the sick, reciting holy texts, whether psalms or parables, and assisting in their washing and feeding. From such ministrations, Father Josephus came forthwith to my needs, something I took for granted. My father paid him for his attendance yet, for certain, every such payment was passed on to poor widows or the destitute.

Father Josephus may have hoped I would prefer his priestly vocation. But each day my pulse quickened towards my true calling. Two hours after noon, another teacher walked to our house prepared and determined to instruct me in the subtle art of the numbers.

This was a merchant skilled in business and finance, whether lending or borrowing, investing, saving, spending or merely hoarding. That he was a Jew meant nothing to me, except for the rumours which always accompany such a person. But in Pisa men pride themselves on tolerance and Abraham da Milano was much sought after as a shrewd adviser in both private finance and affairs of the state.

Abraham was not a true man of science. His concerns were profit and wealth. He knew, from Deuteronomy, the fifth book of Moses, that 'man does not live by bread alone'. But he also observed the Lord's Prayer, 'Give us this day our daily bread', which acknowledges that such an essential substance must be harvested in the fields, baked in the oven by the sweat of man's brow, sold and bought before being eaten and digested. Such processes involve gain, loss, labour, wages, buying, selling, distribution, an inexorable chain of cause and effect, throughout the entire history of humanity.

Thus when he laid six coins in front of me, each of the same value, I became aware of their significance, as numerals, as the bearer of the emblems of authority, as a symbol of what men covet, as a substance, and as a branch of mathematics.

Abraham introduced me to the mysteries of the abacus, which he called the 'bead game'. I was required to touch it with respect like a precious musical instrument. Its vibrations, the music of the spheres, were the unheard harmony of numbers resonating in humanity.

He observed, furthermore, that *abacus* originates from the Hebrew word, *abaq,* dust or sand, the first calculations, whether by philosophers or traders, being scrawled in the earth. This inspired speculation on sin and death, profit and greed, permanence and mortality. (Abraham was always fond of allegorical extensions.)

Though many types of abacus exist according to the culture of countries, Abraham preferred the traditional style of the counting table which presented patterns pleasing to a boy's curiosity:

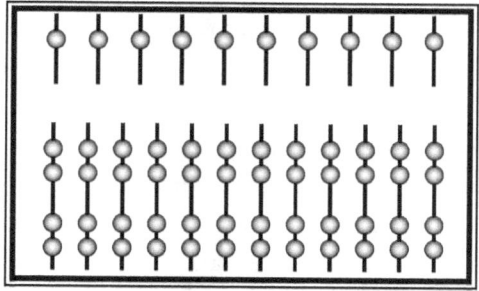

At first, this was only a child's game but from the abacus can be learned not only adding and subtracting but also diverse calculations and other skills in auditing.

Abraham's ancestors, of course, came from biblical lands, some of them willingly, others in dreadful bondage.

Mindful of this, he knew that counting has been present ever since Eve selected a single apple, on the advice of the one snake in the garden, to feed from the one forbidden tree to the one man who existed, Adam, from whose loins all men of all kinds, colours and creeds have sprung. Their expulsion from paradise brought about general barter and trade, exchanging and selling, poverty and wealth.

Thus I imbibed not only the whispering language of the poet but the shouting of the numbers in the marketplace, their problems and solutions.

For all this I am indebted to my father's wisdom in appointing Abraham da Milano, merchant adventurer and money-lender, as my first teacher of the science which shaped my fate.

III

In view of my mother's death and father's long absences, it may be of concern whether my younger years were but a lonely island in a sea of strangers. But for the precocious child, that growing thing accustomed to run ahead of the pack, it is usual to prefer the company of the old and wise.

Risking immodesty, I confess to a certain aptitude in learning, well exceeding my peers. This is not to consider myself superior but to indicate that the journey ahead was long and my voyage needed early preparation to catch the tide.

My father determined I should not be confined to the prison

of a school where the hare waits for the snail and the fleet stallion stands in attendance on the cartwright's jade. He insisted that my masters were appointed directly by himself and that I, the potential reaper of their harvest, would enjoy the sowing of knowledge as they saw fit.

So rather than the casual acquaintanceship of the school yard and the lottery of mercenary tutors, I was the recipient of private learning with noble teachers. My life revolved round their wisdom like a small moon circling a large planet. In such a forum, debate and dissent were twins given liberty to range hither and thither across rainbow seas.

But if among the heady winds of discussion I should, like a poor mariner, lose my bearings and drift beyond the right channels of childhood, that evening or some other time, my friends would visit me, their coming being a corrective to illusion.

Those who assume that the childish state is some brazen court where underlings endlessly compete in envy or malice are mistaken. Among dear companions, brothers under the skin, respect prevails. Friendship among children is thus founded not on baser instincts but shared love which hardly names or knows itself.

Foremost among friends was Angelo, offspring of a clever merchant and a beautiful mother, a dreamer, a poet in the making, inclined to depart on silent journeys within himself, and yet whose words matched wit for wit with the speed of a sword. It was Angelo who first whispered in my ear the rude truths of life, about the planting of seed to engender birth, the rutting of dogs and horses, the mating of birds, the qualities of girls and women, what they wore, their strangeness, their familiarity.

It was Angelo who directed me to poetry and art, his sensitivity exceeding any I knew at that time. When he sang I envied his diction and his sweet mouthing of the words, lips wide parted like a girl.

Alas, that Angelo was fated for an early grave and did not live to see the manhood he desired.

But no matter for the past is buried deep. We can but pray for Angelo's soul. His mortal remains will sanctify for ever that small piece of ground in which he was laid.

Another friend was Marco, strong and fair of limb, with a grin like the devil himself, so opposite in character to Angelo and yet as dear. He was remote from learning, preferring to run and swim or compete in games, aspiring to be a soldier in the Emperor's army, though I know not if he succeeded in this or became a rich grocer like his father.

In his company I was always tempted to mischief, stealing ripe fruit from the trees of neighbours, chasing urchin girls into alleys and pulling their hair, or tormenting the idiot child with one ear who begged on the street corner.

Marco had three sisters, two older and one younger than ourselves. He was adept at spying and I collaborated in his quest to catch them unawares. We would hide in the bushes to watch as they bathed their feet in the river, the oldest one pulling up her long skirt to avoid getting it wet.

It was the deceit which attracted me as much as the prospect of seeing more than we should. But such romping came to a bad end. While out with Marco on one of our evil missions, a summer storm erupted, drenching us. We were quite far from home. Lightning flashed, thunder induced fear of death. We shivered in the ferocity of the downpour.

Going our separate ways. I hurried home, like a half-drowned dog, through empty streets. My duty nurse, Maria, cried out in fear when she saw me, wrapping me at once in warm towels. But to no effect.

In bed I shivered with alternate hot and cold spasms as pains clawed my feet, legs and arms. A physician was summoned in haste, Doctor Benedict, dressed in black, carrying his bag of medical instruments and potions.

While Maria stood close by, like an angel ready to carry me into purgatory, the physician examined his patient.

Maria wept gently. Doctor Benedict drew her out of the room to speak with her in private.

His diagnosis was that scourge of children, rheumatic ague. As a remedy blankets were piled on, blood taken from the leg, foul medicine and broth spooned into the mouth, and the patient confined to bed for many weeks. I prepared for dying while Father Josephus constantly knelt in prayer at my bedside.

One dreadful night I dreamed about the visitation of Death, dressed like Benedict, making his entrance when the sun pierced the bedroom window with its arrow. What horrors I endured, waiting with fear in my throat for the first light of dawn.

My father, being far away, sent comforting letters. After a month the ague dissipated and I attempted small steps round the room.

From the secrecy of my bed I overheard Master Benedict tell Maria, in his physician's whisper, that the force of the malady was spent but care was necessary. His prescription required no excesses of studying lest I become agitated.

The diet was to be regulated with no red meat though chicken and fish were permitted, as were most types of fruit, with goat's cheese and rations of red wine to irrigate the blood and cleanse impurities.

My body was weakened and I had shuddered to hear the passing wings of death. It was time to put away foolishness, to prepare for the voyage of life. That call came soon and all would be changed by water and by land.

IV

My father, Guilielmo Bonacci, arrived home suddenly. One moment he was not in the house and I was absorbed in lessons, teachers, Maria, and my friends. Then things altered for ever. Over the months his face and person had been banished from my mind as I enjoyed that liberty a boy feels when the paternal presence does not watch his every action.

While at calculations in the study, immersed in a problem Abraham had set, I heard noises from the street, some shouting within the house, peals of laughter from Maria, and the rasp of my father's voice with that slight strangeness of intonation, the fruit of much speaking in a foreign tongue.

"Where is the boy?" I heard him exclaim. "Where is he?"

"Leonardo's there!" someone said. "He'll be so pleased to see you, he's been missing you."

I did not move, annoyed that his coming would disturb the household and interfere with friends and our sport. But after that unworthy moment I reverted to notions of filial duty. Besides, I wished him to catch me like a scholar at the table with quill and ink. Also, there would be gifts.

He took but a moment to bound along the hall and enter the study. I could no longer pretend concentration but rose to meet him. His countenance full of anxiety, he clutched me in a fierce embrace.

His rough beard rubbed against my face and he shed a few bitter tears. No weeping welled from my selfish soul to mix with his, though this was of little consequence for he was intent on his own feelings.

"I heard news of your sickness," he whispered, "and I came as soon as I could."

Unable to speak, in the strong clasp of his guilt and washed by his sorrow, I was disturbed by a glimpse of Maria standing in the doorway. My father put me at arm's length, his hands on my shoulders.

"Let me look at you, my son – how thin you are – have they been feeding you? – Have you been working too hard? – You seem smaller than when I went away – though perhaps you have grown in stature…"

Then he snatched me up again, sobbing into my hair, kissing my brow and left ear.

"I thought I had lost you," he whimpered, "never to see you again, except your grave – I thank Our Lord for you – I swear, on the tomb of your dear mother, I shall never leave you again – I have learned, Leonardo, I have learned!"

Entwined tightly within his arms, and a spectacle in front of Maria, I had little chance to reply a single word. But like the release of a summer shower, tears came to my rescue, flooding in unmanly exuberance.

Against his face I breathed forth an infinite number of times, "Father, oh father, father, father," causing him, and our watcher, to descend to passion, whereupon each of us entered into lamentation, our bodies shaking as if with fever and every voice lifted to wild emotion.

V

Maria, in her spirited way, rallied the servants to cook a good supper that evening, and Guilielmo and his Leonardo attempted to balance the equilibrium of a pendulum oscillating beyond its normal arc.

He told many a tale of the Barbary coast, of merchants and ships, of soldiers going to wars from which they would not return, and of women so beautiful a man might both rejoice and weep to see them (a conjunction I did not fully understand).

Foremost was the puzzle my father posed that never again would he leave me, a question best left till answered at his own discretion.

His strategy became clear that very evening. I was to accompany him to Barbary, to study with men of learning, to speak a new language and acquaint myself with the Arabic numbers. He looked closely at me as he talked, as if doubtful that my spirit of adventure would be equal to his plan.

Of course he hardly knew me. I had daydreamed often enough of unknown places across the sea as Father Josephus told his tales of diverse tribes and races. I was eager to rise up as on wings and fly to the ends of the earth. To depart from Pisa was no sorrow except for leaving Maria and Angelo.

Guilielmo indeed confessed how his absences were brought about not only by duty but because my face represented a picture too sadly reminiscent of my mother. This having run its course, he hoped henceforth to become a proper father and for me at last to be a proper son.

On that bright evening I looked to the most propitious planets, unaware that all things change all men and whatever we lay down in the garden of the soul, whether good or bad, determines the course of the subsequent journey. In the cauldron of youth, one is unprepared for the attrition of life, its causes and results, and just as well.

Sufficient to say that on this evening I was reconciled to my poor father and together we drank the wine of hope. This made him maudlin and hopelessly nostalgic, while I became confused with expectation and delusion, which is not inappropriate for the young.

VI

Once a journey has been planned all thoughts bend towards departure. It matters not a jot if that day is distant for everything is already transformed.

In truth, my father's return to Barbary would not be rushed. For weeks, newly established as master of his household, he wished to savour every indulgence, whether lingering over meals, drinking wine, meeting old friends or conversing with neighbours and passers-by.

I wanted to go at once to whatever horizons our stars could guide us. My father's relish in homely delights was obvious and I had no desire to deprive him of a single day of his time of refreshment.

But the young steed, once the saddle is on, smells the chase and cannot be contained. Eagerness irritated like a mosquito and my impatience clouded our mutual path. However, he was tolerant with these tantrums and chose not to rise up in wrath, as he would have done when I was younger.

The memory of the evening of our reunion lay like a prayer on our souls, and its benediction was not to be thwarted.

My father daily gave me the full attention of his discourse, intending I should attempt the dangerous crossing from boy to man with the help of his navigation. He spoke of other lands, the moods of the sea, the practicalities of commerce. Thus, in simple steps, he tried to prepare me for whatever lay ahead.

One particular day he bade me go to the study and wait there. He entered quietly and closed the door, wishing to remain disconnected from the ears of servants. Observing such privacy, I fell prey to an uneasy feeling. His behaviour usually followed well known patterns quite different from this.

My discomfort was matched in the same measure by his own, for having walked three times round the room and looked often, but with little interest, into the street, he descended into his favourite chair, cleared his throat, and, for several long minutes, said precisely nothing.

Like a rat trapped before a cat I remained deathly still, searching his expression for some revelation but not meeting his eyes which responded in like manner.

As it turned out, what was on his mind were those selfsame matters my friend Angelo and I had whispered in dark corners, at that time like a traveller lost for directions but now with a map, hesitantly unrolled.

Guilielmo had resolved in view of our coming adventure to enlighten me about the workings of nature. It agitated him to begin such an epic but his purpose determined that, like Homer, once embarked, he waxed fulsome.

As this narrative progressed I appreciated how Angelo's knowledge had been but partial, comprehended through a glass darkly.

The true saga was like the night sky, full of depths, heights, breadths and mysteries. The tale began with breeding rabbits, thence to the substance of dogs and puppies, cats and kittens, proceeding to pigs, horses and cattle (quite similar), and ultimately to men and women, this being the most interesting.

Though the message in full strength was not easy to take, my father's explanations assumed the elements of a puzzle as I pieced together what I already knew with what he provided. Of the formings of male and female, I appreciated more than hitherto, though beyond certain points lay confusion.

Such details of natural processes require for the innocent a period of reflection before full digestion, like a python having swallowed a goat. The pain of so much revelation disturbed me with waking nightmares which flew around my head in the manner of bats not to be put to rest.

Agitated but still half asleep, I crept from my unquiet bed and, lighting a candle, advanced to the kitchen. Here I sampled various wines, from the powerful to the insipid, adding to the refreshment segments of orange and a quantity of sweet biscuits to which my palate was partial.

Like Odysseus returning through the unknown sea of night, with the wine singing in my veins, I passed once more my father's bedroom, which on my outward journey was as silent as the grave. Now from within I heard a dialogue of mutterings, first low and then louder, modulating towards laughter, and sounds somehow more animal than human.

My father's utterances were harmonised by shriller tones and whisperings, those intonations and cadences I loved from much acquaintance. An impulse to throw open the door shook my soul. But reason counselled and, eavesdropper only, I restrained my hand from the latch.

The voice of Maria was as familiar as if she was my mother, and after the colloquy of the day my understanding was increased a thousandfold.

Salt tears whipped my eyes and bitter jealousy my heart. Like a humbled cur, I turned and carried my candle, their voices an echo. Back in bed I muffled my mouth and howled dog-like into the pillow, no longer an ignorant child but one who had learned too much and indeed knew *that* which must for ever remain locked in the dungeon of his heart.

❧ VII ☙

After a fitful night when the wine slowly enticed me into spasms of sleep, the household appeared normal to the inexperienced eye. But I sat during the early meal like the serpent in the garden, wiser than I seemed, more cunning than they might have believed.

My father, in exceptionally good humour, full of smiles and of great appetite, downed jugs of goat's milk with satisfaction, wiping the ring of residue from his mouth with the back of his hand. Maria bustled round, emitting little peals of laughter, a small bell ringing round a graveyard. She paused behind me to retrieve a plate, placing hands on my shoulders and offering a playful kiss on the top of my head, which pleased my father for he smiled indulgently at her from across the table.

Her affectionate hands and joyful face had yesterday been as dear to me as any, for what had she been but my loveliest companion, who took me into her arms, bathed me, dressed me, comforted me, pressed my face to her bosom when I was melancholy, laughed with me when we played games, cooked good food, read me ancient yarns as I fought the battle between sleep and waking?

But such feelings had drained away. As if touched by a mendicant leper, my body flinched. She noticed nothing and cleared away the dishes humming a merry folk song. A red tide of shame suffused my cheeks and I hid my face behind my food, determined no longer to weep for betrayal or show sorrow.

"You seem feverish this morning!" said my father thoughtfully. "Perhaps we should get the physician to see you – are you ill?"

"Not at all," I muttered, my mouth full. "I didn't sleep very well."

"Hmmm, neither did I!" he replied, leaning across the table and placing a finger on my hot brow. "No, you're all right – it's probably just too much excitement."

Dissimulation masked my features even as nausea gripped my entrails. It was as if I already lived in an unknown land where behaviour was unfamiliar and yet I pretended to be at home. I was a butterfly emerged from the chrysalis, the snake sloughing its skin. In nature all things feel pain through change. Now I was the one watching the universe as earth turns from night to day and back to blackness.

And from that darkness I remembered the pleasure when, in the shame of my bed, images of Maria, of Marco's sisters, of Angelo's mother, of women seen in church, of the pretty beggar girl, of the wimpled novice from the convent, and many another, came to me with soft flesh and, as in a private bower, I sampled the sweet apples of temptation.

I never confessed this to any priest, abundant though such imaginings were as they piled thickly on me. Kneeling before Father Josephus I occasionally threw him a bone of contrition by mentioning 'unclean thoughts' or 'improper thoughts', but never offering any more detailed explanation.

He absolved me readily for he regarded it as natural that absolution will inevitably be followed by further sins in perpetual sequence. But previously I had been childlike, in a state of innocence. Now I was privy to knowledge of my father's sins and the lusts of women.

It was too huge a problem to be solved in a morning. Burdened with such mystery I suffered the pangs of grief.

❧ VIII ❧

After breakfast, I went to find Angelo and Marco, and the three of us went down to the river. They observed, while throwing stones at passing swans, how serious I had become since my father's return.

"I don't recognise you!" said Angelo.

Marco, unskilled in noticing the responses of others, redoubled his efforts to strike a bird. He was selecting larger stones and making his aim more lethal, should the target be hit, though less accurate because of the missile's weight. But even he, the would-be soldier, the granite soul, brusquely expressed a wish I might soon become my former self because such oddities made me a dull comrade.

While we continued our game, each action becoming wilder as the swans retreated from the barrage with much flapping of wings, two of Marco's sisters came upon us.

They protested stridently at our sport, vowing that if we hurt one of these creatures they would never speak to us again, a threat which did not, in the midst of our exertions, immediately deter us.

But armed with the knowledge recently imparted by my father, I cast fresh eyes on the sisters, observing the tossing of hair, smooth arms, small breasts and movements of hips and hindquarters.

They were indeed fair to behold, sweet of eye and lip, and very girlish. I took myself from the water's edge and put down my stone to walk with them.

Just as we prepared to sit down together overlooking the river, the fair Angelo, by the whim of some fate other than his own volition, hurled a large pebble with the force of Hercules.

The projectile curved skywards in beautiful flight, the very air helping it on its way. Swooping down, the stone swung on its axis, a miraculous fluke, and, extending further than any would have thought possible, descended spinning and low, straight against a swan's head.

The bird collapsed, changed from living and swimming to floating and dying. Blood discoloured the water like a rainbow.

"Good shot!" shouted Marco, grinning like a monkey.

"Holy Christ!" shrieked Angelo, from whose mouth such exclamations had never been heard, before bursting into tears.

The sisters in doleful chorus amplified Angelo's grief with shrieks and accusations, pulling at their hair and clothes.

As their outcry subsided to sobs, we moved, as if in a herd, to a vantage point to watch the aftermath. The white rag of our sin bobbed in the stream like a child's boat, before slipping to the middle of the river and drifting out of sight.

We looked in that direction long after it disappeared.

IX

The swan's death created many troubles. For one thing the whole locality got wind of it within an hour. This was not only because Marco's sisters ran home weeping hysterically to create an impression and draw attention to themselves.

More seriously, our escapade was observed by two stalwarts of

Pisan society, members of the guild of shoemakers no less, who, in the act of putting their soles to the test by a brief walk, happened to pass on the opposite bank of the river at the moment our deed was committed.

The bird murderer himself, the hapless Angelo, was chastised by both father and uncle that afternoon, though the whip of conscience was no doubt worse than the flaying of flesh by hand and rod. The situation was complicated as the righteous shoemakers were customers of Angelo's merchant father for various essential commodities.

Marco, the offspring of a less sophisticated household than our friend, and despite vindictive testimony from his sisters, received not the merest iota of retribution. Indeed it was whispered abroad that his father laughed very loudly at every detail, true or false, and even patted his son on the back.

Marco's defence, against the claims of garrulous sisters and the buzz of rumours, was that he was merely tossing stones into the water to watch the widening ripples and had not noticed a single bird near or far.

As I knew him to be the prime cause, it was a hard choice whether to admire him as a fine teller of tales or as a worthy liar.

The evil news reached the ears of my father faster than horses can gallop or birds fly. By the time I reached the house, having circumnavigated the area in order to avoid too rapid a homecoming, the messenger of ill fortune had already winged his way there.

Though dread pounded in my heart as I slunk like a thief through the door, guilty by association, it seemed Guilielmo was anxious to avoid scandal rather than punish me for the morning's work.

The shoemakers of course approached the magistrates to lodge complaints of affray, wilful damage to the swans, disorderliness, and other allegations.

Having received these complaints, the magistrate was compelled to initiate a preliminary hearing at the earliest sitting, a convenient date for him being some ten days into the future.

In like manner to Marco, I constructed my own devices round the problem, presuming to be innocently seated with the sisters on the bank, removed from whatever was going on. At this both my father and Maria, in close attendance, appeared appropriately at ease.

Thus when at noon the next day the magistrate's clerk, a gaunt, pimply, callow youth, arrived with a summons, commanding me to a tribunal within two weeks, my father accompanied him back into town.

Guilielmo, who had been at school with our esteemed magistrate, made two visitations that afternoon, one to a merchant who knew the comings and goings of ships and a social call at the august residence of the law.

Over fine wine, supplied by my father, it was agreed that due to the offices of diplomacy, Bonacci, in the company of his son, now to be apprenticed, had been recalled to Barbary posthaste and would be unable to be present ten days later.

Therefore no testimony could be delivered on the date of the tribunal by either of us, much as we wished for justice to be done.

However, under the circumstances, as recompense for our absence, my father was prepared to offer a donation to the municipal coffers, payable immediately to the person of the magistrate for safekeeping.

Thus it was that my journey to a distant land was brought forward to be rapidly expedited, much to my satisfaction.

Third Letter

*Concerning a voyage to the coast of Barbary,
the boy Cristoforo, and the mysterious activities
of Guilielmo.*

Li venz est en la mer levé
Et fiert soi en milieu du tref,
A terre fait venir la nef.

THOMAS D'ANGLETERRE (c. 1170)

(The wind arises over the sea
Forces itself on the midst of the sail,
Bearing the vessel to the shore.)

~~I~~

Sire, My Esteemed Master Theodorus, Philosopher in the Service of His Glorious Majesty, Frederick II.

After farewells and embraces from Maria, more for my father than myself, we set out from Pisa early one morning accompanied by five serving men with swords. Their task was to drive and guard our baggage cart until we reached the harbour. We rode on reliable geldings, bred for resilience.

Each bend in the road thrust childhood further behind. My father, broodingly pensive as if mindful of hazards to come, said nothing.

Hours later, after several pauses for watering the sweating horses, we arrived at Livorno, a harmless enough hamlet, as my father observed, of fishermen and women grown old before their time. The blue evening sea beckoned and the sun played on the water as if offering a glimpse of paradise itself.

Saddle-sore we approached the harbour area, crammed with boats. My father, eager to be aboard, led us straight to our chosen vessel. While he and I climbed the gangplank the servants were busy with stowage of our belongings, bringing forth much fervent grunting and cursing as the weighty items were dragged one by one and forced down passageways to dark compartments below.

Here I learned the first rule of the sea, that the further an observer is from that mixture of wood and rope we call a ship, the more attractive it appears. A vessel under sail far out on the ocean, viewed from a cliff, is a beauty. Yet stand upon the deck, with its mess of tackle, crew, stores, and odours, and fears of the voyage afflict even the strongest.

The next rule concerns the nature of sailors who live surrounded by space and yet are penned like beasts in a sty. Each hour may bring death so they are inordinately superstitious but appear almost childishly carefree.

They are deprived of the home comforts of a simple peasant and live under perpetual tyranny, but possess a spirit of freedom and adventure denied to many. Nevertheless, these disadvantages give rise to wonder that any sane man follows the unruly sea for a living when he could be safe on dry land.

The captain presented himself as a taciturn man of dignity, whose scowl suggested one unaccustomed to contrary opinions. Our accommodation was a clumsy cubbyhole at the stern, illuminated by light from the passageway, no door being provided but only a heavy leather curtain.

After dark, two tapers secured in iron rings were lit. One crude chair, a table, and a bed and soiled blankets, in addition to a bucket for human needs (to be emptied over the lee side) sufficed for furnishings.

The deck was dominated by two masts, pitched slightly forward the better to sustain the sails, one in the bows, the other amidships, each supported by thick shrouds on either side, and hung with broad crossbeams on which were stitched the twin sails.

At the back of the boat was a pear-shaped steering oar, the contraption being manipulated from the deck by two strong men.

The sailors stared at us strangely as if some untoward animals had appeared amongst them. One stopped to squeeze my shoulder like a farmer assessing a pig for market, whispering comments to an associate in a most sinister manner.

Already the sun was dipping low, though I was surprised we were to confront the ocean by night and not at the crack of dawn.

For in a short time, with the help of rowing boats which tugged at our bows, sails were unfurled, ropes tightened, orders shouted, and we parted from the land.

My father and I watched from a sheltered area of the ship. The deck heaved and the hull palpitated against the waves, with creaking harness and a stiff breeze moaning against tackle and sail.

Heading towards the dying sun and a blood red sea, the land diminished until it became a tiny dark stripe on the horizon. The waves grew more boisterous as we eased out of the coast's comfort, the gusty wind removing some of the odours which tended to accumulate below and above decks when in harbour.

Later, in our private den, my father explained the habits of sailors and their brute lusts which apparently extended in some instances to licentiousness even towards mere youths such as myself. Though I hid my feelings I was nauseated. Such activities seemed entirely out of harmony with logic and ancient religion.

The isolation of the sea, according to Guilielmo, removes all moral decency from men till they sin without restraint. He advised an aloof manner towards these creatures of bestiality.

Though I would be safe on deck, I was not to enter any living quarters. My God! After such admonitions I would sooner have penetrated the gates of hell!

That evening we feasted on bread, cheese, cooked fish, and wine. The waves lifted the ship insistently but my young stomach was resolute. As darkness came we took a promenade round the deck, in awe of the stars and aware of the horror of the night sea as the ship pushed forward and the waves rushed mercilessly past into the blackness.

One could not help but speculate on the universes twinkling above and the baseness of the earth. Could these distances between planets, stars, moon and earth ever be measured? But these musings were cut short for father wished to retire for the night.

Unaccustomed to the intimacy of sharing a cabin together, we prepared for bed by the light of a flickering candle. Following fragments of muttered complaints we lay uncomfortably side by side on the hard wood, pulling the unclean blankets over our bodies against the sea chill.

My father set to snoring. After listening for a while to this unpleasant drone I slipped into fitful sleep, philosophising on things which, like the sea itself, could never be fathomed.

II

Even before dawn the life of the ship was well begun, with strident voices, trimming of sails, and the thudding of energetic movement on deck above us. A bowl of sea water was brought to the cabin for ablutions. My father washed first, splashing his face, ears, and the back of his neck, aware that I was watching him.

I shared the water he had used but was more hurried in my preparations as young men usually are. As he fussed around the cabin, tidying the bed and smoothing the blankets, impatiently I took my leave of him and ventured outside.

It was a fine day with the sun bright in the sky from the port side. Blinking into the light, I saw the land of Corsica a few leagues off as we progressed southwards.

In the stern, the captain barked out commands while matelots climbed aloft like apes among rope and sail and others scurried backwards and forwards below.

As I leaned on the rail admiring the infinite patterns of the water, a sailor, a year or so younger than myself, approached and stood by my side, caught between the Scylla and Charybdis of timidity and curiosity. He was not unlike Angelo in his looks but darker in complexion from exposure to sea and sun, with steadfast eyes searching my countenance as if asking questions to which he knew no answers.

Mindful of the fear of seafarers which my father had aroused, I addressed him somewhat brusquely.

"Why do you stand here, boy? Have you no duties to attend to?"

His response was a smile, revealing white teeth and a gentle face, which charmed and reassured as much as his reply.

"It's a fine morning, sir. I trust you are enjoying the voyage."

"I have never been to sea before," I said. "I find it strange."

"I was born on a boat like this," he replied. "I am the captain's son."

He spoke with authority, quite unlike my young friends in Pisa. During the fleeting years when I had cavorted in carefree child-hood, this individual had known the call of the sea, the uncertainty of weather, the nearness of death, and the hope of fair winds.

While I studied with tutors, his schoolroom was this small wooden prison, his taskmasters the elements themselves.

"My name is Leonardo," I said, offering my hand, ashamed of my impoliteness to this disciple of the ocean, of whom there was surely no reason to be afraid.

"I am Cristoforo," he whispered, clasping my palm.

"There are many things you can teach me. I would like to find out about ships and how they are guided through the waters by day and night."

He smiled scornfully, as if it was impossible for those from the land to know about such matters.

"It takes years to learn about the sea. Here we are all as gypsies, born to it. We know no other life. But ask what you wish – I will try to answer."

"Can you read?"

"Not yet," he replied, "but neither can my father nor any of us aboard. Here we read the sea, the sun, or the stars of the night sky. But I can work out numbers."

"Numbers?"

"Yes, I can add, divide and subtract, count money, and estimate the price of a cargo. The captain taught me that. Sometimes I help him."

"I love the numbers," I said. "In fact, I love them more than anything."

At this, the boy looked at me in disbelief. Anxious he might depart, I tried another way to humour him.

"Your father looks very strict!" I added. The boy knew what I meant for he laughed aloud.

"He is as mean as the devil and as good as gold. Often he beats me but afterwards talks as if nothing happened. I know then that he has forgotten whatever sin I committed."

"Does he beat you if you have not committed any sin?"

"If he has a mind to. But not usually."

Cristoforo shrugged to show there were far worse things in the world to worry about. We strolled the length of the vessel and, like a friend, he put his arm casually round my shoulder.

"We must talk about the numbers," I said. "You could teach me some of the things you know."

"If you prefer, I will teach you what you first asked me, the sea, the ship, and guiding it through the water."

"That too…But most of all the numbers. Of that I could perhaps teach you something."

He gave his little smile as we ducked under the sail awning and came towards the bow of the ship. He waited with me a few moments as we looked ahead at the great blue distance.

"I must work now," he said. "There are decks to clean, food to prepare. We will talk later about the sea and numbers."

He turned his head and kissed me on the cheek and I felt his breath against me. His eyes caught mine as he pulled away.

He left to attend to his duties. I put my fingers where his lips had touched to explore a gift received from a stranger, sensing something to which I would later give the name of love, a small plant hardly rooted, yet surely the harbinger of all affections that would ever follow.

I retraced my steps to the stern, hoping to get another glimpse of him. But Cristoforo had departed, like a mole, into the secret warrens of the ship. I no more dared to follow him than speak with Neptune himself.

I joined my father for an early meal of fish and wine and the sustenance of a few grapes. Casually I mentioned the captain's son, but Guilielmo hardly seemed to listen.

Instead, he rushed on to more pressing matters. In particular, while at sea, he wished to engage me in preliminary studies, covering elements of taxation and relative values of some of the currencies in which we would deal.

Following breakfast, and after voiding my bowels into the bucket and emptying the contents over the side in a ritual not unobserved by sailors, we sat within a shaded portion of the deck and started my tuition.

But just as the lesson began the waves grew disturbed and the wind freshened. So much so, that while I still thirsted after more learning, my father became unwell and was forced to sacrifice his breakfast to the belly of the sea with much vile coughing and gulping before finding a kind of sanctuary in the cabin.

I stayed on deck to taste the good sea breezes.

III

With adverse winds to hamper us the vessel tacked about, keeling over from side to side, manoeuvres which did not please my father. His constant resort to the bucket polluted the cabin's small supply of freshness and it was left to me, as he groaned on the bed before the next seizure, to empty the receptacle, scouring it well with sea water before returning it for further use.

At this time I hoped to keep away from the cabin as such stench can prove contagious even to the strongest stomach.

Thus during the afternoon watch, despite much activity from the crew in manipulation of sails and tackle, my new friend Cristoforo approached, his bare feet slapping on the scrubbed deck mimicking the sound of waves against the hull of the ship.

Without a word he took my arm and insisted on leading me below decks through a number of dark corridors, to his living area, a small patch of space where his meagre belongings, a pillow, a blanket, a knife, some items of clothing, and several pieces of rope, were grouped in neat rows like treasures of the Orient. The light was dim, though there seemed sufficient from some far hatchway to allow the eyes slowly to focus.

He indicated I should sit near him on the blanket. I obeyed. With a magician's art he handed me a wooden object which, despite the gloom, I identified as a small, battered abacus.

Still saying nothing he snatched it back and with keen fingers dragged the beads hither and thither to demonstrate his dexterity.

"Very good!" I said. Encouraged, he spoke, as if imparting a secret.

"From six remove two!" Once more he attacked the beads with vigour. After several minutes he proudly announced, in the tone of one discovering the measurements of the universe, "Four!"

"Very good," I said again, with less conviction than previously.

"Into six divide three."

This was more difficult for he took longer before pronouncing in a voice as serious as that of a teacher, "Two!"

Having proved his worth in subtraction and division, he progressed to multiplication.

"Three times three…" Many rapid bead movements here to impress upon me the wonder of it all. "Nine!"

And thence he proceeded to adding units of tens, in the sequence of ten to ten making twenty, forty to forty making eighty, and ten times ten making one hundred, the exercises demanding increased expenditure of time and movement, each accompanied by knowing glances until further triumphant declarations of the results.

Once started there was no stopping him. Cristoforo's answers were accurate but was this expertise on the abacus or his memory of the numbers?

After an excess of examples to demonstrate ability in simple sums, he allowed me my turn. Indeed I was eager to show off my skill with the abacus. Though semi-darkness made it hard to distinguish one row of beads from another, if he could do it, so must I.

Here Cristoforo revealed his cunning. For rather than setting a simple problem he requested advanced arithmetic, namely the multiplication of twelve times thirty-seven to be divided by four, to be multiplied by three, with thirty-three subtracted from the total.

After trying to recall Abraham's lessons and wishing that certain aspects had been more thoroughly mastered, I became confused by the construction of this particular abacus.

I persevered and began, after the first obstacle of twelve times thirty-seven, amounting to four hundred and forty-four, to move to division of the total by four.

Division proved more hazardous than multiplication. But as I toiled and cogitated, Cristoforo moved his leg smoothly against mine, resting his left hand as gently as a butterfly on the inside of my thigh, while his right arm floated round my shoulders.

Ignoring the sensation of a silken glove moving along the upper part of the leg, I redoubled my efforts at the beads. The logic of the device was now clearer, though I was also making progress by means of appropriate mental calculations.

Cristoforo's breath was warm on my cheek, and with my head down, peering at the infernal counters and trying to decipher columns and lines, his lips brushed my face, his fingers alighting on the front of my garment like a small bird seeking its nest.

The problem had now advanced satisfactorily to the simple sum of one hundred and eleven to be multiplied by three, with thirty-three to be subtracted from the total and thence to victory. I shifted my head slightly to one side to speak, whereupon his mouth met mine in moist union.

For an instant I retreated a thumb's breadth away from him to whisper triumphantly, "Three hundred!"

In reply, or reward, his arm around my shoulder pulled firmly to bring us closer. I cast aside the abacus, letting him embrace me, our eager bodies slowly easing back to lie together on the floor.

Tasting the smoothness of his face and neck, Marco's sisters came to mind. For what was this boy but an image of a girl, with supple and delightful grace, his tanned features just as tempting?

I gave up the ghost of shyness.

But as, eel-like, we twisted against the hard deck, our heads cushioned by his unwashed pillow, locked in desire like wrestlers, I felt patterings along the backs of my legs as if insects had descended to scuttle across my flesh.

Breaking from his strong grip and the allure of his velvet limbs, I glanced backwards and downwards at the source of the tickling.

"Holy Christ!" I shouted, for, with its front paws on my calf, was the largest, most hideous rat imaginable.

Cristoforo merely laughed and clapped his hands.

The creature departed as quickly as it had come, dragging that long, filthy tail, the disappearance as sinister as its arrival, for where had the monster gone?

Would one ever sleep or eat on this vessel again when we shared our space with such an abomination? My cravings evaporated like morning mist.

"I must go," I said.

The poor boy endeavoured to persuade me to stay, his sad face pleading and earnest.

"I'm sorry," I said, nuzzling the top of his head before straightening my clothing and rushing away for the open air.

Once on deck I breathed deeply, Cristoforo's sighs still moist on my skin. But so too was the touch of the rat.

I returned to the cabin. My father was bent double over the bucket, spluttering and gagging. But no bile came for he had expended it in previous spasms.

His groaning agonies were awful to see and hear, but for some reason a smile came involuntarily to my face, which I think Guilielmo noticed.

IV

That night, jammed awkwardly in the narrow bed against my father's snoring body, I slept badly, thinking of Cristoforo on his pillow, wrapped in a blanket. I became drowsily anxious about him, bitten by jealousy at the notion of rough fellows caressing him. When I slipped into slumber, hideous dreams partitioned my brain like slices of cheese and I chased many puzzles but solved none.

Waking, I found myself alone. The ship had lost its rhythm and from afar voices sounded as busy as children at play. Hurriedly putting on fresh garments, I splashed my face with the briny water and went at once to find Guilielmo.

We were docked in Calvi, a port noted for watchtowers and fortifications. Though the sun was only just climbing behind the church, a host of people jostled along the quay.

My father was already ashore and gestured irritably as I appeared on deck, summoning me to traverse the precarious gangplank, thronged with comings and goings as sailors brought provisions on board. I threaded my way between the streams of bearers, causing curses and growls as our paths nearly collided.

As I stepped onto *terra firma* I saw Cristoforo approaching, balancing on his shoulders a large parcel of goods in a line of men waiting their turn to stagger up the wooden board, burdened like pack animals. He glanced in my direction but made no sign of recognition as though the chore of labour blotted me out. I watched him toil up the slope till his slim figure was concealed among companions.

My father shook his head as I drew near.

"What are you thinking about? You're getting in their way!"

"Sorry, father!"

He grasped my arm and strode swiftly along the quay, compelling me to run to keep pace. Guilielmo, his sickness gone, knew an eating house where fresh bread, butter, sheep and goat cheese, olive oil, eggs, milk, chestnuts, vegetables, pasta, cured meat and game, and even cakes and pies, could be bought for cheap prices.

We gorged ourselves on a fine meal, flavoured with the island's famous herbs, rosemary and fennel, the proprietor quick to pile extra food on our plates.

After feasting I expected to sit in the sunlight and take our ease. But Guilielmo had other matters on his mind.

"Go back to the boat – I'll meet you there. I have business to attend to."

"Can't I come with you, father?" I asked.

"No, it's not business for boys. It is business for men!"

Such phrases were fresh currency in his exchequer and stung like hornets. But if honesty was refused, I too could be devious. Accordingly, in filial tones I thanked him for the meal, adding a reminder of our noon departure. In mitigation of his foul mood he handed over a small bribe which I transferred to my purse with exaggerated gratitude.

Rising from the table I inclined my head towards the proprietor and skipped away, rounding the corner with a merry wave and a valedictory shout, while my father fastened his eyes on me as acutely as a hawk watches a tasty mouse.

Once round the corner, roles were reversed – I was the hunter,

Guilielmo my prey. It was a game Marco and myself had perfected as we stalked beggars to their lair, monks to prayers, and girls to the river for bathing.

From cover, I observed Guilielmo pay his dues at the eating house and saw his furtive glances and purposeful steps away from the harbour area.

He knew the streets well, so much so that I became confused among the alleyways. Only the manoeuvres with Marco saved me for at least I did not lose sight of the gamebird.

Eventually Guilielmo seemed to have reached his destination for he stopped outside a particular house. After looking earnestly back and forth he knocked firmly on the door, to be greeted by a woman.

I moved to where I could get a clear view of the windows. After some delay I saw Guilielmo in an upstairs room.

Momentarily he disappeared from sight till suddenly I was rewarded with a glimpse of him, though all was perceived from a distance as passing shapes and apparitions.

It seemed an eternity before the door opened and Guilielmo came out, the woman seeming to cling, as if begging him to stay longer. He embraced her and their mouths crushed in a fervent kiss.

Her features were painted, rouged cheeks like apples, lips crimson as a flower, her long black hair loose to the waist.

Before Guilielmo departed she took a handkerchief and dabbed at his face as if removing a speck of dirt.

Was this one of those whom men call *whore, harlot, prostitute, courtesan,* even as they pay them?

As he left she called his name after him, "Gui-li-el-mo", the shrill syllables ringing like the cry of an animal, echoing among the dingy houses.

My father resumed his rapid walking. The journey back was no less unpleasant than coming hither. Sometimes he slackened his stride as though listening, causing my heart to flutter like a sparrow's wings.

How good it was to regain the main thoroughfare where people crowded and pushed and the masts of vessels loomed through gaps between buildings.

Guilielmo, absent from Pisa for so long, was a kind of stranger to me. As a child I had thought father and son were twin cities with no bridges needing to be built from one to the other and no locked gates between.

All false.

Fourth Letter

Concerning the land of Barbary, the customs house,
Al-Alwah, my Master,
my love for his daughter Akilah,
and how Guilielmo cruelly deceived me.

Ne vous esmerveilliez neant,
Car qui aime moult lealment,
Moult est dolenz et trespensés,
Quant il nen a ses volentés.

MARIE DE FRANCE (*c.* 1150)

(Do not be amazed at all,
  That whoever in love does headlong fall,
  Is most sad and heavy-hearted,
  When he from his sweet love is parted.)

I

Sire, My Dear Friend, Michael Theodorus, Philosopher in the Service of His Majesty, Frederick II.

Long before the Barbary coast appeared on the horizon the routines of slopping out, sharing a bed with my father, and the general shipboard filth, became irksome.

My infatuation with Cristoforo withered when I watched him sport with fellows in the rigging and he pointed and laughed in my direction.

Guilielmo oscillated between silence and subdued conversation – he did not enjoy sea journeys. After bouts of sea sickness, my father even cancelled the promised daily lessons in commerce, muttering that there would be time for such matters at the customs house.

As we drew towards the coast we saw palm trees, mountains beyond, and the town of Bugia, white under the harsh sun. The land smelled of heat, a touch of spices, and more than a hint of decay.

The customs house was a few streets back from the harbour, a spacious white building with flat roof and Moorish windows. My room was on the far side from the thoroughfare, a bead curtain discouraging (with small success) the aggressive flies from entering.

I lay on the bed, watching insects crawling back and forth round the ceiling. In the room's stuffiness it seemed I was still at sea with movement and moments of nausea. After an hour or so a knock at the door aroused me.

"Let's go!" said my father briskly, in the same tone as he usually addressed servants. "We'll have a meal somewhere – it will be good for us."

I dragged myself from the bed, and we tidied ourselves and went out. Along the street father greeted people in every direction, bending his head, chuckling, speaking rapidly in their language. Some stopped to touch my hair or face while we conversed.

Guilielmo smiled and made no objection. One old man could scarcely shift his eyes from me. Clutching me by the shoulders with arms outstretched, he leaned his hooked nose and short beard close enough to puff putrid breath, but I dared not show revulsion.

"It is their way!" Guilielmo explained as we escaped, for he too had been ritually kissed a few times to left and right by all and sundry.

We passed scores of beggars, mainly children and young men, their limbs misshapen, one without the lower part of his right leg, the bare stump an incitement to sympathy.

Guilielmo gave them some small coins, to which they responded with a prayer-like gesture, bowing dusty heads.

My father took me to an eating house with crude tables and wicker stools where a dozen men were gathered. They rose to their feet as we approached, Guilielmo nodded and they resumed activities. The owner, a surly creature with one eye glazed white like an egg, took our order. My father engaged him in rapid talk and the man fetched plates and drinking bowls, and trays of food.

The drink was sweet lemon water and our meal consisted of balls of boiled fish flavoured with onion and garlic, a goodly amount of rice, a dish of ripe dates and oranges, and an assortment of sweet cakes much to my liking.

While we ate I observed our fellow diners. Wearing the long white robes of the country, their garments besmirched with dirt and much use, they deftly balanced food between thumb and forefinger of the right hand, talking quietly but with many gestures.

My father needed to pass water. I accompanied him through the confines of the house and out to a hole dug thirty paces beyond the dwelling. The pit was not seemly to behold and I moved back hastily while Guilielmo carried out his function.

Needless to say, the pit was the habitat of a thousand winged creatures, buzzing like music plucked by primitive hands. Its nearness to the cookhouse was not comforting.

We returned to the gathering and sat for a while. Veiled women strolled past, their eyes peering anxiously from within the visor. Some, encased in black from head to foot, were described as 'married women of the desert' visiting town.

By their side young girls trotted like foals, one or two of reasonable beauty, though when I stared my father nudged me as curiosity should not overcome decorum.

Later I learned my first native utterances for greetings, good morning, and thank you. On the morrow I would meet my new tutor even if as yet we could not communicate much beyond the numbers, though Guilielmo expected me to acquire some knowledge of the Barbary dialect as soon as possible.

That night I dreamed of fishballs, an eye like an egg, and beggars toppling like dolls into the pit. I had hoped to enjoy visions of cakes and girls without veils, but this was not to be.

II

I woke early with excitement at the prospect of meeting my new teacher. As it happened it was hours before a polite knock was heard on the main door, though his presence had been expected sooner.

After some discussion between Guilielmo and the visitor I was summoned to our guest room, notable for its tapestries, sumptuous carved furniture, and carpets as fine as any in Arabia, provided and paid for by the Republic of Pisa to enhance my father's status.

On entering this palatial area, quite distinct from the sparseness of the rest of the house, I clapped eyes on a splendid personage, reclining in the best chair like a monarch, with silver beard, imperious gestures, exquisite robes, and solemn black eyes that pierced to one's very soul in a manner both erudite and alien.

My father, standing by the great man's side, hands clasped behind his back, spoke quietly.

"This, Sire, is Leonardo, my son, who wishes to be your pupil."

I bowed before the Eminence, feeling nervous as never before. He nodded regally.

"Good. I know little speech," he said, in a deep voice, "but enough."

I was thankful for that.

"You will address him as 'Master'," commanded my father, "and we know him as Al-Alwah."

"Yes, Master!" I said.

When Guilielmo left the room after more fawning, Al-Alwah settled in his chair.

He was in no hurry, scrutinising the pupil in the same manner as pondering the sheen of a new falcon. Al-Alwah had a habit of rubbing his hands together, as if drying them after washing, for those moments the friction of palm on palm being the only sound.

Abruptly he coughed, noisily clearing his throat of dust and phlegm. The lesson started.

"Are you good?" (*A-re yo-u go-od?*), was his first question, each word two syllables.

"Good, Master?" I asked.

"Yes! Good? Numbers?"

"I love the numbers," I said.

"Good," he answered, "I too."

Reaching down, he produced a board and a piece of chalk. He indicated I should sit cross-legged at his feet, which I hastened to do.

"We will write out the numbers," was his first command.

When I looked baffled he wrote even numbers on the left and odd numbers to the right. After wiping the board clean he passed it back to me, indicating I should write the figures, even and odd, exactly as he had done. We went on to write bigger numbers, of hundreds and thousands.

From there we explored further elementary arithmetic (addition, division, multiplication, subtraction), problems which I solved with a little scribbling. Much of it would have been easy enough when I was only half my present age. I began to wonder if my father was deceived and whether this so-called master was little more than a simpleton to be humoured.

That he continued to repeat 'Go-od' in that ridiculous way each time I solved these trivial sums seemed no kind of compliment, any more than if he had asked me to hop round the room on one leg.

But after this excess of simple things Al-Alwah threw in a meatier bone and at a stroke displayed his mastery.

His first puzzle involved a lord who sent thirty men to plant trees in a field. When they planted one thousand trees in nine days, the lord wished to know how many days it would take for thirty-six men to plant four thousand four hundred trees.

The attachment of a fable to the sum captured my interest, a fact which did not escape Al-Alwah. He rose from his chair to peer over my shoulder as I scribbled back and forth on the board.

I wrote the essence of the conundrum as follows:

9 (days) x 30 (men) = 1000 (trees)
? (days) x 36 (men) = 4400 (trees)

But if such a thing now appears obvious (for everything is easy when you know how), on that day the answer lay beyond the next bend in the road. My chalk scratchings grew ever more desperate.

Al-Alwah, seeing I was lost, took the board and drew the following diagram:

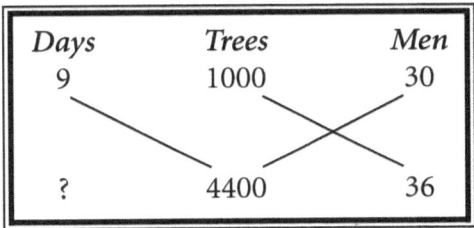

Thus he revealed the measure of his art. For if you multiply thirty men by four thousand four hundred trees and by nine days, and divide the total by thirty-six men multiplied by one thousand trees you will, in one bound, complete your mission and receive the figure of thirty-three days:

(30 x 4400 x 9) divided by (36 x 1000) = 33

This united the known and the unknown. *Ergo* you multiply the known number of men by the desired number of trees by the known number of days, and divide this by the unknown number of men by the known number of trees to receive the answer of the required number of days.

My initial calculations were confused as to which was to be multiplied by what or divided by whatever. But Al-Alwah made the path straight until I perceived a golden road stretching to the stars.

As the lesson was coming to its end Guilielmo entered the room in the company of a girl, Al-Alwah's only daughter, adored as the greatest jewel in her father's possession. This she certainly was, being of such ineffable beauty as I had never before imagined, let alone witnessed. Her smile at once filled me with joy and longing. From that first sight I was afflicted with the passion of Orpheus for Eurydice or Tristan for Isolde.

The four of us sat for a while and drank lemon water. Akilah, for that was her name, proved as vivacious as a cricket, her rapid prattle enticing like the song of a magic bird.

Though her remarks were addressed to her father, whose admiring glances resembled how a rich man looks at a favourite horse, Akilah's eyes occasionally met mine in mischievous asides. I smiled often in her direction. She reciprocated with tiny movements of her head, delightful to behold.

I determined to master her language to reach across the gulf of Babel, though the rock of Al-Alwah would be a hazard to negotiate.

Alas, I knew little of girls, women, traditions, or love. But the young reach out for the overflowing cup and suffer all the consequences thereof.

III

My days were absorbed with the business of the customs house and tuition with Al-Alwah. Transactions were conducted at the front of the building, protected from our living quarters by strong doors through which no stranger entered.

Every vessel visiting Bugia with goods was required to register and be taxed according to the edicts of the Republic of Pisa. This involved contracts, inspections, discussions, evaluations, negotiations, and mountains of paperwork in the reception and accreditation of levies. Negotiating was a vicious bear garden, prone to disagreement as well as appropriate settlements. The foundation concerned the numbers, their assessment and balance.

In accounting, Guilielmo was the arbiter determining all details. The presence of so many complications would have driven many into madness. But my father's competence resolved difficulties before they developed into monsters.

At the root of taxation was a dilemma, the art of valuation. Each cargo, as itemised by captains of vessels and merchants, was of indeterminate worth until assessed by us. This, as one can imagine, stimulated endless bickering.

The men of commerce naturally insisted their goods were worth less on the open market than Guilielmo's inspectors estimated. As a countermeasure, my father overestimated the values of all cargoes. When this framework was established, equilibrium was achieved by compromise.

The rules of the game implied both sides knew the other party was bluffing, the officers asserting that the property was worth far more, the owners arguing for far less.

Guilielmo's art was somehow to provide a kind of philosopher's stone transforming the base metal of dissent into the pure gold of agreement.

As with tax gatherers through the ages, the prime mover (Guilielmo) achieved resolution in each case by what he considered 'fair settlement'. This involved a discount above the sum agreed, wherein the officer of the law secured a specific sum (for himself) beyond that payable to the government. This could create enmity but, if not too rapacious, discounts payable to the officer were a convenient means of adjusting the balance and shortening periods of assessment.

Valuation was thus our problem. The customs house stored dozens of scales, codes and lists dispatched from the authorities. From time to time officials came from Pisa to see the codes were not tampered with and audits were correct. They also satisfied themselves that the corruption of those administering the tax was not excessive. This was resolved, more often than not, by a separate private payment to the visiting official.

But valuation remained the core. The quantity and quality of a hundred cured hides, diverse bales of cloth, commodities such as corn, pepper, Pisan cheese, saffron, nutmeg or oil, enclosed in the belly of a vessel or displayed on the quay, each presented an array of differing appraisals.

In commerce and negotiations, four proportional numbers are of significance, of which three are known and one is unknown:

1) The first of the known numbers is the number of the sale of the merchandise or the measure or weight, according to the goods in question. (Thus one hundred hides can be distinguished from fifty measured rolls of cloth, or so many hundred pounds of corn.)
2) The second number is the price of the sale of the goods, according to the currency we are dealing with.
3) The third number is the price of a certain quantity of such a material, which leads on to an unknown number when the price has to be multiplied.

If one hundred hides are worth, according to official lists, sixty and three-quarter pounds, it might be necessary to estimate the value of thirty-two such hides. Cargoes were not usually bundled together in convenient arithmetical quantities, and so awkward fractions were inevitable in calculations.

It was at this point that Al-Alwah's teachings united with taxation, in a flurry of multiplications, divisions, and subtractions, to be produced to keep up with the volume of goods in and out. Before many weeks passed, Guilielmo gladly provided me with the raw meat of the numbers, requiring solutions in the quickest possible time. Though at first I stumbled, light eventually shone through and for every equation I evolved answers speedily delivered.

It was a question of practice as well as knowledge, though some of the arithmetic would have tried the patience of a saint. But as with saints, perfection is an uphill path. Though at first Guilielmo declined to accept a few of my results and requested further attempts, he was patient with my shortcomings as I toiled hour after hour.

Various merchants were displeased to see a young officer working out taxes. One such man, who often complained of having to visit such a disgusting place as Bugia, attempted to persuade Guilielmo of my errors in a particular transaction.

"The boy is too young to be entrusted with such work!" he whined, his high voice grating on our nerves.

My father was adamant.

"Tell me where he is mistaken and we will pay recompense."

The next hour was spent checking procedures already set out. The man sat in close proximity, the odour of his garments potent, twiddling repulsive fingers on my knee under concealment of the table as we leaned over the figures.

His cargo was cheese, an excessive intake of which perhaps accounted for his corpulence. He also tried to catch me out on currency conversion when units of the Pisan denarius were to be transferred into Barbary bezants.

By using more fractions than necessary, I threw him off track, still arriving at the same answer. When he requested we should go over the numbers once again, my leg still being fondled, I re-wrote the problem and succeeded in reaching the same destination.

Exasperated, he leaned his head close and malevolently whispered an invitation to dine that evening at his friend's house, where food and entertainment would be exceptionally good.

As I guessed what entertainment he and his friend had in mind, I explained how I was compelled to study throughout the evenings.

After murmuring (his lips almost touching my ear), that we should seek pleasure and not just concentrate on work, he approached Guilielmo and now began to sing my praises.

"The boy is splendid!" he cackled loudly, wishing me to eavesdrop. "I want him to visit my friend's house to teach me what he knows. It is useful to be informed about these things."

My father paused before answering most pleasantly and courteously.

"My son is proficient in the numbers though he still has much to learn. But it is a rule that to remain impartial, officers and apprentices consult clients only on the premises. Anything you wish to know, I will gladly instruct you myself."

This was not at all what the man had in mind and his embarrassment was awful to behold.

In addition, Guilielmo cunningly levied a quite exorbitant

discount for his own pocket on the tax payable on a ship's load of cheeses.

Later he congratulated me on bamboozling the merchant with a figure in excess of the correct solution.

"You are doing well," he said, patting me on the back, "You understand this business better than I could have hoped."

As a reward, he pressed several high value coins into my palm. I instantly resolved to buy a present for Akilah with this windfall.

But Guilielmo's assumption that I had falsified the numbers infuriated me, for such thoughts were far from my intentions. In the night, free from any distracting attendance on my person, I wrote out the problem again. Within minutes, I discovered a mistake which enlarged the final sum like a swollen boil. I decided not to confess to Guilielmo as it was better to be thought a knave than a fool.

But that night I did not sleep well for such an error was for me a sin in excess of many other sins.

IV

The gift for Akilah posed dilemmas, what to buy and what Guilielmo might say. But the matter was resolved when, out of the blue, my father casually commented,

"Why not buy a present for Al-Alwah's daughter to show appreciation of his teaching? I gave you money yesterday. You could use that!"

"Good idea!" I answered. "But what should I buy?"

Guilielmo stroked his beard and looked thoughtful.

"An ornament of some kind. That's the best. All young girls love ornaments – jewellery – that sort of thing."

In the evening he took me to a shop near the harbour where trinkets were sold. The proprietor, bowing and scraping, emerged from a back room. Sly as a magician, at Guilielmo's request, he spread out trays of jewels. One had but to point to something and he would raise the bauble, holding it against wrist or neck in a feminine gesture with curious turnings of his head imitating a woman before a mirror.

Tiring of my indecision, he summoned his wife from behind the curtain. Her sullen face did not inspire confidence as she stood, silent as a statue, while our host demonstrated his wares, decorating her with brooches, necklaces and wrist bangles till she was loaded like a camel.

Guilielmo uttered appreciative grunts as the adornments accumulated. But if the articles were confusing enough on the table, their placing *in situ* did not render them more enticing. Then, as if in a moment of inspiration, my eyes alighted on a necklace of the most delicate gold with inset jewels sparkling even in the chiaroscuro of the shop. I imagined Akilah made more radiant by this and myself putting it round her neck, fingers teasing aside her black hair so as to secure the clasp.

"That's the one!" I exclaimed. The delighted shopkeeper eased his hand under the jewel to lift it slightly away from his wife's wrinkled neck.

My father, evidently displeased, engaged the man in a torrent of words. The dialogue moved back and forth like dogs snarling, both being masters of barter. Guilielmo broke off to address me indignantly.

"You've chosen the best jewel. It's worth more than I gave you!"

At this the shopkeeper unlatched the gift from the harridan and, turning my palm upwards, placed the lovely thing in a halo on my hand. He stepped backwards in the manner of an artist before a painting.

"It's wonderful," I muttered. Guilielmo, with a shrug, resumed bargaining. He had got himself into this and he hated being beaten in any contest. The numbers flew round the room in brisk bartering. Finally a sale was agreed.

The jeweller retrieved the necklace, religiously placing the precious object in a case lined with blue silk. I searched my purse, extracting every coin but falling short of what was needed. Guilielmo, with a flourish, saved the day by handing over the amount still owing.

Though harsh words were expected for choosing this expensive item, there was a surprise. Proud that I had vanquished the merchant, my father had augmented my reward. Such generosity on his part was not usual.

I held tight to the gift as we walked home and would have killed any who approached with evil designs. But no thieving took place on these streets for punishments such as removal of ears or limbs were enacted within hours of conviction. The true larcenies were carried out with impunity in the customs house among merchants, dealers and officers.

During the next lessons we studied currencies, a necessary subject though not my main interest. Thinking of Akilah, my concentration drifted like a rudderless ship. Al-Alwah, sensing his pupil's distraction, groaned as my chalk hesitated before I desperately jotted incorrect scribbles.

The problem involved twelve ounces (in weight) of silver sold for seven pounds (in currency) and the best means of reckoning what two ounces would therefore cost. His logic, as always, pierced the darkness. There were no numbers which deceived the Master. Taking over the writing board, he again drew a diagram in two columns, ounces (weight) on the right, pounds (currency) to the left, the question of the unknown figure in the bottom left-hand corner:

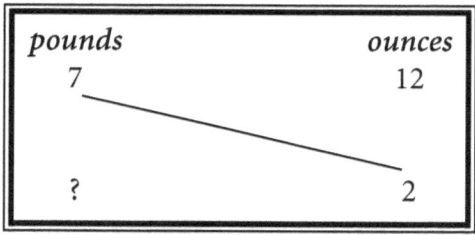

The secret was to multiply the two by the seven, making fourteen and divide by twelve – what could be easier? – a total of one and one sixth Pisan pounds, the equivalent (as it happens) of twenty-three soldi and four denarii. Al-Alwah commented in rebuke, "Your father knows this!"

After this unhappy start we crawled into the swamp of relative currencies. Thus began the juggling of Genoese soldi against Pisan soldi, Magalona soldi in terms of Regal denarii, an Imperial soldo changed to Pisan pounds, a Bolognese pound against Barcelonan soldi, Paduan denarii translated to Venetian pounds, and so on, multiplying and dividing until the mind sickened of such sport.

But I pulled my wits together, that random team of horses, and slowly the chariot struggled uphill.

Al-Alwah, after dwelling on all this paraphernalia, intoned, "Go-od bo-y."

"Thank you, Master!"

I blushed at praise and yet was overjoyed to hear footsteps in the hall. A tap at the door, and Guilielmo entered, followed by Akilah. My father bowed in respect and spoke a few words to which Al-Alwah nodded. I hardly dared look at Akilah. The master turned to me.

"You have gift?"

"For Akilah!" I stuttered.

"For daughter?" he said, pausing. "Go-od. Gi-ve!"

I rose to face her perfection. She had picked up the word for gift in my father's speech and, realising the present was hers and not for Al-Alwah, trembled with excitement.

"Akilah," I said softly, the first time I had ever addressed her by name. It was my opportunity to raise the gift towards her, our fingers brushing as she accepted.

She opened the box, slowly and gently. Her giggling increased then stopped, lips pursed as she glimpsed the gold.

To my delight, Akilah did not touch the necklace but handed back the gift, inclining her head to indicate she wanted me to help her with the adornment.

My pulse quickening, I teased out the necklace. As in a sacred ceremony, I elevated the offering and put the jewel on the goddess, fastening the clasp and fussing it into position.

With a gesture of joy, the gold bright against her skin, she turned to her father who smiled approval. Guilielmo sagely nodded.

Akilah stepped towards me. My face burned like fire, my nostrils imbibed perfume.

"*Shukran!*" she whispered. Reaching out she held both my hands and dipped her lovely head in salutation.

My adoration multiplied feverishly.

VI

So rapid was my advancement under tuition that after a few weeks I requested my father to purchase a quantity of the finest Arabic paper. The paper used in daily taxation, provided at government expense in vast amounts, was inferior, tending to tear, discolour or absorb ink like a sponge if left too long in the cupboard or subjected to heat, sweat or moisture. For daily records it was adequate, final audits being transferred by scribes onto more substantial material in order to withstand the rough handling of inspectors.

Such was my teacher's art that I determined to capture his methods and not allow a single example to escape. At first this was a framework of outlines but the poor skeleton soon begged for flesh to cover its bones.

Hence I began to write my first book, starting with addition, multiplication, subtraction of lesser numbers from greater numbers, division of integral numbers, multiplication of integral numbers with fractions, and so on.

I deemed it prudent not to tell Al-Alwah of this. Even Guilielmo knew nothing, thinking perhaps that the expensive paper was for a diary, poems, descriptions or other trivia.

To set a false trail, I scattered a few sheets round my room with fragments of Arabic texts, Pisan poems, or odd lines from prayers. The book I hid under a loose floorboard directly beneath my bed.

After that blessed day when I bestowed the necklace on his daughter, Al-Alwah waxed ever more benevolent towards me. He still fascinated Guilielmo and myself by his habit of rubbing hands together in that peculiar fashion, a movement more akin to strangling a goat than drying fingers after ablutions. Friendliness on his part increased in proportion to the amount of his language I absorbed. He intimated to Guilielmo that as I was learning to speak his tongue so well he wished to provide a teacher for me to progress further.

The person appointed to improve vocabulary and perfect my accent was none other than Akilah herself. The immediate consequence was that she would come regularly to our house at other times than her father.

I tried to conceal my jubilation from Guilielmo but with limited success for he was nobody's fool. Such was his concern that it brought on another lecture, the third that year.

But among his calculations was that he did not dare to insult Al-Alwah by a refusal of the Master's kind offer. Thus linguistic tuition would be conducted by Akilah according to an agreement between my father and myself.

The details of the covenant evade my failing memory and might be tedious to relate. But the main clauses were obvious, that any relationship between mentor and pupil was meant to be formal not familiar, feelings were subordinate to intellect, lessons would be paid for at the going rate.

As I was already enamoured of the girl, aspects of this contract were null and void before signatures were dry on any imaginary document Guilielmo could have devised. Despite this my father was sufficiently satisfied for instruction to begin.

Akilah arrived one afternoon and she and I were left to get on with the task. At first we were shy as strangers, uncertain of how to proceed.

She was dressed in a long white robe accentuating every movement. My gold necklace swung like a trophy, her eyes, eyebrows, hair, complexion, lips and teeth, a delightful landscape for any young man to contemplate.

After initial silence, we hardly dared to look at each other, let alone speak. A servant brought a jug of lemon drink, and left. We sipped from wooden cups. She put a forefinger to the vessel, suddenly uttering a word, which I attempted to imitate. Having gulped her drink, and placed the empty cup on the table, she muttered incomprehensible phrases in rapid succession, interspersed by laughter.

Akilah set off round the room, pointing at things, exclaiming a word every time. I followed pronouncing each. In headlong flight she touched wall, floor, carpet, pictures, paper, chair, table, ornaments, and the cup again. Tired of the game, she sat cross-legged on the floor and motioned I should sit in front of her, a command I was more than willing to obey.

Here she tried a new trick, reaching out to touch my arm (*dhira*), leg *(rijl)*, foot *(qadam)*, shoulder *(katf)*, each syllable repeated like parrots till mastered. To help things along, I edged closer, my finger first on my nose, then on hers. From here was but a step to ear *(udhun)*, eyebrow *(hajib)*, cheek *(khadd)*, chin *(dhaqan)*, and lip *(shafa)*, around which I drew a slow semi-circle with two fingers, and, in climax, mouth *(fam)*, where I managed to touch her tongue *(lisan)* while sticking out my own.

I took her right hand and indicated each area of it, finger *(isba)*, thumb *(ibham)*, and wrist *(misam)*. Other parts I wished to touch but the game was getting risky.

However, she seemed content, lowering her eyes modestly one second, smiling the next for something else to be nominated.

The chance for revision was too good to miss so I retraced geographies of arm, leg, foot, and shoulder, this time laying *my* hand on the relevant item of *her* body, before progressing to *her* face, hands, arms and legs.

Like a good teacher she tested my knowledge, taking turns to jab at my lips, mouth, cheek, ear, tongue and chin. Laughter flowed and shyness vanished like mist off the sea.

When Guilielmo's footsteps echoed in the hallway, coming to end the lesson, we stood up.

"*Ghadan?*" I asked, wanting another lesson the next day.

"*Ba'd ghad,*" she replied, meaning the day after tomorrow.

Two days was an eternity to endure before we met again. As it turned out I didn't see her for at least a week. At keeping appointments she was never punctual. It was the only fault I ever observed in her.

VII

Akilah and I continued lessons though not always in the house. Once or twice (I know not how we were permitted), we walked by the sea together, just the two of us. She threw pebbles and I watched her throw them.

I was in a state of paradise but clouds lingered. Akilah was contained in a strange separateness, an otherness not to be fathomed. The more I loved her, the greater the distance between us. What I admired snared me daily. That which was beyond knowing, tantalised like fruit out of reach.

Partly the fault was mine. I always felt duty bound to honour at least some of Guilielmo's agreement though not always precisely according to his intentions. Thus occasionally, while out of doors, away from the streets or shaded by palms, we clasped fingers as we walked. She accepted this like an infant of five years old rather than as a comely young woman.

Such a gesture, full of significance for me, meant little to her. In Bugia most people held hands, men in the street, children, relatives, friends, almost everyone except wives and husbands, or lovers. The holding of hands aggravated my desire. I swallowed nervously, pretended everything was normal. She looked sideways, smiled, and said nothing.

I tried to advance progress, putting my arm round her shoulders or waist. Once or twice my lips engaged cheek or hair in semblance of a kiss. Even this for Akilah seemed a kiss delivered as to a child, received as affection but with no hinterland beyond. She showed neither displeasure nor pleasure. The next instant she might break away, laughing, to catch a lizard sunning itself on the path.

The girls of Pisa would have protested, submitted, slapped my face, or refused to see me. Akilah did nothing, as if nothing entered her head. I forced the pace where I could but no passionate fire to equal my own seemed aroused in her heart beyond that of simple friendship.

I concealed my pain always with a smiling face.

VIII

After a while, Akilah no longer came to the house at the end of my lessons with her father. In this country so many unexplained layers of behaviour and etiquette bubbled beneath the surface that it seemed indelicate to enquire about certain matters.

But as my grasp of their language developed so Al-Alwah's instruction became increasingly useful. He was fascinated by diverse problems, dressing them up like riddles in fine words. Each night after such sessions, I entered these jewels into my book of numbers, the concepts growing like the exploration of a new land, each part being continually corrected to bring in different systems of meaning and logic.

I extended the puzzles invented by Al-Alwah with my own tricks and twists.

The master's mathematical problems were calculations dressed not in abstracts but in practical fables. One of these concerned the finding of a purse. Two men who already possessed a certain sum of denarii found a purse containing more of the same coinage. One man, adding the contents of the purse to the previous amount of his money, found he had three times as much money as his companion.

To which the other replied that if only he could have that amount within the purse, he would possess no less than four times that of his companion. I was required to solve how many denarii they each had, and how many denarii were originally in the purse.

Solutions were straightforward once questions were approached in correct sequence. With the men and the purse, the solution could be set out in these terms:

1) *If the first man has three times the amount of the second man, then if the first has three denarii, the second has one, and the purse contains four.*

2) *Thus, as the first with the purse has three, he has three-quarters of the entire sum of their denarii and the purse, and the second, with the purse, has four times as many as the first, which is four-fifths of the same sum.*

3) *Therefore one must find the lowest common denominator of four-fifths and three-quarters which is twenty.*

4) *Thus, with the sum said to be twenty denarii, the first man with three-quarters has fifteen, while the second man with the purse has four-fifths, which is sixteen.*

5) *Therefore, when the purse is counted twice they have between them thirty- one. The difference between thirty-one and twenty is eleven, which was the amount originally contained in the purse.*

But the master did not let the matter rest there. He developed further sums involving three men and a purse, or four or five men and a purse, or two men and two purses, or three men and three purses, or four men and four purses, or when the quantity of the purse is known but only the fractions possessed of the men, and so on.

If such reasonings were often as opaque as mist I excused myself for I was young. With the passing weeks new doors would open and the scales fall from my eyes.

IX

Like a sleepwalker I moved through that halcyon season, accepting greater burdens at the customs house as my expertise improved, attending Al-Alwah's lessons, writing my book, studying the language, and, above all, dreaming of being united for ever in marriage with Akilah.

Some weeks I scarcely saw my father. As I gained experience to deal with taxation and legal niceties, Guilielmo trusted me to work on my own while he visited vessels, negotiated with merchants, ate and drank with friends, or just disappeared from sight without explanation.

During evenings he was rarely at home, excusing himself with a gruff word and going out in haste, usually returning late at night or at dawn. Our lives became separate, united only by the thread of duties.

But in return for estimating values of cargoes and convincing clients of my utter probity, Guilielmo paid a generous salary. I soon amassed a useful hoard of coins including silver and gold pieces.

One day my father approached me at the customs house, just as I was finishing my daily stint.

"Leonardo," he said, in that tone which demanded attention, "I have decided to arrange a banquet in honour of Al-Alwah at our house."

I was surprised for though Guilielmo frequently dined out with his friends, lavish feasts at home were not usual. Before I could bite my tongue I blurted out,

"Will Akilah be there?"

He frowned.

"She could be, if you invite her. But we'll invite many people. Al-Alwah will also bring his associates."

I sensed danger but could not reason why. Being close to Akilah at a social gathering and having to feign indifference would not be pleasant.

Such qualms were associated with my observance of her advancing signs of womanhood. Time was not on my side. Before long other hunters would be in the chase.

I imagined ingenious plots to bring matters to a head. Such longings remained hidden. My lonely secrets hung like chains round my neck, binding me to silence and misery.

Meanwhile, I was busy with details of the banquet. Guilielmo decided the feast would take place in the large room of the customs house itself, with furniture, papers and impedimenta removed, so that we could sit round on cushions and carpets in traditional style. My task was to prepare the room, his was to engage the caterers.

I made out lists of people to invite. Al-Alwah and Akilah were guests of honour, and we hoped for the attendance of various merchants, sea captains and diplomats.

Guilielmo added a few more, including a mysterious widow resident in Bugia to whom I had not, as yet, been introduced.

Menus were left to my father as he was paying a small fraction of the bill, the rest being laid as expenses to the charge of the Republic of Pisa. Guilielmo's share was a fig leaf to avoid any conceivable accusations against his conduct of business.

It was essential to hire extra servants, some to greet the guests, others to help with the preparation of cuisine, yet more to offer an illusion of opulence, a concept not always associated with the ruthless pragmatism of a customs house.

Thus during the days before the dinner, we received a succession of callers seeking employment as servants. Some were no better than beggars, unsuitable for any labour, honest or otherwise. Many of these looked ancient, dirty, and unaccustomed to living in houses. One knocked at the door displaying the raw stump of a left arm, evidence of punishment for some crime. I gave him a coin for his pains, felt sorry for his crestfallen demeanour at being turned away, and that night had a frightful nightmare concerning his grievous affliction.

A number of veiled women came offering small children as servants. While some of these youngsters were pretty and fetching, in the same brood might be scabby little creatures, covered in flies and dirt, marked and scarred by illness. To these pathetic cases I usually offered a few sweet cakes which they immediately set upon as if they had not eaten for days.

When they came in pairs it sometimes proved necessary to

dismiss one of the partners as unsuitable and retain the other. But if a male came with a female, whether wife or relative, it was politic to engage both or reject them together. Men could not bear to be subjected to what they considered loss of face or downright humiliation.

Acceptable applicants were obvious at once. They wore clean clothes, were upright of posture and handsome, spoke with respect but without cringing, and their faces were smooth of complexion without repulsive sores, scabs, or blemishes of any kind.

On the day chosen for the banquet I mobilised my team of temporary servants to move all the official chairs, desks and papers, into the living part of the house, leaving the customs area free for carpets and cushions. This exercise was at first interrupted by mutterings of wonder, for these people had never been in a dwelling inhabited by Europeans before.

Once the novelty was digested, and with dire warnings from our jealous house servants that newcomers were to behave themselves at all times, the work proceeded with only a few minor accidents and breakages.

This was followed by the bringing in of carpets, to be manipulated through the narrow door and unrolled. Synchronisation of efforts was not achieved at first. But with shouting and occasional blows directed by the senior servants at the pates of the more stupid, the task was eventually completed.

The assembled company then enjoyed the scattering of coloured cushions, arrayed round the room like flowers. Whereupon, fatigued by their exertions, many of the hired hands lay prone on the carpeted floor, positioning their heads and limbs in comfort with the aid of the bright pillows.

I found this amusing. But at that very moment Guilielmo, in a foul temper, entered the customs house. Seeing so many recumbent figures he cursed in a most frightening manner and shouted,

"For the love of Christ, stop all this!"

My willing helpers jumped to their feet, wringing their hands. Fastening his evil eye on myself, Guilielmo profaned some more, this time in my direction, threatening that if I was not capable of controlling this rabble I would never be a man of authority, in fact no kind of man at all.

Regrettably I responded to this tirade with Akilah-like laughter, echoed in ripples among one or two of the more audacious servants. At this, my father turned on his heel and stalked out the way he had come.

It took several minutes for us all to stop laughing by which time my cohort of serving men were well won over to my side.

As a reward for their labours, for the dullness of the customs house was truly transformed into magnificence, our regular servants were ordered to prepare lemon drinks for all.

As the gang greedily drank I noticed most of them subsiding back onto the cushions again but did not have the heart to urge them to their feet.

Feeling as weary as my helpers I sat down and listened to their chatter before the next of our chores – decorating the room with silk ribbons, perfumed flowers, and embroidered awnings to cover the austerity of the walls.

X

Before an eagerly awaited event time hangs heavily, its substance wasted in excitement. Yet what will the occasion bring except another apple on the tree of life, almost at once to fall to earth and perish?

But when young we delight in such things, not having lived sufficient days to disregard the limits of possibility. Thus the aura of a banquet beckoned where sparkling lights draw us in like butterflies to flowers.

Guilielmo and I spent a separate hour or two preening, washing, powdering, brushing, cleaning, and putting on choice apparel. Meeting him unexpectedly in the hallway, I hardly recognised him, and he said the same of me.

Flaunting our feathers we went to the social area and fussed around making meaningless adjustments to decorations. The house servants, proud in laundered robes, lined up to welcome guests, though it was as yet only late afternoon.

Unlike earlier that day, Guilielmo was now cheerful and keen to please concerning my efforts with the decor.

"Well done," he said, "You have excelled yourself!"

"The servants helped," I replied, remembering their previous antics on the cushions.

"Now that we are *not* sure about!" Guilielmo said, speaking loudly enough to be heard by those servants hovering at the doorway, but adding a wink.

As dusk fell, with an orange sunset so familiar on the Barbary coast, when the ocean turns to blood and the sky is a flag of colour, guests began to drift in. As usual the first arrivals were the least interesting, merchants dripping with wealth, trading in Bugia for a few weeks.

Servants offered them wine which they downed like thirsty men emerging from the desert rather than in the manner of rich men from sumptuous lodgings. They chatted amiably enough about their enterprises, the lack of viable profit, the inconveniences of the place, and so forth. Guilielmo and I voiced agreement with all they said, commiserating with them for being so far from home.

Soon the room was tingling with laughter, intimacies, jests and cordiality. Some who had disputed nastily over their taxes appeared to be better men here than could be deduced from their usual behaviour. Rituals of drinking helped as excise was temporarily put aside in an unspoken truce.

Disappointingly, Guilielmo's much vaunted widow did not come. In view of conversation being centred mainly on commerce, this was probably just as well.

Al-Alwah's party delayed their arrival till after dark. By then the tapers had been lit and their flickering lights assumed a magical charm. Nevertheless, the lateness of the 'honoured guests' began to try our patience.

Servants were posted to keep watch and welcome them in. The moment of their arrival transformed the mood from irritable anticipation to a sense of fulfilment.

Al-Alwah strode in grandly, splendid to behold, in a black robe embroidered with gold patterns, his turban bearing a mighty jewel, his eyes bright with pleasure. By his side and behind were a dozen kinsmen, some wearing short swords to guard his person.

The merchants ceased chattering and turned and bowed.

Guilielmo and myself, also bowing, approached in welcome. Al-Alwah accepted our greeting with a movement of both hands in blessing.

From the crush my beloved emerged, an angel from heaven. But she was not the Akilah of the day, rather a princess, clad in white with a silk headband, the lamplight flattering her with a luminosity which took one's breath away.

She was not wearing the necklace I gave her but another, more richly jewelled with finer gold, set off by several gold bangles. Beside her were two women, less elegantly clothed, mere shadows.

I addressed Al-Alwah, bowing low.

"Master, how good to see you!"

He smiled, placing a hand on my shoulder.

"I thank your father for this great honour!"

Formalities continued. Al-Alwah introduced us to his kinsmen. Akilah, standing close to her father, said nothing.

Guilielmo and I smiled and bowed in turn to each of the dark warriors who one by one inclined before us, both parties nervously aware of the essential protocol of this welcoming ceremony.

Only when such overtures were completed could the main activity of the evening begin.

Adroitly the dining area was prepared, the places to be occupied by the hosts and chief guests being tactfully indicated by little coloured markers. Once the circle was laid out a procession of servants loaded with plates of food emerged from the inner house, where cooks had laboured all day.

We were arranged like so many planets according to our status. At the centre was Al-Alwah, around whom all things revolved.

To his right was Akilah, and to his left, his men deployed like soldiers.

I seized my chance and, as if casually, sat next to Akilah, Guilielmo on my right. The merchants, making hasty decisions about where and with whom they wished to sit, jostled for places around the ring. With much manipulation of cushions, several for each person, they finally settled themselves.

We looked with amazement as the inner sanctum of the circle filled up with dishes till there was hardly room to place even one more pot. Without further delay we turned to eating. Next to Akilah I breathed deeply her perfumed hair, our elbows touching.

Hands were reaching eagerly towards the regiment of dishes – meats cooked with vinegar and honey, roast chicken and pistachios, sausage and stuffed marrow, breast of lamb, bowls of *mufalfal* rice, fritters dripping with syrup, puff pastry soaked in honey, almond cakes, dried fruits, nuts, fresh dates, and sweetmeats too numerous to mention.

The guests seemed content, discourse diminishing as they concentrated on selection, eagerly loading their plates.

I was happy, Akilah was by my side. I slyly watched her chewing and stuffing her cheeks. How delicious she looked when she ate.

The merchants opposite glanced at us as their hunger found redemption. I observed lustful looks at Akilah.

Al-Alwah spoke occasionally to his daughter but mostly to a man on his left, a warrior hideously scarred on his cheek, who spoke rapidly in the harsh guttural tones of a desert dweller. The conversation, clearly of some significance, continued throughout the meal.

Later, our hunger more than satiated, we indulged in speeches, beginning with Guilielmo, proceeding to Al-Alwah, and then to the merchants, every address more or less the same, the host thanking the guests for coming, the guests thanking the host for inviting them.

Musicians entered to sing plaintive dirges accompanied by lutes, drums and shrill flutes. The wailing music crept into our hearts, filling us with congenial sentimentality about the present, the past, and what was to come.

Eventually, some guests began to slip away, muttering thanks to Guilielmo as they passed, and offering obeisance to Al-Alwah who scarcely noticed them so busy was his colloquy with the man of the scar.

By this time Akilah and myself were somehow closer, edging nearer to each other on our cushions. She looked the very image and fulfilment of my soul's desire.

As the feast drew to an end Akilah asked permission from her father to be excused. Before she departed the girl nudged me and cast such a look that I struggled to decipher what its meaning might be. When she had not returned for some while, with many guests rising and moving round the room to talk, I rose also. As if by instinct, I slipped through the door into the main part of our residence and thence out by the side entrance to move to the front of the building.

Rounding a dark corner I saw Akilah, sweetly alone among the bright shadows of the starry night, under a full moon.

Without a word, but as if expecting me, she led me down the alley by the side of the house. As we stopped she moved closer till our bodies were almost touching. Not sure what was happening I cautiously put my arms round her, protecting her against the night chill. Our lips met, parted, and met again, our actions becoming hasty, almost feverish.

Her tongue penetrated my lips like a flickering snake and she thrust herself against me. My hands lightly caressed the contours of her waist and back, the silk robe tantalising the fingertips, for I had never known such softness.

But as it came, so the moment passed. She kissed me once more, girlish tears running down her face. She breathed a lamenting sigh into my ear. A strange sobbing burst forth within her as if from the depths of a sorrow which I could neither comfort nor interpret.

I understood nothing except she was mine and I was hers, and that this would remain in our hearts for ever.

"I love you, Akilah," I whispered.

"I go!" she said, offering goodbye as if departing on a journey. She slid from my arms and hurried away like Eurydice vanishing from Orpheus.

Shivering a little, I waited a few minutes. By the time I ventured back, Al-Alwah was just leaving, Guilielmo at his side. Akilah, almost hidden in the throng, said nothing. In the half-light I noticed she had dried her tears.

I bowed to the next in line, the man of the scar, and to each of Al-Alwah's party. The group departed into the night, talking loudly. Guilielmo and I waved from the doorway.

For an instant I saw the elfin form of Akilah, her hair like a river caught in the moonlight. They turned the corner and were gone.

XI

Well before dawn that night I awoke from a shallow sleep, nausea clutching at my throat and with severe stomach pains. Making my way outside from bedroom to privy I fell down in a swoon, making a mess from both ends in violent motions.

Guilielmo, having ventured into the town after the feast to consort with one of his friends, arrived back in a drowsy state. By chance he stumbled over my recumbent body, soiling his fine leather shoes with the various fluids saturating my nightclothes and limbs.

Believing his son was sodden with drink, he irritably alerted the chief servant who dutifully carried me back to my room, despite the stained gown.

Three hours later I could not be roused. Those who attended me over the coming days prepared for my death at any time. In fever, I crossed between seas, doors, and deserts.

The faces of those I loved leered at me among reflections and the bright fires of hell. Sometimes I burst through the barriers, finding my brow was bathed by monsters till I slept again.

In my conscious moments they forced milk or wine down my throat. But it all came back, compelling me to choke bile and soil the bed once more with foul liquid and odours.

Guilielmo sent for the physician. I do not remember his coming for I was far away in a silent world. But I was told later that his expression was sombre when he first examined me. Having sniffed the watery stools, felt my pulse, and looked into my eyes, the doctor offered little chance of recovery.

My father gave him a generous payment of gold even before treatment was forthcoming and promised the same amount should I revive and live. Our physician, though spiritually above such worldly concerns, accepted the fee and began the task of restoring me to life.

Al-Mu'allim had studied his profession in Baghdad, the great university of medicine. He claimed not only to cure ailments of the body but to minister to the soul, prescribing a code of conduct such as when and what to pray, what should and should not be eaten and the nature of nourishing herbs.

Some Europeans dismissed him as a quack as he was fond of condemning lascivious behaviour, excessive drinking and self-indulgence, as well as administering malodorous potions. But his reputation was beyond question. It was rumoured that he had once brought a woman back from the dead by breathing into her mouth.

Waking abruptly, I mistook Al-Mu'allim for Al-Alwah, shouted out 'Master', and recited the problem of the two spiders ascending a wall at different speeds.

The physician, assuming this to be a symptom of disorder, forced bitter liquid down my throat till I perceived he was certainly not Al-Alwah. In Pisa I had learned to fear physicians, addicted as they were to letting much blood from arms or legs. But here physicians were nobler. Unlike Pisan doctors they were also clean, purifying their hands frequently and insisting that patients wash daily, especially round those parts from which pollution comes.

Al-Mu'allim visited morning and evening, bringing new medicines or further dosages of the sour liquid. He would massage my aching spine and legs for up to half an hour, whereupon my chest, arms, thighs, calves and feet were pummelled with his strong fingers.

Eventually I was allowed a few steps round the room, my digestion now being robust enough to cope with soup, chicken, bread, and lemon water.

That day Al-Mu'allim put his nose to my stools and urine with more enthusiasm than previously. His diagnosis was contamination from food at the banquet, his prognosis – that such sickness would probably not recur.

He suggested a few minutes of prayer five or six times a day, followed by quiet thought, would disperse false apparitions, nightmares and hallucinations.

I asked if thinking about the numbers might be beneficial. Of this he could not be certain.

Guilielmo paid him the promised gold. Al-Mu'allim was content.

Between the banquet and recovery stretched a gulf of oblivion. Days drifted like smoke.

XII

It was some weeks before I was able to walk to the harbour, or the seashore. My body ached through lack of use, limbs heavy as if bags of wheat were attached. It was such pleasure to breathe the air, watch urchins run back and forth in games, or drink lemon water at the eating house! But I looked as through a veil, for I was not yet entirely of this world.

Thus nature dispatched me to a private chamber until the harvest was ripe. This sickness was a rite of passage filching the dregs of childhood.

Bugia had poisoned me and the draining of the residue left me exhausted. What of the numbers? Did they sleep in my head like hibernating bees? I did not wish to disturb them or hear their buzzing.

Neither was I ready to return to the customs house though Guilielmo was becoming impatient and cursing me for an idle beggar.

"You can't be ill for ever!" he shouted one morning just as I was gathering sufficient energy to visit the beach.

"I won't be!" I said.

"What about your studies? What about Al-Alwah?" His voice took on a dog-like growl, grating on the nerves.

"Summon him," I replied. "Let us begin lessons! Why not?"

"Because I'll not have you shame me in this house!" he snarled. "In your present state you're worth nothing."

"Let us try!" I insisted, though all I felt was weakness like a collapsing cave consumed by the sea.

"And what about your work – your work for me – for which you are paid more than you deserve?"

"You *should* pay me." I said. "I am sick. I am your son!"

My voice rose in anger but without strength to shout. Dizziness made the room move like a vessel.

I slammed the door behind me and went on my way, weeping with frailty.

On the shore I recalled walking with Akilah and watched the waves bobbing. Brown bodies fished in the shallows. Out to sea were two ships under full sail.

I desired to be out there, away from sickness, travelling towards whatever destiny awaited.

That afternoon Al-Alwah called at the house. My father had asked him to come.

"Are you better?" he asked.

"Thank you, Master. Much better now."

"Go-od," he replied. "We work together?"

"Of course. Whenever possible."

"All is possible!" he answered.

"I have not studied my exercises, Master," I said.

"You have been ill!."

We sat in quietness, hearing only distant voices and curtains twitching in the breeze. Neither felt inclined to break the peace. Usually we were too busy to sit idly.

But in my febrile condition, I carelessly broke the stillness and abruptly enquired, "How is Akilah?"

I could have bitten off my tongue and spat it on the ground for asking such a question. But the arrow once released cannot be drawn back.

Al-Alwah paused, seemingly unable to reply.

Eventually he spoke. "Go-od. Akilah is go-od."

"Oh, good!" I said. "Very good."

Having ventured so far, I wanted to go further. For when would I see her again? I leapt once more into the unknown.

"And Master, will Akilah be coming?"

"*Insh'allah – ilHamdu lilaah!*" said Al-Alwah, offering "God willing" and "God be praised" without a single crumb of comfort falling to the love-sick supplicant by his side.

With immense dignity Al-Alwah rose to his feet, as I did too, bowing low, pupil to master. His expression hinted at dark emotions, whether anger, sadness or mere displeasure.

I could not tell. He stooped as if he had aged ten years since entering the room.

Al-Alwah departed without a word of farewell to Guilielmo, a most uncharacteristic discourtesy.

When my father came tapping at the door and saw me alone, he grew anxious.

"Where is the Master?" he asked.

"Gone!" I said curtly.

"No lesson today?"

"Apparently not. We just talked."

"Did you? I hardly pay Al-Alwah just to *talk* to you."

Guilielmo snorted like a bull, manifestly insulted.

"We didn't talk much," I said, in mitigation.

"Obviously enough to upset him!"

I sat down to rest my aching limbs.

"Perhaps!" I whispered in a feeble voice.

"Perhaps? That word contains the biggest concept in the world," snapped Guilielmo scornfully. "Commerce is founded on it, as are wars, philosophy and man's very salvation. You'll have to say more than that."

Deciding I might be flogged twice but only hanged once, I told him the truth, for what it was worth.

"I just asked about Akilah."

"Hmmmm," was his response. "And?"

"I asked if Akilah was coming."

Guilielmo pulled up a chair and sat opposite me. His voice softened.

"Leonardo, what did the Master say?"

"He said nothing. *Insh'allah – ilHamdu lilaah!* That's all."

"No more?"

"Not another word. Then he got up and left."

Guilielmo stroked his beard, as if meditating on a tricky calculation in the customs house.

"Then he left?"

The beard stroking continued. I was feeling dizzy, tired of this twisting path.

"Hmmmm…well, Leonardo, perhaps you shouldn't have mentioned Akilah. It's a sore point. I should have warned you. You weren't to know. I can't blame you."

Bewilderment replaced dizziness.

"*What* didn't I know?" I murmured, panic filling my throat.

"You were fond of Akilah?" replied Guilielmo, sympathetically. I hated his use of the past tense.

"*Fond* of Akilah?" I answered with as much indignation as I could summon. "*Fond?* I *love* her with all my soul. She is all I want, I loved her since I first saw her. I want her for my own."

Guilielmo winced as he saw my eyes fill with tears.

"Don't be upset, Leonardo. You have been sick, just as you were in Pisa. You are very young. Love is not what you think it is."

I could not stomach such condescension.

"But for me it *is* what I think it is. It's what I know it is. That's all there is to it."

"But the numbers, your future? How can such a girl fit into that?"

"*Such a girl?*" (I imitated his voice cruelly.) "The daughter of the greatest scholar! *Such a girl* fits in very well. But whether she does or not I still love *such a girl*. That's all there is. Without her I don't know what I'll do. *Ever!*"

"But, please, please, Leonardo! You are not as other boys. Al-Alwah tells me you have a gift from God for the numbers."

Al-Alwah had never offered any revenue of praise to my face. But I was pleased. His opinion might lead to another gift, that of Akilah herself.

My tears flowed – she seemed to stand before me in her loveliness. Without her my heart would break into a thousand pieces, like a crystal vase smashed by a child.

"Papa!" I said, "I want her. I cannot live without her. It is making me ill to love so much. I never loved anything except the numbers. But I want Akilah, as my wife!"

The poor man tried to interrupt. I quietened him by raising my hand, just as he did to me sometimes.

"God gave me the gift of numbers. But He has also given me the gift of love. Why shouldn't I love? Why not? Love is love! You loved my mother. I love Akilah. She has been in my thoughts ever since I first met her."

Guilielmo stood and raised me to my feet. He took both my hands in his and put his face close to mine.

"Leonardo, you are mistaken!" he whispered. "You do not yet know love. One day you will thank me for what I have to tell you."

How well I understood every inflection of his voice, each expression on his face. It was like looking into a mirror.

"What are you saying?" I said. "What is it I don't know?"

"Sit down first!" Guilielmo commanded. "Be a man! You are my son, not a fool!"

We sat down again.

"Listen!" he said, like a storyteller beginning a tale. "You cannot marry Akilah or any girl from this country."

"Why not?"

"Because…because they have customs which do not permit it!"

"Foreigners have married Barbary women!" I said. "I'm sure they have."

"Perhaps they have! But to marry Akilah is not possible. I am telling you!"

"Why not? For the love of Christ, why not?"

He leaned forward. His next words had the bite of a snake.

"Because Akilah is married!"

The venom spurted from his mouth and I was poisoned.

"Married? Akilah? When?"

"When you were ill. She was sent to be married. They have strange traditions here. She was betrothed from her birth."

My throat constricted.

"But whom did she marry?"

Guilielmo thrust in the last dagger.

"Do you remember the night of the banquet?"

"Yes!"

"Well, the man with Al-Alwah, the man with the scar. He married Akilah. She is with him in the desert. That is why the Master is sad."

Grace departed. I entered a wilderness. The man was with Akilah, she was with him, for ever and ever, and always.

Overcome, I rushed to my room where I fell into a frenzy of fury, insupportable jealousy, and all the extremities of bereavement.

XIII

Some hours later, having considered the matter, I confronted my father with composed features, assuring him I would continue with my studies and forget Akilah. Whereupon he kissed my cheek and wept.

When I heard him leave for his customary assignation with women in the town, I dressed in native clothes borrowed from the servants and retrieved my manuscript and private savings of coinage from their hiding place.

Downstairs I stole every bit of currency from the customs box for daily expenses, a goodly sum, and slipped out into the darkness.

In the port an Egyptian ship was preparing to sail at dawn. Making the acquaintance of the captain I handed him generous coinage to book my passage to another land.

Thus I shook off the dust of Bugia. With Akilah and bitterness in my heart, I passed the night on board in tolerable comfort.

As the sun peeped over the horizon the vessel threw off its ropes and headed east.

Fifth Letter

*Concerning departure from Bugia,
my journey through the desert,
and the redemption of Abdul.*

Ne laisse pas pour reparlance
Qu'el nel voie dedans sa tente;
Dès or est toute en lui s'entente,
Dès or l'aime, dès or le tient...

BENOÎT DE SAINTE-MAURE (*c.* 1150)

(Not hesitant for fear of ill repute
 Within his tent she looks for him there;
 Henceforth her love is all she shares,
 Henceforth in love she holds him near...)

I

Sire, My Eminent Master Michael Theodorus, Philosopher in the Service of His Majesty, Frederick II.

During that journey conscience conflicted with justification for my actions. Conscience punished me for fleeing Bugia and Guilielmo. Justification argued that a young man needs to flex his fledgling wings outside the nest. On that pitching deck, day after day, I balanced right against wrong.

My anguish was but to think of the man with the scar violating my beloved. Passing years have not diminished those images, her subjugation, the brute force of the warrior. A vestige of this poison still lurks within.

But Guilielmo! How much he must have suffered when, returning satiated from a widow's bed, he found his Leonardo gone? He who gave me life surely entered into hell, not knowing whether I had taken ship or ventured to the vast desert to slake my sorrow.

Sailing eastwards, the next dawn, I imagined his weeping, his prayers. Such entreaty came from the very waves, the salt they blew to my lips being the substance of his tears.

Of course there was little I could do. The voyage once undertaken, bracing breezes and the rhythm of the swelling waves somehow dulled guilt.

At first, my moral sense was an irksome see-saw swinging up and down like the realm of Neptune itself. But as nights and days passed, resolve strengthened. Like a novice in unaccustomed delights, I began to glory in my escape, all sickness, of body or soul, dissipated.

Such was my recovery that I took out my book of the numbers and began to fashion improvements. I baptised it with the name *Book of the Abacus,* in part because the voyage recalled Cristoforo, the poor sweet boy with the abacus.

To Al-Alwah I gave scant thought. My theft of his numbers, their burial and resurrection in the book I intended to present to the world, seemed recompense for any injury I had suffered.

Such work was retribution for the Master's callous treatment of that creature whose misfortune it was to be his daughter, like a chattel disposed of in barbaric fashion.

II

Our vessel called at many ports on that voyage, so many that I have forgotten their names. Each landfall was an interruption to the blue serenity of the journey, but, if given an opportunity, I went ashore, visited eating houses, and attended to the native speech, becoming ever more proficient.

At sea I worked on the *Book of the Abacus.* Already the chapters were filling out like spring trees, where buds became leaves, and the greenery clustered to encircle each branch.

I discovered the joy of constructing diagrams and schemes, adjacent to the problems they represented, each aspect of the numbers multiplied till it became fruitful. Thus the division of 780005 by 59 or 81540 by 8190, or 30749 by 307, jostled with the subtraction of 841 from 15738 or the art of dealing with fractions such as multiplying $17^{11}/_{98}$ by $28^{11}/_{173}$ or $^{14}/_{27}$ by $^{22}/_{35}$.

To lovers of the numbers these elements are the foundation from which all things proceed. Therefore I decided that no less than seven chapters were to be devoted to the building blocks of the method. I developed a thousand exercises by which students might progress from the simplest to the most difficult.

So many hours at sea passed in happy fruition. Though the fires of Akilah still burned, by work the heat could be suffocated under a blanket of thought.

On deck, gazing at the sea, it was different, remorse for my lost love haunting me like an evil spirit that comes and goes.

Looking into a mirror after some days I observed my complexion to be nut-brown from sun and wind. My disguise became more plausible as the pallor of illness abated. In this way a man might be born again, changing what had gone before to prepare for that which was to come.

Weeks later, in calm seas, we glimpsed the blessed land of Egypt.

III

I left the vessel at Alexandria, a teeming city with swarms of beggars loitering to pick up scraps from ships. The good captain embraced me warmly, wishing me a fruitful journey for wherever destiny would take me.

In exchange I gave him a letter for Guilielmo to be delivered when the vessel was next in Bugia. This epistle, in the kindest detail, explained my reasoning, reassured him that I was well, and would one day return.

At this moment I would have been ashamed to contemplate Guilielmo's fury. Time might be a great healer but I know it better as the deceiver who sifts our days and nights with fine mesh, waiting to destroy us whatever we do.

I did not linger in Alexandria though many scholars of the numbers live there. Instead, with head hooded against the heat and a cloth round my face, I ventured to the outskirts, carrying my few possessions to where caravans of overloaded camels clustered like pilgrims ready to set forth.

The Leader of the enterprise, swathed in black, looked at the coinage offered. He asked for more, which he received. The extra amount satisfied him so much that he at once selected one of the less bad-tempered camels to be my companion for the journey.

A boy named Abdul was summoned, soundly smacked round the head by the Leader, and thereby appointed as my camel master. He was a wretched parentless runt, the produce of casual dalliance. Whatever the sins of his progenitors, he paid a thousandfold, being the butt of every jest and buffet his companions could bestow on him.

On occasion Abdul became so insolent I was tempted to beat him myself. For instance, the brat laughed hideously when, during my first lesson in riding a camel, I fell heavily from the beast. There was much ridicule to be endured before I was eventually stowed aloft with feet and legs in the correct posture, belongings securely fastened, and the wayward motions of the animal mastered.

When we set off at last in the long line of the caravan the boy walked ahead, shouting for me to do this or that, none of which I performed to his satisfaction. In the end he took himself off to the second camel in arrears of mine where he perched, shrieking with amusement and always at my expense.

As we voyaged step by step into the sandy oblivion each traveller withdrew into private thoughts. Every camel monotonously followed the one in front as hour by hour we endured cramp in shoulders, arms, back and thighs.

As for the sensation of 'thirst' during that morning, this was like nothing previously experienced. The gullet constricted, eyes ceased to water, sand gritted against teeth, and nostrils grew sore as if hot sticks had been inserted. This was accompanied by a swooning sensation.

The eyes began to lose focus on the haze of horizons round and about, mirages took on new meanings. Though such illusions were caused by the desert's reflections, one questioned the senses, wondering if others could also see such marvels.

I hardly dared to drowse as we moved along for that might bring about a dreadful tumble. Yet half-sleep induced hallucinations of shadows, fragments of fables or visions.

As I slid into repose, my fainting dreams full of grapes and wine, the man behind drew level on his camel and lashed me across the shoulders with his whip, commanding me to keep awake. Indignant but grateful, I thanked him, the pain arousing me from lethargy.

At the first oasis I was too tired to speak. Abdul came to aid my dismount. We drank from the same pool as camels and goats. When we had gulped down a sufficiency and splashed our faces, hands and arms, the Leader asked me to accompany him. Wondering if I had caused offence, I meekly followed, the desert making me passive like an inebriated man. From baggage piled on one of the pack camels the Leader pulled out a set of black clothes, just like his, which he handed over with a slight nod of the head. It was a gift from heaven. He pointed, with some disdain, to my white Barbary garment and indicated I should change immediately.

I hurried behind the privacy of the meagre palm trees to disrobe. As if by magic an audience presented itself, including some women, Abdul (of course), and one or two of another party lounging in the shade.

Threats and curses achieving nothing I pulled off my clothes. The observers were intrigued by my fair skin, the females ululating in mock admiration, the men gesturing as if admiring a prize goat, the idiot boy rolling about with exaggerated guffaws.

As I completed the change they grew quieter. By putting on the enveloping headgear with its sinister visor, I became indistinguishable from them.

Before departure a call of nature came on me. I trotted a short way into the wilderness to dig a hole, hitch up my clothing and try my best. Hardly had I turned to bury the evidence when a dozen black dung beetles, their horrid eyes set on stalks, arrived from the depths of the sand to claim their meal, rolling my recent deposit before them, and possibly thanking me for my generosity.

With new clothes, well watered and my bowels cleansed, I returned refreshed to the journey. Once more Abdul assisted my ascent into the saddle and, with more cackles, left me to myself. In less than an hour the oasis seemed but a memory, as we swayed under the sun, just as before.

I was worried towards nightfall about sleeping arrangements, being without personal blankets or other necessities for making myself comfortable. We eventually arrived, God knows how, at a conglomeration of black tents spread across a wide area, near a small pool of water and what appeared to be a dried up well.

I watched as the camels were laboriously unloaded, watered, and taken to be hobbled for the night.

The Leader approached. Putting his arm round me in a friendly manner, he led me to one of the larger tents. Here I found food and tea. Before long every one of the travellers was gathered at the fireside, eating and chattering, though their dialect was difficult to follow.

Eager to find sport they offered me a sheep's eye or a wedge of putrid mutton fat to eat, replenished my cup with more tea, enquiring with many furtive glances where I came from and the purpose of my journey.

They knew nothing of the world beyond. For them Pisa, Bugia and western Barbary might have been on the moon. The sea interested them not at all but they loved to tell legends of the imagined past, long-winded tales and poems. Later, as their spirits mellowed, some intoned songs of love and betrayal, causing one's heart to burn with regret.

When it was time to sleep the Leader came with bedding. He took me on a circuitous route to an outlying tent, indicating I should sleep near a small fire liberally surrounded by spare fuel of dried camel dung. The tent was mine with no other inhabitants to share my dreams. I thanked him, he bowed and departed.

Fatigued and weak, the taste of foul food in the mouth, I sorted out my bedding and crawled into its comforting enclosure. The night was chill and the million lucid stars of the firmament made it colder. I drifted towards sleep, particles of dreams wafting back and forth like circling birds.

I thought of Akilah in a tent like this, caressed and taken by her loathsome husband. From time to time I woke, hearing little noises, rustling sounds, far-off voices, perhaps the distant cry of an animal.

But footsteps kept coming. In sudden fear I sat up abruptly and peered out into the darkness.

A shadowy figure approached. By the light of the fire, my pulse drumming in head and chest, I saw a woman of the tribe, with head uncovered, her long black hair flowing to her waist.

To warn against any salutation, whispered or otherwise, she placed a silencing finger on her lips. With scarcely a pause, she slipped into bed beside me.

She was not young. With such nomads it is difficult to assess their age once the youthful bloom has faded. Certainly she was strong for she began to embrace me firmly. Deftly she removed her scant upper garment to reveal herself.

As the joust began in earnest and her mouth touched my face, I threw caution to the wind. When I fondled her breasts she moaned and writhed like a snake. One body excited the other, and groping beneath her dress, I explored for the first time the secrets of a woman.

Did she sense I was virgin? It did not matter for what was needed was forthcoming and my teacher was thorough.

How long we twisted and turned like fish on a golden hook, I could not estimate. But too quickly I dispersed my seed. After that she muttered soft words, incomprehensible but comforting while I stroked her face tenderly.

All too soon the game ended. She sat up, put on her clothes, and left.

Lapsing into contented sleep, I hardly knew whether I had been visited by an angel or an apparition of evil.

IV

At dawn the sand shimmered like gold coins. Walking to the communal tent I looked for the woman but all had covered their faces. It was impossible to recognise one from another.

I crouched to partake of food and water. The company said little, mumbling occasionally as they ate as if contemplating the day to come. I kept my head down, wondering if any knew of my adventure.

Soon, in accordance with their usual morning ritual, the men brought the camels closer to the encampment and began to load the baggage.

I helped as best I could, straining to lift the weight and sweating profusely with the effort. Three or four women stood idly round, mocking my attempts to assist their masters. Perhaps my unexpected paramour was among them but their anonymous attire preserved discretion.

The boy came late, his face blotched with purple bruising. He did little to assist me. It was sad to observe how he had momentarily lost his laughter and that defiance which carried him through tormented days.

The caravan set out once more. Slyly proud, at ease with myself, I relished the hours of travel and discomfort to come.

When we were next granted landfall among palms and dunes, our party dismounted, crushing together round a small discoloured pool. Like a herd of monkeys we bent to its benediction and drank noisily. In my haste, I took no notice of those next to me.

During this ritual the women discarded their veils, the better to drink. Being nudged, I looked towards my neighbour and saw my partner and mentor of the previous night.

In the dappled sunlight among the palms all faults stood revealed. By firelight her features had looked quite attractive. But she was hardly the same woman by day. Her hair was greasy and matted, her complexion pitted with deprivation, her wrists thin. She laid a hand on my arm to show friendship.

"*Shukran,*" I said, unable to think of anything else.

"*Armala,*" she muttered, a new word.

I shook my head to indicate I did not understand. She nodded as if to say *she* understood everything. With that she replaced her veil and moved into the crowd of dark-clad figures.

As we reclaimed our camels I found much to think about. She was not pretty, such a woman wore life on her face. But we had come together and I remembered everything and was grateful.

The word *armala* echoed like a sounding bell, a lyrical word, which she pronounced almost as if she was singing. Perhaps this was her name. Desert tribes often assumed peculiar forms of address, quite different from those of Bugia.

But it was no comfort when the boy, once he condescended to help, also sang out the word, *armala,* as if in harmonious conversation with himself.

"*Armala?*" I asked, pitying his bruised face and glad that he had resumed some semblance of his usual self.

"*Armala,*" he replied, smiling. "*Armala. Bushra.*"

I knew then that *Bushra* was her name. But how could he have noticed that she had spoken to me at the water hole?

When I was at last perched in my high seat and ready to travel, he looked up and rudely repeated, "*Armala! Armala!*"

Screeching with laughter he went back to his mount, his high voice resonating like a mynah bird.

That night in camp the Leader again approached after the meal. He carried bedding for me and escorted me to my solitary tent, I thanked him. With a curt nod he left.

I crawled under the blankets curious to see if my visitor would come. Just when I was falling asleep, a rough tap on my shoulder gave me a shock. There she was, snuggling in beside me.

Now that I knew what was expected, I ministered with more competence than the previous night for I had become the teacher and she my pupil.

We pleasured for time infinite, lost in ourselves, naked against the coarse blankets. When matters were resolved we slept like children embracing.

I woke in the budding dawn and she was still there. With an anxious look at the brightening sky, she indulged me again with her passion before hastily dressing and departing.

I fell into a satisfied sleep. But in dreams the word *armala* resounded like a gong from a cavern. In panic I sat up, my head full of visions of widows such as Guilielmo courted in Bugia.

Bushra, like a thief in the night, had indeed visited. The Leader had given me a widow.

Even the boy knew. Perhaps they all knew.

VI

The wilderness breeds bad thoughts. Among these wastes people are different. They could cut my throat with no qualms. Their code follows survival and those who infringe the code are not left unpunished. Untutored one might be, but sinners pay the price even if the nomads had tricked them into transgression.

It was like playing chess without knowing the rules. Shifting pieces round the board gave the game to those who knew the moves. I was less than a pawn. Explanations, contrition – nothing would be accepted – a curse was on me. Despite my borrowed clothes I believed my life to be reaching a premature conclusion.

One hope sustained me. With these travellers I had broken bread. Having gifted me with a widow they might be content if I took her in wedlock, a thought as nauseous as swallowing dust. Thus I resolved to do whatever they demanded. In a lonely stupor induced by the sun I prayed for the protection of their desert God.

Later that day, as we made camp, Abdul, the hated bastard child, fell sick with vomiting and emissions of bile. His condition was considered such a threat to the tribe's well-being that, in accordance with their customs, they carried the boy's inert body into the dunes, abandoning him well beyond the tents.

The Leader announced that the boy was as good as dead and any ministering to this untouchable would be punished. As I had retired to bed early I knew nothing of this.

I might have remained oblivious to Abdul's banishment till morning. But walking out to present my usual moonlight offering to the dung beetles I tripped over what seemed like a dead animal half-covered with sand. At first I thought it was a decayed goat but its smell was of a more human kind.

Overcoming my repulsion I kneeled to look. At my touch Abdul shivered, breathing out a strange mournful gasp which dislodged some of the dirt from his clogged nostrils. Thinking he had collapsed from the heat and was not yet found, I lifted him away from that awful place and took him to my tent.

I gingerly stripped off his polluted clothes, committing the dirty rags to the fire, laid him on the ground outside and fetched water from the oasis. With a cloth I washed away the filth, cleared sand from his eyes and ears, and found his brow only slightly fevered. Using a fresh towel and a little water, I cleansed his entire body, including the parts where he had soiled himself. I doubt whether the child had ever been so pampered in all his life.

I brought out the robes borrowed from Bugia and put them on him, including an undergarment, all too big but they would do for now. I carried him inside the tent, wrapped him in blankets and placed pillows behind his head.

When eventually his eyes opened he shied away in trepidation as if expecting punishment. But I stroked his forehead and spoke gently.

I insisted he should drink water, which he then gulped so eagerly he could have drowned in its excess. Having imbibed enough to fill a camel he settled to sleep as sweetly as a baby.

Pleased with the night's work I anticipated a grateful response from the Leader that Abdul had been saved from a premature death.

As I once more felt his brow to check his condition, soft footsteps approached. Bushra crept in. By the firelight, the boy's pale face was that of a spectre, a sight sufficient to quench her usual ardour. Her relief, as I interpreted it, at the boy's appearance in white apparel, his scrubbed countenance shining like a bright coin, was demonstrated most oddly. She let out a sequence of distressing sobs, covering her face with her hands.

She seemed in a state of mourning, ready to tear her clothing or beat her bosom with clenched fists. When she recovered her voice she became furtive, looking constantly beyond the firelight to the other tents, then back again and all round, as if wild beasts were preparing to attack. I laid a hand on her shoulder but she flinched, for it was the same hand with which I had soothed the boy's brow.

"*Mawt, mawt, mawt!*" she muttered as if demented. I assured her there was no death in this tent. But she reiterated "*Mawt, mawt, mawt!*" in rising urgency, jabbing her forefinger towards my nose, though careful not to touch.

I took a fresh cloth to comfort the boy's face, at which he woke up, looking up at the two of us, his childish expression as innocent as a kitten. Without another word Bushra hurried from the tent. I attributed this to the unpredictable ways of the nomads of whose customs I had so much to learn.

But in a few minutes she returned, this time with some kind of linctus which she administered as gently as his own mother might have done. Whatever the medication was he licked his lips, liked its flavour, and fell into a deep sleep, a little colour coming back into his face.

Bushra gazed at me with a tenderness quite distinct from desire. But when assured that the boy was truly sleeping, she made me understand with gestures and a few words that she did not wish to be associated in any way with our patient.

I nodded agreement, past caring about anything except that the boy should be well. Before leaving Bushra waved her palms at me in disappointment that there would be no dalliance this time. I was so weary that oblivion came at once, toppling me into a dreamless slumber.

When I woke, shortly after dawn, Abdul was still asleep. At my touch his eyes opened. Without moving he giggled in that mocking sound which formerly I had hated so much. But this time I joined in with his merriment, surprising both of us.

Having ordered him not to move, I went to the main tent where the early meal was under way accompanied by the usual soft grunting and muttering.

The men looked inquisitively as I scooped up several slices of cold mutton, two lumps of cheese, and three pieces of bread, and filled two cups with milk from the pot. Perhaps they thought the woman had stayed through the night. But I was becoming reckless, caring little for their foibles or curiosity.

Abdul consumed his portion as if accustomed to being waited on at this hour. Obediently he was still in bed and turned his face to permit me to check whether his brow was cool. That he appeared refreshed and well I attributed more to Bushra's potion than my efforts on his behalf.

When raised to his feet the boy was once more sturdily himself. Compared to the previous night he was surely none other than my little Lazarus, risen from the dead and from the desert.

On an impulse I embraced him, seeing myself as a kind of Guilielmo welcoming his son back from the brink of nothingness.

Abdul, familiar with blows and curses but never affection, threw his thin arms round my neck. I wept with shame to think how only yesterday I had so despised him.

VII

Without a thought in my head, except a kind of joy, we walked together to the scenes of activity near the watering hole. I felt him stumble in his weakness. But he chattered happily and his incorrigible laughter cheered me.

As we approached, the men broke from their work of baggage and camels to surround us, standing a few steps away as if we were contagious. Such was their commotion that the Leader himself appeared in our midst like an angel of doom.

Sensing danger I held Abdul closer, smiling foolishly in appeasement at the angry faces, bowing my head to the Leader towering like a colossus.

So extreme were the circumstances that the man tore off his headdress, turning on me the majesty of his sullen countenance, his dark eyes ominous with menace.

In the torrent of foul curses and spittle that came forth from his mouth, I comprehended more the spirit than the letter of what was uttered. But one could not avoid notice of the repetition in various forms of a word familiar in Abdul's daily life signifying filth and uncleanliness.

At that moment I remembered not only Al-Mu'allim who once restored my health, but also Guilielmo's gift of lies, words flowing from his lips so sincerely that all present instantly began to believe that which was manifestly untrue.

Casting caution aside I searched my heart and found there the deception needed. I looked straight into his harsh visage, drummed my knuckles against my chest and shouted *'Tabib, ilhamdu lillaah',* identifying myself as none other than a physician and praising God for it.

A gasp of astonishment emanated from the watchers. The Leader twisted his mouth horribly, disbelieving my falsehood but unable to refute it. For here beside me was the evidence of my skill, Abdul resurrected by a miracle.

After further furious grimaces the Leader turned on his heel as if to attend a more urgent meeting. The nomads dropped to their knees, hands held up in prayer.

I passed through their ranks holding the boy to me, a lucky omen that I too was now safely untouchable.

VIII

Having fallen into necessary deception I both enjoyed and suffered the fruits of duplicity. The nomads henceforth no longer jested against me but offered undeserved awe and deference to my role as healer.

The message was communicated, with a certain amount of exaggeration, to all whose paths we crossed, increasing both my own value and the esteem of the bearers of this good news.

As a consequence a parade of loathsome ailments plagued my tent each evening. Sick children, ulcerated legs, infected eyes, bloated stomachs, as well as a quantity of yellow abscesses, were brought to me in orderly succession at the end of every travelling day.

Aping from afar the methods of Al-Mu'allim, I insisted on much washing of wounds and binding them in strips of clean cloth, fasting for abdominal complaints, piercing of abscesses with a red-hot knife, and massage for muscular conditions.

My patients were disappointed that I had no medicine with me. But I informed them that these techniques relied entirely on natural concepts rather than disturbances of the body's functions or humours.

With my new friend Abdul as an eager assistant during consultation times, it was a pleasurable moment when none other than the Leader himself presented an old injury for inspection.

He had sustained a knife thrust to the stomach some years before, leaving an impressive scar, a thumb's length from his navel. From time to time the wound played up, giving him a rancid, hot taste in his gullet and acute pain as if the blade were still in his flesh, especially after riding for several days. For this condition I prescribed extra doses of goat's milk to soothe the throat and comfort the intestines.

The Leader appeared pathetically grateful for these crumbs of advice and departed backwards from the tent bowing low.

Though I was a charlatan in this enterprise, it was no worse than the ministrations of physicians in my native land and I hastened nobody's death.

As the days passed our caravan entered the cultivated lands adjoining the delta. The diet began to improve as many types of fruit, a better quality of date, superior rice, and a variety of fish, became available.

I soon assumed the role of guest of honour at evening meals though my demeanour remained aloof as befits someone of my alleged status.

Of Bushra, little was seen though she smiled whenever our paths crossed. I missed her nightly visits but, having escaped the perils of entrapment, I no longer wished to return like Daniel to the lion's den.

Meanwhile, Abdul clung to my heels to repay whatever debt he owed. Within the tribe his position advanced from pariah to living miracle, a being brought back from the groves of darkness, and therefore blessed. Even to touch the hem of his garment was considered lucky by some.

Abdul was consequently promoted from camel boy to first servant to the Leader. Given respect, the transformation from runt to dignified youth was testament to the healing powers of kindness.

In the time remaining I grew very fond of him. His help

during sessions with patients was invaluable. He ran every errand willingly, fetching water and cloth, bathing putrid sores without squeamishness, and offering explanations when their dialect was incomprehensible.

Nevertheless, as we approached within sight of Cairo, I desired to return to my studies as a man wishes to be reunited with his wife.

Therefore, well before dawn one day, a good walking distance from the city, offering no farewells, I slipped away from the caravan carrying my book of the numbers, coinage, and a few other belongings.

I hurried on, clothed in the apparel loaned to me by the Leader, the rays of the sun rising in a halo from behind the buildings. Thus disguised as a nomad I joined the throng of workers on their way to labour.

Two hours later, having crossed the old bridge from Ibaba, amazed and enchanted by my first acquaintance with the mighty Nile, I edged through the city gate like a fugitive.

Sixth Letter

Concerning my sojourn in Egypt,
my studies with Al-Kabir,
a visit to the Great Pyramid with Ibrahim,
and departure from the Nile.

Or potess'eo venire a voi, amorosa,
Come larone ascoso e non paresse!

PIER DELLA VIGNA (1190–*c.* 1249)

(If only I could come to you now, my darling,
Like a thief in the night and never be seen!)

I

Sire, My Most Revered Master Michael Theodorus,
Philosopher in the Service of His Imperial Majesty,
Frederick II.

Entry by the north gate, the square-towered Bab-an Nasr, into the great city filled me with excitement and fear. To left and right guards in rusty armour detained certain individuals, for no apparent reason hauling them roughly from the crowd.

But they paid no undue attention to my nomad semblance.

I passed on among the swarms of day labourers pressing forward to whatever tasks awaited them.

Once beyond the portal I hurried through the streets, my nostrils, accustomed to pure desert air, now assailed by intermingled smells of cooking and garbage.

When I sighted an array of vestments for sale, pausing to touch one of the exhibits, a pleasant looking individual enticed me in with welcoming words.

From his store I selected a decorated skullcap, and a rakish *imama* or turban, complete with a superbly woven *khirqa* to flow under the turban and across my shoulders. Several types of white mantle were shown to me, some from Persia (few Egyptians wore them). I chose a cool cotton cloth, soothing the body with its light caress, surmounted by a cloak with an embroidered border.

Behind an ornate screen I discarded my old attire, leaving it on the floor, to emerge in new clothes from head to foot. The proprietor exclaimed aloud at the transformation.

Even with my turban appropriately adjusted, I probably looked as enigmatic to him as I would to myself. But he uttered appreciative grunts and called his mother from behind the arras to share his admiration.

The man was no amateur when it came to extracting payment. We bargained for many minutes. In the end I gave him more than intended but less than he demanded, leaving both parties slightly dissatisfied. Moreover, having acquired my discarded remnants, he gathered them up with care before handing them to the old woman.

I emerged into the streets holding close my bundle of worldly goods. The passers-by were cautious in their response to such white-robed splendour. Rather than bending my head humbly forwards, I squared my shoulders to walk boldly, ignoring beggars and glances from the inquisitive.

At a dining house I enjoyed beans and fish washed down with goat's milk. I brooded on the adoption of a name and finally settled on Al-Abbas, the Frowner, to blend modesty and curiosity.

Fortified by food, drink, and the benediction of a new title, I set out for the Mosque of Al-Azhar where learned men congregated. Its minarets were visible from afar but the sun was near its highest point by the time I approached.

Having reverently removed my shoes, I entered the holy place, the building's magnitude overwhelming my thoughts. I drank in its space knowing this was the finest architecture of the East. The noon heat shimmered oven-like on marbled terraces. But inside the precincts, multiple arches miraculously captured cooler air, refreshing body and soul.

I gave a coin to an old blind man at the entrance, pleading for alms in a singsong voice, cross-legged in the dust as if he had been sitting there for ever. Not expecting much of a reply, I enquired where the learned teachers of this place might be found. Without pausing in his chant, he lifted a scrawny claw to point across the street to the scholars residence, conveniently adjacent to the mosque itself.

Full of apprehension I ventured into a courtyard leading to a grand building of some splendour. Near the gateway a porter sat at a table, casting a cautious eye on all who came near. He seemed reluctant to answer any of my questions or even to have a civil tongue in his head.

Just as I was becoming irritated, a young man, emerging from a side door, came to my rescue. The porter relapsed into sulky silence while the helper asked the purpose of my visit.

"I wish to study the numbers," I said. "I have travelled from Barbary."

Showing no surprise he announced his name as Ibrahim, a disciple of this school. He led me without further ado across the wide courtyard and into the building beyond. After requesting I should wait in an anteroom, Ibrahim went off to consult his masters.

On his return I was ushered into the presence of an elderly scholar. Ibrahim left with a bow. At the sage's gesture with open palm, I obediently seated myself on the floor in front of him.

"What is your name?" he asked.

"My name is Al-Abbas." I replied. "I am from Bugia, where I was a student of Al-Alwah."

My name obviously puzzled him.

"Al-Abbas? Al-Abbas! I am Sa'id al-Kabir, scholar of the numbers."

The man paused as if hoping his fame extended as far as Bugia, wherever that might be.

I bowed my head. This appeared to please him for he smiled benignly.

"Before we proceed, there are a few formalities."

"Certainly," I said.

"What is 300 multiplied by 49?"

With only the slightest hesitation I replied, "14,700."

"What is 300 divided by 49."

This was more difficult.

"Six, remainder six."

"1692 divided by 18?"

"92, sorry, 94."

And so it continued, cat and mouse, the mouse replying until the cat was impressed.

Al-Kabir switched tactics. He asked about valuations of currencies and the relative amounts paid by four men with diverse sums of money in the purchase of three horses. Each of these, in one form or another, was in my private book. I was well prepared. So Al-Kabir tried fresh tricks, probing weaknesses rather than strengths.

"Tell me about the *Method Elchataym* and problems solved with it?"

Alas, I could not.

"What about finding square and cubic roots or the treatment of binomials and apotomes?"

I confessed defeat.

"Have you studied the rules of geometry and the problems of algebra and almuchabala?"

My head lowered in shame. Such things were known to me as children know of exotic animals in distant countries. My triumph was halted. But Al-Kabir, observing my hangdog face, abruptly ended the interview with a moment of encouragement.

"Do not be dismayed, Al-Abbas, or whatever you call yourself. Rarely does anyone impress me. To pay for your keep, you may be required to teach some of our younger pupils."

"But Master," I stammered, "I have never given instruction."

"No matter – they will learn much from you."

Al-Kabir rang the bell and Ibrahim returned.

"Take Al-Abbas to one of the rooms set aside!" said Al-Kabir. "Al-Abbas, I will see you tomorrow."

I followed the young man through many corridors. My room, when at last we came to it, was small and stuffy like a monk's cell, its solitary window overlooking the courtyard. Clean bedding was set out. The meagre furniture included a chair, a table with writing materials, a bowl of water, a faded flower in a vase. Ibrahim gestured like a proud landlord and, commenting that his own room was just along the hall, promised to return later.

II

Within an hour, Ibrahim woke me from a nap. He insisted on showing me round the establishment, visiting the refectory, library, gardens, washrooms and privies.

Rules were strict, especially concerning the bearing of false witness, spreading gossip, arbitrary absence from class, or failure to uphold the dignity of the establishment.

Ibrahim reeled off a list of horrendous punishments for failure to observe the code, from mild caning to suspension, expulsion, litigation and incarceration, by which time I had begun earnestly to despise him.

As I had been appointed by Sa'id al-Kabir as a tutor, Ibrahim made it clear that a high level of moral conduct was expected from me. No tolerance was allowed for any scandal or dishonour.

Ibrahim was no ordinary student but a kind of watchdog to induct newcomers, monitor behaviour and to report back what he discovered. His words betrayed no cravings or weaknesses. Even asked about so simple a matter as the porter at the gate, Ibrahim put a finger to his lips in a vow of silence.

Caution was necessary with such a paragon of perfection. As helpmate, guide, keeper and spy, Ibrahim was useful but treacherous. Beneath deceptively calm waters lurked a shark who could devour me, his rectitude being in contrast to my own dabblings in the puddles of human squalor. Naturally I felt both inferior to his spirituality and superior to his priggishness. While Ibrahim was entering life by the narrow gate, my net had already been cast into more polluted waters.

He did not treat me as a colleague but vomited in my face a rule book only partially ingested. Fortunately the customs house had offered generous schooling in hypocrisy. It was no hardship nodding at his superficial wisdoms while inwardly laughing up my sleeve.

Ibrahim's concern was avoidance of petty sins such as speaking badly of the porter, being late for class, not cleaning the room, dirty garments, running in the corridors, and so on. Most sins, apart from pride and envy, had passed him by.

We ate a meal together in the refectory. A few students gathered. As a monastic tone was obligatory, conversation tended to be in hushed whispers.

Afterwards I invited Ibrahim to accompany me in a walk through the streets. He was reluctant but I spun a yarn about needing to know the district. So together we wandered hither and thither through mazes of alleys, Ibrahim anxious lest we become lost. Once beyond the precincts of the residence, he cast fearful looks from side to side, especially when accosted by lewd women who invited us to enter their abode.

One of them was exceptionally blatant, arms open in welcome, her dishevelled garments most provocative. Poor Ibrahim blushed, obviously never having thought about or seen such things. We moved on, leaving their importuning.

Ibrahim was silent.

"What is wrong, brother?" I asked, more from malice than concern.

"Nothing. I do not walk these streets often."

"This is new to me also!" I replied.

"We go back now?"
"Of course!" I said.

⚜ III ⚜

The next morning, awoken early by birdsong, I presented myself, armed with chalk and writing slate, at Sa'id al-Kabir's teaching room where he sat deep in thought. I bowed and crouched respectfully on the floor before him.

Al-Kabir launched into a problem. A tree in the courtyard has seven-twelfths of its length underground and above the ground twenty cubits. How tall is the tree?

Thus I came face to face with the *hisab al-Khataayn*, later identified in my *Book of the Abacus* as the *Method Elchataym* or the *rule of false position*. How simple was his outline of the question, how elusive the solution.

The principle of the method was, on the surface, straightforward. Its essence was to postulate imaginary measurements and progress by calculated falsehood towards the truth. At first I traversed a dozen corners, as I clung to the two fundamental elements of the problem – the height of the tree above ground and the seven-twelfths buried in the earth.

Following much contemplation and writing, I arrived at a conclusion which was *not* the correct answer. Baffled, I shrugged my shoulders.

The Master grunted that he could understand why my name was Al-Abbas for my brow wrinkled like an old woman's hand as

I worked. But he taunted with good humour, aware that solutions are achieved through method not intuition.

His explanation was precise, as pure as running water, as intricate as mosaic:

1) *Everything must be logically integral to everything else.*
2) *Move away from the problem to look at it in a different way.*
3) *Do not be afraid to travel in order to return.*

He proceeded:

Seven-twelfths is the core of what we know. Therefore if the tree is twelve cubits in its entire length, seven cubits will be below the ground and five cubits above the ground.

I scribbled it down, imagining the tree, its greater part under the soil. Al-Kabir continued.

"But the tree is not five cubits above the ground, it is twenty. So in our first estimation we are still fifteen cubits out! Fifteen entire cubits!"

I wrote this down too. His voice became serious.

"Listen! We are at the crossroads! If we suggest another position – that the tree is not twelve cubits in its entire length, but double that – what would we have?"

I replied that fourteen cubits of the tree would be below ground and ten cubits above and that we were only seven cubits from the height above ground.

This caused him to smile.

"Good. Now we draw the diagram!"

Turning triumphantly back to his board, he wrote in large figures the four-sided gateway to truth:

	cubits
5	12
10	24

The secret was to multiply ten, representing cubits above ground, by twelve in the opposite corner and divide by five, the result being twenty-four cubits.

Next, the sum of twenty-four was added to the twenty-four cubits of the second position, making a total of forty-eight cubits for the tree's length.

A moment's thought concerning the seven-twelfths of the hidden tree produced the sum of twenty-eight cubits beneath the soil, and twenty cubits of visible tree.

I was not sure of being able to solve this by myself. Al-Kabir then analysed the problem in detail – what we started with, what we knew, how the diagram was constructed.

When the lesson ended, he announced that my teaching of young boys must begin the next day. Bad pupils should be punished by application of the cane to soles of the feet or palms of hands.

My plea, that love of study is not taught by beating any more than birds learn to sing by having their feathers plucked out, fell on deaf ears.

❧ IV ❧

At dinner that evening Ibrahim was nowhere to be seen, his absence being very welcome for I had no desire to run the gauntlet of his questioning. After the meal I slipped out through the main gate, though unable to avoid the evil eye of the porter who was leaning against the doorway as I left.

It was a relief to walk normal streets again and shake off the petty oppressiveness of the residence. I sought the route followed with Ibrahim the previous evening, finding my way slowly among twisting alleys. By pure chance, after meandering far too long, I recognised the place where we had encountered the gang of women.

Still loitering for trade, a collection of females, some younger, some older, preening, stroking their thighs and moving their hips like dancers, spread across the street. When they caught sight of a man they ran to him as if greeting a beloved friend.

They seemed particularly pleased to see me and crowded round, fondling my arms and shoulders, their smooth fingers exploring the texture of my foreign face.

One woman took me gently by the hand. She was pretty enough and I nodded. She smiled, showing uneven teeth. The others circled and pushed to gain attention. When I attempted to follow this particular woman, her associates drifted away according to their own protocol.

Through a narrow doorway we passed deserted rooms, till we came to an area at the back of the house with carpets, cushions, and bedding.

She drew back a curtain across the entrance to one of the rooms with a practised movement. Not sure what might happen next but interested in finding out, I willingly entered the lair of the temptress.

We sat together for a while on the soft ornate rugs. She offered sweet tea. I drank slowly, licking my lips, enjoying the flavour and her increasing closeness. I gave her a coin or two. She looked sulky and wanted more. The glint of another made her expression brighten.

As if by magic, we moved together onto the comfort of the bedding. Thereafter she enticed me gently, each step quite logical, from first to last, from presentation to consummation.

When the matter was resolved, falling back on the bed, she feigned sleep, flicking her long eyelashes open and shut to show she was but pretending. I rested beside her till I fell asleep.

V

When I awoke tapers had been lit round the room, but the woman was gone. By night it would be difficult to find my way back to the school.

I listened for sounds, the stillness making the house eerie. I eased from the bed and, hastily pulling on clothes, began a retreat, treading tiptoe along passageways, past closed curtains, where hidden sleepers sighed or snored.

On reaching the entrance I breathed cooler air. In the alleys, boys and beggars, wrapped in rags, were dispersed among the shadows, a dim moon picking out thin legs and calloused feet.

They slept with heads covered. I kept as far away from them as possible. Turning one corner then many others, the way became confused as I entered empty streets that no longer attracted vagrant sleepers.

By three hundred paces I was lost. But spotting a dark gap between the hovels, earnestly hoping not to encounter rats, I crouched down to await dawn. Hours passed, my ears attuned to every sound near or far.

When light appeared, a blushing suffusion, the day straining to be born, I crept from my shabby cave and set off, very soon observing familiar landmarks as good as a map.

Near the mosque a man was setting out his tables and chairs. I requested tea and a meal. After food and drink my spirits revived. I did not move till the call from the minaret announced the time of activity was upon us. Within seconds crowds of eager young men were flocking from the residence on their way to prayer.

Casting off my shoes at the entrance, I joined them. As they prayed, so did I, bowing my head, the devoted rising and falling like white waves against the marble floor.

On the way out, jostling through the throng, I almost collided with Sa'id al-Kabir, walking arm in arm with Ibrahim. They looked startled as if they were just talking about me.

"Good morning, Master," I said.

"Al-Abbas? This is a surprise."

"For me also!" I murmured.

"Remember the tree problem?" asked Al-Kabir out of the blue. "Two things are known, one thing is not. So with life!"

"Did you sleep in your room?" snapped Ibrahim.

"Of course!" I answered. "Where else could I go?"

"I came. Your room was empty."

"Perhaps I was visiting the privy!"

"The porter saw you go out!" said Ibrahim.

"Is it forbidden? If a porter sleeps, I wouldn't wish to disturb him."

"The porter never sleeps!" replied Ibrahim.

Al-Kabir turned with an angry frown towards Ibrahim.

"Al-Abbas is our honoured guest – I expect you to be friends."

"Forgive me, Master," muttered Ibrahim.

"Good!" said Al-Kabir. "Al-Abbas, you will not forget what I said about teaching, will you?"

"No, Master," I said.

VI

I hurried back to my room, washed from head to toe, put on clean attire, and set off like a gladiator to the arena. After a short social visit to the refectory with Ibrahim, who watched me like a sulky child, it was time to confront the class.

Striding the criss-cross of corridors I made certain which room it was to be. My classroom was on the ground floor at the rear. Without much of a view, it suffered annoyance from students sticking their faces in to see what was going on. An occasional breeze carried certain odours causing pupils to pinch their noses and giggle.

The boys, fifteen altogether, were sitting cross-legged on the floor, each with board and chalk. As I came in they jumped up like soldiers, scrutinising the unknown tutor with anxious eyes.

I motioned them to be seated. A willowy cane, like a snake ready to bite, rested meaningfully on the desk. How kind of Al-Kabir to be so considerate.

When I greeted the boys they replied in unison, their shrill voices echoing round the walls. We began the lesson. First their names. They were about twelve or thirteen years old. One boy seemed bigger and older than the others, an individual of low intelligence, scorned by all whenever his stuttering voice failed to provide an appropriate answer.

First, simple addition, two plus three, five plus seven, and so on, before moving to larger amounts and, apart from the stutterer, the class did quite well. I dictated a list of sums to be solved, they obediently wrote them down. As they toiled over these simple calculations, I patrolled behind the class, observing each pupil in his style of writing.

One peered sideways at the efforts of another, hoping to copy from his neighbour who shielded his own scribblings with a scrawny brown arm. Another stuck out a pink tongue in concentration as his chalk scratched on the board, others glanced furtively around.

Later they became restless. Some had completed every question, others were marooned. The stuttering one was bent over like a hunchback but wrote nothing.

Engrossed in observing them, I casually picked up the cane and ran my fingers along its length, testing the springiness. Some boys saw my action and nudged partners, returning their gaze quickly to the boards. Abruptly I stood up, cane in hand. In an instant, each boy looked from the puzzles to the Master.

Holding the stick firmly at each end, I raised it, lowered it, and snapped the rod over my knee. Walking to the end of the room, I threw the pieces out of the window, hurling them as far as I could. The boys broke into applause, laughing, patting each other on the back, some beginning to lounge about in relaxation, losing their fear.

It occurred to me I had fallen short of the standards of my own mentors. They taught me the value of spice and flavour. What could be duller than five plus four or twenty plus seven? Far better to offer six camels in an enclosure, five monkeys on the roof, seven rabbits in a hutch – and so, how many animals do we have there?

I moved at once to this superior method. The excitement of the boys was beyond belief as they competed to find answers.

I enquired how many eyes these animals possessed, how many legs, how many tails, how many ears, how many teeth. As with all scholars, an impossible question aroused so much discussion they began to guess at possible answers.

We progressed from addition to multiplication. If six donkeys have two offspring each year and breed the following year and the year after that, how many donkeys would a farmer have? Even the poor stutterer took part in the debate.

In the middle of this turmoil Al-Kabir, accompanied by Ibrahim, entered the room, causing the pupils to jump to their feet in genuine terror until, at his imperious nod, being permitted to crouch back onto the floor.

While Al-Kabir and Ibrahim stood on guard like inquisitors, I introduced fractions. The questions were about sharing a cake between seven pupils, an orange between five, or a melon between eleven thirsty workers.

Each boy drew diagrams and in pairs argued like old men over the division of the spoils. When the class was dismissed they trooped out, looking back over their shoulders towards me as they went.

Al-Kabir came forward, oozing benevolence like a lion who had just devoured an antelope. Ibrahim remained silent as the Master bowed and murmured,

"Excellent, Al-Abbas! We will continue with our studies two days from now, *Insh'allah!* Tomorrow Ibrahim will take you to see our monuments."

"Thank you, Master!" I said.

Ibrahim did not look overjoyed.

~VII~

The following morning Ibrahim duly arrived at the appointed hour with two horses bearing ornamented saddles. By long custom it is preferable for Europeans to ride horses rather than camels. Mine was an adequate beast but slightly smaller than Ibrahim's steed.

We ambled along, the sun on our backs, crossing the languid Nile and its dirty little tributary, the Al-Bahr al-Ama. Houses and alleys were left behind and the Pyramids sprawled in the distant heat. Our horses walked ever more lazily. No drumming of heels, blows or entreaties could hurry them.

I began swaying in the saddle as heat confused me into a state of trance. Ibrahim became concerned, handing over his water bottle and commanding me to drink. By the time we reached the foot of the Sphinx I felt sick and dizzy. But the awe of gazing into that animal face eased the spasm.

As we came to the Great Pyramid Ibrahim commented, as if reading from a list, on the weight of the stones, how they were transported, the number of men who died in its building and the cost to the Pharaohs. He was trying to please. His statistics were surely imaginary though I was in no condition to argue.

Ibrahim suggested we climb to the top. At this my stomach grew weak as I loathe heights. But he laughed and said it was usual to try. If I felt tired we need not go right to the summit. Some attendant nomads, hopeful for our trade or any other, took care of the horses as we dismounted.

Ibrahim did not hesitate but shouted and ran to the first obstacle. Within minutes he was as high above us as an eagle, waving mockingly. Not wishing to be beaten I made a jovial gesture of futility towards the horse minders and, with some scraping of flesh on stone, pulled myself up onto the nearest lump of rock.

As I ventured from one block to another, Ibrahim became a marker above, moving fast, often perched out of sight. As the desert fell away below, my limbs shook with exertion. But I was determined my companion would not outclimb me.

Near the halfway point I rested, chafed from the sharp edges of the masonry. Below, the nomads appeared like so many ants, strolling around enviably at their ease, occasionally looking up, as if assessing our painful progress to the dreadful summit.

Thus I edged nervously towards the accursed Ibrahim, though it proved impossible to keep him in view for long. An infinity later I neared the peak and there he sat, as fearless as a pirate. My face drenched with anguish at the hideous perspectives of stone beneath us, I reached his side and stretched out on the immense slab which pinpointed the summit. Such was my vertigo and fear, a sickness pouring from my throat could not be contained.

He ignored me at first, shading his eyes and surveying the distance. Though the view was unlike anything ever seen before, its very vastness was discomforting as if enlarging the drop to the sand. I looked to the four corners of the compass, dreading the descent.

Ibrahim slipped an arm round my shoulder and I leaned against him. In weakness of spirit I embraced him, clinging to the soaked sweat of his garment as a frightened girl grasps a doll.

"We go down now?" I asked.

"Yes, down," he answered.

"You will help?"

"Yes, *Insh'allah!*"

And so he did, not going too far ahead, assisting by holding my arm or leg if the block down which I was shinning was larger than others.

Several times, I almost swooned while sickness flowed. Ibraham pretended not to notice.

As with all things, an end eventually came. I thanked Ibrahim for his trouble in bringing me here and spat on my blistered hands.

The ride back was in silence.

VIII

At our next lesson, Al-Kabir launched directly into the Method Elchataym. His first problem concerned a man who went on business to Damanhur, then to Tanta, and on to Zagazig, doubling his money in each place and paying out twelve denarii as expenses in every town.

In the end, the man had no money left. How much therefore did he take with him at the beginning?

The solution once more involved supposition, false estimation and progress by error. This departure from normal calculation teased the brain. But the principle to keep in mind was that to depart from previously learned systems of logic involves skill not intuition, procedure not chance. I started the new curriculum with relish, hoping to impress Al-Kabir.

The first step postulated that the man began with twelve denarii:
1) To Damanhur with 12 denarii, doubles his money = 24 minus 12 for expenses = 12
2) To Tanta with 12 denarii, doubles his money = 24 minus 12 for expenses = 12
3) To Zagazig with 12 denarii, doubles his money = 24 minus 12 for expenses = 12
Final value errs by plus 12 (too much)

Next, what if the man set out with eleven denarii?
1) To Damanhur with 11 denarii, doubles his money = 22 minus 12 for expenses = 10
2) To Tanta with 10 denarii, doubles his money = 20 minus 12 for expenses = 8
3) To Zagazig with 8 denarii, doubles his money = 16 minus 12 for expenses = 14
Final value errs by plus 4 (too much)

In the second supposition, when the capital was decreased by one, we were nearer the target by eight than in the first. To discover by how much more the capital must be decreased, multiply the four by the one and divide by eight, the result being one half denarius:

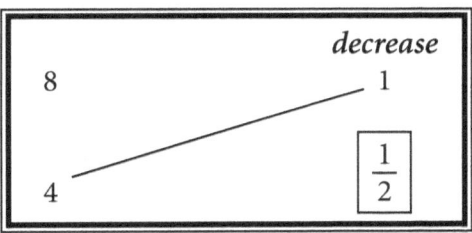

This half denarius subtracted from eleven denarii gives the final tally of ten and a half. When I arrived at this conclusion, Al-Kabir scratched his head and sat speechless.

But this was merely preliminary to similar problems. Concerning five men who bought a horse, two men who found a purse, of a man who invested money, four men who bought a horse, and so on – each delivered with such speed my writing was scarcely able to keep up.

These tutorial encounters were but a sort of war between the Master and myself. When I defeated him, he provided further obstacles. Thus Al-Kabir kept his dominance while I struggled.

With these tactics we moved on. After the lesson I spent hours noting down Al-Kabir's *Elchatayms*, inventing a few of my own to consolidate the method.

IX

That evening I ventured out again to satisfy other needs. This time finding the way was easy. Some inhabitants of the streets waved in greeting as if they already knew me.

The quite attractive woman with dishevelled garments was waiting outside the house in company with the creature of uneven teeth who had previously taken me to her bed.

But somehow, after the initial hubbub of welcome, I found myself paired with the same one as before, more through her intentions than mine.

Once again we reclined on the soft rugs and drank tea. However, progress was at first slow. She insisted on enquiring about things of interest to her – my name, where I lived, my country, my occupation, how many wives, and so on.

The questions were interspersed with drinking, caressing, and kissing. I deflected each inquisitive dart. My name became 'Ibrahim', my country 'Greece', my occupation 'scribe'. The only truth admitted was that I had no wife.

She gave her name as Afifah, requesting that I repeat it several times to secure the correct pronunciation according to her Cairo dialect. At the end of this linguistic exercise it became clear that I had not yet achieved perfection and further practice was necessary.

Above all, her profession required simplicity. For example, she grasped perfectly the principles of supply and demand, never giving less than I asked nor more than she needed to. Moreover, her trade being pleasure, she seldom failed to please. *Ergo,* I was fond of her.

"Two things are known and one thing is not!" I said quite out of the blue, for no other reason than to mock Al-Kabir.

Afifah swooped on the comment like a hawk on a mouse.

"What is not known?" she asked. "And why not?" To such astute questions no answer was possible, not even a lie. She emitted a peal of girlish laughter at my inability to reply.

Afifah took my hand in hers, tenderly touching my fingers skinned and chafed after the Pyramid climb, examining my palm like a fortune-teller, gently smoothing the abrasions as if to heal them.

To encourage advancement I produced two coins, and a third, holding each in turn between thumb and forefinger as if offering a morsel to a parrot.

Afifah was truly as great a practitioner of her particular profession as Al-Kabir of his. She accepted each coin and asked for a fourth and a fifth, which I gave her. In exchange, she disrobed as shyly as a bride.

When at last our bodies writhed together, wrapped in blankets of silk, her flesh as fresh as water to a nomad's mouth, she murmured in urgent crescendo against my ear,

"Ibrahim – Ibrahim – Ibrahim – *Ibrahim!*"

From the *Method Elchataym*, Al-Kabir moved to geometry, *algebra*, and *almuchabala*. For the first of this trinity, we became good friends with Euclid and Pythagoras, their triangles, circles and

squares, and the perennial proofs of the dimensions of space in measured areas.

In accordance with this I introduced simpler aspects of angles and diagrams to my own pupils, who took special delight in drawing shapes and geometrical designs each to be measured and discussed.

Algebra and *almuchabala*, differentiated by Al-Kabir as *Proportion* and *Restoration,* enticed me into roots, squares and equations. Receiving the teachings of Abu Ja'Far Mohamed ibn Musa al-Khwarizimi, dead for two and a half centuries, whose concepts Al-Kabir propounded with extraordinary passion, I thus began to savour the true elixir of knowledge.

After wrestling with these problems most of the day, it became a blessed relief to visit Afifah by night.

At first she was tender, gentle and undemanding, and her company was pure pleasure. I looked forward eagerly to the silky embraces with her lithe brown flesh and her little animal sounds of satisfaction. In a short time I almost believed myself to be in love with her because of her obliging nature and submissive charms.

Unfortunately, after this early spirit of romance, a change occurred, perhaps at the promptings of her companions in the house. First she began putting on a show of becoming jealous and possessive, demanding I was never to have lovers other than herself.

Then, requesting more payment, she offered as part of the new bargain, meals, impromptu dances (scantily clad she throbbed her abdomen rhythmically before disrobing), massages, longer hours and vows of devotion. She also took to scolding me roundly if I displeased in any way.

When it was inconvenient for me to visit her on a particular evening, Afifah was so incensed she would not come to bed till I begged forgiveness. In justification she claimed to have abandoned all others to devote herself exclusively to my welfare. This was not beyond the bounds of possibility for our hours together elicited so much coinage from the suitor that her fidelity had become a sufficient profession in itself.

Her friends occasionally attended our meals or arrived for conversation. Each showed interest and vied like children for my attention. I observed their names and characters – the vivacious Aida, the sulky Fadwa, the reticent Nawar, the extraordinarily beautiful Zafira, the happy Samira.

Afifah, however, took good care of her property, clearly indicating when their presence was no longer welcome.

Unfortunately, my outings did not escape attention at the residence, mainly because of the porter who observed all things. Moreover, Ibrahim became increasingly intrigued by the mystery of my nocturnal excursions, so much so that I often took a circuitous path to Afifah to avoid any possibility of being followed.

Looking over my shoulder while dodging through back alleys, doorways and diversions, I endeavoured to shake off pursuers, real or imaginary.

This worked well until one morning, on stepping out of Afifah's house, I thought I saw Ibrahim waiting across the street. Fortunately, I was wearing new garments which he may not have recognised and my head was covered.

Nevertheless the return to the residence was a merry dance, considerably longer by many diverse streets.

Once back, I changed into other clothes, kept out of sight and sent messages to Al-Kabir that through temporary illness I was not able to give or take lessons that morning.

By this deceit I avoided Ibrahim for a day or two but later decided it had perhaps not been him outside the house after all.

XI

Despite abundant misgivings my assignations with Afifah continued with reliable frequency. But one night a routine visit found her mood transformed into angry darkness. She had no immediate appetite for dalliance and would not in any way be persuaded to fulfil her normal functions.

As I considered that I usually responded fondly and tolerantly to most of her whims, this black despair was neither anticipated nor desirable. But after many kind words, coaxing, and much passing over of coinage, Afifah shyly confessed herself to be 'with child'.

As the alleged begetter, or scapegoat, for this deed, I bit my tongue and said nothing. With the cat out of the bag she assured me, accompanied by a profusion of tears, that she was indeed with child and not in error.

Alas, the scales instantly fell from my eyes. Afifah was, as I had surely guessed all along, a wretched scheming creature, surrounded by pitiful women of similar tendencies. From pure love for Akilah I had descended to Afifah, falling pathetically like Icarus from brilliant heights to sordid depths!

A stag seeking flight, over the next hour I promised Afifah the earth itself, support, friendship, love, even marriage. Eventually her moody tantrum ceased. She drew close and we lay together. Following the briefest of couplings, as we caressed in the aftermath, Afifah let slip that she admired all who studied at the *madrasa* but would never tell anybody there about me or the baby or anything else. This proved she was no fool and knew far more than she should.

She was reluctant to allow me to depart. From time to time she patted her stomach, pointing to the putative father and uttering a deal of baby talk, as if to please. Eventually even Afifah became bored with this game and released me from her bondage.

I promised with kisses and embraces to return the next night and the night after that and all would be for the best. She was to fear nothing.

I gave her extra coinage and promised more. She replied that money meant less than other things. She trusted me and would make a good wife. I answered that I knew she could be, that I was happy, she was happy, and we were both happy.

Once away from the house I ran like the wind, regardless of the sharp moon filling alleys with sinister shadows.

Back at the residence, though the hour was abysmally late, as always the porter prowled at the entrance. I went directly to my room, full of alarm and fear.

Gathering together my meagre possessions, book, coinage and clothing, I wrote a letter to Al-Kabir pleading the receipt of bad news from my family which meant that I must leave at once. One hour before dawn I left this place of learning.

As I went out of the gate the porter was for once deceived. My vigilant enemy was nowhere to be seen.

I made my way to the Nile where many vessels were gathered.

With money, nothing is impossible. It took but a short time to find a trader eager to transport my tired body northwards to the sea.

As we took to the stream, I crept beneath an awning and fell into a deep sleep.

I was on my way back to Bugia.

Letter from Guilielmo Bonacci
to Leonardo Pisano

*From Guilielmo Bonacci,
for Leonardo Pisano, formerly apprentice in Bugia at the
Customs House of the Republic of Pisa.*

My dearest and most precious son, sweet Leonardo,

Your letter having been delivered by an Egyptian shipmaster, I write for my own solace, doubtful whether you will ever read these few words. I live in the hope of further news of you but so far in vain.

Though it has been some while since you left Bugia, the wounds of your departure have not healed. In like manner as you lost your dreams of fulfilment, so I was bereft of that which is most precious.

But whereas you parted from me in falsehood and illusion, a play of shadows in fantasy, my bereavement is true loss. But no more of this, for sickness is not cured by words nor grief by lamentation.

Such events offer occasion for much casting back to half-forgotten things. It is not generally in the nature of fathers to confide in children for it is better some elements be hidden. But I confess my grievous shortcomings in being absent from your side when you were a child, the sum of which contributes to present difficulties.

In particular I remember the happiness we shared in Pisa during my last visit there, your joy at my homecoming, our many conversations, and our journey by sea. The time together in Bugia was most fruitful and progress in the apprenticeship of your duties exemplary. The loss of your assistance here has been too much to bear.

The burden of your illness in Bugia affected me more than words could express. The physician believed you to be in mortal danger and only Providence redeemed you to life.

What a change came after your sickness. You were no longer my familiar son but a being impelled by fantasies. Whether this was a surfeit of study or vile fever in the blood, it needed but one straw to drive you to madness. For your flight from this place was untoward. All could have been resolved in honesty and love.

That you should blame your father for your misdemeanours is but part of the disease which carried you to action so wilfully undertaken. But I intend no further comment, content as I am to hear that you are safe though in a far country.

Following grief for your departure, I have taken stock of my own behaviour. My life has not been without sin and shame. But it is better if a son knows little about his father's frailties.

As a consequence I am now betrothed to a widow and we are to be wedded within the month. She inherited a worthy estate and has two daughters.

If you come back to me, you will discover I am wiser but with further responsibilities, to love and honour a wife, your stepmother, and to be a good father to her children.

May God give me strength to fulfil my obligations that we be not blamed, neither here on earth nor in the world to come.

Your loving and ever devoted father,

Guilielmo Bonacci

Seventh Letter

Concerning my return to Bugia,
Guilielmo's marriage,
Giovanna and my friendship with a rich man.

Arriere en ses chambres s'en entre.
Moult li tressaut li cuers el ventre;
Esprise l'a forment Amours.
Moult li ennuie que li jours...

BENOÎT DE SAINTE-MAURE (*c.* 1150)

(To her bedchamber she retreats.
 Her heart within her wildly beats;
 Love has filled her soul with fire,
 The day is too tedious to endure...)

I

Sire, My Most Eminent Master Michael Theodorus,
Philosopher in the Service of His Majesty, Frederick II.

Anxious that my father might regard me more as Thief of Baghdad than Prodigal Son, I did not altogether relish the prospect of returning to Bugia. Joy at the possibilities of reunion with Guilielmo warred against fear of consequences, the easy carelessness of youth mingling with those shadows which experience breeds.

I had travelled the upper reaches of the Nile to the harbour of Damietta with impatience, for the little vessel was as lazy as the river itself. But the sights and smells of the open sea dispelled melancholy and I was fortunate in being recommended a ship for the voyage home by the skipper of the river boat.

After some haggling with the new master, a price was agreed and a small but adequate living space provided for me at the stern of his shabby barque. He was carrying a cargo of silks and spices, some part of it bound for Algiers, but hoping to pick up other goods to deliver on the way.

He expected to call at Bugia but would make a special visit there for me even if further trade was not forthcoming. Over the days to come we had many landfalls, driven by favourable winds to rotting towns and dilapidated ports.

Whether among troubled seas or absence of waves like a smooth lake, I calculated the numbers in my book or stared at the horizon till my eyes smarted.

To the left the jagged coast beckoned as we followed its contours, a marker for our course. The wild sea thus rubbed shoulders with barren desert, such thoughts making me nostalgic for the winter rain of Pisa and its spring flowers.

I pondered how each ocean journey shapes and changes us. We embark, endure the leagues, philosophise and fret, and finally our destination arrives within thinking distance, while the past recedes day by day beyond the waves and is cleansed from our blood.

Sunsets and dawns come and go in sudden beauty. Yet we cannot remember them as separate events when each day imitates those that came before.

I lost track of days, calendars, places, and horizons. Finally the captain told me to expect to be in Bugia soon.

So it happened, some time later, with my earthly possessions in a bag on my shoulder, I was able to step ashore.

II

A hot wind wrapped the town in a shroud of sand. Gathering a wide scarf round my face, head down against the blast, I set off through the streets, battling towards the customs house. Within minutes my clothes and face were filthy, the granules of desert dust tasting foul on tongue and teeth.

The customs house was closed against the blizzard.

I knocked loudly at the door many times. When at last it was opened, I saw not a familiar servant, but a female of European birth.

"Yes?" she asked, with the voice this kind of woman uses to address a native, for such she thought me to be with my flowing garments and face concealed from the gale.

"Is Guilielmo Bonacci at home?" I enquired.

"There is no business today!" was her reply.

"I would like to see Guilielmo Bonacci!" I shouted over the howling wind. "I am his son, Leonardo."

If I had claimed to be the devil himself, I think she might have been more polite and less surprised. The woman clearly believed me to be an imposter. Perhaps my voice, like my father's after long service abroad, had taken on the accent of a foreigner. Her response was to slam the door, leaving me huddled in the archway as the sand redoubled its attack.

Not certain what strategy to adopt, I cowered in the doorway, waiting for something to happen. When nothing did, I banged on the door with fists, feet, and elbows, furious that I was thus thwarted. At this angle, cornered against the house, the storm was virulent. Sand infiltrated ears, nose, eyes, mouth, and hair, causing me to pound with greater urgency.

I presumed the woman, whoever she was, had gone to warn Guilielmo. In view of the quantity of money in the house, he might be cautious about opening the door.

But I put down my sack of belongings and began to shout as well as thump the wood. Like a man drowning in the wind I called, "Leonardo, Leonardo!" covering my mouth with the cloth and thus muffling my cries for help.

But it did the trick. After much of this the portal opened the breadth of a man's hand.

In the crack of the opening was Guilielmo's startled face. Still uncertain at the turn of events, he waited for revelation. But I picked up the bag and pushed past him into the customs house to escape the tumult of the wind.

"I am Leonardo...I am your son!" I exclaimed. He at first seemed doubtful of any such thing. Once inside the house I carefully placed my possessions on the floor and removed my scarf and turban to reveal my features to him.

Even so he could scarcely recognise me, standing far back as if greeting a stranger. When he seemed assured that this was indeed his son, he did not embrace me but led me into the sitting room.

The woman was seated on the best chair, looking exceedingly frightened at this visitation. Guilielmo stared too, confronting the apparition of a living ghost. He collapsed back onto the chaise-longue as if his legs could support him no more. I sat down on a chair, sprinkling sand onto the fine carpet.

"You've changed!" he said, when he found use of his voice. So had my father, for Guilielmo looked much older than how I remembered him.

He presented me with a mirror from the table. Looking into it I saw a stained, weathered face, brown as leather, the visage of a man not recognisably European nor a youth.

"My God, what's happened?" he said, tears like stones welling from his eyes. "Is it really you, Leonardo?"

He spoke my name as if it was difficult to pronounce.

I embraced him, emotion aroused in my breast like fire. But the wind outside had drained my tears for I did not weep. His flow of anguish washed some of the dust from my neck as he clasped me to him.

His unmanly sobbing was a river which overflowed its banks and flooded the surrounding pastures. Each moment was a knife straight into the heart, for my folly had caused this grief and more. The woman was crying also, dabbing her nose with a lace embroidered handkerchief.

She rose and spread her arms round Guilielmo and myself like a hen with a comforting wing. When the torrents of sorrow subsided we all sat down, wearied by this expenditure of feelings, silent as we waited for the next fall of the dice. Guilielmo's features slowly regained their composure.

He motioned towards the woman.

"This is Sara, from Florence. She is my wife – and now your stepmother."

I stood up and formally shook hands with her. She inclined her head, a little moisture running down her rouged cheeks.

"We missed you so much!" whispered Guilielmo.

"I am sorry, father," I replied.

"There will be time for that!" he said.

"I travelled," I said." I have much to tell."

"So I believe."

"How long was I away?"

"We will talk later. Please go and change your clothes."

Before I could leave the room two girls entered. They were as shocked to see me as I was astonished to see them.

"This is Leonardo – son of Guilielmo," said Sara, taking charge of the matter. "These are my daughters."

Their faces were masks of disdain at this intruder in their

midst. But I raised myself, squared my shoulders, and bowed to them as I would have done to a teacher. To meet these fair-skinned girls after so long in distant lands seemed a kind of absurdity. The elder was Giovanna, the younger, Elisabetta. After all my wanderings they appeared hardly more than simple children who had not yet tasted the world, nor been tasted by it.

Like a mendicant, unwelcome in my own home, I took my belongings and went towards what was previously my room. My clothes and chattels were stored there as if waiting for their owner's return.

I fetched water and washed myself, shaved off the knotty beard, brushed unkempt hair, put on usual clothes and concealed my book in its original hiding place. Dressed once more as a man from Pisa I returned to the sitting room. Giovanna and Elisabetta gazed with increased interest. Sara even smiled slightly. Guilielmo stared, weeping from time to time.

III

In my new role as cuckoo in the nest I woke the next morning after many strange dreams. At breakfast I scrutinised the faces of this unexpected 'family', especially my stepsisters.

It transpired that Guilielmo had regularly boasted about me to the widow and her daughters. My first appearance with sunburned complexion and clothes covered in sand hardly matched expectations.

He had described this legendary son as a studious boy, gifted at the numbers, innocent, and vulnerable, who, after an illness and perturbed in mind, departed by night, rumours of his whereabouts coming from various quarters.

Some had spread whispers of my return to Pisa, others suggested that I disappeared into the desert wilderness. One or two speculated about a youth running away to sea where he was drowned.

Offering Guilielmo an explanation I presented a version of events, omitting some aspects, embellishing others. The purpose of my journey became erudition, not escape, pursuit rather than retreat. Mention of my stay in Cairo evoked disbelief from my listeners though I did not dwell too much on the means of arriving there.

Neither did I indicate why leaving that city was as hurried as my earlier departure from Bugia. I depicted myself as a hero. While Guilielmo and Sara might be impossible to convince, the gullible girls were a fine canvas on which to paint fables in bright colours.

They were amused by the antics of camel riding, screeched in repulsion at dung beetles, cooed at my descriptions of the Pyramids and the face of the Sphinx, which I claimed resembled the features of my own father.

They admired tales of bazaars, shipboard, ports, high seas, banquets and the characters of the boys to whom I taught the numbers.

Guilielmo, as was his wont, said little. Sara was polite but reserved, for who could ever fathom what lurked behind her specious smile?

Elisabetta, the younger of the daughters, was inquisitive. But Giovanna, sitting next to me at the table, became most forward, touching my hand at more poignant moments of the narrative, involving herself with responsive grimaces, laughter, or nudges with her knee.

By the end of the saga, garnished with tributes to the excellence of my masters in Egypt, I saw in Giovanna's smiles that I had gained an admirer. She even seemed eager to have lessons in the numbers herself despite her mother's opinion that such knowledge was of no use to those unable to participate in commerce.

Guilielmo's expression asked unspoken questions throughout my monologue. But I avoided the unmentionable, such as the presence of women or otherwise, explaining instead how an unveiled female was rarely seen for Egypt was strict in such matters.

This seemed of special interest to Giovanna. She enquired whether desert travelling compelled men to consort closely with female companions. This was easily brushed aside on grounds of tribal custom, conveniently omitting my experiences of the laxity of etiquette in the case of nomad widows.

IV

As my epic waned, Guilielmo and Sara tentatively began their own narrative.

Sara was not long a widow, the former wife of a rich Florentine merchant, acquainted with my father for some time. Uniting through matrimony her inherited wealth with Guilielmo's expertise in finance was the nature of their romance. As they knew all too well, it was something other than love which drew them together.

When it was my turn to speak again (for clearly they wished

to hear my views on the new situation), I put my father's case as strongly as possible, emphasising how lonely he had been since my mother's demise, how this marriage must be the best thing for him. I spoke in praise of the excellence of his choice and my hopes for their happy future.

Surely my father could sniff duplicity in this. Even as I mouthed the words our eyes met as if he instantly deduced my true feelings.

Sara appeared deeply moved. She came over to my side of the table to embrace me with all the fervour of a stepmother.

I felt her fulsome body against me and could scarcely imagine why Guilielmo had married this one and not a woman such as our beloved Maria of Pisa.

But as Sara hugged me, a great bear loosed from a cage, I touched the expensive fabric of her raiment and in that moment understood precisely why my father had taken her to be his bride.

Giovanna and Elisabetta joined in with their mother's embrace. As she returned to Guilielmo's side, they threw their arms round me. I kissed them as a new brother ought. Elisabetta was but a little thing, unformed and skittish. Giovanna was more artful for she touched the back of my neck in a tender way without arousing any suspicions that this caress could inspire beyond sisterhood.

When Guilielmo and I were alone, I expressed remorse at taking coinage from the customs house. Could he possibly pardon such a deed?

He laughed at this, being more concerned about my abrupt departure. Such was the corruption of taxes that little record was kept of currency secreted from the main coffers for private use. Truth to tell, Guilielmo was unaware any money had been taken, let alone the precise amount.

More significantly he enquired whether the morals of Egypt were really as rigorous as I had asserted. I put on a mask of simplicity to explain how in the *madrasa* strict regulations applied to students and teachers, wanting him to believe my younger self still kept sentinel over my desires.

Guilielmo asked if I had given them a true and honest opinion of his marriage to Sara. I reassured him, commenting that Sara was a good woman, that Guilielmo knew best, and so forth, to the point he became almost embarrassed.

"I thought you to be full of jealousy!" he said. "But you are not."

"My travels have taught me wisdom, father," I replied.

"Good!" he exclaimed. "And what do you think of Giovanna? Isn't she a fine girl to have for a sister?"

"Indeed!"

In this I spoke the truth for she seemed a very fine girl.

V

To make amends to my father I began work in the customs house almost at once. Guilielmo urgently needed assistance. My absence, followed by his marriage, had caused him to neglect his duties. The accounts were less well ordered than before.

Sitting side by side, we pored for long hours over lists of taxes, cargoes, invoices, receipts, bills of trade, regulations, notices, amendments and sheets of calculations and records. Inadequacies were more or less corrected.

By day, we met merchants, bailiffs and officers. This involved visiting ships, negotiating details of currency, loading, importation and taxing. We were swamped in a backlog of finance and yet forced to confront incoming floods of new business.

Sara became ever more affectionate, instructing me to address her in whatever manner I preferred such as 'mama', 'mother', or even 'stepmother'.

I did not rise to this bait. To my father I called her 'your wife', to the daughters 'your mother'. To Sara's face I omitted any appellation of the maternal kind.

My reluctance in this matter set me apart from Sara as if a river flowed between us. My father became annoyed with Sara and myself, but particularly with his wife. I overheard him telling her that "Leonardo should be allowed time!"

Elisabetta found that a young man about the house was a novelty to her liking. She incessantly solicited my attention, proudly showing me her embroidery, singing a folk song she claimed to have composed herself, or asking help to mend a doll or stitch clothing.

Sara often told her not to pester me for reasons of my presumed weariness. But the girl, sensing that I liked to indulge her whims, took refuge in repeating like a parrot, "Leonardo likes me! Leonardo likes me!"

Giovanna was somewhat distant in her demeanour when Sara or Guilielmo were present but became friendly at other times. She entered my room occasionally in the evenings while I worked on the book of numbers, leaning over as if to look at the pages, her long hair brushing my face or the back of my neck.

I claimed such writing was to do with the customs house. But she was not actually interested in my scribbles, preferring to walk round the room as if in private exhibition, swishing her skirt, gesturing like a magician weaving a spell. By means of this spectacle she invariably gained my full attention.

We began strolling out to the port area together. Then further along the shore. She liked clambering up steep rocks. I would assist her by lifting, pushing or pulling, according to the need.

Soon natural attraction overcame us so that we clasped hands as we walked. She smiled and clung to me.

"You are my stepsister!" I would say.

"And you are my stepbrother!" she replied.

Such behaviour, despite Giovanna's play-acting of apparent remoteness in the presence of parents, was soon uncovered. One evening Elisabetta spied on us from a distance. Next morning she blurted out to her mother that we had been seen embracing and kissing behind the rounding of the cliff.

Sara hastened with the news to Guilielmo. He threw his arms up in despair and hurried to the counting room.

At that moment I was engaged in negotiation with a merchant desirous of a good deal on a shipping of fine leather. Just as I prepared to clinch a useful emolument, Guilielmo's impatient face appeared behind the client, indicating, like imperial Caesar, that I must shorten the interview and follow him to the anteroom.

The bartering concluded too hastily, with the inevitable *lower* rate of private return, our customer being very pleased by this outcome.

Guilielmo, slumped in his chair by the time I reached him, motioned I was to sit by his side. His mute indecision, as I discovered later, was grounded on two things, one known, the other unknown.

That Giovanna was his wife's daughter was known. What was unknown was whether the son of Guilielmo remained innocent and untainted or had become a sinner exiled from Eden having tasted the fruit of the tree. The art of gaining the upper hand was, as always, to be as wise as an owl, cunning as a serpent, and pure as an angel.

Poor Guilielmo, unable, past or present, to understand his son! Such was his inability to speak I thought he was ill. In truth his complexion did look ashen around the perimeter of his beard.

But as I rose to comfort whatever ailed him, he waved his hand to command me to remain seated.

At last he spoke.

"There is a problem…"

Guilielmo paused, looking round the room like a trapped animal.

"It's to do with Sara…or rather to do with Elisabetta…Did I say Elisabetta?…I meant Giovanna!"

"Giovanna?" I said. "My sister?"

"Of course, your sister!" he growled. "What other Giovanna is there?"

"None," I said, "none at all!"

Guilielmo sighed out loud, burying his face in both hands, leaning forward as if in mourning.

"This is very difficult!" he exclaimed. "Leonardo, I have no wish to offend you if you are not guilty."

"Not guilty?" I protested. "I have no idea what you're talking about."

Guilielmo stood up, looming over me. But he raised me to

my feet, embraced me and revealed his heart, as if throwing off all constraint.

"Let me explain. Elisabetta saw you and Giovanna near the cliffs. Is this true or not?"

I sat down, suddenly sensing what might be in the air. Elisabetta was no longer my favourite. Never again, I silently vowed, would she be permitted to sit on my lap or put her little arms round my neck.

"We did go for a walk," I admitted. "What's wrong with that?"

Guilielmo collapsed back into his chair as if his troubles were too terrible to suffer standing up.

"Nothing, Leonardo, nothing. But Elisabetta…"

"Elisabetta?"

"She said…you were together…"

"Together?" I asked, as innocent as a lamb.

"You were…embracing."

I settled myself quietly, to reply in the mildest voice.

"Father, she was mistaken."

"I hope to God she was."

"I removed a speck of dirt from Giovanna's eye. Elisabetta must have imagined something else."

"A speck?" whispered Guilielmo as if receiving a precious lifeline.

"A speck!" I said.

"Thank God!" he exclaimed, laughing loudly for the first time since my return.

VI

I met Giovanna, quite by chance, an hour later in the street. The tale of Elisabetta's treachery frightened her. But this was quickly transmuted into the more usable currency of fury.

Giovanna stamped her feet and threw her hands about, attracting the attention of the ever watchful mendicants who converged like a swarm of flies.

After we drove them off with curses and threats, Giovanna was relieved to hear of the alleged speck of dirt in her eye and Guilielmo's response. But if Elisabetta had happened to appear round the corner at that moment, her sister might well have committed murder!

We rehearsed our story till each matched the other in vocabulary and conviction. She was a willing pupil in deception. Yet before we parted she kissed me sweetly and deeply in the selfsame manner that had already compromised us.

That evening in the sitting room a hearing was arranged in a quasi-court with Sara as judge, and Giovanna and myself as false witnesses.

Unaware of the hornet's nest stirred up, let alone the ordeal ahead, the felon, the hapless Elisabetta, was summoned to the proceedings. She arrived dancing and jumping, her usual behaviour.

Transfixed by her sister's basilisk stare, the cold dignity of her mother, the presence of the stepfather, and my own unaccustomed reticence, the poor creature looked sadly around the room and began to whimper most pitifully.

Sara grabbed the child with two powerful hands. Putting her

rouged face close to Elisabetta's nose, she shouted that she could not permit a liar to remain unpunished in her house. At this Guilielmo nodded sagely.

"You have spoken dreadful, untrue things about your sister," continued my stepmother. "What have you to say for yourself?"

Elisabetta, observing angry expressions ranged about like waiting wolves, burst into extravagant moaning, her movement restricted by her mother's grip.

The weeping and inability to say anything in her own defence were natural indications of guilt for the gathering. No further evidence was deemed necessary. Judgement followed.

The woman decreed the child was to be soundly whipped and never to tell lies again. Sara, now judge, jury, *and* executioner, rose to her feet, swivelled Elisabetta a full circle, and propelled her to an adjacent room. As the girl was turned forcibly, her eyes red with misery, she flicked a glance at myself and Giovanna, a look so potent with sorrow none could have read its message without remorse.

After a brief pause, from the neighbouring room came sounds of the cane and high treble shrieking. Guilielmo and Giovanna remained passive as if thoughtful.

I felt sick but relieved that the young one's perfidy was deflected from its proper target.

Sara was most vindictive for we heard the rhythm of the beating for far more strokes than the lesson needed. Elisabetta's clamour reached a howling climax half-way through, modulating to subdued whining for the rest.

A supplementary penalty banished Elisabetta to bed without

supper, a welcome respite, for nobody relished the spectacle of her tear-stained visage across the table.

The evening meal passed in uneasy silence. Sara florid of complexion, Guilielmo, at the head of the table, drinking much wine, refilling my glass liberally.

Giovanna's expression was of a studied indignation, head held high, her neck arched like a swan, a slight flush on each cheek, a younger image of her mother.

When all was completed and servants had cleared away the plates and debris, Sara and Guilielmo made their excuses. They departed rapidly for bed as if exhausted by the day's events.

Giovanna and I stared at each other. She winked at me, and I winked back. She wrinkled her nose, I did the same.

She shook her head from side to side and I performed a mirror image of all she did. She raised her left palm and I raised my right one, she tweaked her right ear and I pinched mine.

"What about Elisabetta?" I asked, anxious to expiate our deeds.

"Oh dear," she said, giggling gently as if not sure what to say. "Your mother was so *angry*!"

"Not as angry as me! The little snake deserved it!"

"We should be careful," I replied.

This amused her even more. Coming over to me she stroked my face and laid her lips on my brow.

In mischief, she whispered, "I'm going to bed. Sweet dreams, Leonardo!" Without further ado, except the hint of an innocent smile, she turned on her heel and departed humming, as if devoid of a single care in all the world.

I sat thinking everything over. A sadness possessed me for Elisabetta, scapegoat and victim.

After drinking more wine to soothe my conscience, I crept quietly to my bedroom.

I retrieved my book from the hiding place and idly perused its pages without comfort or satisfaction. I washed, put on my night attire, and extinguished the candles.

Laying my troubled head on the pillow, I drifted towards sleep, dreaming of weeping and apparitions. I half woke on hearing a sound. My door opened and closed.

Giovanna whispered through the darkness. I knew it was her and why she was with me.

She infiltrated my bed without a word. Having cast off her clothes, we completed what we had begun.

I found no means of resisting her that night or any other night.

VII

Breakfast the next morning was not an auspicious occasion. Elisabetta, hungry after her night of fasting, glanced accusingly at each of us, her doleful eyes resentful rather than contrite.

Guilielmo remained taciturn as if matters of state troubled him. Sara was triumphant, munching loudly on a bunch of grapes, noisily drinking numerous cups of goat's milk.

Only Giovanna, brisk, bright and chatty, seemed her normal self, eating plenty, ignoring Elisabetta, and, in my opinion, smiling more than was wise.

Towards the end of this awkward meal I casually announced

a desire to walk by the sea before beginning duties at the customs house. As hoped for, Giovanna opted to join me, Elisabetta being subtly warned by our frigid manner that she was not welcome in her present state of shame. Nevertheless, on our amble towards the beach, I took care to glance behind and make sure our little spy was not up to her tricks.

Giovanna, it transpired, was in a tetchy mood, complaining about my silence during breakfast and saying she really wanted to spend the whole day with me.

Why couldn't I leave work for a few hours and be with her? As she had made a sacrifice for me why should I not make a lesser one for her? Now we were 'together', I was to be less selfish, accede to her demands, and remember her welfare came first.

In return I agreed with all she said, apologised for the self-absorption which represented one of my true weaknesses, promised to watch over her, and emphasised that I was obligated to her as much as any man to any woman.

This was insufficient for, having traversed the sea of chastity and reached the further side, she became a polluted river which had broken its banks rather than a beautiful butterfly emerged from a chrysalis. As we spoke, minute by minute unforeseen fissures appeared in the sandstone of her character, Giovanna's hidden self coming to light in a displeasing manner.

By the time we reached the cliffs Giovanna had revealed herself as possessive and demanding, as well as supercilious and unpredictable. Her language to me was but a perfect imitation of her mother when speaking to Guilielmo.

I had opened Pandora's box and felt myself wilting at such discoveries. To be with her when she was thus was to wish not to be with her. I questioned whether I liked her in the least, for what I saw at this moment was hateful.

These revelations persisted in burgeoning forth like slime from the bottom of a barrel. Giovanna was even impertinent enough to suggest how she disliked certain characteristics within me that resembled Guilielmo, for he was not the kind of man she would have chosen for a stepfather.

Shocked by all this, I put on my best bland face of patience and reticence. But she was not to be quietened. Giovanna was ruthless in her analysis of my inadequacies, citing my previous adventures as indicative of what was wrong with me. Moreover, she had heard rumours of my infatuation for a worthless slut of a native girl. She would not be surprised to learn that other women had entered my bed. But Giovanna trusted this had not happened for she would not be pleased if it had.

As we turned the corner of the cliff into the sheltered privacy of that part of the shore, Giovanna abruptly burst into tears and embraced me fiercely.

She asked forgiveness for her loose tongue, explaining how everything had upset her. She said she loved me to distraction and knew that I felt the same as she did. If I ever stopped loving her, her heart and soul would break into a thousand fragments.

With our bodies entwined and her lips moist on my mouth, all resolve expired. I put aside thoughts of her former frailties, embracing her with an intensity appropriate to the moment.

We went back home almost healed of rancour. I worked out the day in the customs house in unhelpful mood, my attention on matters closer to the heart than routine negotiations and calculations. Even Guilielmo noticed my discomfiture and asked whether I was unwell. I assured him everything was fine.

Our evening passed much as usual. Elisabetta was still cautious, knowing Giovanna and myself to be untrustworthy. But before bedtime she came forward in her child's innocence to be hugged and comforted. I kissed her warm face and whispered a few affectionate words, promising to be kind. In response, sad tears filled her sweet brown eyes.

In due order and routine I departed to my room, worked for a while on my book, then retired to bed with many questions on my mind.

Of these, the first was soon answered. After a sleepless interim, the door opened and closed. Giovanna once more entranced me with her presence.

All her foolish ways faded to nothingness. I entered that state of ecstasy where my soul quivered like a bee exploring the velvet petals of a flower.

My passion flickered into flame. For the duration of that heat all adverse things were forgotten, as if lost for ever.

VIII

Giovanna and I continued to quarrel but by night negotiated a blissful truce. Yet each day she yielded up more secrets. The open book of her mind exposed many flaws.

She claimed devotion to this and that, contrasting her alleged piety against my laxity. There was disagreement on the significance of astrological omens, she disputed the validity of numbers, disliked poetry, and despised Guilielmo.

Her model of perfection was her mother, concerning whom not a single criticism was acceptable. Elisabetta, on the other hand, was the object of her worst jibes, certain remarks illuminating the dark chambers of Giovanna's private jealousies.

Yet all adverse things vanished in the night. Our bodies joined and her mouth, the vehicle of quiet poison from dawn to dusk, became the giver of joy along infinite paths of delight.

Regrettably, as weeks passed, I took account of the sum of my feelings, arriving always at the same conclusion. How often the scales were set out in my mind, with different weights and balances apportioned to left and right. Yet the answer remained constant.

In the case of Giovanna I found few redeeming graces beyond that of physical union. How was such a thing possible, that one loved her touch to distraction, yet her habits and characteristics did not please? The result was that I lapsed into a misery of spirit which she scarcely noticed, continuing with her prattle and disputes.

My melancholy was observed first by Guilielmo, then by Elisabetta and even Sara after that. They attributed it to the dullness of Bugia following the excitement of travel. All three conspired to help me to regain levity. But I was not to be won over.

Instead, I plunged into the work of the customs house, leaving no tally unaudited, no client unattended, no taxes subject to shortfall, no paper work neglected, no profit ungathered.

⚜ IX ⚜

One morning Guilielmo introduced me to a gentleman of great esteem. This person had recently arrived, intending to reside in Barbary for a while after voyages to many places. An owner of ships, property, lands, vineyards and goods, he was rumoured to be one of the wealthiest men ever to have traded in Bugia.

"This is the noble Don Umberto di Salerno!" said Guilielmo. "His presence here will be of great value."

The man's firm handshake and piercing gaze were impressive. About the same age as my father, his exquisite clothes marked him out from the usual run of merchants, mostly dishonest by nature whom we cheated in our official way, while they, in their turn, gained recompense from their own clients.

Umberto di Salerno was different. One might have assumed by his bearing that he was an ambassador, an eminent scholar, or a courtier. Instead he chose to embrace the profession of merchant adventurer though many other destinies surely lay within his reach.

Talking to him I became shy, conscious of the crassness of youth, the folly of young men, the pretences we assume to hide weakness. Umberto immediately put me at my ease with his kind words.

"Leonardo – I am very pleased to meet you. Your father has told me various things. I understand you are a scholar of the numbers."

I bowed in modest acquiescence.

"You look too young to be erudite. But Guilielmo said you have studied with esteemed masters, here and abroad."

"I confess I have had that honour, Sir," I said humbly, inclining my head.

"You must tell me more," replied Umberto in a tone of one who truly wished to be told much more. Already I felt an overwhelming admiration for him.

That afternoon Guilielmo afforded me the responsibility of negotiating with such a man. The subsequent discussions proved to be lengthy battles, Umberto unyielding till the end. I was compelled many times to retreat in order to advance, to be honest to deceive, and to feign surrender at the point where victory seemed assured. The results were the lucrative compromises hoped for from the outset. Umberto seemed amused by both my impertinence and my competence.

"Well, I'll be confounded, beaten by a boy!" he exclaimed when the calculations of his cargoes were completed to our mutual satisfaction.

"Beaten, sir?" I said in mock surprise. "It is rather you who defeated a somewhat inexperienced officer."

"I have never known such sprightly numbers," he replied. "I must tell your father how much we have enjoyed ourselves."

At this point Guilielmo came over, having gauged the strategic moment of the deal, and, to my surprise, invited Umberto to accompany us to our living quarters.

This pleased me immensely for never had I met so formidable and yet so agreeable a person.

We shared with him some of our best wine. As a man of taste he exclaimed at every kind of excellence, draining his cup to the dregs to be refilled by an eager Guilielmo.

We discussed how we could be of assistance in his enterprises.

In return Umberto told tales of fine horses, of his wife recently deceased, and of the dangers of investing in ships.

Guilielmo thereupon invited Umberto to dinner the following evening, an honour extended to very few of our clients. The great man arrived at the appointed hour, his elegant apparel putting us slightly to shame. Sara, Giovanna and Elisabetta trooped in like choristers to stand before him and have the privilege of being introduced one by one.

"These are your lovely daughters?" remarked Umberto in a tone midway between exclamation and polite question.

"My stepdaughters, sir!" answered Guilielmo. "My wife and I married recently."

"What a wedding that must have been," said Umberto.

"It was!" replied Sara. "Almost as fine as my first wedding." We all laughed, taking it as a jest but knowing it was nothing of the kind.

Throughout the meal Umberto spun stories like an inspired wizard. I had never before heard a man who could speak thus. So transparent was his diction, images etched with extraordinary clarity, characters evoked so vividly, places springing to life as we listened, his voice varied and lyrical, the flow of his narrative organic to its substance with not a single word wasted.

As he talked on I glanced at the faces round the table, Elisabetta enchanted as with a fairy tale, Giovanna glowing in the candlelight like an attentive goddess, Sara silent against the majestic flow of language, Guilielmo leaning forward to catch every syllable as if each was a precious bird loosed from a gilded cage.

Umberto, like myself, had visited Egypt. But instead of my stories of scholars and beggars, he spoke of leaders and princesses, of palaces lined with gold, of a Nile flowing like a holy flood to irrigate the land, his voice evoking the hot breath of the desert or thirst under the sun.

When his legends ended we sat silent, deep in thought, not wishing to break the spell. Each stared at our guest, lost in awe at what he said and the way he expressed it. But, as with good wine, we had imbibed our fill of fables and more might be too much.

Guilielmo sighed as if thinking of things past, Elisabetta stifled an excited giggle, Sara mopped her brow. Only Giovanna remained inscrutable.

Umberto looked directly at me.

"Leonardo, I'm sure you must have a few tales to tell."

"He has told us most of them," said Sara, a shade too precipitately, "but *never* as you tell them!"

"I am afraid my inclination is more to the numbers," I confessed, "but to speak as you do, sir, is indeed a precious gift."

"Thank you," he said. "And Giovanna, young lady, do you tell tales?"

"I do!" piped up Elisabetta and we all roared with laughter.

꧁ X ꧂

Over the next few weeks Umberto di Salerno invited me to visit him at his house on various occasions. Like a camel shedding its load, I was relieved to retreat for a while from Sara's domain, where she ruled like a queen over her subservient Guilielmo.

Umberto resided in a stylish mansion overlooking the sea, just out of the town. In his company the hours passed in pleasant enlightenment. Some of our sessions became a means of tuition in etiquette whereby I became educated in those elements a young man can hardly imagine without a mentor to guide him.

He spoke of the importance of choosing attire. Clothes needed to be of a certain cut and quality rather than merely expensive. To this was added the matter of appearance. Brushing one's hair, trimming a beard, or having no beard at all, fragrance about one's person, care of fingernails, good teeth and sweet breath, sitting with dignity in a chair, bowing gracefully, and so on, all these things needed careful attention to create a good impression on others of whatever rank.

Umberto explained how in the presence of a great man – emperor, prince, general, or archbishop – one's qualities were judged on various factors. Rules for each occasion could be formulated. This was the courtly art, to learn established etiquette and follow its precepts.

Bugia seemed far from such demands. Guilielmo, a devoted servant of Pisa, had never been near a court let alone in the presence of princes or emperors. How could a person such as myself presume ever to receive so singular an honour?

Umberto frowned but continued to instruct in the skills of gaining preferment, the science of defeating enemies, encouraging allies, and how to conspire and vanquish possible rivals. Beyond this, Umberto related the history of kings and wars, of soldiers, of corrupt rulers and prelates, of the Emperor Frederick Barbarossa and his son, Henry of Swabia, married to Constance, the aunt of King William II, whose offspring, Frederick, became heir to the empire.

On other evenings he embarked on topics such as philosophy, law, legends, saintliness, and the ancient world.

Umberto, however, knew little about the science of the numbers. So in order to show off my own expertise, I decided on a whim to smuggle my book from home and seek his comments. Thus, on an occasion when Guilielmo was out of the house, I transported the bulky script to my new friend.

Once the manuscript was in his hands Umberto began, with immense care, to scrutinise each page. After a process of slow consideration covering almost every page, with many questions asked, he complimented me on the ingenuity of the problems and the fine quality of the solutions.

Abruptly digressing, he enquired with a quizzical expression, "Does your father know about this?"

I confessed that Guilielmo knew nothing of it.

"When the work is completed, I may ask his opinion," I said. "Till then, I follow my own ideas."

He turned over a few more chapters, stopping here and there with finger poised to decipher a sentence or two.

"And how much of this is taken from your masters?"

I hesitated, calculating how things might seem to such a man.

"Everything is founded on what I have been taught. The synthesis is my own."

Such an answer seemed to satisfy him. Umberto continued to examine the text.

"This is excellent paper, exquisite!"

"My father acquired it. He thought I wished to write poems or a diary."

"I see."

Umberto became thoughtful again, as if mulling over some secret intent.

"May I borrow your book to read it more closely?" he enquired.

I could not speak. In my travels the manuscript had always been by my side, hence the smear of grime on its covers.

To lend such a thing was to yield my life into another's keeping. The studies there were more valuable than treasure. Did he want me to deliver my very soul into his keeping?

He looked displeased at my hesitation.

"Well, Leonardo, what is your answer? May I borrow the book?"

I plunged into the abyss.

"Of course."

He smiled.

"Good. That's settled then."

He gathered up the work and placed it gently on his desk, like a priest handling a sacred relic.

XI

During the following few weeks Umberto di Salerno did not honour us with his company at the customs house. His absence plagued me less than the lack of my book, concerning which I entertained a thousand fantasies. Destruction by fire, theft, or careless servants – each prospect troubled me greatly.

Giovanna, usually unresponsive to the moods of others, attributed my distraction to a lessening of ardour. As a result her attentiveness to me increased. She became more affectionate, smiling often and talking far less.

Her nightly visits lengthened so that she usually lingered in dalliance almost till dawn. I worked my hours in the customs house assailed by fatigue.

Several times I fell asleep at the desk, which did not go unnoticed by Guilielmo. But he frequently slipped into drowsiness himself, attributing this habit to our inherited similarities. As with various things, when I feared his wrath he responded with good humour.

"Too many evenings carousing with Umberto!" he laughed, in mock rebuke.

"Have you seen him over the last week or so?" I asked. Guilielmo scratched his head.

"I can't say I have. But he deals entirely with you. He is *your* responsibility."

In reply I could but express concern for Umberto's health. At this Guilielmo decided the man should be invited for dinner on the Sabbath, today being Tuesday. It was up to me to discuss the matter with him.

Entrusted with this mission, I was pleased to walk the league or so to Umberto's dwelling, the sea air being a contrast to the oppressive heat where the merchants gathered.

Servants clustering round the door took me into the house.

They showed me to the sitting room, provided lemon water, and went to find their master.

I looked swiftly round for my manuscript but it was not on the desk nor elsewhere. Giving up the pursuit, I lounged in the chair and, lulled by the murmur of the surf, promptly fell asleep.

When I awoke Umberto was seated behind the desk, writing a letter. I apologised for my lack of manners. He smiled and waved his hand, his noble eyebrows lifting in reassurance that he was by no means offended.

"Sir, my father wishes to invite you for dinner this Sabbath evening, if it is possible for you to attend."

"Of course," he said, "Thank you."

Umberto carried on writing. I sipped my lemon water, as drowsiness descended again, covertly pinching the back of my hand to fend off discourteous sleep.

After a few minutes, Umberto, having finished whatever he was writing, placed his arms on the desk, staring with a strangely anguished expression.

"Leonardo…" he began. "If you are not too tired…I would like your advice on a private matter."

My head cleared as I hastened to reply.

"I would be very pleased to help…Is it a problem of commerce?"

Umberto frowned, slightly irritated.

"Not at all. I said a 'private' matter, did I not?"

"Indeed you did, sir," I answered contritely.

"Good. I need your help…"

But Umberto's flow of language faltered. He became uncharacteristically tongue-tied, weaving about, not making sense. Entirely unaware of what was on his mind, I leaned forward to listen.

Eventually, from the untidy fragments of his words, I grasped the elements of the problem, summarised as follows:

i) Umberto was a widower.

ii) This sad situation of being a widower occurred through the premature decease of his former wife.

iii) The aforesaid former wife was a woman of incomparable superiority to all others, however beautiful, intelligent or wealthy all others might be.

iv) Umberto was therefore in a state of permanent bereavement because of the perfection of his former wife.

v) However, even given the perfection of the dear departed, any man might find it necessary, after a suitable mourning interval (despite reluctance and regret), to take to himself another wife.

vi) This statement of intent was not to be interpreted as any kind of disrespect to the memory of the deceased wife.

Concerning Umberto's predicament as set out above, I was in no position to pass comment. How could the advice of a young man be of any assistance in such discussions? Would not the advice of Guilielmo, a recently married widower, be of greater relevance?

Such reservations however remained unspoken. Umberto, minute by minute, was regaining his powers of oratory.

I was torn between listening to the music of his utterance and analysing the substance. For the man had already given serious thought to the question of who would make a suitable bride for him.

Umberto was apparently well acquainted with several excellent women of the court in our native land who would willingly proffer their hand in marriage as he was renowned for his wealth and investments. To this assertion, I nodded. But Umberto was only in the middle of his story. Despite the miasma into which he now and then stumbled, lines of clarity emerged, as when a painter begins his canvas with lack of luminosity, but later an entire picture springs to life whether of knights, landscapes, or the Virgin Mary. Like a drowning man aiming towards the shore and, just in time, treading on firm ground, Umberto ultimately unveiled his meaning.

After consideration of various women eligible to walk down the aisle with him, Umberto confessed to having fallen entirely, deeply, irrevocably, in love with one of them. Could I not guess the identity of this fortunate lady?

I confessed I could not. After all, Umberto and myself had never been in social company beyond the confines of the customs house or his own residence. One might presume that of the few rich widows who lived in Bugia, at least one would prove suitable in status and wealth for such a person.

I remained unable to comprehend how a young man might offer advice on marriage to Umberto. Certainly any insights might promote me in his estimation, a longed for outcome. But to appoint me as his counsellor in affairs of the heart was surely inappropriate. My knowledge of widows was restricted to a nomad in a distant desert and the unfortunate example of Sara, my father's corpulent new wife.

Umberto now became reticent, to the point of stuttering. But after reaching for a flagon of wine concealed on the floor by his feet, pouring some into a receptacle, and taking large mouthfuls, he recovered his equilibrium and came to the heart of the matter.

"The truth is…" (I nodded in expectation…)

"The truth is…" that Umberto was now hopelessly in love with "an angel, a goddess, a virginal creature of beauty and virtue, the apple of my eye, my joy, my hope, my life's dream, my everything".

As if intoning the name of a deity in prayer, the great Umberto, determined to prove that every man in love is a kind of fool, whispered reverentially, "Giovanna! Giovanna! Giovanna!"

I could have dissolved into a thousand fits of laughter. Instead I emitted a spasm of dire coughing before exclaiming in a somewhat strangulated voice,

"My sister! My sister!"

"Ah yes, exactly, Leonardo! Now you see why I need your help!"

XII

It would not have been possible or polite to explain that Giovanna was my stepsister and lover, that he was too old for such a young girl, that the prospect of the two of them together was ridiculous, that his protestations of love were rooted in a shallow ignorance of Giovanna's true character.

For in that instant I was propelled into silence by the mere fact that Umberto had concocted such absurd notions. In truth, I was shocked, to an extent violated, as if a lecher had designs on my own wife and I was unable to defend her honour.

But once again the fortunate blankness of my face concealed the inner tumult of feelings. I even attempted a kind of smile by way of response. Words, further words, stuck in my throat as if a fishbone remained lodged in the gullet.

The sensation was of foreboding, disaster, a collapse of reason, an awareness of catastrophe rising like the full moon out of a dark nocturnal sea.

Umberto, however, interpreted my lack of speech as acquiescence. He rose to his feet, circumnavigated the desk, and shook my hand warmly.

"My dear young friend, I knew I could count on you!"

Umberto could not hide his pleasure at what he thought had occurred. He poured wine. We foolishly clinked cups in the manner of celebrating a betrothal.

He was beside himself with satisfaction, smiling as if I had thrown him a lifeline – love, or whatever it was, having obviously addled his wits.

After we had drunk more wine he progressed to the subject of my book, forgotten in the heat of the moment.

From a nearby chest of drawers, Umberto lifted out the manuscript, congratulated me on its depth, breadth, length and scope. Then, as if by magic, he produced (from behind his desk) a copy of my precious text, exquisitely and perfectly handwritten by scribes, including a beautifully ornate title page, bearing the words – *Liber Abaci, Leonardo Pisano's Book of Calculation.*

Speechless now for different reasons, I breathlessly and slowly perused each individual paragraph and page of this glorious treasure.

Umberto came forward to watch my happiness. Tears trickled down my cheeks at the homecoming of my work, a sight which moved him.

He began to apologise for not being more explicit about his intentions. But he wished to surprise me with this token of his esteem.

Recovering my voice for a moment or two, I expressed my profoundest thanks for such a marvellous gift, so generously bestowed.

This gratitude graciously accepted, Umberto returned to the Giovanna question.

XIII

The subject having been resumed, Umberto was interested in whether Giovanna's mother would approve. I was careful not to express too definite an opinion.

But in my heart I knew, without being told, that Sara's consent would be forthcoming. She admired wealth and wanted the best for her daughters.

I did venture to wonder out loud about Giovanna's own feelings. This seemed of little interest to Umberto, coming as he did from that level of society where young women's whims were subordinate to parental authority and expediency.

In the event Umberto interpreted my position as promising to do my best for his chances of landing the prize fish. In fact, I had merely suggested that he should enquire of Sara and find out the situation for himself. Thus my stance of neutrality was misunderstood by Umberto as friendly agreement.

Furthermore, I realised how the gift of my scribe-copied book was an incentive, a donation, towards Umberto's success in achieving his objective.

Unsure of the ground under my feet or the sky above my head, I took my leave, befuddled with wine, bearing my trophy and in much confusion.

XIV

Such was my anxiety that when I shook off the dust of Umberto's abode my thoughts came as if in equations. Among things known and unknown it was necessary to fathom my reasoning, discovering the solution which best fulfilled my purposes.

The central question was whether Giovanna was to be *my* wife, whom I would love and cherish for ever, till death did us part. Or was she to be thrust wilfully into the arms of another?

In this bright light, looking out to a sea caressed by balmy breezes, I pondered the dilemma. In such moments is one's destiny, and that of others, irrevocably chosen.

By night Giovanna's touch was truly heavenly, by day her tongue tortured me in hell. I loved her body, disliked her company. The girl had been sweeter of late. But the long haul of marriage with her was dreadful for a young man to contemplate.

Of course it seemed hateful to entertain thoughts of my beautiful Giovanna mated with an old ram. Her bedroom whimpers of broken innocence still haunted me, her warm kisses, her intimacy, resonated like sirens calling across a dangerous ocean.

This, however, was not the kind of love I had felt for Akilah, image and emblem of all that love might be. Nostalgia and regrets flooded me with weeping.

I brushed the tears from my face and set off back to town.

XV

On strolling by way of the quay I paused to admire a large military vessel moored preparatory to its journey east. This brought to mind that Guilielmo would be absent from the customs house on the afternoon of the next day. He was taking myself, Giovanna and Elisabetta, on a tour of this ship at the captain's invitation.

Thus by the time of my return to the customs house a strategy was formed and ready to be hatched.

Firstly the manuscript and the copy needed to be in their hiding place. Next, making sure Giovanna and Elisabetta were well out of the way, I cornered Sara in the kitchen area and requested a moment in private.

The woman showed no urgency. I was compelled to kick my heels in the sitting room for far too long before she made her entry. That Guilielmo might unexpectedly appear added to my consternation.

But time passes. The moment arrived when Sara, like a huge ship underway in a narrow channel, swept through the door, motioned me to be seated, and perched herself on Guilielmo's favourite chair.

"You want to see me?"

I gathered my resources. The best spun words prepared in advance often fly like sparrows before the wind when the stage is set.

"I have a message from Don Umberto," I began.

She smiled as if preening herself.

"Oh, that wonderful man! Did Guilielmo give you my instructions to invite him this Sabbath?"

"I have done so."

"Excellent!"

My serious expression caught her attention.

"Anything else?" she asked. "No difficulties?"

"No difficulties. It is just that Don Umberto…wishes to see you."

"To see *me?*" she said, her face a mask of pride and curiosity.

"Yes, in private."

She tossed her chin towards the ceiling with pursed mouth, showing the lines of her neck.

"I will ask Guilielmo."

I coughed gently.

"I think Don Umberto prefers…in private. Better not to worry Guilielmo."

"I'm not to mention anything of this to your father?" "That's right…Not yet…The good gentleman wishes to see you…*in private.*"

The woman blushed beneath her rouge, confused by the message and my amiability.

"What does he want?" she murmured, "Why should such a man wish to *see me?* In private? I am a married woman."

She shook her head coquettishly as if I was arranging a secret assignation of a dubious kind.

"Don Umberto is the soul of discretion and politeness!" I suggested.

"Of course, of course!" she said, dabbing at her brow and wet lips with her customary lace handkerchief. "So when can we meet?"

"I will arrange an appointment. Perhaps tomorrow afternoon is possible. We're going out to see the ship."

"Of course. Tomorrow afternoon would be fine!"

Still patting her flushed face, Sara flounced from the room, triumphant but subdued.

With the first part of the conundrum solved, I composed a letter to Umberto with details of the appointment.

I gave it to one of the servants with orders to tell nobody, just to hand it to the gentleman himself and wait for an answer. The servant was not very intelligent. I was compelled to repeat the instructions several times till almost overcome with impatience.

I watched his departure as he ran up the street like a schoolboy. At that moment Guilielmo emerged from the customs house. Always inquisitive and alert, he caught sight of the scurrying servant.

I explained that a letter had been dispatched to Umberto to confirm the Sabbath invitation. Guilielmo nodded in approval and returned to his work.

I later apprehended the servant slinking back from his mission. He informed me of Umberto's willingness to attend during the following afternoon.

Once more I enjoined the boy to secrecy, uttering dire threats should a single breath of this reach ears other than our own.

It was a difficult message for him to grasp, accustomed as he was to spreading gossip. But grabbing hold of his collar and putting my face close to his as I shouted seemed to convince him of my sincerity.

XVI

The following morning, consumed in anxiety, I fretted about how many things could go wrong.

Shortly after noon, Giovanna, Elisabetta, my father and myself, went to an eating house for lunch. Intent not to spend too much time on the street, I kept a good lookout for Umberto in case he came earlier than planned.

My letter had informed him of the proposed hour of our visit to the port and the time when Sara would be alone in the house. Though the slow pace of Barbary did not usually lend itself to punctuality, the hot suitor in this instance might prove to be uniquely prompt.

Giovanna looked at me fondly during the meal. At one point she leaned over and wiped a crumb from my mouth with the back of her hand, her skin so smooth that on any other day I would have darted a lustful glance.

Elisabetta meanwhile was so busy filling her belly with sweet cakes that she would not have noticed if I dropped through the floor.

We arrived at the ship to be met by an officer stationed on the gangplank. The vessel was an impressive sight, its vast oars stored below, the rowing pews fashioned from polished oak. The masts were as big as I had ever seen while the scrubbed decks stretched spacious and gleaming.

The crew went about their business under the haughty eye of an adjacent officer. In one corner a sailor, his mouth clogged with a bung, was being informally flogged by a sweating bosun. While the lash was applied with a skilful rhythmic thumping, the matelots tried not to stare unduly at this *pas de deux* as they hurried about their duties.

At the sight of an amount of blood, Elisabetta began to sob. Giovanna could not resist ogling the poor fellow's suffering. Guilielmo, as ever, shrugged his shoulders.

I pretended to be unmoved by such a scene, musing instead out loud on its daily ordinariness for a ship of war.

After the penalty had reached its peak in a flurry of brutal strokes, the agent of this horror cut down his victim. As if tenderly embracing a child, the bosun carried him away, minding not at all the gore which spattered his own shirt and trousers.

Our accompanying lieutenant hardly deigned to notice, commenting only that this would teach an insolent wretch a well deserved lesson.

After a thorough tour, we were granted the privilege of a brief audience with the captain in his spacious state room. This polite formality concluded, we expressed gratitude for his courtesy and departed the vessel.

Once ashore, Elisabetta began singing her latest song, a sure sign that no irreparable misery had been inflicted on her girlish mind by the sight of blood.

Giovanna became positively skittish, bumping against me, claiming it was accidental, and then knocking into Guilielmo in like manner.

We responded, my father and I, by pushing her bodily from one to the other, a sport she enjoyed until Elisabetta joined in, upsetting the balance of the game.

Whereupon Giovanna pulled Elisabetta's hair, making her cry again.

XVII

Once back at the customs house I went in search of Sara. She was in the kitchen, clearly agitated.

Umberto had indeed kept his appointment. She wished to say nothing more till 'the others' had been spoken to. Her face was stricter, more austere than usual, her rouge slightly smudged.

An hour or so later, Sara summoned Guilielmo to their bedroom. He eventually came back to the sitting room with an expression akin to a hound brought to heel.

Giovanna and Elisabetta were at their ease quarrelling. I kept my eyes down to the scrap of parchment on which I was scribbling a few calculations.

"You are to go to your mother!" said Guilielmo, in that special voice he reserved for Giovanna, part stepfather, part supplicant.

Giovanna was not pleased, presuming the teasing of Elisabetta, for which Sara constantly rebuked her, had brought forth the order. My innards were sick with apprehension as I saw the game develop. But I moved not a muscle of my face and did not look up.

Giovanna's light steps pranced like a dancer up the stairs. I heard the bedroom door close firmly.

A slight ripple of voices, some shouting, and a climax of shrieking and wailing, were succeeded by the scurrying of feet and Giovanna's hysterical return, her features contorted with extreme grief and anguish.

I stood up. Giovanna threw herself into my arms, her cheeks on fire with heat of a different passion than usual. Elisabetta looked up cheerfully, exclaiming innocently, "What *is* the matter with you?"

Giovanna, after one more hug, released herself from my grasp, to rush back upstairs to her room, where she slammed the door with a mighty bang. We heard the noise increase, her uncontrollable lamentations audible in every room of the house.

"Go out!" snapped Guilielmo to Elisabetta. "I wish to speak to Leonardo!"

Such was his tone that the girl ran off as if pursued by a thousand devils. I spread my hands in a gesture of innocent interrogation. He motioned me to sit.

Guilielmo mopped his brow, twitched his face, and sniffed several times.

"Umberto di Salerno has requested the hand of Giovanna in marriage!" he said stiffly.

I groped for words but found none. The mood of general dislocation was affecting each of us. The dice had been tossed into the air. Its long fall was awful.

"Your stepmother has given consent…" he added in absent-minded afterthought.

Fear gripped me. I felt more guilty than the sailor whipped that afternoon for some trivial fluffball.

"Holy God!" I exclaimed. "He's old enough to be her grand-father."

"And she is old enough to be married," said Guilielmo.

This encounter was terminated by Sara's entrance, her face like a furnace, now over-rouged and overwrought.

"Did you tell him the news?" she barked.

"Yes, my dear."

She sat down heavily.

"Good! So that's all dealt with!"

I looked at the monster in amazement.

"What does Giovanna say?" I asked quietly.

Sara glared towards me in that way she had, suggesting how in all things she knew better.

"She agrees!" she said, her jaw jutting like a ferret.

"Was that terrible noise 'agreement'?" I enquired.

"Girls always cry on these occasions."

I could have beaten my head against the wall and hers as well.

"She will get used to it!" said Sara. "I did when I was her age."

I imagined a million such scenes as daughters of all faiths, nations, races, were plummeted into destinies far from their desires. I had expected coaxing, reason and logic, not the maiming of a young woman's will, this forcing of a poor horse to water, making it drink till it burst.

How naive I was. The grip of custom strangles each of us. In this age, as in every other, we are powerless to speak and impotent to act when it is most needed.

I glanced at Guilielmo. He turned his face away.

Complicit in Giovanna's betrayal, I said nothing when I should have advanced, a knight in brilliant armour, to rescue my princess from the dragon.

But I did not and would not.

XVIII

As with executions, weddings take place quite soon after sentence is passed. Many negotiations are necessary, nuptials demanding more ceremony than justice and greater expense than burials.

Priests, caterers, servants, musicians, menus, guest lists, transport, venue, attire, gifts, dowry and decor must be provided. A date was set at just over four weeks after that meeting when Umberto first confided in me.

During the interim, he often came courting. On such occasions he wore expensive clothes, his hair and eyebrows dyed to a darker shade, his manner that of a lowly suitor rather than a wealthy sire. Our household responded with each person arrayed in finest feathers, especially Sara.

Giovanna was the recipient of an abundance of new garments, worn with no pleasure.

Only Elisabetta revelled in the coming prospects, displaying her collection of pretty dresses and attracting many admiring glances. Sara appeared somewhat puffed out, excitement making her eat even more than usual. Guilielmo looked much the same as always and said little.

Following the betrothal, Giovanna ceased her nocturnal visits to my room. At home, her behaviour resembled widowhood rather than that of one about to be married.

She spent hours in her room weeping, her visage stained with sadness at breakfast, noon, and supper, casting brown eyes towards me with such poignant glances that my very soul shrivelled in shame.

On those evenings when Umberto arrived to get acquainted with his bride-to-be, Giovanna was worse, venting irritation on Elisabetta who, saint-like, tolerated every insult.

With the betrothed couple closeted in the sitting room, we were exiled out of earshot. When they emerged, after half an hour or so, Umberto beamed as he departed. Giovanna, eyes cast down, resumed her sepulchral mask. She would go to her room, slamming the door, while we waited for bursts of wailing to follow.

One evening, to resolve the issue, when the house appeared quiet except for Giovanna's soft sobbing from inside her chamber, I tapped on her door and made my entrance. She was lying on the bed, wiping her eyes with a towel.

I sat down, head in hands, and cried with her, sharing a prayer of sorrow. She ran kind fingers through my hair.

"Don't weep, Leonardo, it's no use."

This increased the deluge, breaking my heart. I turned towards her. We embraced, not as lovers but like siblings seeking comfort.

"I'm so sorry!" I mumbled, her hair fragrant, her body against mine. I would have succumbed that instant to her charm. But she untwined herself and leaned against the bedhead, making use of the towel to dry my face. We sat in silence as if everything between us was said and done.

She took my right hand in hers and placed it against her left breast. Looking at me with a doomed expression, she whispered, "Don't worry. I'll tell nobody about our love."

When I tiptoed from the room, doubts assailed me. Could Giovanna and I have shared a happy life? Had I misjudged everything? To some questions there are no answers.

Besides, it was too late to turn back.

XIX

Umberto di Salerno came to dinner every Sabbath and many other evenings. Sara was enchanted, being somewhat in love with him herself. Guilielmo spoke less and less. Elisabetta shrieked with joy whenever she saw the suitor approaching. Poor Giovanna looked mournful.

The meals were protracted affairs. Umberto dipped into his bag of stories and spun them at length. The delights of his eloquence dimmed after a few suppers as repetition crept in. His attempts to coax anecdotes from others were futile for nobody felt able to compete.

When I tried to save the day by reminiscences of Egyptian sights, riding a camel or travels at sea, everything sounded as out of tune as an old lute. Even when Umberto dazzled we tired of his shining excellence. Never again did he release those butterflies of delight which enthralled us at first hearing. From time to time Guilielmo stifled yawns.

Sara made sure that Umberto and Giovanna sat side by side at the table, leaving Elisabetta and myself on the opposing parallel, Guilielmo to my right as the nominal head of family and Sara seated queen-like at the far end.

Our main *dramatis personae* presented a pretty picture suggesting 'Grandfather with Maiden in Fine Flower', despite Umberto's attempts to make himself appear a year or two younger by trimming his beard and wearing new clothes.

That these two were to become man and wife destroyed my enjoyment of any meal. If, by chance, his fingers brushed her arm, I observed it.

That his bearded mouth would meet her soft sweet lips, that his large hands would caress and fondle her milk-white breasts, that their legs would entwine – such images were so galling that more than once I had to apologise and leave the room, overcome by nausea.

One evening after supper Umberto drew me to one side to repeat for the thousandth time his gratitude for my intercession on his behalf.

"Without you, Leonardo, I would not be in this happy situation."

My protests that I had little to do with the matter were brushed aside. "You will be my stepbrother-in-law!" he murmured, putting a fraternal hand on my arm.

"And Sara will be your mother-in-law!" I retorted.

"What a beautiful woman!" he intoned.

But other things were on his mind that night for he wished

to discuss matters of currency. I went into my recitation about Imperial, Genoese, Barcelonan and Magalono soldos, Pisan and Bolognese denarii, Paduan, Regal and Venetian pounds, Saracen bezants, the weight of silver and the price of gold. He admitted that too much detail made him drowsy. I promised to inform him further when he felt sufficiently awake.

Umberto's alleged indebtedness to me in the business of marriage was of such concern to him that he returned to the subject many times, rather as a dog searches for buried bones. Our intimate conclaves were noted in the household enough to arouse suspicion, especially in Guilielmo who would enquire why we were talking so earnestly together.

"Business, commerce, currency!" was my reply. Guilielmo sniffed irritably and muttered, "I didn't know these subjects were so amusing!"

Umberto could not keep away from me. I was promoted from an underling addressing him as 'Sir' to a future relative and confidant.

He acquired the habit of sidling up with sly questions about Giovanna. I fobbed him off but he persisted along such lines as "Is Giovanna religious?" or "Is she happy?"

My fear was not only that we were seen putting heads together but that we would be overheard. Elisabetta in particular could be relied on to tittle-tattle any juicy scraps of hearsay around the house.

Another evening, somewhat drunk, prior to setting off home, Umberto approached me in the hallway.

"Leonardo, thank you for everything you have done."

"I have done nothing!"

"You have brought me happiness!"

I shook my head.

"I cannot claim such honour."

He grasped me in a massive embrace.

As I writhed like prey in a snare, I glimpsed behind him a reflection in a tall mirror of Giovanna watching round the corner of the corridor.

Umberto, releasing me from his clutches, unaware of the phantom spectator, promptly produced a bag which he handed to me, announcing like a town crier in a wine-laden voice, "This is for all you have done for me!"

He thrust the gift clumsily into my palm.

Trapped between Giovanna's image in the mirror and her actual presence behind me, I untied the string at the mouth of the bag. A number of gold coins glimmered in the candlelight.

"What is this?" I asked.

"Yours! Yours for the keeping."

Once more he hugged me close, tears filled his eyes.

By the time I had sufficiently expressed gratitude for his gift, the apparition of the hallway was no longer to be seen.

Umberto's gift gave me no pleasure. I deposited his purse in the usual hiding place next to the precious copy of my book he had given me, and slipped out for a walk by the quay. The night was glorious with a silver moon and flickering lights from moored ships. I returned late, padding up the stairs as quietly as a thief.

But in vain. Giovanna was waiting for me, seated on a chair in my bedroom, a sour expression on her face.

"Giovanna!" I exclaimed, startled.

"Yes, *Giovanna!*" she threw at me, imitating my voice. "What was all that about?"

I was too weary to cheat her further.

"You mean Umberto?"

"Yes, I mean *you* and Umberto, talking! '*This is for all you have done for me.*' What *have* you done for him?"

I paused, sucked my lower lip before replying.

"I made him a lot of money!"

"Money? He doesn't care about money. He doesn't need to."

"Well perhaps he *does* care. More than you think. You don't know him as I do."

Even as the words came out, I knew it was a bad error.

"'*You don't know him as I do!*' True, but *I* have to marry the man. And he gave *you* a gift."

"I am sorry. I did nothing to deserve anything. I was doing my duty."

She was silent for a moment.

"Duty?" she enquired. "You don't know the meaning of *duty!* Soldiers have *duties,* sailors have *duties*, priests have *duties.* You, however, do exactly what you want!"

"Perhaps you are right!" I answered. "But I do no more for Umberto than what is done for other merchants."

"Do *they* reward you with bags of money?"

"Sometimes. They offer money. That's how business is conducted!"

Her dear face expressed contempt for all I had become in recent weeks.

My heart heaved with remorse. I longed to hold her close, to put back the clock, to make amends.

"Giovanna," I murmured, "I love you so much. I am sorry for what has happened."

"Well," she replied, with a sardonic smile that would have graced an abdicating monarch, "It's the first time you ever said you *love* me!"

"But I do love you!"

"It's too late," she said. "I am promised to Umberto. That is what I shall do. You and I have become souls apart."

"Do you love *me?*" I asked.

"Sometimes! Sometimes not. But it's neither here nor there. We know what we have to do. We shall do it."

Giovanna stood up.

She did not want me to touch her. Having been embraced by Umberto, I was as a leper in her sight, his gift of gold a noose around my neck.

Giovanna moved to depart, never to return, her whole body drooping with despair. On reaching the door, she stared in a manner most strange.

"I have a gift for you. But you will never receive it!" she said, speaking as softly as a rustling of silk.

And, like a will-o'-the-wisp, she was gone.

ᘓᕦ XXI ᕤᘔ

From then on Giovanna remained in her bedchamber, taking her meals alone, living the existence of a nun. Sara took this in her stride, convinced that a fear of losing their maidenhead induces seclusion in girls. Guilielmo said less and less to any of us, as if the whole affair was nothing to do with him.

To make things worse, Elisabetta was taken into a corner by Sara to be given a talk on marriage, its function and purpose. This caused further unhappiness. The girl tried in the same manner as her sister to take to her room, moping and sobbing, vowing that if things were as Sara described them she would never wed nor allow a man to do *that* to her.

Sara drove her downstairs with blows and shouts, ordering her to join in family life and not be so silly. But the knowledge made Elisabetta shy with Guilielmo and myself.

I overheard Sara explain to my father that Elisabetta had recently crossed the border from child to woman. Discipline was required or she would become as wilful as her sister. With enough troubles of my own, I kept a good distance from such conversations.

At first I avoided any chores to do with organising the wedding, leaving everything to Sara at the centre of the whirlwind. My neutrality went well until Umberto requested me to act as his *testimone dello sposo,* an honour which, in view of his various kindnesses to me, could not be refused.

As his 'best man', Umberto called upon my services many times, sending me to recruit caterers, musicians, servants, suppliers, cooks, and miscellaneous others. I spent hours running in circles, negotiating prices, discounts, deals, and bargains.

Each instance had to be referred back for Umberto's *imprimatur* on bills of sale. His scrutiny of accounts was an art in itself. Not a single item missed his eagle eye and he was quick to spot any party who exceeded permitted limits.

Such was my conscience in these days before the wedding that my passion for Giovanna intensified. By night her image floated before my eyes like a mirage. With each dawn I mourned her absence from me and her coming fate.

Apart from this, my anxieties centred on the wedding night. Umberto would easily discover that Giovanna's ripe cherry had been snatched from the tree. When the virgin goddess was revealed as stained lace, prospects of catastrophe were plentiful. Either way there was much to think about.

One touch from Giovanna, a look, a gesture, would reveal her skill in the school of dalliance. A person such as Umberto would demand answers, whatever casual vows of silence Giovanna had given to me.

I decided it would be prudent to leave Bugia after the wedding. Umberto's gold had given me wings to fly. Like Icarus, I intended to launch towards the sun.

I perused the records at the customs house, noting the log of every ship in harbour or forthcoming. Pending supplies of cargo, captains often gave notice of their itineraries in advance. The imminent departure of a suitable vessel might coincide with my plan. All I needed was a little luck.

For this reason I made sure Guilielmo paid me everything owing for work on his behalf.

Indeed, he asked no questions and even increased payment with a generous bonus. Furthermore, he supplied a certificate establishing I was no longer his apprentice but master in my own right, competent to conduct all tasks pertaining to taxes of the Republic of Pisa.

At the same time I drove hard bargains with each merchant whose work I handled, forcing them so close to the edge they rewarded me with fine bribes to wriggle off the hooks on which they were impaled.

Within two days of the wedding a suitable ship came in. Outbound from Bugia, she was scheduled to proceed via various ports towards Syria. Her master, a Greek, I liked on sight. Recently promoted, he knew neither Bugia nor my father, having spent much time in home waters. Our contract of passage was sealed with some of the coins Umberto had given me.

I assured the captain that before we sailed, as part of our bargain, I would attempt to complete much of his port business, charging no excess in our favour. The tax on his cargo, whatever it was, would be reduced to a bare minimum.

His only condition, for reasons of space on board, was that I would have to share a cabin with another passenger. I had no alternative but, with some anxiety, to accept this.

XXII

The day of the wedding dawned, much like any other, the turnings of the earth and its dances with sun and moon being unaltered by anything we contrive.

I woke to hear Guilielmo and Sara arguing somewhere in the house. The previous night, very late, I had packed my few belongings and taken them to the ship. I placed some money in a belt to wear round my waist beneath the tunic, the rest slipped into a smaller bag to accompany me.

Later that morning I departed for Umberto's house, the ceremony to take place at noon in the chapel along the quay. He greeted me with great cordiality. I said as little as possible, hiding my tormented anxieties beneath a mask of quietness appropriate and fitting for a responsible *testimone dello sposo*.

We drank some wine together. I tried to imagine how Giovanna would fare in this spacious dwelling.

At one point Umberto sent me upstairs to fetch a handkerchief for him. I peered into the main bedroom. How galling it was to think of Giovanna on her back among these furnishings and fine linen.

Reluctant to dwell more on such painful remembrances than is strictly necessary, I hasten to tell of the wedding itself. Umberto had kindly enriched me with new clothes for the occasion, fit for a prince, his further gift for what I had allegedly achieved on his behalf. Feeling slightly foolish in this new attire, I accepted his compliments on my appearance with what he assumed to be 'youthful modesty'.

Umberto's own garments were only slightly more magnificent. Given his straight back and dignified bearing, he could have been my father escorting his son to union with a beautiful bride.

At the appointed hour, priest and guests assembled at the chapel door. Sara, her fulsome form enveloped in rich cloth, was very much at the centre of things, accompanied by merchants, servants, and a number of wealthy widows.

She greeted Umberto with an extravagant display of affection before turning her weasel gaze towards me.

"How handsome you look, Leonardo. I haven't seen you in such splendour before."

"Thank you," I replied, succumbing to a slightly less fervent embrace than that afforded to Umberto.

After much chattering, extending for half an hour beyond the designated time, Giovanna arrived with Guilielmo, delegated to the duty of giving her away to Umberto.

The first sight of the bride, in traditional blue, with a sardonyx brooch signifying chastity, set my pulse beating like a wild sea. Elisabetta, *damigella d'onore,* wore matching silk which clung to her diminutive body, her face shining with the crispness of a young flower.

All passed as in a blur. But unforgettable was the light in Umberto's eyes as his bride stepped from the carriage.

I observed how possessively he touched her hand, her arm, her waist.

And when Guilielmo gave Giovanna to him, with the words *Ego in nomine domini eam tibi trado,* I knew for sure that I should have been standing in that place where Umberto was now proclaimed for ever as her lord and master.

My eyes filled with massive tears, which Sara noticed, for she wiped my face with her perfumed handkerchief.

The couple were pronounced man and wife. Giovanna smiled at her husband like a woman resurrected on the day of judgement. He smiled back and kissed her on the lips. My heart heaved with regret.

We moved to the body of the chapel for the Nuptial Mass, I found myself once again next to Sara. In the heat and babble, the clerks intoning *Beati Omnes,* a weakness afflicted me, my senses reeled.

I swooned onto Sara's shoulder before slipping like a drunkard to the floor.

For several long moments I lay prone and half conscious, Sara's rouged face leering over me. Giovanna in that magnificent dress and Umberto in his finery stared disconsolately down. Guilielmo knelt beside me. While they ministered to the fallen, the choir sang on.

I was lifted to my feet. Sara took charge, putting her powerful arms round me. I leaned wearily against her. They attributed this fainting to my having fasted before Mass. Feebly I nodded in agreement.

We retreated after the ceremony for a reception in the customs house. The musicians were playing loudly with much percussion and caterwauling. People kept approaching to ask if I had recovered, to which I could but mumble assent.

The feast began, though I had no stomach for it, the very sight of food inducing nausea. Sara suggested that to sip from a small cup of milk would stifle my sickness.

Doing their rounds among the guests, the newly wedded couple eventually approached me, Giovanna walking stiffly, constrained by the tightness of the dress, while Umberto imperiously dangled his chosen fruit from an uxorious arm.

Giovanna looked pale. She afforded me a light sisterly kiss, a hint of wine on her breath.

Umberto thumped me heartily on the back, guffawed, shook my hand. I traded on my swoon and kept my voice low, wishing them happiness.

Such a comment occasioned a slight flicker across Giovanna's face and a sideways glance. Umberto, noticing nothing amiss, continued to strut and preen as a man should on his wedding day.

Guilielmo approached with anxiety, wondering why on earth I should be so frail on this of all days. I made excuses and apologised for my weakness. He hastened to reassure me that my own mother had also been given to such ailments. We embraced, sorrow plaguing me like a rock strapped to my chest.

With the party at its height, and before the couple left the hall, I whispered in a few ears, danced with Elisabetta, kissed Sara, and expressed the need to breathe some fresh air.

I went directly to my room, took off the wedding clothes and hung them in the closet, put on daily garments, including the belt of coinage, and left by the back door.

Within minutes I boarded the chosen vessel, busy with departure, its rigging full of men and boys. Without a backward look, I traversed the gangplank and made my way aft to greet the captain.

He nodded curtly and ordered an underling to escort me to my quarters.

XXIII

In the allotted cabin, kneeling at his bedside, was my companion for the journey, his back to me as he prayed towards the light from a small porthole, a massive sword held before him in the manner of a cross.

He prayed on silently, undisturbed by my arrival. Only when

the devotions were completed did he rise to his feet, a little unsteadily, then turning abruptly as if just realising my presence.

I observed the eagle-like intensity of his eyes, the closely cropped grey hair, a face as clean shaven as a monk. He was dressed in a brown velvet tunic and a cord belt like a friar, with black military-style breeches and heavy boots.

"I am Guy de Poitiers," he said, "a soldier in the service of God."

"I am Leonardo Pisano, a scholar."

We sat on our respective couches. He seemed eager to talk, having spent much time on his own.

His profession intrigued me though I knew nothing about the ways of warriors. In these matters Guy de Poitiers would attempt to instruct me, starting at once.

He pursued God as others devote themselves to worldly ambition. Yet his hands were 'saturated', as he expressed it, with the blood of those he had killed.

He felt as if he were already dead on some distant field of battle, that very sensation proving he was still alive.

Such was the intensity of his discourse I scarcely noticed that the vessel was already gently moving and the voyage beginning.

At Guy's suggestion, I was persuaded on deck to watch the setting sun illuminating Bugia, while the boat trembled in the choppy sea like a nervous bride.

"There will be plenty of time to talk on this voyage," said Guy, with obvious relish.

We stood side by side, watching the azure strip of water widen between us and the land.

I imagined Giovanna and Umberto in their first embrace, and Sara and Guilielmo reading the letter I had left for them.

"You look thoughtful!" said Guy. "Almost guilty!"
"I have much to think about!" I murmured.
But already the sea breeze tasted sweetly fresh.

Letter from Giovanna
to Leonardo Pisano

To Leonardo Pisano, son of Guilielmo Bonacci,
from Giovanna, wife of Umberto di Salerno.

I cannot be certain whether you will ever read this letter, not being acquainted with your present circumstances or whereabouts. But some letters are written for the purposes of those who send them. I will attempt to set out the truth as I understand it.

Neither, dear Leonardo, am I aware if you are a great letter writer yourself. My husband informs me you have written a book about the numbers but I do not know if you write many letters.

In the seven and a half months since you went from Bugia, I have never ceased to wonder where you might be. Your absence is a burden and I regret it more than words can say. The day you left was, you will recall, my wedding day, following my hasty betrothal to Umberto di Salerno. Since then many things have happened.

Six months later I gave birth to a boy who died, cut off from life by the very cord which sustained him in the womb. It was the saddest moment of my life, even more so than my wedding day. For he was the child of none other than my beloved Leonardo, now departed into foreign lands.

My husband believes this was a miscarriage. Through the good offices of a midwife, she and I were fortunate to conceal the true facts. Thus I escaped scandal to my reputation and remain virtuous in the opinion of all.

On my wedding night, I deceived Umberto about my unvirginal condition. That is not difficult with a gullible man and a guileful woman.

He proved in view of his age to be an unreliable lover, having difficulties arousing the stag to jump to its duties, this through no fault of his own. However, he managed the task at least once, hence providing an excuse for my being with child.

In general, Umberto is a kind, forbearing husband who lavishes much on me by way of clothes, jewellery, servants and fine food.

My mother thinks it is a marriage made in heaven and visits us often to converse with Umberto. Your father remains pensive, says little, weeps much, and misses you more than he admits.

Despite the comforts of home I would have preferred another road. If only you and I could have united together and defied protocol I might have been as happy as a queen. But, alas, it was never to be.

I am the more sorry for that as the days pass in endless progression towards whatever fate God has decreed for us in this world or the next.

How well do I remember when I first laid eyes on you, Leonardo returned from his travels, accoutred like a native, dark skinned, garments soiled with the desert dust. You were a figure of legend that night. When you had washed and shaved, you returned to us like a new creation, a kind of miracle, a being rescued from oblivion.

Already we were drunk on a thousand tales told by your father of your exploits in Pisa and Bugia, of your wondrous ease with the numbers, your childhood escapades, your apartness from the world, your ambitions, your follies, your goodness.

When I saw you, I fell headlong into the depths of love, that abyss from which there is no earthly escape. I determined I would marry you one day. Your tales of distant lands, your bravado, your exquisite description of unknown things, carried me further into the snare of love.

When you began work in the customs house I saw you as my captive pigeon, ready to be tamed. I was even annoyed with Elisabetta as she stole your time from me and you were kind to her.

Then our souls became more and more entwined till, in a rash moment, Elisabetta gave us away. With that deceit we strengthened our affection. My sister's chastisement bound us in chains of falsehood.

Later I comforted Elisabetta by telling her there were things beyond her comprehension which would one day be revealed. She trusted me and held no grudge, dear angel that she is.

I came to your bed and you were mine. You were experienced in dalliance. I was envious of those who first instructed you. But in the light of day, petulance possessed me. I became like my mother, criticising where I should not, blaming without reason, my tongue wounding you whom I most adored. Each night I attempted to repair the damage and you responded with unfailing ardour, winning my heart and sealing my destiny.

I spoke much foolishness in my green days as a girl in love, for example praising wealth but never meaning such things. Now that I live abundantly in daily extravagance, how sad it is without you beside me.

Quite soon I was with child. Then Umberto entered our lives and my mother saw union between him and myself as the marriage of her dreams. Umberto spun his tales and told them well. But I preferred those of my Leonardo. I feared most when you became friends with Umberto. Beneath the surface, like an earthquake under the sea, were events which destroyed my happiness.

You, Leonardo, seemed star-struck by Umberto's wealth and authority, so beholden to the man, that you became servile in order to advance your ambitions.

It was my mother who told me of Umberto's proposal and that he had first asked you about it. What a betrayal of love and hope! I was offered one road to travel, my mother blocked all others.

Somehow, Umberto came to believe that I accepted his proposal. Then I saw you taking money from Umberto. Trapped like a rabbit by ferrets, I surrendered to fate. I vowed you would be punished, that the gift I carried for you, your child in my womb, would never be received by you nor ever known.

But when I saw you fall to the floor in the chapel, my heart ached as if I would die. I saw your dear face that day and knew that you could not be responsible for what happened. The world has become confused and awful. That which I did not wish to do, I did. What I desired seemed forbidden. I was lost for ever in unhappiness.

It might be better, dearest Leonardo, if you never receive this letter. However, I will keep it safe against the day of your return. Now that everything has been decided and settled, it would perhaps be preferable for you to live in ignorance of what has come to pass and how love was betrayed. But as a scholar you should rejoice in what is true.

Your nature, Leonardo, is flawed. One day you must come to terms with that. The numbers have become your master when you should be master of them. You can be duped by the sparkle of false jewels and yet at other times fail to recognise pure gold.

You have a long and difficult road ahead. I wish you had shared the journey with me, with myself happy by your side and you safe in my loving arms. But this was not to be and while you travel I go in an opposite direction, my hopes lost, our child dead, living with a husband who cannot fathom my mind but knows my regrets for they are written on my face and body.

Will we ever meet again? Perhaps it is true that the stars exert influence over us and that God knows our little histories before we live them, that each of us is doomed to sorrow. Although He knows our desires, perhaps He thwarts them to bring us closer to what He wants us to be.

What am I therefore? A broken reed, a memory of love, an image in your soul, a neglected wife in harness with an old horse.

I should not be these things. Yet in my married state I speak with other wives, each with blighted dreams that marriage could not repair, despite so many promises and vows.

I send you the only gifts I have left, my broken heart, my loving thoughts.

I shall remember you however old I become. I hope and pray you will never forget the love of your Giovanna.

If you receive this letter, whether in one year or ten, it will remain a faithful testimony of my thoughts.

May God in His mercy keep you safe,

Giovanna

Eighth Letter

Concerning a voyage from Bugia,
the madness of Guy de Poitiers,
and the death of a sailor.

Veriedes tantas lanças – premer e alçar,
tanta adágara – foradar e passar,
tanta loriga – falssar e desmanchar,
tantos pendones blancos – salir vermejos en sangre,
tantos buenos cavallos – sin sos dueños andar.

Poema de Mío Cid (12th century)

(You would see so many lances, raised and crushed,
so many shields pierced and smashed,
so many coats of mail destroyed and lashed,
so many flags with hot blood flushed,
so many riderless horses rush.)

I

Sire, My Most Admired Master Michael Theodorus,
Philosopher in the Service of His Majesty, Frederick II.

As our vessel ventured along the Barbary coast Guy de Poitiers had much to say. Most of all he was concerned for my immortal soul, advising confession, fasting, and constant prayer, as the means of passing through the gates of heaven.

Conversely, he dreamed often of hellfire, waking in the middle of the night with sweats and swearing, demanding tapers be lit and that I should talk to him through the long hours till dawn. His visions of hell were plainly drawn from experiences of battle. Yet his claim to have no fear of death but only of spiritual extinction or desertion by God was entirely credible.

The equation of this man's goodness balanced against the horrors of his profession was the opposite of reason. But perhaps his beliefs preserved him from worse madness. He was convinced of the powers of witchcraft, Satan, and devils, for he had seen such things with his own eyes and heard their diabolical cries with his own ears.

Hitherto I had never exercised my mind much on these things, preferring to believe that God was more logical than His followers and therefore less to be feared than legions of priests and monks.

Guy de Poitiers distrusted scholarship, terrified that Lucifer himself lurked within the numbers. I explained a few practical mathematical problems but even then the chevalier seemed only slightly reassured about the innocence of this kind of questioning and answering.

Guy, who could scarcely write his own name, possessed a peasant's suspicion about the magical properties of the written word. To this end, I began to instruct him in literacy. With a piece of chalk we spent many an hour, sometimes in the periods when he could not sleep, scribbling letters and words on scraps of wood.

He proved an able student but only if certain aspects were left untouched. He had qualms, for example, about writing the word *God* and I recalled the Hebrew belief that God was not to be named.

On the other hand, Guy de Poitiers was content to write *Devil* or *Satan* for this implied a certain disrespect for these entities.

He was not however averse to reading the word *God*. When it became apparent that Holy Scripture constantly used the word, he eventually considered it permissible to write it, with appropriate reverence, on the page.

His reluctance caused me to think that such notions had been absorbed as a boy training with sword, shield, bow, and knife. For those accustomed to facing death in battle, it is essential to take no chances with the Deity. Hence, soldiers and sailors, as a matter of course, follow many unwritten traditions of this kind, which others call 'superstitions'.

In speech Guy was chaste and reticent, no oaths permitted to pass his lips. It therefore proved intriguing when he woke from nightmares with the foulest curses coming from his mouth, like a man gone berserk. His sudden tirades did not engender happy sleep on my part.

For who could know when Guy de Poitiers might suddenly awake from his slumbers with an angry roar? Any companion of his could be casually killed by this sleepwalking leviathan on the rampage.

When taking him to task for the contrast between his usual restraint and the stream of blasphemies on waking, he denied everything, possessing no recollection of any of these utterances. I assured him on the salvation of my soul that what I said was the gospel truth.

Following incredulity, he fell to his knees and begged God for forgiveness, requesting me to repeat exactly what he had said, omitting nothing. To humour him, I pronounced a few of the choicest fruits of his nightly vocabulary, though not all, for some outbursts might have offended the devil himself.

II

During the voyage we dined with the captain in his comfortable quarters equipped with a solid table and sturdy chairs. Captain Mitsos of Athens enjoyed our company, offered many cups of wine, and the food on board was as palatable as could be expected under the circumstances.

Mitsos told tales of storms at sea, shipwreck, the beauties of his native land, and the ancient civilisation of Greece. He quoted poetry in his own tongue about Achilles and Hector which sounded remarkably like music.

On the third evening, Mitsos, speaking softly, presented Guy de Poitiers with a special problem. A particular sailor, a giant of a man, refused to be disciplined, his behaviour inciting the crew against Mitsos himself. The captain, though not a coward, could see no easy way of resolving this dilemma.

I looked towards Guy as the details of the matter were explained, like a sickness being described to a physician.

"Could you help?" said the captain, with the air of a man who for the life of him could find no remedy.

"I am a soldier, not a sailor." said Guy de Poitiers. "But men are men and all the same under the skin. Tell me more."

"This individual is a threat to the ship!" said Mitsos. Guy drank a sip of wine, looking at me as if I might be able to suggest a solution. I bit my lip and said nothing. Such matters were to do with experience and instinct, not reason.

"Do you want him dead?" asked Guy casually, as if he were requesting Mitsos to pass a slice of cheese. It was the captain's moment to pause. I watched his dark brow furrow as he pondered the question.

"Whatever is necessary!" said Mitsos when his mind was made up. "Do as you think. But he is a Goliath of a man."

Guy de Poitiers chuckled.

"The size is of no concern. It is what is in a man's soul that matters. I have seen a dwarf fight in battle with the vigour of twenty men and mighty warriors pleading for mercy on their knees."

Mitsos smiled, the burden of responsibility satisfactorily transferred to another's conscience.

"In the morning, point him out!" said Guy.

"Thank you!" exclaimed Mitsos.

He clapped his hands for the steward to enter, ordering more wine, cheese, and fruit before embarking on another batch of fables.

In the unlikely event that such a task was laid at my door, I could not have slept. But Guy de Poitiers that night fell into a snoring sleep. For this was one occasion when he did *not* wake from nightmare to engage in distracting conversation.

Shortly after dawn we ventured out to greet Mitsos on the afterdeck. It was a beautiful day with a calm sea and soft breeze, the coast just visible to starboard as we progressed eastwards. At first we chatted about the pleasures of the previous evening's meal, complimenting the captain on his food and his yarns.

As we stood looking towards the bow, a huge man emerged from below decks, striding arrogantly across the planks, ducking beneath the boom, and sweeping aside a wretch who impeded his path.

Aware of our trio at the steerage point, he leered rudely as if mocking, turned his back ostentatiously, and swaggered away. Naked to the waist, with shaven head, the breadth of his shoulders recalled Atlas supporting the globe.

His arms were massive, embroidered with fibres of muscles honed by hard exercise in rigging and manual work. The erect neck and tilt of body suggested a Roman gladiator.

"That's the man!" whispered Mitsos, somewhat unnecessarily.

I glanced at Guy de Poitiers. He too was well-built but against that giant he was diminished, as were all others. I was intrigued how Guy would deal with a matter which clearly needed to be settled.

"Wait here a moment, Sir," said Guy to the captain. "Leonardo, come with me!"

Before I could protest, Guy moved down the steps of the raised afterdeck, walking slowly. By and by, pausing a few times to survey the ocean, Guy pointed to the waves as if watching a fish or swooping bird. We came to where the giant lounged near the ratlines.

"Stand behind me," muttered Guy, "but gently!"

I needed no second bidding.

Guy de Poitiers walked forward while I hesitated a few paces back. The giant sensed we were stalking him for he sneered dreadfully. The soldier spoke to the man in a low persuasive voice, rather as one might address a child.

"Sailor! The captain would like you to attend on the afterdeck."

"The captain can go hang!" said the giant. "If he wants to say something, he can come himself."

There was a pause, the very motion of the ship seeming to hold its breath. Members of the crew turned from their work, waiting to see whatever was about to happen.

"As you wish," said Guy. "I am only the messenger."

The giant relaxed, grinning hideously, confident of his victory.

Yet even as that great body stooped ever so slightly towards his unknown foe, the soldier struck like a bolt of lightning across his opponent's throat, driving his hand into the Adam's apple, somehow upending the man, swinging him backwards over the side, straight into the sea.

There were two sounds, the choke of the initial blow and a gurgle as the giant was propelled beyond the ship into the water.

It was so quick, so deliberate, that each of us could hardly believe what we had seen. The crew let out a sustained cheer, relieved the tyrant was destroyed.

I looked into the waves but the vessel's movement impaired sight of the body caught beneath the hull. I hurried aft to the rail to catch a glimpse of the man should he be swept away in the momentum. He never reappeared, presumably dragged down by the keel and current to meet his Maker.

Guy de Poitiers ambled back the way he had come without a glance of curiosity concerning his quarry. He appeared no more interested than if he had thrown a rat into the water. Thus he returned alone to our cabin.

"Holy Christ preserve us!" mumbled Captain Mitsos.

I decided it was best to stay on deck and let the soldier pray in private for a while.

III

When I returned much later to the cabin Guy de Poitiers was still praying, his sword held before him cross-like in the accustomed manner, his torso hunched in contrition. After emerging from the state of trance such devotions induced, he seated himself, eager to converse. Sin was on his mind.

"You must consider me a great sinner, Leonardo!" he began.

"I do not judge you," I replied. "I am also a sinner!"

"What have you done you are sorry for?" he said, like a father confessor. So I confessed.

"I have betrayed those I love, lusted after immoral women, practised deceit, borne false witness against a child, conspired for a person to be married against her will, shown disrespect to my father, and other things."

Guy de Poitiers paused to let the enormity of these transgressions sink in.

"Some are unusual. I will not ask what the 'other things' are. But each stems from our sinful nature inherited from Adam."

That a man who had committed murder before my very eyes was discussing *my* sins, not his own, did not strike me as incongruous. Guy de Poitiers, risen from prayer, was refreshed, forgiven.

He began a long monologue, fascinating in both logic and incoherence. As I understood it, his thesis centred on divine accountancy, whereby a monk envying a grape on his neighbour's plate could be judged as sinful as any soldier killing in the course of duty. To this principle he clung as a shipwrecked sailor holds fast to a piece of rotten driftwood.

Guy de Poitiers, warming to his subject, cited sins against the Holy Ghost as the greatest evil, followed by sins of the flesh, disobedience, covetousness, murder, sins of omission and commission, of greed, sloth, envy, and despair.

His voice rising, I saw the man was possessed of many devils, unhinged on one side of his nature. The killing of the sailor had released the hindrances which bound his tongue.

With myself as a frightened audience, the torrent continued. He had such a look in his eyes I feared becoming his next victim.

The cabin, hitherto spacious enough, gave pause for thought as a cage in which I was imprisoned with a deranged animal.

But once his tirade reached its climax, Guy de Poitiers sneezed twice, laughed, shook my hand and clapped me on the back, commending me for my patience in listening to his opinions.

With that he moved over to his bed, fell on it with his back to the door, and began snoring loudly.

Aware of the paradoxes of my own soul, I pondered on his. A knight with speech unblemished by profanity except when waking from bad dreams, a diligent man of prayer till his legs groaned from kneeling, yet able to kill another without remorse, a proud soldier, strict in routine, casual in murder.

Within his skull, he was not one but many – soldier, monk, penitent, sinner, killer, theologian, leader, both reticent of speech and loquacious.

My appreciation of his virtues became confused with fear of his vices. Such a man might kill me as I slept and thereafter begin to pray. I worried how the problem might be solved considering he and I were enclosed upon the emptiness of the ocean.

As I wallowed in this quandary, Guy de Poitiers ceased his slumbers and sat upright. His face, transformed from the earnestness affected during his harangue, looked boyish as he scanned me up and down with a kind of delight.

"Let's go and eat!" he exclaimed. "I am extremely hungry."

Assuming the pretence that this was an ordinary morning on an ordinary ship, we made our way to the captain's quarters.

To my surprise, a celebratory feast of soup, fish, nuts, cheese, bread, lemon water, wine, hard biscuits, dates and grapes, had been prepared. I joined in with a will, discovering a sudden appetite.

Guy de Poitiers and the captain jested as if neither had a care in the world.

✥ IV ✥

Later that afternoon, with Guy de Poitiers again sleeping as if shaking off the consequences of the day, I made my way to the captain for a confidential word. My request for a separate cabin was denied despite much pleading that Guy was noisy in the night and disturbed my rest.

Mitsos insisted that the knight would be offended if I moved out. The captain emphasised how our arrangements were by mutual consent. I should keep to the initial agreement as he intended to do.

In a more pleasing tone, he thanked me for helping Guy de Poitiers rid the vessel of an evil curse. Captain and crew now regarded us as benefactors who by our valour had averted a host of troubles.

It was futile for me to protest that I was a bystander not an accomplice, a suggestion which Mitsos deemed merely admirable modesty on my part.

The captain apologised for his inability to meet my need for different quarters. But conditions on board, regrettably, did not permit privileges even to special guests. He would try to make up any deficiency with extra food.

Having been spun out of my purpose by this Greek spider, I offered my salutation and left. After drifting idly round the deck, pausing to offer a brief prayer in memory of the departed giant, I reluctantly returned to the cabin.

Guy de Poitiers was sitting on the bed, his head in his hands. He looked up.

"I slept well," he said.

"Good," I replied. As madmen do, he caught the essence of my mood in an instant, rising to his feet.

"Leonardo, my dear friend! Let us not be sad about this morning. I know it upset you. Believe me, such a thing was necessary."

Gloomily, I offered a nod of agreement.

"Sit down, Leonardo, I want to tell you a story."

I had no choice but to do what he said. He made himself comfortable. Reading my thoughts from my tense frown, he began.

"Dear Leonardo, you are distraught. I know that. But, compared with what I have seen, you are an innocent boy. If you live long, you will see worse things."

I grunted in noncommittal manner.

"You are a scholar, Leonardo. At your age you think you will live for ever. But I am a soldier. I know how short life is. In the end each of us will be buried in the same earth or drowned in the same ocean."

The sense of his guilt being cleansed by the flow of speech, I became the chosen receptacle for confession. That I was a mouse helpless before the cat's claws mattered not a jot. We were alone in a wooden cell on an endless sea.

He cleared his throat before continuing, this time in a whisper more frightening than normal speech.

"God has two faces, darkness and light, wrath and love. We

are created in His image. Age and youth, sickness and health, experience and innocence, betrayal and faith."

The man was undoubtedly mad. Yet his words were cast in shadows which played around the edge of truth. He embarked once more on his narrative, a player on a stage where none dared interrupt.

"I was in the Holy Land," he said softly, tears welling into his eyes. "Nothing was holy except the ground itself. Have you heard of the Horns of Hattin?"

I admitted I had not.

"I was there. I followed Raymond of Tripoli against Saladin, hard by the Sea of Galilee, from the Jordan River to Tiberias."

The man spoke in riddles. The rumours that had floated to my ears took scant cognisance of deeds of valour. In the Bugia customs house we were remote from these events.

"Tell me," I said. "I know little about such things."

"Too much to speak," he muttered, "far too much. Thousands died there, slaughtered by the sword, the rich earth steeped in blood, other men dying from thirst."

He put his head in his hands, making a dreadful groaning noise, then wiping his wet nose on his sleeve.

"Forgive me, Leonardo. I am like a woman...I have told nobody what happened. But I shall tell you, Leonardo, before my chest bursts with grief. You are my friend..."

He spilled out an awful tale of misery, death and battle. Men transfixed by arrows or gutted by sword thrusts, bodies on spears, the hordes of Saladin, so many that the sun on their armour dazzled the foe.

Guy de Poiters had been one of the personal guards of Raymond of Tripoli, trapped by the enemy in the inferno of Galilee, the main body of the army far behind.

Raymond's warriors were too eager to charge headlong into the conflict. Those in the rear could not follow and camped for the night, exhausted by heat and thirst. Raymond of Tripoli and his soldiers were isolated leagues ahead.

And so their general learned of defeat, howling in anguish at betrayal and the end of everything.

"The Horns of Hattin!" said Guy de Poitiers with a heart-rending sigh. "I dream of that every night."

The charge against the enemy was mounted. The massed formations of Taliq-al-Din parted like the waves of the sea to let them through. But the thrust met no resistance. Behind their advance a wall of the finest of Saladin's troops formed impenetrable columns, blocking them from their allies.

"We retreated till we came to the coast," blubbered Guy de Poitiers, "leaving them to die. They perished or were captured, the head of every Templar and Hospitaler severed one by one. Can you imagine it? Hundreds sent into slavery, one man bartered for a pair of shoes, others sold like beasts in the markets of Damascus!"

Here he broke into uncontrollable moans, a terrible sound like the wailing of wolves.

"Our shame remains…We escaped…Raymond died before the year was out…I got on a ship and went home to France…My poor wife…buried so young…dying in my arms…So much loss!"

Such was his grief that I too was moved beyond words.

We rose to embrace like brothers, his sobbing awful to witness.

I understood only part of his tale. But the intensity of its telling was beyond all words.

I still feared Guy de Poitiers though not quite as much as before. There is a pit into which any of us may fall. Terrible deeds are enacted perpetually and for no reason or profit. Once committed there can be no redemption in this life, only the torment of memory.

His sad song over, I helped the weeping warrior onto his bed, where he cried himself to sleep like a hurt boy.

V

Guy de Poitiers slept peacefully that night. In the morning, to humour him, I related stories of my escape from Bugia disguised as a native, journeying over the desert to Cairo to study the numbers. Guy took to these tales with many questions, becoming alarmingly thoughtful as he chewed over each episode.

The vessel docked in a small harbour to stock up on victuals. The two of us went ashore, savouring firm earth under our feet. We enjoyed a meal despite the inquisitiveness of the inhabitants who stared most strangely at my companion. While I drank cup after cup of sweet tea, Guy de Poitiers left to visit a neighbouring shop.

Various customers of the eating house crowded round, at first keeping their distance but then familiarly touching my hair, laying hands on my garments as if testing the quality of the cloth. They showed surprise at my facility in their tongue, and were particularly sociable when I ordered food and drink for them.

Before long, we were a swelling congregation with beggars and ragged children venturing nearer to feast their eyes on this infidel.

Our discourse was friendly. I explained, as best I could, where I was born, that I was a scholar, not married and with no offspring that I knew of (this made them laugh).

They enquired whether my companion was also a scholar. In answering, I was reticent. A man of arms invariably excites curiosity. If he wished to explain, he could do so himself.

One ragamuffin did progress as far as wondering whether my friend was *jundi,* a soldier, perhaps because Guy had crossed the gangplank wearing his military short sword in its black leather scabbard, a procedure so natural I had hardly noticed it.

I countered by explaining that my comrade was actually a seafarer, which aroused loud dissent. Their curiosity soon grew tedious, though it seemed difficult to change the subject.

Fortunately Guy de Poitiers returned to relieve the siege, carrying a small bundle under his arm. Finding me in the centre of a throng, he gave the crowd just one glance. My admirers abruptly took their leave, their treats of food and drink going with them.

"How did you do that?" I asked.

He shrugged.

"Practice?" he suggested. "Or perhaps they can smell the blood on me!"

I wondered if his madness might be coming again into its season. But he sat down, quiet as a ghost, and ordered more tea.

VI

Beggars on the quay made no attempt to importune Guy de Poitiers as he swaggered along. Whereas I was usually a target for every mendicant, in his company I became immune from pestering. Back on board, we shook the dust of that flyblown hamlet from shoes, clothes and hair, our cabin presenting an illusion of home.

What joy it was to slip from our moorings and set out to sea, the scattering of decrepit huts and hovels growing ever more picturesque the further we progressed from land. I began to see virtues in the mariner's life, the cutting of ties, the tantalising horizons, the endless sky, the singing of the wind in the rigging, the movement towards we know not what.

Guy de Poitiers, as usual, had things on his mind. After uncharacteristic hesitation, he revealed the contents of that mysterious bundle purchased ashore. This proved to be two sets of native garments, including an embroidered belt and a most elegant white turban.

"Is this not excellent cloth?" he urged, holding out the material for me to touch. I obliged with forefinger and thumb, agreeing it was of fine quality. This added to his pleasure. But I could in no way fathom his purpose.

It transpired, after some evasiveness, that this was a gift for me. The tale of my disguise in Egypt seemed to have inflamed his imagination. However, I willingly accepted this token of his esteem. When he later took a stroll round the deck, I donned the garments to humour him.

On his return, the manifestation of this exotic being pleased him greatly. He adjusted the turban on my head to his soldierly satisfaction, ensured the belt was aligned, and spun me round and round with his rough grip to assess the disguise.

When, as a further joke, I spoke to him in a gruff nomadic dialect, he seemed delighted.

"You will have to grow a beard, darken your hair, and sit for hours in the sun," he said, his mind like a horse out of control.

"Grow a beard?" I queried, for I preferred to be clean-shaven.

"Yes, to complete the picture," he growled. "The picture must be complete."

I let this go as springing from his sickness. But he went on.

"Where do you intend to disembark?"

It was a question I could have asked myself, lacking any desire to return to Cairo. The Holy Land would have been tempting except that Guy de Poitiers described it as a perpetual battlefield.

"I am not sure," I answered.

"Good. Then I have something here for you."

Guy de Poitiers rummaged among his belongings for several moments. He came up with a leather bag, similar to that which Umberto had given me. With a conspiratorial glance, Guy emptied coinage into his palm, a flow of gold and silver trickled in a tinkling shower, a mere fraction of the total contents. I had not known he was so well provided for.

"This is yours!" he announced.

Having poured the coins back and tightened the fastening, he playfully flung the bag at me as if it was a child's toy. Accustomed as I was to handling money, I knew that here was abundance indeed.

To receive a gift of clothes was one thing but his generosity was becoming embarrassing. The soldier took the opportunity of my surprise to continue his train of thought.

"I have a proposition!" he exclaimed. "You must not refuse me."

"What would you like me to do?" I asked, grasping the nettle.

"You should go to Syria. Some of the finest scholars are in Damascus."

Guy's knowledge of scholars was surely unreliable, his intent becoming more obscure with every word.

"Yes, Leonardo, I will pay for you to study in Damascus with the best scholars."

My perplexity increased.

"Listen," he insisted, "You *could* do it!."

"Do what?" I said, trying to keep my voice calm.

"Study in Syria, as I told you."

I placed the bag on the bed, tired of its weight.

"What will *you* do?" I enquired. "Where will *you* go?"

"To the Holy Land of course. I'll find something there, a battle or two to restore my honour. But if you could do this for me, I shall go to my grave more or less content."

"I regret, Guy, I do not understand."

The knight looked exasperated.

"I'll explain again," he replied, speaking slowly but firmly. "I want to pay for you to study with great teachers."

Stupefaction silenced me. Tears came to his eyes, rolling down tired cheeks towards his mouth.

"In Syria, with this coinage, you could do something for me." Guy de Poitiers was close to breaking down. His hands trembled as he reached the climax of what he intended.

"In that country are men captured in the desert. Some were taken to Damascus. Leonardo, do some good with your life. Learn from the best scholars. But also buy back a slave or two, they are soldiers, they will know what to do."

"I'll have to consider this carefully!" I said, not keen to reject him outright in view of what kind of man he was.

"Think of it," said Guy de Poitiers, "as a burden laid upon you. I am giving you a chance to be charitable and rich."

"How will I be rich," I asked, "when money must be spent in the freeing of those in captivity?"

"That is the beauty of it. They took so many slaves that the market value plummeted like a stone. As I told you, one man was bought for a pair of sandals of the crudest leather. I heard this on good authority. With this money you could buy half a dozen poor wretches, perhaps more. But three or four will do. Or less. Even one would be something."

I lifted the bag again, and tipped the coins onto the bed in a river of abundance.

"Perhaps I'll consider it," I exclaimed, "not for the money, but for you!"

Guy de Poitiers embraced me like a father and shed more tears, staining the new white cloth of my disguise.

"Thank you!" he whispered. "I never thought I'd persuade you. You are a nobler person than I took you for."

⟨⟨VII⟩⟩

Days came and went, harbours hove into sight, were briefly visited, and left to their fate. As the time of parting drew nearer, Guy de Poitiers became withdrawn, hardly uttering a word, preferring to pray or sleep.

The voyage was nearly over. Sadness enveloped us as we thought of our separate paths. Even Captain Mitsos and his crew appeared downcast, almost sullen.

A storm blew up, making our cabin uncomfortable and the decks overflow with waves. Tempest tossed, we wondered if the end was nigh. But the vessel was strong, Mitsos at the helm, and the Almighty saw fit to let us pass unscathed through the briny valleys of death.

For some hours during the gale we lost sight of land as the ship was driven out to sea to give her room to romp and roam. Once the terror let us out of its clutches, we steered southeast to pick up the coast again, the distant outline as comforting as a mother's smile.

Preparing to disembark at Caesarea, Guy de Poitiers put on his soldier's gear, light chain mail over the tunic, leather breeches, the belt with scabbards for large and small swords, as well as his personal dagger. His pack was fetched from storage, a heavy bundle as much as a strong man could lift.

Guy's departure was solemn, as befits a knight soon to attend his own funeral. Such was the sorrow of his going that I could not restrain a few mournful tears.

"Have no fear, Leonardo," he whispered. "Do just what I asked and I shall be fortunate in whatever I find."

"Stay with me!" I said. "Come to Damascus."

"The die is cast." he answered. "Besides, I'd not be welcome there."

The crew, including the captain, formed a kind of guard of honour to watch him leave. He traversed their lines like a true dignitary and they applauded.

I was privileged to accompany him across the gangplank and into the harbour. We were already divided as travelling companions are when they part. His mind was in another place and so was mine.

Our final valedictions completed, we shook hands and he hugged me briefly as if in blessing. Then hoisting his baggage across his shoulders, he staggered away humped like a camel, his knees buckling under the strain.

Now that Guy de Poitiers had gone, I missed him and his mad presence with a strange nostalgia. His soldier's aura hung round like a spirit.

I lingered on the image of dear Guy bent for hours in prayer, the sword before his face, the warrior pressing his lips against its ornate handle with saintly devotion.

As the vessel struggled out to sea again, I stood in the bows, watching the coast to the east. The captain beckoned and handed over a letter, not to be opened till the port was well cleared.

I thanked Mitsos and hurried to my cabin.

Letter and Last Testament
of Guy de Poitiers

To the esteemed Scholar, Leonardo Pisano,
from Guy de Poitiers, an epistle taken down by his
amanuensis, Captain Mitsos.

Dear Leonardo,

You will be surprised by this letter. But I requested Captain
Mitsos to write down these thoughts for me. The captain spent some
considerable time on my behalf to produce this document appropriate
to my need.

We have but brief acquaintance. Yet in a short time I have seen
in you much that is admirable, some things that are despicable, and
other seeds waiting to burst forth. It is rare I tarry long with scholars or
philosophers. At first I requested the captain private space for myself.
But he gave assurances our partnership would prove amicable.

I admire your spirit of enquiry. You are not suited to a soldier's
life though the art of politics would not be incompatible with your
talents. Being a soldier it falls to me to estimate the character of men
and to make decisions. In this we share similarities of purpose.

However, between us are many differences. The sins I have
committed are nameless and legion. Visions torment me each
time I lay my head down to sleep. May you ever be preserved from
such dreams.

At the Day of Judgement, I shall not be able to justify my deeds
however many prayers I stitch together before my dying breath.

On behalf of others, I have committed crimes they would not do themselves. My soul is in peril and may not be redeemed.

I have done my soldier's duty to God and the Church. This has damned me for ever. When the fiends come for my soul, I shall suffer in hellfire for a thousand million centuries and more on account of the wrongs I inflicted on others. This is my cross to bear, to be a believer denied the prospect of heaven because of all I have seen and done. When I was young, my deeds hardly troubled me. Later, after the siege of a city, the remains of women and children in every street, the old cut down like wheat, things were not the same. Madness came like a blanket, my nights disturbed.

Moreover, I was most unkind to a precious wife on my return from the wars, could not speak with a civil tongue, and troubled her with my own burden of guilt. She tolerated my follies but, taking ill, died in my arms. I cherished her memory thereafter more than I ever did her presence during her wretched life. Thus to the mountain of my iniquity, another molehill was added.

I shall soon, God willing, face death in the thickest part of battle, and fall as soldiers fall, frightened and lost. But in that pit that armies dig for their fallen after battle, there may be peace such as we know not of on earth. I tell you this because I fear for your salvation. The art of the numbers is close to witchcraft, heresy, necromancy, the denial of God's sufficiency. I have this on the authority of many a saintly priest. Be careful in your path, redeem yourself by good works.

This, my last testament, bequeaths to you the money I gave you. Search Damascus for slaves who should be freed. It will need all the resources of your devious cunning. As I have used my skills in war to achieve higher purposes, though to my eternal cost, so you must endeavour to bring these men back into the light. If you do this, God will surely reward you with good things.

My wits fail and I find it hard to remember what I should. My mind is a torn curtain through which I see the world in strange colours.

That you suffered my infirmity with kindness, leaves me in your debt. I thank you for your forbearance, irksome as this must have been for a young man. We achieve patience through experience. That is a lesson you have begun to learn.

I hope to be remembered by your deeds on my behalf and in your heart. You are my memorial on earth. However long you live, you will not forget me.

I shall rejoice in the tales you told me till like a tree I am cut down and burned in the fire.

Do not think too severely concerning my frailties. We all reap that which we sow. I go to gather my harvest in an unknown place.

When we meet again it will be in a kingdom beyond our understanding, if such a realm exists for us poor sinners.

Farewell, Leonardo, think of me sometimes.

Guy de Poitiers, soldier in the service of God

Ninth Letter

Concerning Damascus, my studies with Al-Nahar,
and the liberation of Guillaume de Lyons.

Però priego, Dolcietto,
che sai la pena mia,
che men facie un sonetto
e mandilo in Soria,
ch'io non posso abentare
la notte nè la dia,
in terra d'oltra mare
istà la vita mia

RINALDO D'AQUINO (*fl.* 1240–50)

(Thus I beseech you, Poppet,
who knows my sad nostalgia,
to write me a sonnet
and send it to Syria,
for I can have no peace
whether by night or day,
when in lands beyond the seas
my true love is away.)

I

Sire, My Most Esteemed Master Michael Theodorus,
Philosopher in the Service of His Majesty, Frederick II.

Ibade farewell to Mitsos at Sidon, its harbour crammed with vessels. Attired in my new garments, with thickening beard and swarthy complexion, I disembarked.

It was an uneasy town, scarred by recent pillaging especially on its ramparts, fought over every now and then by the comrades of Guy de Poitiers and their enemies, none of whom could leave the place alone for long. However, I happily trod its picturesque streets during this lull between hostilities, savouring the breezes, cuisine and monuments.

After a day or two I came upon the ruined Temple of Echmoun in a citrus grove near the river. As I pottered among stones and flowers, an old man came to my side, holding out his hand. "Here," he informed me in a quavery voice, "is the Pool of Astarte, where Echmoun, a mortal loved by the goddess Astarte, mutilated himself and perished. His lover resurrected him as the god of healing, symbolised by a snake coiled round a staff."

Perhaps I was none other than a true child of Echmoun, pursued by goddesses, self-wounding, re-born. This line of meditation was, however, interrupted by the story-teller pulling at my garment, eager for payment. Caught in the labyrinth of his fable, I put a small coin into his gnarled hand and thanked him for his wisdom.

At the end of an idle week, I prepared to travel to Damascus. For this I purchased four fine horses, along with food and equipment for the journey. A guide and two bodyguards were recruited.

We set off early one morning, though not soon enough to avoid a gang of shouting children and yapping dogs at our heels.

The guide, a small slip of a man, claimed to know every settlement between Sidon and Damascus. The bodyguards were not soldiers but wore swords and showed alertness. Thus we followed the winding thread of valleys and mountain passes, sleeping each night on the hard ground wrapped in rough blankets.

My companions spoke a dialect impossible to decipher beyond a few words. Though they did not understand everything I said, they quickly grasped the false premise that if harm came to me, punishment would be meted out by the rulers of Damascus.

For this purpose I showed them the epistle of Guy de Poitiers, which impressed them as an official document. Any kind of calligraphy fascinated them. So I gave each a fragment of paper on which their names were inscribed, causing much excited discussion round the camp fire.

We saw many villages, some little more than a grouping of primitive huts, others with cultivated fields and good irrigation. At Bayy Sur a high fort guarded dwellings below. At Jezzine we saw vineyards, orchards heavy with fruit, waterfalls gushing from the high cliffs.

Following the river, we advanced to Niha, Khout, Kamed el Laouz and Aita el Foukhar, beyond which sinister forests aroused concerns of ambush and robbery.

At such moments my guards looked shiftily from side to side and at each other. But these woods were devoid of evil. We continued safely, in danger of nothing except our own wild imaginings.

Eventually we caught our first sight of the Nahr Barada, flowing to Damascus. The men laughed and sang. I shared their levity.

From that moment our steeds had winged hooves and we lengthened our stride. Under the river's nurture, we saw a thousand gardens ripe with flowers and fruit, the scent of jasmine and citrus intoxicating us with freshness.

Such was the fertility of this region as we traversed the domain of the Ghouta Oasis, that one could wish it never ended.

But before long the oncoming city shadowed our thoughts. When eventually the black spider of Damascus loomed so dominantly we were sucked into its spreading web like helpless flies, the men uttered agitated whispers.

As we approached the gates on the last morning of our journey, a mist hung over the rooftops, birds of prey wheeled above domes and minarets.

It was time to bid farewell to my companions and allow them the horses and saddles for their return to Sidon. On parting we embraced like brothers, never to meet again.

I entered Damascus on foot through Bab al Jabiye, the west gate. With my bundle of coinage, books, and belongings, I jostled through the crowds of Souk Medhat Pasha until, almost fainting in the dusty bustle, I reached Straight Street.

II

With much hot breath on me among the thicket of passers-by, I was glad to sit at a table and order a meal. Good fresh flat bread, stuffed with spinach, complemented by yoghurt and tea, was brought by a proprietor, whose willingness to please extended to a knowledge of suitable lodgings.

I intended to keep clear of Christians and Jews and found a place with an old Damascene couple, eager for a pittance to gain a small income.

I took up residence in two rooms of their house, confining my hosts to their meagre living room and kitchen. Abdul-Hafiz and his wife fussed round, bringing lemon water and sweet cakes, offering respectful salutations and advice about the ways of the city.

They were unsure what kind of scholar I might be, whether religious, astronomer or physician. My assumed name was Halim ibn-Bonaj (Patient Son of Bonacci), which they considered unusual.

For days I explored the streets and alleys, discovering a number of *madrasas* each crammed with erudites or *shaykhs* with whom one might enrol as a disciple.

Some teachers aspired to instruct combinations of law, theology, philosophy, natural sciences, and literature, such a scholar being known as *kamil,* 'a complete man'. I hoped to find a mentor dedicated only to the numbers.

Growing in confidence, I made enquiries at the eating houses where scholars congregated. Here I realised the garments Guy de Poitiers had purchased, though elegant, marked me as an outsider.

Learned men of Damascus wore large turbans and wide sleeves, calling themselves *muta'ammamin* ('wearers of the turban'), the most eminent adorned with the *taylasan* (a covering over the turban running down the back). For these reasons I purchased a quite capacious turban, though certainly not the biggest available, and sported the wide sleeves like a hovering white bird. This appeared to command respect, especially from younger alumni.

With the size of my head seemingly increased, the crowd, gathering round my table at the eating house near one of the city's most esteemed *madrasas*, swelled almost to the point of embarrassment. Since these students were eager for debate, what could be construed as lessons, but were actually discussions, started to flourish.

The owner of the establishment, seeing how my adherents were buying quantities of food and drink, insisted on providing chalk and a writing board, reserving space in a shaded area for the sessions at regular times.

During what turned out to be the final occasion, with a score of my supporters gathered, I observed three huge turbans arrive, positioning themselves at the back. On standing up to investigate the newcomers, I discovered a trio of ancient greybeards scrutinising my diagrams with expressions of a most unpleasant kind. When those immediately in front of the large turbans noticed their presence, they whispered in the ears of those before them, the process spreading like disease.

Without a word of apology, starting from the rear of the assembly, the students rose one by one and left. In less than two minutes, only the three wise men remained. As these gentlemen wore the dress of the most esteemed masters, my big turban and wide sleeves now put me to shame.

Insecure in protocol, concealed behind my beard and tanned complexion, I had no choice but to stay the course.

"Do you have a licence to teach?" asked the scholar in the middle. I paused and bowed.

"I beg forgiveness. This was debate, not instruction."

"That is not what we heard," said the right hand member of the group. "You give lessons. We were told."

"We have discussions," I replied. "I would not dare to instruct, only to…"

Here my voice trailed off for I knew no appropriate word in their language or my own.

"Come with us!" commanded the third sage.

Like a prisoner with an escort for each arm and a guard behind, I was frogmarched to the school, my turban in danger of flopping to one side unless I kept my head still.

Inside one of the inner chambers of the establishment the interrogation continued. Further *ahl al-imama* (people of the turban) were summoned. My spirits flagged when soldiers with scimitars were stationed round the room, glaring as if I was about to attempt escape. They were nothing if not thorough. Moreover, the tribunal seemed mystified by my name, Halim ibn-Bonaj, and repeated it in chorus, exclaiming they had never heard anything so extraordinary.

When the privilege of speaking to them was finally granted, though it took some time coming, I explained my intention to study with a master, the reputation of Damascus in the field of the numbers being as great as that of Baghdad or Cairo.

My inquisitors forthwith demanded whether I was interested

in other studies, theology, medicine, or law. To this I replied that the numbers were my sole preoccupation.

Attempting to win their favour, I gave my parentage as that of a European father and Egyptian mother, stressing how I was not brought up to speak her language as she died soon after my birth.

When this inquisition came to an end, the jury retired to consider their verdict, leaving the soldiers to watch me. I was permitted to sit on the marble floor to wait an hour or so before they reached their decision.

The man who had first addressed me at the eating house returned to urge the prisoner to his feet. I scrambled up as best I could, conscious of the wobblings of the turban and that my robe might be soiled with squatting in the dust.

However, this time he smiled and held out his hand.

"I am Abu al-Nahar," he announced, "I teach mathematics and astronomy."

Bowing, I wondered whether the entire pack would reappear. But they had left as abruptly as they came. Even the soldiers turned smartly to the right and marched out.

"Master," I muttered in homage, my eyes down.

"You will study with me, *insh'allah!*" he said.

"I am honoured," I replied.

"And so am I!" he exclaimed.

In this way my greatest master and I found each other.

❧ III ❧

Al-Nahar, unlike my previous teachers, was enamoured of small talk, discourse, and digressions from whatever subject was the focus of the day. As the lessons were lengthy, this was of little consequence, indeed, quite the opposite. His ramblings were as illuminating as specific instruction.

In our first session he spoke of Muhammad ibn Musa al-Khwarizmi in such intimate terms one would never have imagined the man had died some centuries past. From Al-Khwarizmi it was a short step to the esteemed Caliph al-Mamun and problems measuring distance between meridians.

Other topics included *Kitab al-jahr wa al-muqabalah (Calculation by Restoration and Reduction)*, the glories of algebra, the astronomer Abul Hassan al-Uqlidisi, and the work of Abu Rayhan al-Biruni, mathematician and poet. Each was spoken of as a friend and colleague despite having passed from this earth generations before.

It was during the second and third lessons, when Al-Nahar mentioned the same names and subjects, but in a different order, that the mists cleared and I glimpsed a shape or two of the landscape beyond. As several lessons were provided each week, my being was often in turmoil, the pace exceeding my abilities to digest the feast of numbers laid out day after day.

Fortunately Al-Nahar frequently seemed to forget what had been taught earlier, regressing to elements already dealt with. Thanks to this, I was able to revisit the more baffling investigations and gain clearer insight.

Al-Nahar's system of teaching soon drew me into square and

cubic roots, the multiplication and subtraction of such, and the treatment of binomials, apotomes, and their roots. From here he transported me to geometric rules concerning proportions of three and four quantities, as well as the realms of *algebra* and *almuchabala*.

At night in my lodgings, I extracted my *Liber Abaci* manuscript and added to the store of information. Every nugget from Al-Nahar was written down. Such was the progress that it became necessary to buy more paper as the book grew like a healthy child.

Al-Nahar was paid handsomely though his tuition was of a value beyond price. His beard twitched with pleasure when it was time to pay his fee, especially if I offered a little more.

Transactions were conducted delicately. It was not seemly that scholars should relish too much the benefits of financial gain. But as he lovingly transferred the coinage to his purse, I recognised the symptoms of avarice, an aspect of his character well worth knowing about.

IV

Despite these weeks of study I did not forget the responsibility Guy de Poitiers had laid on me of liberating a slave or two. The difficulty was discretion. Asking about European prisoners of previous wars would arouse suspicion. My hosts, who knew hardly anything of who I was or where I came from, seemed to have accepted me as a scholar, no more, no less.

I prayed regularly in the mosque with my fellow students, though I struck up no friendships. After the incident in the eating house, I had acquired a somewhat awkward reputation. Many disciples became reticent as if I were someone with whom it would not be prudent to fraternise.

I spent much time exploring the streets and sampling the cuisine of Damascus in eating houses of many kinds, some disgracefully unkempt, others intended for richer clients.

The best meals were cooked by my landlord's wife. I feasted daily on *mujadarra* (a dish consisting of lentils), fried slices of *kibbeb* (dough stuffed with beef), chicken breast with artichokes or garlic and coriander, *s'fiha* (flat bread with meat, pine nuts, yoghurt and pomegranate juice), *ful* (broad beans boiled and garnished with a piquant sauce), or green beans with aubergines, *tis'yye,* (chickpea soup), a myriad of spices, and a supply of sweet cakes, fruit, and much tea.

Needless to say, I was getting fatter but portliness increased my *gravitas,* adding to the impression I wished to create. Henceforth I walked slower, with augmented dignity.

During my strolls into every part of Damascus I glimpsed a number of slaves, some from Africa, others of lighter complexion, a few boys in bondage to overweening masters, and the rest, of nondescript appearance, put to labour repairing buildings and roads.

According to Guy de Poitiers, so many had been captured at the battle of Hattin that the value of slaves diminished. But there appeared to be none of European origin out in the open.

Till one day, halfway through a meal near Bab as Salaam, the north gate, I chanced to see a man passing in company with a young girl.

His face was cruelly mutilated across the brow with a brand, similar to that on the rumps of cattle at market. Yet his bearing, the straight back, agile movements, suggested the deportment and physique of a former soldier.

Casting a coin or two at the proprietor, I reluctantly abandoned my food and set off in pursuit.

The girl skipped and laughed loudly while they dawdled in front of shops and stalls. When they turned off the main street, I continued after them, trailing by a hundred paces or more. The man, aware of my presence, frequently glanced back.

After a while, he stopped to confront me, pushing the child behind him to shield her from harm.

Without his blemish he might have been handsome, but the disfigurement gave him the ghastly look of a leper, set apart from others.

I approached cautiously. He stared like a Cyclops.

Quickly I spoke up.

"Excuse me, sir, are you from Europe?"

To my amazement, he replied in French.

"*Je suis français!*"

"*Je suis Chrétien!*" I answered, "*Je viens de la République de Pisa.*"

The girl peered round his waist, bemused by the strange language.

"Wait here…I'll meet you," he whispered urgently.

Taking the child by the hand, the man led her to the end of the street where they disappeared round the corner. The main thoroughfare, visible from here, was crowded with people but this alley was a tributary, consisting of disused hovels.

Growing uneasy, I waited. Just as I was deciding it was time to depart, the man returned, idling along as if without a care in the world.

"Follow me!" he said, and went back the way he had come. I set off after him, almost having to run to keep him in view. After a dozen twists and turns he led me into an abandoned shack awaiting repair. As my eyes readjusted to the poor light, he pulled forward a couple of old chairs.

We sat down to size each other up.

"I haven't heard French for a few years," he said.

"I haven't spoken it for years either!" I replied.

"My name is Guillaume de Lyons. But they don't call me that here."

He began talking and talking. I was surprised how trusting he seemed. Speech flowed from him like a river, his captivity, the branding, the grief.

He was now owned as a slave by a lenient master who entrusted a beloved daughter to his daily care and protection. To make things easier, Guillaume de Lyons had converted to his master's faith, reaping many benefits.

After these revelations came to a close, he indicated that he wished to hear my story.

Mindful of the peril of Damascus towards enemies, with no desire to end up like this man, I presented my own version of a tale, true in part but with much omitted.

I gave my name as Halim ibn-Bonaj and enquired about the chances of buying him from his owner and if he knew others in need of release.

"There are scores of us here," he whispered, "many like broken pack animals."

Pressed on the purchasing of slaves, he could only see difficulties, such was his desire not to make things worse.

I was anxious his present absence might be noticed. He assured me that since his conversion, his master had treated him as a faithful and beloved servant rather than abject bondsman and he was free, within reason, to come and go.

I racked my brains for solutions, looking for some omen to lift his heart. But conversation with a kindred spirit was already illuminating his darkness.

"Who is the girl?" I asked.

"That is Zahirah, my master's youngest child. I love her dearly."

"Who *is* your master?"

"He is a scholar," replied Guillaume with a hint of pride.

"A scholar?" I said, assuming owners of slaves were usually merchants or rich officials.

"Yes, the finest. He is Abu al-Nahar."

The blood drained from my face, my legs weakened, my stomach contracted with fear. I said nothing but even in this dim light Guillaume perceived the disturbance.

"Do you know him?" he asked.

"Yes!" I said. "Yes."

"Then it might be possible!" he exclaimed, hope in his voice.

"No, it is *impossible!*" I said. "But I will try!"

∽෴ V ෴∾

Al-Nahar, when he desisted from his voyages round a verbal ocean, was eager to plumb geometric proportions. To this end we spent many a sticky hour.

Sailing close to the realm of Euclid (whom the master revered almost as much as his beloved Al-Khwarizmi), my teacher repeated constantly that it had been Moorish scholars who first translated Byzantine manuscripts from Greek and rescued the Ancients from antiquity. Our investigations into Euclid began with Book II, where fourteen propositions deal with the transformation of areas and Pythagorean geometrical algebra.

Until this encounter with Al-Nahar, my knowledge of Euclid had remained neglected, the main concerns having been commerce, taxation and currency. Yet as doors swung open, I perceived geometry conjunct through angles and measurements with the visible universe itself. But at this stage my feet were on the ground with eyes not on the stars but on a scribbled page.

One of Al-Nahar's relished topics, *proportions,* made the brain groan if indulged throughout entire lessons. For example, take three numbers, the first and third being known, the second unknown, the proportion of the greatest minus the middle to the middle minus the smallest in proportion as the greatest number to the smallest. Al-Nahar proceeded thus:

i)   *Let the known numbers be 20 and 12*
ii)   *Thus 12 subtracted from 20 = 8*
(the proportion the 20 is to the 12)
iii)   *Therefore add 20 to the 12 = 32*

iv)   Therefore as 32 is to 12 so will be 8 to the difference between middle and smallest
v)   Therefore multiply 8 by 12 = 96, and divide by 32 (see iv), giving 3 for the difference between middle and smallest
vi)   Therefore if 3 is added to 12 the middle number = 15
vii)   Answer = 20, 15, 12

From here Al-Nahar pursued problems where either the greatest or the least figure was unknown, and the other two known, or the smallest unknown, and the proportions of one to another similarly differed – all at first somewhat confusing.

Such was our concentration, matched with the heat in the room, that before solutions were reached, the paper became sodden with sweat. However, after a dozen such puzzles, light began to penetrate.

We moved to measurement, conjecturing that a pole, twenty feet in length, leans against a tower, the foot of the pole being of the distance of twelve feet from the tower. How many feet does the end of the pole fall below the top of the tower?

Going on from proportion to line in sequence, so did Al-Nahar lead me by steps:

i)   Let the tower be ab
ii)   The pole intersects the tower at c
iii)   The line on the ground is bd = 12 feet
iv)   Thus a triangle with a right angle is created
v)   As Euclid proves in a right angled triangle the square of the side opposite the right angle = the sum of the squares of the remaining two sides

vi)   Thus the square of the pole, cd = 400
vii) The sum of the squares bd and bc = cd
viii) Square of bd is known = 144
ix)   400 (square of cd) – 144 (square of bd) = 256,
the square of which = 16
x)   Thus 20 (ab) – 16 = 4

From the acorn of geometry we progressed to small shoots, young trees, and finally to mature oaks.

We grappled with the problems of estimated distances of birds flying from towers, as well as calculations of columns and circular pyramids, each element later transcribed into my book now bulging at the seams with fresh knowledge.

Add to this, proportional problems of merchants gaining ratios of profit from multiple visits to markets, and study of the elements of square roots. One may deduce that Al-Nahar was nothing if not rigorous.

VI

As athletes gain from exercise so the muscles of the mind improve with endeavour. Not only did I labour in lessons but for hours in my lodgings I wrestled with every aspect of all I had been taught that day.

The landlady, fearful for my health, often insisted I should cease work for a while and eat in their company. With this I usually complied, though after meals Al-Nahar's secrets drew me to further study.

Meanwhile severe dilemmas plagued me concerning Guillaume de Lyons. Suspended between anxiety and despair, I put together a few of the difficulties to be solved. With Al-Nahar's estimation of my abilities rising, evidenced by his praise and courteous manner, it was time to prepare an ambush.

Accordingly I arranged an appointment with the Master on a personal matter. With unkempt hair and dishevelled clothing, I appeared before him in a nervous state, trembling like a leaf, waving hands about, twitching with agitation, unable to settle to normal composure.

The climax of this performance was to stutter out that as a foreigner, I no longer felt safe on the streets, having been jostled near my lodgings by individuals of evil intent.

Al-Nahar doubted whether this behaviour was directed towards a 'foreigner' or merely at a man who looked prosperous. Scholars *were* harassed in particular districts, the area of my lodgings being notorious.

In his opinion, I did not appear too obviously like a 'foreigner' as I had an Egyptian mother, prayed in the mosque, and was welcome here as a disciple.

Calming myself down, I suggested that the only possible remedy was to hire a bodyguard. For this purpose, I was prepared to go to 'considerable expense'. Al-Nahar became momentarily speechless.

When he recovered he explained that learned *shaykhs* and men of the turban, ruling families and merchants, indeed possessed slaves, male and female. But his pupils did not usually have similar aspirations.

I responded that one could not be too careful. Having been

attacked, who knows what might happen next! I began to sob, shivering with emotion, tears trickling down my cheeks.

The Master, visibly moved, reassured me he had no intention of allowing me to leave his tutelage for reasons which could so easily be resolved. After a moment or two of further thought, he changed tack entirely, explaining how protection of this kind need not involve 'considerable expense', but just a 'reasonable' amount.

He recommended African slaves as fine for this purpose, being tall and of a forbidding appearance. He knew a dealer who would be interested in discussing the matter.

I asserted such men seemed far too frightening, especially in close daily proximity. I took the opportunity to quote an alleged remark from my landlord that Europeans were cheaper than Africans, and, as former soldiers, made excellent guards. Al-Nahar, pensive again, stroked his beard and advanced to the window to look out.

Turning to me, he advised against hiring Europeans. For one thing these men might be dangerous if their defensive skills were ever directed against owners. I replied hastily that, having a European mother, I would understand men from Europe more easily than any from Africa.

Al-Nahar became perplexed, pointing out that he thought my *father* was European, my mother Egyptian, not vice versa. Tripping over my own tongue, I contrived more lamentation, muttering that my mother had various nationalities among her ancestry. Fortunately, scenting possible profit, Al-Nahar was not paying much attention to my confused words.

After much pacing and pondering, he swooped to ask just

how much I could afford. I replied that my welfare was at stake. Nothing must be spared to restore peace of mind.

Following another spasm of hesitation, clearing his throat a few times, Al-Nahar got down to business, while I dabbed at my face with a handkerchief.

"I think I may know of a property in my own household," he said. "But he is not handsome."

"Thank you, Master. You are my greatest friend. Thank you."

Cautiously at first, we began to haggle. I beat about the bush under cover of ruses often deployed in Bugia, querying his price to entrap him, withdrawing an offer only to make a better offer, and leapfrogging back and forth till in the end a deal was concluded.

Despite all this, it soon became obvious that at every point Al-Nahar was ahead of me. Each thrust was politely parried, every initiative turned to his advantage. Our final transaction amounted to an agreement in which I paid far more than intended. My sole consolation was that we had achieved a solution and Guillaume, at least, was rescued from bondage.

Al-Nahar fixed an appointment that afternoon when the merchandise would be handed over. We were to meet outside the institution to avoid conducting such business within its hallowed precincts.

VII

At the given time I perched myself on a chair at a nearby eating house to await proceedings. Al-Nahar, never the most punctual of men, delayed his appearance by a tiresome margin, causing me to drink a superfluity of sweet tea affecting my bladder and my nervousness.

When Al-Nahar at last came into view, Guillaume de Lyons was with him and so was Zahirah. She was holding hands with Guillaume, looking up with the adoration a child has for a nurse or defender. I remembered that during our first encounter in the alley, I was bareheaded. So at the sight of the trio coming down the crowded street, I donned my turban and walked towards them.

Al-Nahar introduced me to Guillaume with ceremony and no condescension. Zahirah, at the prospect of losing her friend, began to weep. I ignored her, standing at my full height and paying her no attention. Neither did I speak much to Guillaume beyond politeness. Zahirah, once her crying fit was over, scrutinised the new owner, wrinkling her eyes and blinking as she stared at me. As soon as convenient, I handed over the agreed coinage to her father.

After a respectful farewell I moved away, Guillaume trotting after me like a faithful pony. I could not forbear a glance back to Al-Nahar and his daughter. His left ear was inclined towards her. She was pulling at his sleeve and pointing in my direction. But I walked on like a lord with my new trophy.

On the way back I called at a house available for rent, which had attracted my attention over recent days. The proprietor, keen for business, was content with a modest fee each month. I now had rooms, downstairs and up, where my companion could live without prying eyes. I left Guillaume there and hurried to my former lodgings.

Having fabricated a tale about an offer from a friendly *shaykh* at the *madrasa,* I gathered my belongings, and handed over more money, leaving the erstwhile hosts richer by one month's rent. The landlady, who had begun to grow fond of me, looked dreadfully downcast. Her husband, on the other hand, was jubilant, especially with the generous bonus in hand.

At our new dwelling I informed Guillaume that my real name was Leonardo Pisano and told him the tangled tale of Guy de Poitiers, by whose beneficence I now studied in Damascus.

Later, when some of our initial happiness had dispersed, I mentioned my fear that Zahirah might recognise me and inform her father. Guillaume refused to let any anxiety trouble him as he felt free and happy for the first time in years, never having anticipated any prospect of liberation.

"She is very short-sighted. I doubt she could even see your face!" he said. "I shall miss her!"

"You could visit her if you wanted!" I suggested.

"That would not be in our best interests," he replied. "We must be very careful."

VIII

Guillaume de Lyons was eager to leave Syria very soon. This was surely not the best strategy. My studies demanded fulfilment, premature flight would be dangerous. Guillaume was also concerned about his status as technically, under the laws of Damascus, if I died he could be returned to his original owner.

However the act of granting his freedom was a legal matter. I could not consult a notary without some whiff being carried to Al-Nahar's nostrils. This kind of enquiry was bound to attract gossip like flies to a dunghill. The yielding of freedom to former soldiers of the Christian God was a sensitive issue to those who had suffered under alien invaders.

Naturally, Guillaume was no more my slave than he could be my father. However, his purchase had not solved difficulties but increased them. He understood this while never ceasing to thank me for my intercession.

I tried in return not to become too obsessed with the horror of becoming a slave myself, discovered, branded, hounded, and dragged through the dust. Guillaume, well acquainted with the ways of Damascus, agreed that this could easily come to pass if the full truth was revealed.

I felt something of a coward, especially in the night, when voices whispered from the stillness. I began to fear the knock on the porch, torture, sojourns in dungeons, hostile courts, walls and deprivation, in essence a terror of every violation previously inflicted on dear Guillaume. Neighbours, teachers, landlords, the friendly proprietor at the eating house, not a single one was to be trusted.

No man can estimate his proportion of bravery until he at last confronts the heated tongs, the rack, the masked torturers. When I awoke from awful dreams, each image persisted from half sleep into full alertness. Guillaume came to my bedside on several nights, shaking me, for I was shouting like a madman in my sleep. His remedy for such agitation was to recite poems, soothing in their lilting French:

> *Paien s'adobent des osbercs sarazineis,*
> *Tuit li plusor en sont doblés en treis;*

Lacent lor helmes molt bons sarragozeis,
Ceignent espees de l'acier vianeis...

It was not the sense *(Paynims arming themselves with Saracen hauberks, with triple thickness of chain mail, putting on their marvellous Zaragozan helmets, girding swords of Viana steel)* which restored serenity, but Guillaume's magical gift of incantation. His memory was a bottomless well into which he lowered his bucket and retrieved it full of silver.

Was he inventing these embroidered verses? How could a man remember so much for so long in an alien land?

In daylight I recovered sanity. He smiled at me, his deformed face ugly but kind. My fears subsided as at sea when a storm has died down but waves still shake the vessel.

In the manner of Guy de Poitiers, Guillaume told me about war. He recalled battlefields, hundreds of horses, the sun scintillating on armoured men, spears and swords raised like fire to the leader. In the distance, an enemy, similarly splendid. Then the engagement was on. Men stabbed, thrust, parried and lunged. If you lived and won, dead companions were buried and a few fine words spoken on their behalf.

Defeat brought horror – cruelty beyond imaginings, the unrestrained evil of men revenging fallen comrades. Guillaume's capture, though terrible, might have been worse. Bound, whipped, hungry, he was held by four men, the red-hot iron rammed to his forehead till the brand was impressed. Others had been less fortunate, losing ears and nose, testicles or limbs, in the aftermath.

"Oh," sighed Guillaume, "to look at a baby and imagine what his hands might one day commit! It shames God Himself."

Having recited his adventures, he turned to another tack to whistle up our spirits.

"Have no fear, Leonardo!" he urged. "We are braver than we think. Let us do our best. We will leave Damascus when it is appropriate to do so."

In the morning light the wound on his face gleamed like a monstrous slice of meat. The scar extended the length of his forehead and, his brows being cauterised, the skull above his eyes was damaged by the force of the branding.

To fulfil his role as bodyguard, I purchased for him a short sword with holster and belt, and a dagger with jewelled sheath. He was as pleased as a child with these toys for Al-Nahar had not allowed him to handle weapons.

When Guillaume girded his sword around his waist, his back stiffened, his chin proudly jutted, and his head was held higher. He drew the steel from its scabbard and swished it through the air.

IX

Al-Nahar, having taught me some geometry, pressed on to *algebra* and *almuchabala*. In these studies, three properties contained in any numbers were considered, namely roots, squares and simple numbers.

When a number is multiplied by itself the result is a square, the number being multiplied is a root. Three multiplied by itself equals nine, and three is the root of nine and nine the square of three. But a number not considered in respect of a root or square is deemed to be a simple number.

In the solving of problems are six modes, three simple and three composite:

Simple modes:
First mode: when the square which is called the census is equal to a number of roots
Second mode: when the census is equal to a number
Third mode: when the root is equal to a number

Composite modes:
First mode: when the census plus roots are equal to a number
Second mode: when roots plus a number are equal to the census
Third mode: when the census plus a number is equal to roots

These truths were the teachings of Al-Khwarizmi, whom my teacher also called by the name of *Maumeht*. From here we progressed to the introduction of unknowns (which we called the thing, the part or the sum), and the creation and solutions of equations.

This provided what would become the fifteenth chapter of my *Liber Abaci*, two or three hundred pages of writing, including an introduction to *algebra* and *almuchabala*, and a multitude of scribblings. (If you wished, for example, to separate the number ten into two parts so that their product makes one fourth of the greater part multiplied by itself, seven pages explain such procedures step by step.)

One morning Al-Nahar asked me to give a course of instruction to some students. Despite my reluctance to waste time in this way, he gained the upper hand as ever. Consequently I was compelled to teach pupils, such duties enacted without payment as a service to the school.

Half a dozen of these youths requested the pleasure of my company at the eating house. I agreed, treating them to substantial helpings of food and drink. But they seemed unduly intent on discovering details of my birthplace, pastimes and experiences. These inquisitions I parried with humour suspecting Al-Nahar was setting bloodhounds on my trail.

Al-Nahar, when he was not waxing eloquent about Al-Khwarizmi, Moorish history, Caliphs, Baghdad and astronomy, threw out peculiar asides which put me on my guard.

For instance, he suddenly brought up the subject of Guillaume, starting in a neutral tone and tightening the trap as we progressed. From a simple 'How is Guillaj?' (the pet name for his former slave), he moved sideways like a crab to ask what I gave him to eat, whether he was trustworthy, and if I was satisfied.

"I am pleased, Master," I replied, "and feel safe now he is with me."

But a further question also needed an answer.

"Did you ever see Guillaj before you bought him?"

I preserved a mask of innocence, though if he had struck me across the face I could not have been more astonished.

As I pondered a response, silence hung like a noose. In those fateful seconds I decided to take a chance for none could fathom what this fox already knew.

"Yes, Master, I saw him near the Bab as Salaam."

Al-Nahar leaned forward.

"Did you speak?"

"I was lost in the street and asked directions. He had a child with him."

Al-Nahar put his hands together, like a judge about to pronounce sentence.

"Good!" he said. "My daughter has poor sight but excellent ears. She recognised your voice."

With that he slid off into his usual discourse, passing on to the lesson without a backward glance.

For the rest of the day his guile haunted me. When I told Guillaume, he seemed nonchalant.

"Well, at least you spoke the truth!"

We ate our meal in gloomy quiet, the presence of Al-Nahar a nagging ghost. When our bellies were full, we felt better and he slapped me on the back, imitating Al-Nahar's voice so perfectly that we both cheered up.

Guillaume said later he knew the part of the city where some of his comrades lived. I vowed that if they existed, we would find them.

Though I expected a wild-goose chase, it was worth such promises to see the sudden joy on his misshapen face.

X

Next morning we set off in search of the Europeans. Guillaume believed they were in the south-eastern quarter of the city, not far from Bab Kisan.

It was a long walk as we picked our way through a maze of

backstreets. From Bab Sharqui we wandered towards the gate itself, the high city wall sharp and brutal in the heat.

Here Guillaume became lost, thinking it was this street or another one, or one round the corner, or perhaps not that one. At first, we saw many people but no slaves.

After rounding the hundredth corner of our quest, we came on a group of men digging out the foundations of an old house. An overseer with a whip lashed their bent backs which hurried them hardly at all, so exhausted they seemed.

"Look!" exclaimed Guillaume. "I knew they were here!"

Each victim digging the hole was blackened by the filth of his labour. But as they glanced up from their drudgery, it was clear who they were and where they came from.

Even in the pit one or two preserved a quasi-soldierly bearing, swinging their shovels as if against an enemy, in this instance the earth itself.

We stared, unsure of ourselves.

"Go and ask the man," suggested Guillaume.

"Certainly," I replied. "But ask him what?"

"If these workers can be hired, of course!"

I paused to think. If we hired them, for whatever purpose, an overseer would accompany them. I wanted to purchase them for freedom, not shackle them to further punishment.

"Stay here!" I said. "I will try."

I approached the gangmaster, a vile-looking man, with a broken tooth at the front of his mouth, and a demeanour of such arrogance that his slightest glance inspired fear.

Taking me for a person of substance he drooped his body

obsequiously, saluting by a touch on his forehead with the whip, changing instantly from lordly thug to creeping creature.

I smiled and slipped him a couple of coins. He knew the ropes, pocketed the money like a magician, and waited to know my pleasure.

"They are fine men!" I said. "You clearly know how to get the most work out of them."

He dipped his head in assent.

"Who owns these slaves?" I asked.

"Sire, they belong to the great Ibn al-Hajj."

"I would like to meet your master."

"Certainly, your honour," he replied, making a slight movement with his right hand. I responded by more coinage at which his head dipped once more. "My master does not live far away. I will take you."

Swinging to confront his prisoners, he changed to his previous persona, cracking his whip and snarling how he would chastise slackers.

I nodded to Guillaume before leaving. He would find out in my absence whatever we needed to know.

Ibn al-Hajj's residence was further than the overseer had implied. He set off at a pace and we passed markets, alleys, doorways, arches, and many fine houses.

Once at the residence, the creature re-assumed cringing humility. A luxurious mansion met my eyes. Outside, liveried guards looked vigilant as if tending the very gates of hell.

A word from my guide saw them move back in well drilled order, permitting entry. We progressed through a cool courtyard, along carpeted corridors. I waited in a gilded hallway while the messenger went ahead.

Soon I was ushered into a sultan-like splendour, where a thin-faced lord, clad in silk apparel, reclined on a golden sofa. By his side were two boys and a woman of outstanding beauty. Ibn al-Hajj's sovereignly bearing was displayed in his reception, for he rose from the couch, placed his hands together and *salaamed*. The woman gave a curtsey before leaving, taking the children with her.

"Sir, I am Halim ibn-Bonaj!" I said.

He gestured me to the comfort of the pillowed sofa opposite his golden furniture. A servant appeared bearing a tray of drinks, lemon water and tea. I chose tea and this was duly handed to me.

"I am pleased to meet you," he answered, his voice elevated like that of a poet. "I suppose it is business you come about."

"Yes, Sir."

"It is not often I do business with strangers," he proclaimed. "Especially with foreigners."

My feathers slightly ruffled, I savoured the hot sweet tea.

"Sir, I am grateful for your kindness. I am studying in Damascus with great scholars."

"You are a scholar?" he said abruptly. "I understood you were in trade."

"That too. I studied commerce with my father and the numbers also. The two are siblings, one depends on the other."

He mused for a moment.

"I am not learned in numbers or astronomy, but some in my

employment are. They would willingly discuss these things with you. But what is your business?"

"I saw your workers near Bab Kisan. I wish to enquire about the purchase of such men."

"Bab Kisan?" he replied, trying to recall what anybody might be doing there. "Ah yes, Bab Kisan! The dilapidated houses. It's expensive repairing these places."

"I wish to buy one, or perhaps two men, as servants,"

"One or two?" he queried. "These are infidels, are they not?"

"Yes. I was told they are cheaper than others."

"They *were* cheaper," he said, with an ugly little chuckle, "when they were first brought here! But if you are in commerce you know that values can rise as well as fall."

I offered a furtive nod. He continued.

"When they arrived, there were many. Now there are fewer. Some died. Those left are more valuable."

It was a familiar ploy, talking up the worth of goods to a customer, whether cloth, cattle, or, in this case, men.

"That is why I would like to purchase some," I said.

"Some?" he enquired. "I thought you said one or two."

"Well, one or two or more," I replied. "If goods are worthwhile, we should buy more of them."

"What need has a scholar of servants?" he asked slyly.

"Many scholars have them. My teacher at the school has several."

"Would that be my friend, Al-Nahar?" he asked.

"Indeed!" I answered. "Al-Nahar is my teacher. I even purchased a servant from him."

Ibn al-Hajj frowned.

"I think you are mistaken. Al-Nahar would never sell to *you*."

"But I gave him a goodly sum. In return I have a servant. He is a very fine servant."

Ibn al-Hajj moved his lips in a mock smile, shaking his head from side to side, as if pitying my foolishness.

"You are quite mistaken." he said once more, speaking very quietly. "I am the slave master of Damascus. Not pleasant. But I follow my esteemed father in this." He gestured to emphasise the extent of his property and furnishings.

I tried again, sensing some peril here.

"But as I explained, I do have a servant. He guards me day and night. He is with me. I bought him."

"Good," he said, "I am glad you are pleased. But you are still in error. Al-Nahar has *lent* you his man, hired for payment of course, but he is no more *yours* than you are mine."

"But we have an agreement!" I persisted.

"I doubt it!" he replied. "Is it an agreement in writing? Signed and delivered by a notary?"

I recalled my negotiations with Al-Nahar. No written contract. He had utterly deceived and outwitted me.

"No," I confessed.

"Then," said Ibn al-Hajj," you have no slave, only a slave's *lease*. When you leave Damascus, he will return to Al-Nahar. Or perhaps even *before* you leave."

He carried on, wilfully inflicting more distress on me.

"Now, would you like to do business? How many infidels do you wish to hire?"

"I wanted to purchase, not hire."

"That is impossible!" he replied. "The laws of Damascus forbid it. But you can *hire* as many as you want."

I explained I would consider further, and was sorry to have troubled him. He answered that he looked forward very much to seeing me again. He would arrange the discussion with his colleagues concerning the numbers. For the sake of etiquette, I agreed, speedily taking my leave.

The gangmaster was waiting. Like a lost sheep, I followed him through the streets.

The wretches in the pit wearily pointed their shovels at the ground when they saw the overseer coming. He sprang into action with lashing and cursing, offering fawning apologies to me for having to fulfil his duty.

Guillaume, standing some distance away, was overjoyed to see me. I tried to smile, but it was difficult.

"They are all from Europe!" he murmured with evident elation. "I told them that help is at hand."

We moved away through the streets.

"I saw their master," I whispered. "He is only interested in *hiring*."

"Surely if you raise the price, you can get one or two."

"No, Guillaume. This is a man who does not bargain. I have lost."

Wistfully, he clutched my arm, and with slightly raised voice remarked,

"Well, at least you did your best."

His words hammered nails into my heart.

But before informing Guillaume of the full details of our dilemma, it would be necessary to sound out Al-Nahar and glean whatever one could of the truth of the matter.

⚜ XI ⚜

During the next lesson Al-Nahar concentrated on the astronomy of Abu Allah Mohammed ibn-Jabir al-Battani and Umar ibn-Ibrahim al-Khayyami. The former sage studied the stars and discovered from Indian trigonometry that distances from earth to sun are not necessarily constant, varying throughout the year. This would find little favour with European astronomers who prefer concepts of perfect circular orbits as the universe revolves round the earth.

In like vein, Al-Khayyami had suggested measurements for the solar year equalling 365.24219858156 days, a strange figure for how could the Almighty create a universe with numbers as bizarre as that?

Al-Nahar, supporting his beloved master, insisted that measurements of time are more intricate than those of business. Whereas wealth is calculated in goods, property and income, time is measured by movements of the sun and planets, gyrations of the moon, and diverse infinite mysteries.

These matters appeared more relevant to theology than science. I preferred to concentrate on commerce, being nearer to Euclid than Ptolemy. Al-Nahar despised such narrowness. In the end I pleaded ignorance of the heavens, agreeing such things were beyond my competence.

Concerning Guillaume, I plucked up courage to broach the

subject not head on but from an oblique angle. As the session drew to an end, I casually remarked how my father, not being of sound health, required a visit shortly. Thereafter I would return to Al-Nahar for further study.

I expressed anxieties about Guillaj, who would of course, being my bodyguard, have to accompany me on the journey. Al-Nahar replied he was willing to take him back during my absence. His daughter would be especially delighted at the news. To the plea that I needed Guillaume for protection, Al-Nahar retorted that my unguarded person had previously got on very well without him.

I went step by step to questions of legality. We swayed back and forth in discourse, polite on the surface but with hidden barbs.

The upshot was that I expressed a fervent desire to obtain documents clarifying my claim on Guillaj. Al-Nahar, thereupon, became circumspect, asserting paperwork was not needed and then admitting it probably was.

This discussion drew to a close with a question to Al-Nahar concerning whether I 'owned' Guillaj as my property. He affirmed that if one master left Damascus, a slave normally reverted to his previous overlord.

I now understood that the argument was lost, less by reason than false premises. Any implication of my departure from Syria caused Al-Nahar to reiterate his strange concept of ownership where the object of possession in dispute seemed to belong to both of us at the same time.

His mastery of digression, displayed in every lesson, served him well. However much the bone was gnawed by two competing dogs, agreement would never be reached.

Finally, defeated by the impossibility of bargaining with such a man, I acknowledged meekly that all rights indeed pertained to him, emphasising how fortunate I was to have so eminent a master and so competent a slave.

The corollary to this was that I had to say that my intentions were to stay in Damascus for months to come.

Al-Nahar ostensibly accepted the change of tack for he embraced me, assured me of his kind attention at all times, and asked no further questions about my father's failing health or the date when I would depart to visit my family.

XII

I left the lesson with a suspicion that Guillaume de Lyons might be snatched from me at any moment, perhaps that very evening. It was a day or two since my visit to the slavemaster. Despite the lazy pace of eastern life, Al-Nahar would soon hear of my attempt to purchase infidels.

At the house I was relieved to find Guillaume sleeping peacefully. I roused him and told him to gather up whatever we possessed.

"There is a problem," I said, "which must be resolved."

While Guillaume fussed around our belongings, I visited a shop some minutes away, purchasing a *chador,* an ideal garment for married women, black from head to foot, as well as a comely veil to hide the face, leaving only the eyes modestly visible to a stranger's stare.

I informed the proprietor of my hopes for an imminent union with a bride of peerless beauty needing shelter from the lustful gaze of men.

The shopkeeper was so excited at the sight of money that he suggested certain accessories for the wedding night. I promised to see him again the next day to complete such purchases.

Before returning to the house I bought cheese, bread, sweet cakes, dates, figs, nuts, and leather water flasks, sufficient supplies for several days.

Guillaume, indignant to learn he was to be my wife that night, at least in terms of costume, was overjoyed at the prospect of escape. He promptly shaved, strapped on sword and dagger, and donned his disguise with good humour.

For my part I left scholarly clothes behind and put on those given to me by Guy de Poitiers. I bound up the possessions into a tight bundle, dividing the remaining money between Guillaume and myself.

Putting our heads together, we decided to escape that evening through Bab ash Sharqi, the most eastern gate, making our way first to the north and then west to the coast.

An hour before nightfall we emerged, Guillaume trailing behind with mincing tiny steps like a female, his branded brow and soldierly form concealed by veil and *chador*.

At the gate itself an overloaded cart preceded us. This occupied the attention of the guards far more than the jostling crowd returning to nearby villages before the sunset curfew.

Guillaume stayed invisible in the throng, a tall woman apparently following her husband. Once outside the city, the mass of people quickly diminished to smaller groups, some turning south, others to the east.

Before long we were two alone on a darkening road, the land's immensity stretching about us.

Tenth Letter

Concerning a journey through the wilderness.

le navi sono al porto
e vogliono colare:

RINALDO D'AQUINO (*fl.* 1240–50)

(the ships are in port
and eager to set sail:)

I

Sire, My Most Esteemed Master Michael Theodorus,
Philosopher in the Service of His Majesty, Frederick II.

For such a campaign Guillaume de Lyons was the best of company. He decided we should rest by day, venturing forth during the final moments of twilight, to be guided through the night by the stars which Guillaume could read like a navigator.

Within hours of stepping onto our chosen route he became a warrior again. He needed little sleep, keeping watch while we waited for sunset. Once far enough from the city, he dispensed with disguise unless near a habitation. We walked silently the first night under a harsh moon.

To the north of Damascus there is a kind of road, beaten out by the feet of many generations, sometimes hardly discernible but elsewhere as clear as a compass. At dawn we separated ourselves from the track to hide among ravines and rocks, our eyes open for whatever traversed that pitiless highway.

I feared guards might be dispatched to search for an escaped slave and his abductor. Though none knew through which gate we had fled, I never ceased imagining, especially at dawn, that clouds of dust from approaching horsemen were visible on the horizon. Eventually, tired of such fantasies, I wrapped a cloth round my head and slept as best I could.

Not far off the road, here and there, were various small settlements. We usually shunned them like the plague, creeping past at night. As soon as they came into view I believed our enemies might, like hawks, pick us out from a distance and fall upon us.

Guillaume was less pessimistic. Concealment was an art. Whereas we were looking out for them, they were not watching for us. Nevertheless, when dwellings were situated quite close to the track, we held our breath and tiptoed by, taking care not to kick up stones or trip over our own feet.

After some days of this, we reached the village of Art Nabk, a decent distance from Damascus and worth a gamble. Guillaume resumed his accoutrement of disguise and we ventured among the cluster of huts and alleys. Our entry was noticed but no undue alarm followed.

Dirty children giggled from doorways, running to meet us but mothers ushered them back into their homes. An old man called greetings and I replied politely. Having been acknowledged, he turned again to his dwelling.

We found a filthy place claiming to offer meals, but little to suggest any customers had ever eaten there. Importuned by a wretchedly poor man and his wife, we accepted what was offered. This consisted of thin gruel, unleavened bread, a few vegetables, and the legs of a scrawny chicken.

When the woman insisted on attempting to talk to Guillaume, I explained that my wife was deaf, dumb, and not beautiful. Guillaume remained calm and still, his brown eyes through the visor blinking coyly. Eating was not easy for him as for obvious reasons he had to push each mouthful under the veil while inquisitive infants crowded round. Neighbours came flocking to enjoy the entertainment.

Some, apparently intending gestures of friendship, patted Guillaume on the head till I raised my hand and they desisted. Confusion followed concerning my accent. This brought on comic imitations of my voice with much bantering.

To keep them amused I spoke in guttural tones, throwing out a few phrases from Egypt. Failing to comprehend what I was saying, especially as my mouth was stuffed with their awful food, they became bored and melted away.

Paying for the meal was a ritual we could have done without. They said the food was a gift but when I insisted on offering a few coins, they wanted more.

I gave them more. Still they appeared discontented. To resolve the rising tension, I gave a coin or two to the infants, who passed them on swiftly to their parents for safekeeping. Thus honour was satisfied.

When the villagers grew ever more inquisitive, it was time to depart. I bade farewell to each interested party and set off towards the road. Guillaume rose and padded after me, remembering to shorten his stride and not hurry.

With many farewells we retraced our footsteps. At the village oasis we asked permission to fill our leather flasks with their abominable greenish water.

Once on the northward path we quickened our step. After an hour or two of urgent ambling we found a hiding place and made ourselves secure.

Nobody followed us. But taking turns at sentry duty, we waited until complete darkness before resuming our travels.

II

With blistered feet and parched throats we entered the territory of despair. Guillaume was losing his usual good humour, I stumbled as dizzy as a drunkard. The land mocked our frailty. Each night we seemed to cover less ground than the one before. Our pace was more limping than walking and every step pained ankles and calves.

The dawn sun across the desert rim hurt the eyes. Like dying moles, we hated the light. Crawling into a gully down a long incline from the road, sleep was elusive, the day hotter than any other. Our lair was never too far from the track as we lacked strength to retreat further.

An hour before dark, Guillaume saw travellers on the road from the south. Our dust-ridden vision could not quite make them out. Were they soldiers?

As they approached, Guillaume whistled through his teeth and muttered, "This is a piece of luck!" The falling sun illuminated three horses and a single rider. The animals walked slowly. The man was hunched in his saddle, head covered against the dust.

I had no idea how *this* could be 'a piece of luck'. But Guillaume, as a soldier, saw all things from different perspectives. The military mind thrives on agitation rather than reflection. The sight of an unpolished button or a dirty sword fills the lowest corporal with spleen – a philosopher or teacher ignores such scraps.

However, in this world there exist so many filthy buttons, boots, buckles, badges, medals, suits of armour, guns, doors, floors, and entire buildings, as well as unkempt horses, untrimmed beards, sloppy attire and slovenly posture, that men trained to arms are in a perpetual frenzy. The sum of these activities is unhappiness for all concerned, whether as a leader dispensing such edicts or as a hapless victim of this striving towards artificial perfection.

Its strength is simplicity. When a crisis comes, the soldier sees a problem and solves it almost in the moment the proposition is imagined. Swift and appropriate response is the secret of winning battles.

Even as I glimpsed the traveller, Guillaume formulated equations and resolved them. He pulled on the *chador,* adjusting his veil with newly acquired expertise. His voice, muffled beneath the cloth, commanded me to remain hidden. In my befuddled state I was very content to stay exactly where I was, uncomfortable though the rocks might be.

He set off over the rough ground, climbing up to the road, his movements constricted by the costume, a sight so ridiculous it was almost laughable. Reaching the track, he turned south to walk towards the rider, unhurried, the very image of a nomad at home in the wilderness.

The traveller lifted his head as if unable to believe the mirage. The horses quickened their pace. Guillaume took longer strides. As the two sides closed, the rider broke into a trot, his steed jerking the accompanying horses from their torpor and causing them to jostle. The man sat upright, alert, consumed with the encounter. Guillaume's gait altered again. He was walking on water, his motion suspended as the gentle crepuscular light silhouetted him against the sky.

The angle of my perception lengthened the distance. I could hardly estimate how long till they collided, time hanging in the air like the sun itself.

The rider pulled on the reins and drew adjacent. Guillaume was near the traveller, his arm raised as if in greeting. My vision blurred and I rubbed my eyes.

When I looked again the traveller was out of the saddle and on the ground. I ran helter-skelter from the hide-out, tripping over in my haste. It was further than I thought, the rising ground creating an illusion of nearness.

Out of breath, I reached Guillaume at last. The poor victim was on his back, as dead as a stone, his face uncovered, the mouth gaping to show yellow and black teeth,

"Grab the horses!" shouted Guillaume. I gathered the three lots of reins, the animals becoming unruly. One attempted to rear, unsettling the others.

"Hold them tight!" he ordered. "I'll deal with this."

He lifted the body off the ground with the same care as a man might carry his bride over the threshold. Guillaume left the track and disappeared from view.

I stroked the necks of the horses and stilled their fear, straining my eyes to look south and north, but seeing no other travellers.

When Guillaume returned he seemed highly pleased with himself, especially when he discovered that each horse carried two saddlebags packed with food, a little money, leather water flasks full to the brim, and a set of clean clothes.

Guillaume tried on these garments and was surprised how well they fitted. He patted the rump of the horse on which the man had ridden with a gesture of ownership.

"I'll ride this horse. You take the other and lead the third."

I said nothing. There was nothing to be said. At least not just then. I strapped on my bundle of possessions, placed my foot in the embroidered stirrup.

We set off, the sky reddening to a sunset of tragic beauty.

III

That night the moon hung in the sky like a gold piece scarred with use. The man's gaping mouth and discoloured teeth haunted me as shadows of rocks threatened. I rode ahead, not wanting to look at Guillaume. For his part, he occasionally whistled a ballad. When dawn came we found a place ample enough to hide the horses from the road.

My head was cast down. Guillaume gripped my arm.

"What is the matter?" he asked.

"You killed him!" I said.

"He would have killed us. He had a knife."

"Poor man," I muttered.

"Lucky for us!" he replied. "These horses saved us."

My will was numb. I nibbled on a biscuit and drank a mouthful of water, almost choking on it.

Guillaume, whistling again as he unsaddled the horses, placed the panniers and our possessions on a pile of stones. He took a few rapid bites of the dead man's rations.

Dressed in his new garments, he made himself as comfortable as possible on the brutal ground and promptly fell asleep.

I could neither sleep nor keep properly awake. My eyelids closed. Peculiar shapes came before my vision, rocks moved, sounds became shuffling sandals or animals.

Drowsiness touched me but did not take me into its comfort. Somewhere a body lay in its shallow grave.

I pitched into a nasty dream. When I awoke, Guillaume was on guard, watching from the hideout. The killing had sharpened him. He seemed at ease with himself.

After food and water, we talked. I expressed anxieties that the stolen horses or saddlebags might somehow be recognised along the journey. Guillaume did not share my gloom. His logic was that as I once saved his life, now he had saved mine.

It was impossible to argue. His mind moved in straight lines, like a true disciple of Greek geometry, from a to b and from b to c, without a qualm. Since leaving Damascus his confidence had grown. Guillaume understood my frailty but having slaughtered so many, one more would not tip his scales.

"Accept necessity!" he grunted, an aphorism dressed as philosophy. But what about God seeing every sparrow fall, the Almighty watching a man toppled from his horse?

My companion responded by pointing out it was unwise for humans to judge themselves by standards of divine perfection. Our frailties were surely comprehended by any Deity that was Himself perfect.

"One does not live with clean hands!" he declared. "Even saints wash several times a day."

⟨⟨⟨ IV ⟩⟩⟩

For a while we exchanged few words. The filth of the desert, the heat by day, difficulties of sleeping, exhausted horses, and a long trek each night, robbed us of discourse.

The man we killed might have been travelling to any of the settlements or to our destination, the town of Homs.

So we avoided dwellings, tents, and signs of a community. The further the journey, the more fugitive our senses.

After interminable days and nights the walls of Homs blocked our way. We had no choice but to enter. Guillaume resumed his woman's apparel and we ventured through the south gate with trepidation. We found lodgings, stabled the horses, ate and drank till our bellies were full, and kept in the shadows.

Guillaume in his veil seemed invisible but I was a source of curiosity. It started with beggars and continued with children tugging at my garments to demand coins. I gave them hardly anything. We retreated to shelter uneasily in our shabby room.

The landlord was intrigued, seeking details of our travels. But my suspicions guarded every word, which served only to fatten his curiosity.

Two nights later we rode out through the west gate shortly after dawn. Even the horses pranced as the town was put behind us. With equal joy we crossed the Al-Assi river, following its northern bank to the edge of the great lake, Buhayrat Qattinah. We passed orchards full of singing birds, entering the enchantment of a veritable Garden of Eden, the bad land behind, the good and best to come.

Riding each night under the cold stars, we soon arrived at the castle of Krak des Chevaliers, also known as Hisn al-Akrad. Guillaume would not approach too closely. He had fought there in days gone by. He refused to speak of it, wiping his eyes as if removing sweat from his brow rather than tears shed in bitter memory.

Our relief at reaching the sea knew no bounds. We were children re-born, bathing in the surf to emerge baptised. From there we turned towards Tortosa, called Antaradus by the Romans, where, after much bloodshed, Christian soldiers had constructed a worthy cathedral to the Virgin half a century before.

Guillaume remembered the story of how Saladin's army took the town. The Templars, led by Gerard of Ridefort, barricaded the Keep till their retreat to Arwad Island not long after the battle of Hattin.

But he had only heard this boasted about by his masters in Damascus. To separate truth from falsehood was difficult in these matters.

The nearer to freedom, the more we feared capture. Having stabled our horses away from the quay, and with Guillaume quarantined in a lodging house, I trod carefully among vessels in the harbour, seeking only foreign ships. My apparel worked in my favour, attracting no undue attention as I spied out the possibilities.

Talking to the master of this or that craft, it was possible to let the mask slip a little, introducing myself as a scholar travelling to Europe. On the fourth attempt after negotiating with various characters whose ships matched their disarray, I encountered a

Spanish captain, well attired, of respectful manner, due to leave port that very evening.

Our conversation involved delicate diplomacy. However, the presence of a large crucifix dangling against his hairy chest, and his frequent references to the holy saints and similar subjects, encouraged me to match his piety with gracious sanctimony.

Over a glass of wine in his quarters, Don Francisco even addressed me as 'Brother', presuming that I represented some form of sacred order.

So I took on a new identity as Brother Leonardo of Pisa, hinted at adherence to chastity and obedience but for his peace of mind made no mention of poverty. With veiled references to the Holy Father I implied further duties laid to my charge. Thereupon Don Francisco dropped his voice to a conspiratorial whisper. As the wine soothed our gullets, I mentioned how a certain Chevalier Guillaume also required passage on his ship.

Don Francisco's face twitched gently at this unexpected information but relaxed at the prospect of double payment.

I fetched Guillaume, leaving the horses and saddles to the dispensation of the stables. Once within reasonable distance of the vessel, Guillaume de Lyons shed his disguise and became himself again with leather tunic and disfigured face. We arrived on board without further incident.

As the dying sun smeared sky and sea with crimson and purple, our vessel set out from the harbour. We watched the land recede till it disappeared into the lonely distance.

Letter from Guillaume de Lyons to Leonardo Pisano

From Guillaume de Lyons
To the Esteemed Master and Scholar, Leonardo Pisano

It seems a long while since we sailed from that Syrian shore into a sunset which neither of us will forget. We shall also preserve in memory the conversations with Captain Don Francisco over wine. His mind seemed much possessed with religion, heretics, blasphemies, and their proper correction.

Yet he was a good man, though as Brother Leonardo and Chevalier Guillaume, we led him a merry dance.

My blessings to you for your kindness. Not just for the freedom you won for me at great risk to your own person. But also for the generous division of money which the good knight, Guy de Poitiers, bestowed on you. You did not leave me destitute and with gold in my purse I was able to return home, head held high.

My wife had given me up for dead and my homecoming was not joyous. She now loved another, having entered into wedlock and given birth to several of his children. It was difficult to drive him from my dwelling despite proofs of my identity, and ratification with priests. Neither was my wife pleased with the scar on my face.

But I maintained my rights as a husband. With much weeping from the woman and her children I saw off the usurper by fair means and foul till he no longer dared to come hither. Perhaps through the example of your own forbearance I did not kill that knave who stole my wife, though he deserved it.

He was frightened by my visage and recoiled from it as from the evil mask of Satan. I praise you that never once did you show repugnance at my appearance but treated me from first to last with compassionate understanding.

Some in this parish sympathised with the wretch whose bastards now populate my home. I felt no pity. He had ruined everything I hoped for when I set foot over the threshold of my beloved house in Lyons, the home where I lived as child and man.

Seeing him there, at ease, was another bondage for me. When I entered the house, the children screamed at this monstrous visitation.

I curse that man who thieved love from me. He was the recipient of my wrath. It was by God's grace I did not sever his head from his body. He was no soldier but a coward who crept like a snake between my sheets.

Though you are fearful, Leonardo, you are no coward. Your ability to deceive the gullible and the wise could make you a courtier or a diplomat. Whatever you are, you will never be a coward.

This man was a coward, unwilling to die for the woman he believed to be his wife. Under my curses and avowals of vengeance, he sank to his knees, pleading for mercy, bleating like a goat.

I drew my short sword and waved it before his face. But his children let out such lamentations and excess of noise, embracing the coward with their thin, feeble arms, showing more courage than this fool and thereby putting themselves in mortal danger.

In that instant my fury weakened and I felt pity, not for him, but for them.

I did not therefore give in to my anger and do what I intended with him. Instead I sheathed my sword, smacked the miscreant on the head and kicked him out of my house, deaf to his entreaties but sparing his miserable life for the sake of his brood.

He departed to fetch sheriffs, officers, priests, and kinsmen. But I swore to kill the first man who trespassed over my threshold. Not a soul dared place a toe one single cubit beyond where he stood at a distance. I slammed the door and placed a wooden keep across it.

My wife and the children within the house were mightily afraid. I banished the young to a higher room in order that I might talk privately with my wife. They feared with all their little hearts that I might hurt her. But she commanded them to go and they did her bidding.

I gave her no quarter, claiming my marital rights before God and the law, for she had sinned deeply in her haste to couple with another. I offered the signals of potential violence and many unkind words till in her weakness she capitulated like a wrecked ship against a stormy tide.

That night, as I had vowed when first approaching the walls of Lyons, I subdued my dear lost wife to my lust, though little pleasure it gave me. My jealousy burned her. I strutted in possession and she lay in the path of my domination.

For weeks our only music was her weeping and the crying of the poor children. Till things became quiet as they do after a battle and the victors accept victory and the defeated come to terms with loss. I tell you this, Leonardo, so that you need feel no responsibility for this unhappiness. I am sure you will not.

But the best deeds in the world, even the releasing of a slave, may have consequences beyond our expectations and understanding.

Our vessel, you will remember, travelled from Tortosa, skirted the island of Cyprus, and called in at Constantinople. Here, dear Leonardo, you spent time in the marketplace observing the merchants and their methods of counting. This was beyond me and I tired of such things, searching for more exciting sights than selling and buying, bargaining and cheating.

But foremost in my thoughts was your fascination with the rabbit hutch on board our vessel, where several adults of that species and a few young ones nibbled prior to arriving, garnished with spices, on our plates. As prepared by the cook in his special way, I did not appreciate till then the utter delight of roast rabbit, the light meat washed down with good wine.

Your mind was elsewhere, calculating with chalk and board, quill and paper, till I was forced to ask through curiosity what your sums involved. Never did I imagine a scholar such as yourself might be absorbed with a problem relating to rabbits.

After much pleading on my part, you told me your secret on condition I informed nobody else. Your obsession with the procreation of rabbits became a glass through which I perceived the magic of your calling.

In my profession numbers refer to men and equipment, food, arrows, water, wine, shields, shoes, boots, tunics, swords, horses, maps, and are matched against the enemy's potential. The latter involves terrain, weather, season, cavalry, infantry, scouts, generals, courage, and a thousand other things.

We march to battle, win, perish or are captured, and the victors *prepare to fight again. Such numbers bear witness to the follies of humanity and the self-destructive pride of armies. At the same time, it goes beyond the accustomed limits of imagination. Remembering the thousands of graves, the wounded, the slaves, the destruction, memory fails.*

Your numbers are entirely the opposite – trivial and sublime, parochial and universal, the product of individual minds yet reaching out to entire civilisations.

In your mathematical conundrum concerning the breeding of rabbits, you posed a question that would never occur to a soldier.

But once you opened my eyes to this I could not shake off my fascination with the puzzle you set:

If a keeper places one pair of rabbits in an enclosed place, how many rabbits would be created from the pair and its descendants in one year when it is their capability in a single month to breed another pair and in the second month the young rabbits are also ready to breed?

You did not, at first, provide an answer. For weeks I was left to agonise fruitlessly, walking my rusty mind up and down many a hillock to no avail.

My route towards failure was of misdirection, false trails, paths away from the main highway, which appeared promising but were not correct.

I began with the first breeding pair, imagined their offspring but ended with a mess of random figures. I believed that the matter could not be resolved, not even by you, Leonardo.

After calculating only a few weeks of rabbit breeding, I was lost, my head inhabited by hordes of them procreating incessantly, their long ears, short tails and foolish movements repellent, smelling of wet fur, excrement, and regurgitated food.

I would gladly have exterminated them all, by strangling or disembowelling with sword and dagger, chasing them like lemmings over cliffs. Despite this, each rabbit tasted exquisite raising the jest that Leonardo's conundrum did not anticipate eating the stupid creatures every night.

Eventually I asked for the explanation. I would willingly have given you gold coins for a glimpse of the answer. But of course I admitted no such thing. How you tantalised me, exhorting me to try again with chalk and board and never to surrender.

For days we played this game. You knew the answer by now. I chided myself for impatience.

What did it matter how many mythical rabbits spawned how many more over a certain length of time? But this is the nature of numbers, that we care despite ourselves.

I felt like forcing you to the deck, with my dagger at your throat, wrenching the answer from you. Your mocking manner made me extremely annoyed.

Even you, Leonardo, came to realise that I too, like most soldiers, was tainted with a touch of insanity, that the glint in my eye could become anger if matters were not soon settled.

How blessed I felt, when you promised to give me your solution. It was, in fact, a simple sequence so full of majesty that one could imagine elements of witchcraft there. When the answer was presented, rabbits disappeared from the mind.

It was the symmetry which delighted, rather than images of creatures extending their breeding. Like an alchemist changing metal into gold, you unveiled your thoughts with this explanation:

i)   At the beginning, month 0, there is 1 mature pair.
ii) For month 1, this mature pair breeds offspring of an immature pair, giving us 1 mature pair and 1 immature pair – 2 in all.
iii) In month 2 the mature pair breeds another immature pair while the immature pair breeds nothing as they grow towards maturity.

This gives us 2 mature pairs and 1 immature pair, 3 altogether.
iv) Month 3 sees the 2 mature pairs breed two further immature pairs, the immature pair breeding nothing. This totals 3 mature pairs and 2 immature pairs, giving us 5 in all.
v)   For month 4 we now have 3 mature pairs breeding 3 more immature pairs, the 2 immature pairs producing nothing as yet. Thus we have 5 mature pairs and 3 immature pairs, the sum of 8.
vi) Continuing the same reasoning produces these numbers:
1, 2, 3, 5, 8, 13, 21, 34, 55, 89, 144, 233, 377

The answer to how many such creatures were bred by the end of the year was therefore no less than 377 (sufficient to keep a soldier in rabbit pie till sick to his stomach).

I began to understand the beauty of this sequence, adding each number to the one before it to produce a new number, though the processes of reaching such perfection remain for ever beyond my grasp.

But here was an answer so perfect a child could savour it, so complex a grown person might offer homage in humility.

"What of your teachers?" I enquired foolishly. "Could they have solved this problem?"

You paused before whispering so eloquently an enigmatic 'perhaps', I ought to have shaken your hand in admiration. I never doubted that such teachers would not have been able to solve the problem for the reason that they could never have dreamed up such a question in the first place.

Do not forget to include this problem in your book, dear Leonardo. It will not take up much space compared with all the other things.

How do I know about your book? You certainly did not tell me about it. But a soldier has to find out what he can. Once in Damascus, when you were safely away from the house, I unpacked that bundle you hid so carefully. I saw your handwritten manuscript in the making, and that pure copy by an excellent scribe. I understood little except that it seemed an omen of good things to come.

Dearest Leonardo, do you remember how excited you were when our vessel visited the land of Pythagoras? Your eyes were like saucers with amazement as we trod the Athenian streets.

How marvellously those young women flaunted themselves in the sun, dancing like goddesses, speaking as eloquently as Homer, even if we did not understand a word of their lovely language. In such a place the old gods live.

I hesitate to remind you of how we surrendered, lured to their lair, where we bathed in scented water and cavorted on silk beds with nymphs whose bodies tasted of divinity. Their demands were not excessive, at least not in terms of payment, though each knew how to get the best from a man. Such memories tease me like spirits from another world.

I am not now in good health. I have suffered a wasting disease and am as emaciated as it is possible to be. The physicians have given me up for dead. But I linger on, my body discomforted and all movement difficult.

My wife says this is punishment for my sins. I think she awaits my ultimate departure with a sense of longing. When I breathe my last, the usurper will creep back like a dog returning to its vomit. But he dare not come while I have a single curse left in my throat.

I often dream of death. Not my own but of those I killed in the line of duty. I saw their faces as my sword finished them.

As each falls, a soldier moves to the next, and the next. After a victory we often visited the ground where we had fought, allowing time for reflective thoughts and sorrow for the fallen and maimed.

If we lost, we could only run and save our own skins. But things come back to mind. The young boys struggling against us, old men weak in arm and leg, the strong who pushed us to the brink, lines advancing and shouting, rising, falling, retreating, the melee, the smell of blood and excrement, silence after the shame.

I shall look towards the grave shortly. I am not afraid now, though at that moment I may well be more than afraid. I am too torn by sickness to think of anything but this present hour, seeking remedies in bed or chair, by opiates, strong drink, or snatching at sleep.

The old priest comes to see me and is concerned. When I confess my sins to him he becomes confused, accusing me of admitting the same offences on separate occasions. I correct him, pleading that my crimes are similar but committed in diverse places, again and again.

I am in a twilight where shadows fall across my vision. It is perpetual dusk. My eyes fail, speech hesitates, fingers grow weak. My wife brings milk flavoured as if polluted with some subtle poison, but perhaps it is not so. My tongue is swollen, my hearing poor.

I think of you daily. I am passing on but not in bondage. You have my eternal gratitude for that. I pray that you have a successful life and ask forgiveness for the burdens I put upon you.

I am too frail to write more. What kind of mystery was our life and into what do we descend? A thousand million soldiers have disappeared into dust since time began. There's a simple number for a scholar! And the sum of that dust and all those ashes? As light as a feather, as heavy as God.

I have bequeathed the gold you gave me to my wife. She may forgive my homecoming when I am gone. I have wronged her and others.

On my last day I shall hold the priest's hand like a frightened child.

Your dearest friend for ever, in this world or the next,

Guillaume de Lyons

Eleventh Letter

*Concerning Master John of Palermo,
Signor Goffredo Pugliese, wealthy merchant,
the beauty of his son, Ludovico, and my
union with his daughter, Lucia.*

Que vaut beauté, que vaut richece,
Que vaut honeur? que vaut hautece,
Puis que Mort tout à sa devise
Fait sor nous pluie et secherece,
Puis qu'ele a tout en sa destrece,
Quanqu'on despise et quanqu'on prise?

HÉLINAND (c. 1160–1229)

(What use is beauty? What use prosperity?
 What use is honour? What use nobility?
 Since Death entirely at his own sweet will
 Brings down upon us flood and sterility,
 Since Death has such utter capability
 To destroy all we despise and all we value still?)

❧ I ❧

Sire, My Most Esteemed Master Michael Theodorus,
Philosopher in the service of His Majesty, Frederick II.

return now, like a lost traveller, from early journeys to my late maturity, back to my native soil of Pisa, passing to serious matters. No doubt in confessing all I shall be dragged to the mythology of memory wherein each thing is changed from that which it truly was. But I can only write as I remember.

My troubles began, as I said before, when Master Dominick introduced me to His Celestial Majesty, my Lord Frederick II, Emperor of the Holy Roman Empire. By this act of kindness, I encountered that ill-tongued, devious Master John of Palermo.

You may recall that it was Master John of Palermo who first proposed a riddle of the numbers – *To find a square number from which, when five is added or subtracted, always arises a square number.*

From this imposition came much toil and anguish but, in due course, my *Liber Quadratorum,* also known as *The Book of Squares,* was brought with much labour into the world.

Here I considered the origin of square numbers, arising from this increasing sequence of odd numbers:

1) For 1 is the first square number
(being perfect unity). (1 = 1 × 1)
2) When 3 is added to 1 we have the second
square 4 with root of 2. (1 + 3 = 2 × 2)
3) If to 4 the third odd number 5 is added, the third square
occurs, which is 9, with root of 3. (1 + 3 + 5 = 3 × 3)
4) If to 9 the fourth odd number of 7 is added, the fourth square
occurs, which is 16 with root of 4. (1 + 3 + 5 + 7= 4 × 4)

Beginning with this introduction, I proceeded to explore twenty-four such propositions.

These concerned puzzles such as finding:

1) two square numbers which add together to form
a square number [(1+3+5+7) + 9 = (1+3+5+7+9)
or (4 × 4) + (3 × 3) = 5 × 5]
2) any square number which exceeds the square
immediately before it by the sum of the roots
[(11 × 11) − (10 × 10) = 21 = 11 + 10]
3) two squares which added together make a square
number with their sum [(5 × 5) + (12 × 12) = 13 × 13]

When this was explained to Master John, the result was a yawn as big as the moon, followed by a drooping head the more I persisted.

I wrestled with each problem for more months than I dare admit. In writing this treatise I came close to madness. The squares are stubborn children with minds of their own.

As for Master John's original enquiry I demonstrated there is no whole number solution, but only fractions. This annoyed him. Was it the reason he later sought my ruin?

My thoughts concerning square numbers were subject to complication. At an advanced age I took to myself a wife. Our nuptials were celebrated a few months after I first encountered the riddles of the squares.

These two became grievously intermingled, calculations and marriage. When a man undertakes steps into matrimony, he may find his nature is in inverse proportion to the purity of numbers. Squares, circles, tables, and equations pursue logical courses. The hearts of men and women, whether separate or conjoined, follow no such ordered path. Though I soared like a bird over scholarship, I stumbled like a blind man into wedlock, suffering unimaginable remorse.

I was reminded of many another who experienced similar sorrow within marriage. There was cause to curse not only my bad luck but also Master John of Palermo, who enticed me into the trap, as well as to lament the fate of the poor woman who shared my vows.

II

Out of the blue I was summoned by letter to arrange an appointment with Master John of Palermo. Marooned in the thicket of my calculations, I was reluctant to set foot out of doors. But anticipating some advantage I decided to do his bidding.

He in his turn, having put forward an invitation, wilfully delayed our meeting, rejecting various possible dates to offer others less to my liking. But after much tiresome marking of calendars, the precise hour was eventually decided.

I have mentioned how Master John with his dirty beard and bad teeth was married to Beatrice of the swan-like neck, the white skin, the rose lips, the alabaster hands, the dove's voice, and angelic disposition. Just to think of her was to stand tiptoe by a sea of sensuality, her breath sweet, her perfume as fragrant as a flower.

On arrival at their house it became usual to linger with Beatrice while the servants summoned Master John from some far corner. I longed for him to be so detained he might never arrive.

During one visit the fair Beatrice asked me to remove a speck of dust from her left eye. To achieve this I placed the palm of my hand on her face to hold her steady. That particular day her dark hair flowed exquisitely across her shoulders, sufficient to tempt the heart of a saint into unfulfilled longing.

In close proximity, I admired the ivory perfection of her lake-smooth cheeks, the infinitely delicate filigree of eyebrows and lashes, the light sprinkling of down on that peerless neck, and (all the time I was close to her) the satin folds of her *décolletage,* rising and falling like a gentle ocean swell.

Naturally I did not hurry, slowly teasing out the impediment with the corner of a silk handkerchief.

After the mite was extracted I whispered she should look left and right. She blinked, her lovely eyes obedient to my instructions.

I was reluctant to desist, fussing over the details, not removing my hand till compelled by decency.

By the time the shuffling gait of Master John in his slippers was audible, I was somewhat short of breath with desire, my palms warm from touching her.

Though fire burned in me, Beatrice was calm as a statue, thanking me for my pains, such innocence adding fuel to the blaze.

But I digress. For on the morning of this other meeting, there was little opportunity to dally before that snuffling husband made his entrance, acknowledging my presence by a supercilious lift of the hand.

Beatrice, with curt words from him, was dispatched to an outer room. I watched her go, my feelings inflamed like a boil.

Master John came quickly to his point. A wealthy merchant, Signor Goffredo Pugliese, a newcomer to Pisa, required a tutor to instruct his son in the numbers, preparatory to an apprenticeship in the family business.

The gentleman would pay me well but I was reluctant to waste hours teaching. A less busy scholar could surely be found to fulfil this task. Master John countenanced no refusal.

Following fruitless discussion, I was forced to yield against my better judgement. That I gave in so easily haunts me, for this was my undoing.

But the plainest path is fraught with thorns and barriers. None can know the outcome be the choice ever so simple.

III

Signor Goffredo Pugliese owned a splendid house, full of fine furniture, paintings, tapestries, carpets and valuable ornaments. Softly spoken, he was a man of authority who had no need to raise his voice to enforce his will.

"So you are the great Master Leonardo?" he said at our first meeting. "Master John has spoken well of you."

"I am honoured!" I replied.

He introduced his wife, Francesca, a woman whose lease of beauty had expired though she retained a little of the sparkle of lost youth. To this lady, dressed in bright red set off by gold bracelets and a diamond necklace, I bowed. She exclaimed "Oh, Master Leonardo!" as if somehow surprised.

The three of us took wine and cakes in the sitting room. Goffredo, no friend of small talk, dived at once into matters relevant to his interests. After trade, currencies and maritime commerce, he talked of courtiers and aristocrats, en route praising Master John of Palermo as 'a man of distinction'.

I ignored the bitter gall on my palate at this, nodding vigorously when Francesca joined in to speak well of Beatrice. Goffredo, in the belief that I was agreeing with his sentiments rather than hers, proceeded to lavish yet more praise on Master John.

The subject of Ludovico came next. The son and heir to all this wealth was judged by his father to be lazy. Signora Pugliese, a gentler advocate, pleaded that Ludovico's deficiencies were from inadequate tuition. She preferred to emphasise his sweet nature, an attribute superior, in her view, to any scholarly tendencies.

Puzzled by such varying assessments, I said nothing, frowning at Goffredo and offering smiles for Francesca. Diverse opinions continued awhile. The boy was, according to his parents, either an idle weakling with much to learn or a saintly character of generosity and purity blessed by heaven above.

Aware how a father's love mingles with jealousy, while wives see in their sons what their husbands might have been, I decided these remarks amounted to a simple truth – Ludovico was not yet a scholar but possessed an exquisite soul.

Even as I pondered, Goffredo's cheeks grew florid, his gestures extreme, though his voice did not increase in volume.

"You may school him as you will, Master Leonardo," his hand flailing the air as if in chastisement, "whether with voice or birch, but learn he *must!*"

At this, Francesca lost her tranquillity.

"Oh Master Leonardo, take no notice! My husband lacks all patience. Ludovico is a fine boy!"

Goffredo made no reply. After a pause, I replied boldly,

"Have no fear. If I teach him, he *will* learn. And, Signora, if pupils do not learn by fair means, they cannot learn by foul."

Goffredo continued to the matter of payment for lessons. His first offer needed but a slight adjustment upwards, which I put to him. Goffredo's mouth opened like a fish but no sound came forth. Francesca intervened with the assurance that any fee requested would be met. Her husband said nothing but inclined his head in what I assumed was affirmation.

IV

A servant was sent to summon young Ludovico. We waited in silence.

"Where is the boy?" mumbled Goffredo as minutes passed. Francesca frowned and tutted to quieten his irritability.

Goffredo, unable to restrain himself, muttering under his breath, rose and left the room. Francesca exchanged humorous glances with me. This was the way of the world with little to be done about it.

We heard Goffredo rebuking the servant for failing in his duties. In a few minutes he returned, the boy preceding him, gently pushed along by his father.

"This is Ludovico!" announced Francesca, placing a motherly arm round his shoulders. "My dear, this is your new tutor, Master Leonardo."

"I am honoured to meet you," he said. I stood up and shook his hand.

He was twelve years old, still hugging the coasts of childhood before embarking on the troubled sea of puberty. His face possessed an extraordinary beauty with profound dark eyes, a soft feminine mouth, and a perfect symmetry of form. I felt as when I had first seen Akilah, struck dumb by her presence. Words curdled in my throat. I touched his hand, overcome, mesmerised as if by a work of art.

We seated ourselves. Even the servants were feasting their eyes, just as the pious gaze on holy statues. Ludovico himself was modest, respectful, the goodness of his nature apparent in his serenity.

He sat close to his mother on the couch and she looked at him with proud reverence, occasionally brushing aside a stray wisp of hair from the young god's forehead.

A servant brought Ludovico a cup of milk. He drank it as sweetly as a faun sipping at a stream.

For want of something better to do, I announced my syllabus of learning (addition, multiplication, division, fractions), the basis of the numbers.

After I had burbled on, the boy replied quietly.

"But, sir, I know these things."

I gulped nervously.

"But your father…" I began.

"Yes," interrupted Francesca, "his father gives him no credit for what he has already studied."

Goffredo rose to his feet to reply.

"I apologise if I gave a false impression. What I meant was that Ludovico certainly knows far less for his age than he should, given his abilities."

"In which case," I suggested, "we must begin lessons at once."

"Good," replied Goffredo. "Ludovico, take Master Leonardo to the study and follow his instructions."

The boy jumped up as if there was nothing better that he could wish for. Thus, sooner than expected, I found myself, seated next to my new pupil at a large oak table in a sumptuous room.

V

Ludovico was not lazy, as his father had alleged. The boy was actually full of curiosity concerning the numbers, wars and history. Indeed, he spoke with such respect for learning I considered myself in the presence of a friend.

He was aware of his remarkable beauty, how could he not be? He took this in his stride for what it was, just as others have to come to terms with their ugliness, deformity or stupidity. But Ludovico's character remained of sublime purity and humility, unspoiled by any praises showered upon him.

Certainly his comeliness was *sui generis,* a thing apart, a phenomenon. Such a sight must be seen to be believed, comparable with shining gold, evoking perfection hitherto glimpsed only in idealised figurines or the finest ancient art. Perhaps I say too much but one must tell a truthful tale.

Ludovico confessed that from his earliest years, strangers often came forward to offer admiration, sometimes with a kiss. When I chanced to accompany him through the streets, I myself observed the turning heads, the astonishment, the amazement at this Adonis in our midst. His very presence brought about that reaction which causes the people of the east to veil their women against the evil eye.

Concerning studies, Ludovico was well advanced. Whether multiplying equal numbers such as 607 by 607 to produce 368,449 or unequals such as 123 times 456 to make 56,088 or the division of integral numbers or multiplication of integral numbers with fractions, or addition and subtraction, or division of numbers with fractions – these were but child's play to him.

We moved to practical problems, to the fox fleeing fifty paces ahead of a dog, the former running at six paces for every nine of the latter, requiring calculation of the distance within which the unfortunate fox will be caught.

Ludovico proved most adept at dogs and foxes. But to each problem he applied himself thoroughly, filling up pages with rows and sequences of reasoning. As the journey progressed, my reward would be his smile followed by the correct answer.

In further lessons the slopes were steeper. If solutions evaded him, he wept in exasperation. When a path through the forest presented itself, he threw his arms round my neck, bestowing a tiny kiss like benediction from a visiting angel.

Where problems proved insoluble, he led me to the chessboard on a table in the corner and we would play a game or two. At first, I let him win. But he soon fathomed my lack of strategy and became difficult to defeat.

On the appointed day of a lesson, I rushed from my dwelling, a man possessed, desperate to see him. The boy became a strange wound in my heart. Only by his side did contentment come. My work suffered, my nights were anguish, for waking or dreaming I saw his face. Often I arrived unexpectedly at his house in the hope of seeing him, offering by way of excuse a new sum to be solved.

Such was my turmoil that sometimes I became surly, chiding faults which were no more than minor blemishes. On those occasions, his eyes grew troubled, looking at me with such sadness I felt almost inclined to beg his forgiveness.

But children are forbearing with elders, as they need to be, for often we are guilty of grievous errors in our treatment of them.

VI

Some weeks later, as I shared wine and cakes one morning with Goffredo, Francesca, and Ludovico, a young girl entered the sitting room. I caught my breath.

Apart from her dark hair, drifting to the waist, and the splendour of her elegant dress, she appeared as a veritable twin to my pupil. But this could not be for she was surely a few years older.

"My sister, Lucia," announced Ludovico, giggling at my shocked expression. "She has been away and returned yesterday."

The likeness between brother and sister was truly remarkable. We have all marvelled at identical twins as well as those of diverse appearances and varied dispositions. Here, like peas in a pod, nature, as if in defiance of her own laws, had created two images of the selfsame perfection.

I rose to my feet. Lucia smiled in response, her eyes flickering to my face and downwards in modesty.

"I was told by Ludovico of your excellent tuition," she said, causing me to blush at this compliment from her lips. When the five of us sat down together, Lucia took a small cup of wine, choosing a coloured cake to go with it.

Comparing one sibling with the other, I decided not to comment on the wonder of this double image. Obligingly, Signor Goffredo said it for me, muttering "Aren't they alike?"

"I would never have believed such a thing!" I replied, my gaze fixed on the girl, her brother eclipsed by a brighter planet.

It was difficult to stop staring like a beggar at a queen. Lucia, accustomed like her brother to a birthright of admiration, returned discreet glances.

Her figure was shapely, with slender hips, her form so perfectly proportioned that the eye returned to the contours of her face. She seemed the embodiment of a reincarnated goddess fallen to earth. I felt like a watcher of the stars seeing celestial mysteries, a traveller discovering an unknown land.

My face, I expect, gave little hint of currents beneath. We reposed in pleasant sociability. I drank her smiles like strong wine, chatting about baubles and nothings.

Thereafter, perturbed by dreams of her, I rose often from my bed to divert myself with problems of the square roots.

To no avail. My head drowsy, I sank into a trance-like state in which Lucia was my only contemplation, drifting for days, wondering if I was ill but knowing I was not.

VII

Some weeks later Master John invited me to his house for an evening meal. I was royally treated with dinner and wine and Beatrice smiled at me throughout the evening. I bathed in her benevolence. Bemused by excess of wine, temporarily distracted from obsessions, I was in a congenial mood.

Lounging in comfort, Master John entertained with his usual anecdotes of no point or consequence. But on the back of one of these monologues, Beatrice, as if by chance, mentioned Goffredo's family.

"That story reminds me to enquire whether you have visited Signor Pugliese of late?" she said.

"Yes," I replied, "Some days ago."

"Did you see his daughter? I understand that she has just returned from Rome?"

"Yes, I believe I did."

"Come, come!" interrupted Master John. "If you saw *that* girl, a man like you would surely remember!"

I coughed gently.

"Master John, I have many things on my mind at present."

"I am sure you have!" he remarked. "But do continue, Beatrice."

"Well," said Beatrice happily, "it is rumoured that Signor Pugliese wishes to find his daughter a husband! And fairly soon."

"Really," I muttered, "and why is that?"

"It is difficult. The girl is becoming something of a problem."

"Problem? Lucia?" I asked, shocked.

"Ah!" chuckled Master John. "So you did meet her!"

"I did not deny it," I hastily replied.

"Well," said Beatrice, "apart from that, Signor Pugliese wishes his daughter to have a suitable husband."

"Indeed!" I said, trying to sound detached.

"We thought," said Master John, "a man such as yourself might be appropriate."

A strange silence enveloped the room. I took a small sip of wine, a hesitation they observed.

"Master John," I said quietly, "I have never *yet* married."

"Precisely!" interrupted Beatrice. "For that reason you could be the perfect choice. Signor Pugliese admires you."

"And," said Master John, "on the matter of your age, that need be no impediment. I have it on good authority."

Out of my depth, I floundered.

"But what makes anyone presume I am considering the taking of a wife?"

"Don't be offended!" said Master John, in a more abrupt tone. "We are sounding you out, as we know you so well. It is a good proposition. The girl will have a handsome dowry, Signor Pugliese's problem will be solved. You will be in possession of a beautiful wife whom many would like to have. Think before you turn from it."

I *was* thinking. A peach offered on a gilded tray tempted the appetite. But caution was paramount.

We sparred back and forth like knights at play with wooden swords. Eventually I hit the target.

"What Master John, is the problem which troubles the good Signor?"

Master John smiled broadly, showing his bad teeth.

"Dear Leonardo, you need not concern yourself. It is a family affair. The truth is Signor Pugliese wishes his daughter to marry. Within the law of this land he has every right to choose her husband."

"I am flattered!" I replied, my mind unable to perceive the elements of this conundrum.

But no matter. The possibility of Lucia hung in the air like a gift from the gods or an illusion of the devil.

I took more wine and warmed to the topic, receiving fervent encouragement from Beatrice and Master John.

I left their house in a mist.

A vile eagerness filled my soul. I had not felt so prime for years.

VIII

There was much to think about. Under our laws fathers are legally entitled to dispose of their daughters in marriage whichever way their fancy moves them. Nevertheless, Lucia's possibly adverse opinion concerning my mature age and declining appearance was, in my estimation, not to be taken lightly.

Conflicting against all this, beyond restraint, was my *desire*, to have her, to be with her. I could not return to my previous state of mind before that first sight of her.

Taking my cue from Master John, I eventually decided to direct my creaking body towards Goffredo's house. Though my arrival was without a prior appointment, he seemed not entirely surprised or displeased to see me.

I explained my visit was for personal reasons. Signor Pugliese nodded brusquely, leading me to the sitting room.

We positioned ourselves on upright chairs as if preparing for debate. He called for wine. The servants left, closing the door behind them.

Until a little drinking and chitchat dulled the edge of our blades, he seemed no more concerned to begin serious business than I was.

I waited for a sign. After a while, he placed his cup on the table, looked me in the eye, and enquired,

"Master Leonardo, you have come here for a purpose. Please explain. What could that be?"

I was in the situation of a man requesting the gift of a pedigree horse with little to offer except being able to ride the animal round the yard. Such a gift would have to be stabled, nurtured, cared for. How could one achieve such a thing?

In a weak bargaining position, when asking for the earth, it is best to come straight to the point.

"Sir, it has been suggested you wish your daughter to marry. I come as a suitor for her hand. And, of course, for your permission."

He appeared disconcerted, face reddening, fingers trembling slightly. He glanced away and back again, his emotion not reined in.

He coughed as if his throat troubled him before whispering, in a somewhat croaky voice,

"You may have her, Master Leonardo. It is past the time to consider trifles such as your age and hers. Besides, my father's marriage to my dear departed mother was of similar kind."

Overcome by joy, I fell to my knees like a pilgrim in a shrine, seized his hand and kissed it.

Such a response discomforted him considerably, for he raised me to my feet and, muttering something about going to tell Francesca, left the room in haste.

He returned almost at once, then went out again, announcing he preferred after all to convey the news to his daughter himself.

IX

While Signor Pugliese was imparting his message to Lucia, I was greeted by Ludovico. In his boyish enthusiasm, he wheedled me to the study for a game of chess. So distraught were my nerves that after twenty-five moves I conceded defeat and set up the ivory pieces for a further contest.

Ludovico, sensing my lack of concentration, opted for additional sport. We played two more games, both of which I lost, and began another. Staring at the sunlit board caused my poor eyes to water, the squares shifting and dissembling in distorted perspectives.

At various moments I thought I heard raised voices. But the window was open to the noisy street. Nothing was certain.

It was a relief when Goffredo finally burst through the door with much brouhaha of "Where is he?" Having looked in the sitting room, and finding nobody there, he had concluded the suitor must have fled.

He was therefore most put out to discover the two of us innocently playing chess. Ludovico, having been harshly scolded for his participation, retreated in hangdog manner, pulling sulky faces.

I was left alone once more as Goffredo, consumed with irritation, ventured off again. This time his mission was to retrieve Lucia who, dismissed from her father's presence after my supposed departure, had retired to her bedchamber.

Their subsequent entry proved vivid, Goffredo grasping his daughter by the arm while murmuring in angry monosyllables.

Lucia's peerless eyes were rich with sadness, her cheeks dripping tears. She emitted a few racking sobs which could not signify happiness.

"She will marry in three weeks," said the merchant, "or later if you prefer."

"Let it be three weeks," I replied in a voice so tremulous it was scarcely my own.

I glanced at my beloved with a desire that proposed and resolved every question. She said not a word but nodded as if sentence of death had been passed.

"Lucia, what do you say?" I uttered, glimpsing Ludovico beyond the doorway. Tears were streaming in tragic profusion down his beautiful face, the first time I had ever seen him weep.

"The answer," snapped her father, "is *Yes*! Should we discuss matters further in the sitting room, Master Leonardo?"

Like a pariah I slouched out, taking care to look away from

Lucia and pretending to ignore Ludovico, who stared in my direction with extraordinary malevolence.

Goffredo patted me on the back as I brushed past while Francesca stood astride the hallway like a dragon guarding the gate. Unexpectedly she embraced me, whispering in my ear, "Thank you, Leonardo!" as if I was responsible for some kindness.

I did not have long to wait before Goffredo returned pell-mell, a man on urgent business. He shook my hand, bade me sit, and provided a cup of strong liquor which burned the throat and revived the heart.

"I must apologise," he said, "…the dowry!"

"It is of little significance…" I began. He brushed this aside like a man flicking away a troublesome wasp.

"Listen!" he replied. "There is a house provided for you. A dowry will be paid. *And* an allowance."

Goffredo rummaged in a drawer and handed me a bag. Whether this was dowry or allowance was not manifest.

I neither quibbled nor questioned but as soon as convenient took my leave. In a quiet side street I opened the bag. An array of fine coins caught the light, gleaming like gold and silver fish in a dark net.

X

During those weeks of preparation, like any man entering matrimony, I was busy. There was apparel to purchase and barbers trimmed my thinning hair.

The tailors were delighted at the prospect of good coinage for new garments, measuring my chest, shoulders, waist, arms, and legs, with due ceremony.

I visited a jewel merchant and, after much shilly-shallying, two gold rings, a necklace, and a bracelet were purchased. Content with my selection, I carried the treasures home with pride.

Concerning the forthcoming adventure, I felt excitement, my head full of Lucia and delights in store. I desired nothing but to have her till death us did part.

But the nights were long. It seemed as if she already lay beside me, that I had only to light a candle to see her. But when I shook my head awake and lit a taper, I was as solitary as a monk, the bare walls mocking my fantasies.

As if with a worm in my brain, I became a stranger to sleep, enduring the hours until first light filtered through the curtain.

XI

Whatever our doubts, time still runs. The appointed hour comes, the requisite number of dawns and dusks measure our path to the door of desire.

On the wedding day, I tried to rid myself of misgivings. I tidied my hair, examined my face in a mirror and polished my teeth till purified of all taint. Putting on and adjusting my new clothes with the utmost care, I waited impatiently for the hour of departure.

Previously I had packed up my belongings and dispatched them to our marital home, a stylish residence, equipped with carpets, curtains, paintings, furniture, and sundry extras, as well as various servants including a cook.

When, with much clattering of hooves on the cobbles, the coach arranged by Goffredo arrived, I asked the postillion to step down and remove all specks of dust adhering to my costume, to straighten my hat, and to give a rub to my new leather shoes.

With rings and jewellery safe beside me, I was taken at a fair trot to the Church of San Zeno, where a few guests already gathered. The most gaudy was Master John of Palermo, an exotic bird of prey, accompanied by Beatrice in purple silk.

It was well past noon when the bridal coach, ornamented with flowers and ribbons, came round the corner at a dignified pace.

I hastened to the church door, to be greeted by whispered blessings from the young priest.

XII

The memory chooses only a few moments as keepsakes, though not necessarily the things one wants to remember. In the muddy pool of recollection some memories float to the surface, others must be dredged forth by stirring to the depths with a long stick.

What has occurred since that day fogs my thoughts, causing the nuptials to fade distantly like ghosts.

I recall my bride's arrival clad in a pleated ankle-length dress, long sleeves, a bouquet of flowers and herbs tied with ribbons, her face more attuned to a wake than a wedding.

Goffredo gave away his daughter with an expression as neutral as a judge. Only the bridegroom appeared happy. Truth to tell, I felt as joyful as a songbird.

I remember the blessing of the rings and kneeling at the altar for Mass. In the carriage taking us to the celebrations, I kissed her mouth, her breath as pure as honey, though she held back a little in what I assumed to be natural shyness.

The feast was the usual confusion of people, speeches, food and wine, against a chorus of pipes, drums, lutes and all manner of loud voices, with greetings from Lucia's cousins, aunts, second cousins, and friends of the family.

Goffredo beckoned me to one side. He handed over the dowry money, the previous coinage apparently representing the first instalment of a generous allowance.

Following ceremony and cackle, we waved to the revellers. The coachman drove us to our new home where the servants were lined up to greet us on arrival.

A small meal was set out in the dining room, as if we had not stuffed ourselves enough already. Etiquette demanded we taste a little. The servants fussed round, plying us with tempting extras of cakes, nuts and fruit.

Lucia ate as daintily as a bird. I could not take my gaze from her.

But she deliberately prolonged her stay, whispering to the maidservant, smiling as if in response to some private jest from which I was excluded.

I waited with a hunter's patience for the quarry to emerge from the bramble.

Twelfth Letter

Concerning my marriage to Lucia, the arrival of the student Antonio, a meeting with the Emperor, and other diverse matters towards my life's close.

Al cor m'arde una doglia
com om che tene 'l foco ·a lo suo seno ascoso,
e quando più lo 'nvoglia
alora arde più loco e non po' stare incluso...

GIACOMO DA LENTINI (*fl.* 1200–50)

(My heart with sorrow burns inside
like a man who keeps fire hidden in his breast,
and the more he tries his sadness then to hide
the more it burns and cannot be at rest...)

Oi lasso! non pensai
sì forte mi parisse
lo dipartire da Madonna mia;
ca poi che m'alontai,
ben paria ch'eo morisse,
membrando di sua dolze compagnia...

FREDERICK II (1194–1250)

(Alas! I never thought one day
without my lady by my side
I would know such misery;
for since I went away,
it truly seems as if I died,
remembering her sweet company...)

I

Sire, My Most Esteemed Master Michael Theodorus,
Philosopher in the Service of His Majesty, Frederick II.

ventually Lucia was coaxed upstairs. The door closed. We stood as man and wife, in nuptial clothes, wearing our gold rings.

"I have gifts for you," I whispered. Her face in the lamplight was from another world, too lovely for this spoiled earth.

I drew my wife to me, intending to kiss her. But she remained curiously aloof.

"Gifts?" she asked, so quietly a ghost might have spoken.

I brought out the two jewel boxes containing the necklace and bracelet and opened them. The necklace glinted under the flickering tapers. Without taking the objects from their containers, she placed the boxes gently on the chest of drawers.

As she moved through the interplay of soft shadows and subdued light, her beauty was illuminated as if a master painter had caught her in an immortal frieze.

Not wishing to startle her, I caressed her hair. But after more touching and finding her at arm's length, I wearied of distance and swooped on the prey.

Though she protested, I laid her swiftly on the bed in the

creased wedding dress. Removing the garment from her shoulders, I feasted on those pastures and drank from her lips. I uncovered in haste the hills of her breasts, grasping their summits in turn with hands and mouth. At this she moaned, as if in pain.

I sought and found the buttons, laces, fastenings and trappings of her outer apparel, removing them, incensed by the embroidered lace, her perfumed skin, and the struggle to disrobe her.

Layers of silk clothing were cast to the floor till the prize was hidden by just one intimate item of clothing.

Discarding the remnants of my own attire, I fondled her with lips and fingers. She groaned, pushing at my head to avert such movements. This but further drove me on, my fingers savouring the feel of lace and flesh almost to the centre of the citadel itself.

It was but a moment to ease down the final impediment and clasp her groin. The heaven-sent ram forced the gates, causing her to shriek, and with a single thrust, penetrated.

Such was the allure of her milk-white thighs that almost too soon the seed pulsed. It was my turn to gasp with ecstasy.

I lodged in her until the grape shrivelled on the vine.

In gratitude, I kissed my bride with love and devotion, united in God's matrimony, which neither priest nor notary could now undo.

II

Separating from our embrace, she put on a nightgown. We made ourselves comfortable beneath a single sheet.

Lucia not desirous of further activity, reclined her head in a contrary direction, her dark hair flowing over the pillow. She said nothing, stifling tears and sobs.

Naturally all this and her proximity brought me to visit the well again. Having begun my advance, she attempted a muttered rebuff, claiming to be exhausted after the day's endeavours.

With scant heed I persisted, stroking her hair, face and neck, wandering beneath the rim of the nightdress to touch the warm swelling of her bosom.

In the end, to be thwarted no more, I compelled her to her back and lifted up her shift, concluding with an assault which culminated in satisfaction.

When, an hour later, my passion again ascended from whim to necessity, she surrendered with less complaint, pulling up her damp skirt and, having raised the portcullis, allowed entrance. There being no outgoing flood on this third errand, I had opportunity to explore the sacred palace, its limits, its gardens, its approaches, its everything.

Between much entering and exiting of the velvet mansion, I looked further afield, adoring with lips, eyes, and fingertips every aspect of her delights from head to toe.

Her damp nightgown discarded like a crumpled rag, she lay passive and mute, whimpering pitifully.

After so many unions with her perfect beauty, the stag had run its course.

Baptised in the moisture of the chase, I reposed my head on the pillow and, without dousing the tapers, stared up at the painted ceiling.

My wife wept gently beside me till sleep coaxed us both into oblivion.

⸎ III ⸎

When I woke, just after dawn, Lucia, her hair secured with a ribbon, was out of bed and in the far corner, bent over the chamber pot into which she coughed painfully.

I wrapped a gown round my unclothed body and went to comfort her.

"It must be the wedding food," I murmured, fondling her back. She shivered as if the Evil One had placed his hand upon her.

"Don't touch me," she said half choking. With another fit of straining, a yellow-green gruel of sickness flowed into the receptacle.

"My God!" I uttered. "You are ill. We must get a physician."

"Idiot!" she exclaimed, her head still down, her hands restraining her hair from pollution. "I thought you had been told!"

"Told?" I said. "About your illness?"

"Not my illness. But no matter…"

"I have been told nothing!" I replied.

She retched some more, a distasteful sound, signifying unhappiness as well as whatever it was.

"Let me help you," I urged, holding her arm.

"Don't touch me. Please!"

"What should I do?" I asked, putting on a gentle husbandly voice.

"Nothing!" she said. "Nothing at all! Everything has been done."

I sat down on the bed and, contrary to what I intended, burst into unmanly tears. Following the night's indulgences, my nerves jangled like an old harp hung up in the wind.

"I'm sorry. Forgive me." I said. "I'll kneel and ask forgiveness."

She stood like a warrior in front of me, her arms crossed, her lovely face pallid with anger or sickness.

"Forgiveness for what?" she asked, her voice heavy with contempt.

"For everything!" I said, "Everything."

She sat on the bed next to me. Weeping engulfed me as if from every pore of my skin. I felt her hand fall no heavier than a leaf on my arm. We sat there for a moment or two.

"Listen, Leonardo," she whispered in a solemn voice, "I too am sorry."

"What are you sorry for?" I asked. "For marrying an old man?"

"You're no older than many others," she said, though it was not much consolation.

"Then why apologise?"

"Because," she said firmly," perhaps we're all in the dark here."

I dried my eyes and turned to look at her, the symmetry of her features exquisite beyond compare.

"Tell me," I said, "how dark is dark?"

She laughed, the first time brightness had come to her.

"Darker than you think, but never as dark as it could be."

"Extraordinary," I said, "you should be a philosopher!"

"Have you," she enquired, "ever heard of a female philosopher?"

"I've heard of female witches!" I replied as a jest.

"I've met many a warlock in this life. They're just as evil as witches."

"If you have things to say," I said, "please tell me now, at the beginning, not later."

"Poor Leonardo. You're an innocent. You're not made for this world."

"Perhaps not. But I've lived in this world longer than you."

"Then how can you know so little? You have spent your years on the numbers. It has sharpened your mind but diminished your understanding."

"I understand as much as any man," I protested. "I've travelled much and seen much, yet I don't understand you. But I hope to."

A tear or two trickled down Lucia's face. I wiped them away with a gentle finger.

"I'm sorry!" I said once more. "For everything."

"It's not your fault," she replied, "it's in the stars, it's fate."

My heart heaved like an ocean for love of her.

"Can't we enjoy our fate, together?" I enquired.

"I don't love you," she answered, "and in that way, I never will."

It was a savage blow expressed in a sweet voice.

"But I love you!" I pleaded. "More than I've ever loved any woman."

"That I can't answer," she said. She hesitated, chancing a side-long glance as if to see if she dared say it. "But I've loved another. For that I am punished."

"Punished?"

"In a manner of speaking. You have saved my good name. Didn't Master John tell you?"

"Master John?" I said. "What is he to do with anything?"

"He was the go-between," she said. "He suggested you for my husband."

"I loathe that man more than I hate stinging insects or rats in filthy holes," I replied.

"Good!" she answered. "Yet you accepted his proposal."

I tried another question.

"So how did I save your good name?"

"By marrying me."

The equations did not match, solutions hidden behind clouds.

"I am a fallen woman."

"Fallen?"

"Into the deepest pit."

She was sitting upright now.

"I am with child!" she exclaimed, spitting out the poison, followed by an outburst of sobbing.

Lightning stabbed my heart. My marriage was a walk along a beaten path where others had gone before.

Her tempest of tears lasted for minutes. When her grief subsided, she looked up at me as if to assess the wounds gouged by her words. She saw only a blank board, a clean slate.

"For the love of God, say something!" she said.

I could not speak. Words stifled in the mouth. I could have vomited bile for an hour. But I did not and kept quiet.

"Will you send me back to my father?" she cried.

I shook my head, remembering Giovanna, betrayed into marriage. I made up my mind that instant.

"Let us be man and wife!" I blurted. "Those that know, will know. Those who do not, will know *nothing!*"

"Are you angry?" she said, throwing herself at my feet.

I raised her as I had when she bent over the pot. This time she did not shrink from my touch.

"I also have done things of which I am ashamed!" I confessed. "But I intend no shame here."

Lucia appeared relieved, even pleased. Lithe and youthful, she put her arms around me. I vowed to seek no details of this sorry state, neither her lover's name nor the circumstances.

We returned to bed and she yielded, mindful that I was her lawful husband.

Within locked doors what dreadful sins are committed in the name of matrimony. On the empty pages of that book I now began to write in my own vile script.

IV

Thus began, and so continued, our union. Whatever faults, disjunctions or other elements were revealed during the first weeks, increased in proportion thereafter.

The poor child in her womb, the cuckoo in our nest, grew apace, causing discomfort to its mother. Had it not been for that rising bump, *aide-mémoire* to the entire catalogue of our misfortune, my jealousy might have dissipated.

Moreover, Lucia suffered almost every ailment of a woman with child such as frequent urination, constipation, faintness, food cravings (she became obsessed with figs, yet her constipation remained severe), sore and swollen breasts, stomach cramps, nausea, rages followed by calm, weeping, lack of appetite, prostration and insomnia, the permutations being variable and the despair of physicians, midwives and especially myself.

Her beauty declined as the months crawled by, her features becoming fretful, puffy and peevish. Both of us were touched with a kind of madness, our fears and anguish resonating like a clown's toy drum.

With symptoms exceeding what even doctors considered the bounds of normality, before long she slept in a separate room.

Her maidservant bustled round with drinks, trays of food, sponges, towels, handkerchiefs, medicaments, and bowls of water, hurrying out with chamber pots, uneaten food, saturated sponges and towels, and water bowls to be refilled.

For the first month or so I availed myself of every pleasure, whether morning or afternoon and especially by night. She remarked how my vigour exceeded many a young man, touching off my jealousy, foul imaginings which could never rest.

Thoughts of unknown men incensed me. I fell into the lower fantasies, as if a leper had drunk from a golden goblet and I licked the dregs from the same cup.

Or was it the beggar with a single eye who had rutted astride her? The soldier clattering through the courtyard may have tasted her, implanting seed with his long lance. Or the young man, touching a lute, who sang for her while the duped husband listened.

Lucia scarcely tolerated sight or sound of me. Though she could embroider and dance, she possessed little learning. In this her father had neglected her education. As a consequence, Lucia despised the numbers.

Few callers came. We lived in solitude, serving our sentence in the castle of desolation which the state of matrimony so often becomes.

V

Amidst this wilderness, my *Book of Squares* struggled on.

I still hoped to conquer the territory into which Pythagoras and Euclid had ventured, admiring Aristotle's remark concerning Thales, that illustrious seer who traced numbers in the dust of Greece six centuries before the birth of Our Lord: *For Thales, the main question was not, WHAT DO YOU KNOW but HOW DO WE KNOW IT?*

Thales predicted eclipses, inscribed angles in semicircles and prophesied good harvests. Only Pythagoras, who said *ALL IS NUMBER*, may be compared with him.

I began with origins, discovering how square numbers come from an increasing sequence of odd numbers.

Consider how *ONE* represents *UNITY*. God is *ONE*, an undivided kingdom is *ONE*, man and wife are *ONE* and the earth itself is *ONE*. *ONE* is therefore the beginning of wisdom. Multiply *ONE* by *ONE*. The result is *ONE*. God remains *ONE*, through the *ONENESS* of man and wife, children are brought forth.

After *ONE* (the perfect square of itself when multiplied by *ONE*), we come to the next odd number, *THREE*.

THREE indicates the Blessed Trinity, the *THREE-IN-ONE*, the triple crown of the Holy Father, the *THREE* fingers when thumb and little finger meet across the palm.

Add *ONE* and *THREE* to enter the squares.

ONE multiplied by *ONE* is *ONE SQUARED*,

ONE added to *THREE* is *TWO SQUARED*.

Thus square numbers originate in this increasing sequence of odd numbers:

1+1= **ONE** SQUARED *(1)*
1+3= **TWO** SQUARED *(4)*
1+3+5 = **THREE** SQUARED *(9)*
1+3+5+7= **FOUR** SQUARED *(16)*
1+3+5 +7+9= **FIVE** SQUARED *(25)*
1+3+5+7+9+11= **SIX** SQUARED *(36)*
1+3+5 +7+9+11+13= **SEVEN** SQUARED *(49)*
1+3+5+7+9+11+13+15= **EIGHT** SQUARED *(64)*
1+3+5 +7+9+11+13+15+17= **NINE** SQUARED *(81)*
1+3 +5+7+9+11+13+15+17+19= **TEN** SQUARED *(100)*
1+3+5+7+9+11+13+15+17+19+21=**ELEVEN** SQUARED *(121)*
(etc.)

When I first approached this sequence, I was speechless, convinced this was in itself a small image of divine perfection.

But I could never persuade Lucia of the essential beauty in any of this. She could see nothing in it except a kind of coincidence or pretty patterns on the page.

VI

Eventually, after many setbacks, I completed my *Book of Squares,* dedicating the work to His Majesty, Emperor Frederick II, with the following *Prologue:*

Brought to Pisa by Master Dominick, to the feet of your most celestial Highness, Lord Frederick, I met Master John of Palermo. He proposed a problem which had occurred to him concerning geometry and arithmetic:

Find a square number from which,
when five is added or subtracted,
a square number always arises.

Beyond this problem, the solution to which I have found already, I realised, upon reflection, that this solution and others derive their origin from the squares and the numbers which fall between the squares.

When recently I heard from a report from Pisa and another from the Imperial Court that your Imperial Majesty had deigned to read the book I composed concerning the numbers, the Liber Abaci, and that you were pleased to attend to various subtleties relating to geometry and the numbers, I remembered the question proposed at your court by Master John of Palermo, your philosopher.

Thus I undertook this matter and began to compose in your honour this work entitled The Book of Squares.

I beg your indulgence if its pages contain something more or less than is correct or necessary; for to remember all things and never be mistaken is not human but divine and no one is wise in every respect or free from making mistakes.

Leonardo Pisano

ᘓᘏᕦᕤ VII ᕥᕣᘊᘋ

Yet in the midst of success came trouble. My wife seemed to believe, by virtue of the evidence of this book, that I was distraught, and prone to insanity.

With the obstinacy of an unschooled girl, she insisted all my scribbled figures were merely the doodlings of a man demented and possibly the work of the devil drawing me into madness.

Following a scholar's logic, I tried to demonstrate how the art of the numbers was sanity itself.

She responded that this line of reasoning was sufficient to prove beyond all doubt how I was truly out of my wits.

ᘓᘏᕦᕤ VIII ᕥᕣᘊᘋ

Her baby boy was born following painful labour. We baptised him, Luciano Pisano, at the very church where we were wed. From his birth I loved him. I had shared his mother's troubles. Having paid the price I wished to claim the prize of at least a partial state of fatherhood.

Lucia's body, injured by parturition, took time to heal, her spirit likewise. After a few weeks of suckling, her milk ran dry and a wet nurse was engaged. To see the babe at another's breast caused the mother anxiety. She disliked entrusting Luciano to a stranger's embrace but there was no other remedy.

The nurse, a simple creature of peasant stock, lived in an attic room, accommodating the feeding, changing, cleaning, crying and squealing. This left more congenial chores to the parents, such as dandling the child, clucking over his little tricks and gestures, and marvelling at his tiny feet and fingers.

Lucia and I fussed over the cot like any mother and father. She encouraged me to soothe him to sleep with a lullaby crudely hummed, jesting how I might enhance his slumbers by reading out a page or two of the *Book of Squares.*

When I pretended to do just this, reciting mathematical sentences, it was Lucia who fell asleep while the baby bawled and wriggled till I reverted to humming.

These omens boded well. Encouraged by a smile or two from her, I eventually made a foray into Lucia's room. She was displeased when I slipped naked between her sheets but my appetites were not to be denied indefinitely.

Once this precedent was established, my thirst quenched after months of deprivation, she was fair game. From then on I visited most nights before retreating to my own room to sleep soundly. Routine restored, my studies progressed apace.

With the passing of the months, Luciano became my very own. I loved him jealously, uniquely, beyond reason, just as I loved his mother.

IX

When the child was but ten months old, I received a letter from a certain Antonio, who wished to study the numbers. Considering from the extravagance of his letter that the student might prove to be another Euclid or Pythagoras, I overcame my reluctance and agreed to meet the young man.

Precisely at the appointed hour came a clanging of the bell at the gate. I was at my desk, well prepared. The servant tapped on the door and ushered in the new disciple. I rose to my feet, the young man bowed his head and murmured, "Thank you, Master."

I poured wine, we chatted. I was impressed for the youth was most affable, with fetching demeanour and calm voice.

Progressing to the numbers, his answers came back with speed and accuracy. He appeared to have ingested whole my *Liber Abaci*, presumably in some library, being able to quote from several chapters and produce solutions.

My face, I expect, betrayed not too much. But as the lesson advanced, compliments oozed from me till at last I shook him by the hand, expressing admiration. Just as Luciano was heir to my property, so this brilliant Antonio might one day inherit the legacy of my studies.

From that time forth I enjoyed several months of reasonable content, adoring Luciano, tutoring Antonio and making headway with my studies. For the latter, my new disciple helped as amanuensis and secretary.

After some weeks, I allowed Antonio to meet Lucia. She was modest and the young man reticent. Lucia remarked later on Antonio's handsomeness but only after I fished for opinions.

She expressed disdain at the fellow's cold manner which surprised me. That she found a flaw in Antonio's perfect armour seemed somehow satisfactory.

◆ X ◆

I had not forgotten Master John of Palermo though with all the busy minutiae of wedlock it had become easy to cast him from my thoughts. But one day he sent a gilded invitation summoning me to attend at the Court of Frederick II, who was travelling via Pisa en route to Palermo.

My commission was to address the distinguished gathering on my treatise before presenting the completed *Book of Squares* to His Majesty, the Emperor.

Lucia began talking of new garments and shoes to purchase for the banquet. To this purpose I handed over considerable coinage so she could bloom on that day like a perfect flower.

With Lucia's consent, I asked Antonio to accompany us for this occasion. The young man, visibly moved with gratitude, accepted the invitation almost on bended knee.

But his face clouded when I talked of the need to obtain apparel fit for the court. Realising his lack of means, I gave him more than enough silver pieces to improve his situation.

Naturally I acquired costly fresh raiment for myself. Lucia, at the first fitting of my fine clothes, exclaimed that this surely transformed me into a most distinguished personage.

When I paraded up and down like a vain courtier, speaking mock courtly jargon, she threw her head back and laughed, shouting that I needed no full moon to make me entirely mad.

⚜ XI ⚜

This mood shattered like a fragile bowl. Three days before the ceremony, Antonio wrote to inform me that his father was close to death. He emphasised his regret at this enforced absence from the Emperor's gathering. But filial duty demanded his immediate return to the family home.

Antonio omitted any reference to the money I had given him. Seeking Lucia's opinion, she advised that it would be inappropriate for his teacher to demand redress from a youth devastated by his father's imminent death.

So I put this to rest and made my own preparations. Court officials would send a carriage to take us through the city in royal style, my wife, of course, by my side. I looked forward to this opportunity to impress the citizens of Pisa, many of whom were reluctant to offer respect to scholars.

But even these arrangements were cruelly disrupted. On the morning of the ceremony, it transpired that Lucia was afflicted with cramps and bleeding.

Though I suggested taking a chance, she was adamant no sane person would appear before an Emperor doubled up in pain and leaking blood as she curtsied.

There was no remedy but to put on my finery, kiss Lucia and lift our son fondly out of his cot. Luciano startled by my unfamiliar garb, began a noisy tantrum and would not be quiet till put back on the pillow with his toys around him.

Subsequently I cut a pathetic figure alone in the coach and shrank down among the lush upholstery to avoid being seen. But few people seemed particularly interested in the Emperor's crested coach with its four white horses.

I crouched dejected, holding the manuscript, cheering up only when we set off into the countryside. Here the court had made its temporary lodgings in an aristocrat's mansion, erecting many splendid marquees for the ceremonies.

XII

My presentation of the treatise, in a massive tent crowded with arrogant noblemen, went as well as could be expected. I kept it fairly short, outlining the main features of only some of the twenty-four propositions.

Though my occasional attempts at humour were generally misunderstood, everybody laughed when a spare page from the manuscript fluttered like an escaped bird from hand to floor. The final applause was fulsome, perhaps in some relief that my speech was at last concluded.

The Emperor expressed both his appreciation and the sincere hope that some in the gathering might have grasped the details of the exposition more securely than His Majesty did himself. This was taken as a profoundly witty jest with every courtier guffawing without restraint for several minutes, each unwilling to be the first to cease.

But in his next comment, the Emperor awarded me an annual stipend in honour of my scholarship, an act of generosity which removed the self-righteous smiles from the faces of those who had previously mocked.

After all this we watched a display of juggling by Turkish acrobats, publicly rewarded with a show of coinage which they pretended to make disappear and reappear as if by magic. The court applauded with extravagant enthusiasm.

For how could a discourse on the mystery of squares and square roots ever compete with the manic frenzy of coloured balls and clubs, some of them spouting fire?

I was almost pleased that Lucia was not present for she would certainly have admired the acrobats more than my exposition.

The Emperor later afforded me a brief audition for private talk, accepting the Dedication, and promising publication of my treatise in due course once the scribes had finished producing two hundred copies of His Majesty's own book on falconry.

Furthermore he suggested I should thank Master John of Palermo for the commissioning of the treatise in the first place. Such a command seemed less than magnanimous for I had written the book through my own efforts. But in His Majesty's presence I could only be deeply grateful for any crumbs falling from the table and abide by his commands.

The Emperor thought he recalled our previous meeting, though he got both the date and the place incorrect, and announced his expectation of my attendance at court whenever it passed through Pisa or I happened to be in Palermo.

This I promised faithfully to fulfil.

⊰ XIII ⊱

The evening banquet was an event when a man could consider himself at the centre of the universe and on top of the world. The court of Frederick II travelled the length and breadth of sundry kingdoms, in each country sucking in the finest cuisine, the best wines, the fastest horses, the richest aristocrats, the most expert musicians, and courtesans of such beauty that they appeared like envoys from paradise itself.

Thus we dined on succulent cuts of venison, fish, and game, as well as dishes from Turkey and Arabia, suckling pig, ornamental cakes shaped like castles or palaces, and sweetmeats, all in abundance beyond belief.

In the dining tent, two hundred were seated at various tables, the Emperor's entourage at the furthest end just visible from where I was sitting.

Not too distant from the Emperor, Master John of Palermo and Beatrice sat in close proximity to Master Dominick who, years before, first brought me to court and to whom I am for ever indebted.

In their own corner sat a galaxy of aristocrats, some true gentlemen, courteous and *galant,* while others of their company could be unpleasant, talking in raucous voices and slyly ascertaining your rank before engaging in discourse.

Meanwhile a band of musicians performed, aided by a choir of women singing folk songs in plaintive tones, receiving spasmodic applause until the hubbub of conversation during eating drowned them out almost entirely.

The servants tempted us to a variety of wines and strong

spirits. At my table, many officials were gathered. To these, such dining was routine, tomorrow night, the night after, and so forth, there would be similar events. With the serving wenches offering more liquor, I soon found myself in merry humour. I continued sampling whatever was offered.

At the appropriate moment we all adjourned, following behind the Emperor's party, to arrive at a marquee where musicians were playing lively dances. The tent filled up and half a dozen couples prepared for the *saltarello*. More joined for the *carole*, a dance beloved by the French. A number of *espringales, reiens, hovetänze, estampies* and *stantipes* covered the ground with colour. Following a fanfare of trumpets, the Emperor danced, receiving fervent applause for his nimbleness.

Shortly after, the Emperor having been installed on a small throne, dancing was interrupted by more entertainment. This ranged from elaborate poems praising His Majesty to an Egyptian girl, accompanied by drums and flutes, who cavorted wonderfully, her gyrations almost exceeding the credible limits of nature.

Through excess of fine wine, my vision became as blurred as my speech. The gentry, also in their cups, seemed oblivious to my stupor though unknown friends continued to offer beverages it would have been churlish to refuse.

Some time after midnight, a flunkey announced my carriage was available. Revellers, kicking up their heels fore and aft, escorted me to the coach, helped me aboard and waved with many cheers as we departed into the night.

I sank sleepily into the velvet cushions, mulling over the finest day of my life.

❧❧ XIV ❧❧

Having arrived at a convenient point to disembark near our house, the postillion came respectfully to offer assistance for my return to *terra firma*.

After the rigours of the day I felt as deflated as a pig's bladder. My apparel, a perfect fit that morning, now seemed to hang heavily, causing me to perspire. The cloth's thickness prevented ventilation while a certain tightness afforded no margin for comfort.

I bade the coachman goodnight with a handful of coinage, slightly confused which way to go. It was late. No lights shone within my residence nor any other.

Nausea gripped me. Falling to my knees, I unleashed a tide through gullet and nostrils, choking to release the last dregs. Thus the Emperor's wine, and all the rest, were dished up for some dog to savour the next day.

After more gripes, I succeeded in approaching my own dwelling, the front door presenting itself in an unlocked state.

On stumbling through the entrance, how strange it was to discover every room devoid of light. Cursing, bumping into furniture, I began to shout.

By some miracle, I laid hands on a flint and lit the tapers, calling out meanwhile. My ridiculous garments hindering movement, the task began of tracking down every candle, lamp and taper, lighting wicks and flares as I went.

I found a temporary haven in the drawing room, where, sprawled on a couch, I paused to wipe my evil-tasting mouth on the ornate sleeve. It seemed they must all have taken opiates for my cries and blundering seemed not to have disturbed a single soul.

I thought of Lucia. Desirous of telling her about my adventures, I eased up the stairs, illuminating my progress with inept flicking of the flint.

Her bedroom door was closed but I thrust it open, the light from the corridor falling on her bed. Except that she was not in it.

Caution cast to the wind, I bellowed, "Lucia! Lucia! Lucia! where are you?" calling till the sickness returned, compelling me to slump on the bed for respite.

By the light of a candle, I ventured to the wet nurse's room, where the baby slept. This room too was empty.

Puffing with the climb, ready to vomit forth, I rested, face in hands. Some catastrophe must have dragged my wife away. Either her bleeding had worsened or the baby was sick and they were visiting the caring nuns.

Like a blind man I groped my way downstairs, the halls and rooms shadowy and unreal. Ensconced once more on the familiar couch, I poured wine, its taste repellent, and racked my addled brain for solutions to the mystery.

Not wishing to wait till morning, I decided to enquire of the neighbours. I picked a path to the opposite dwelling, avoiding the mess in the road, and banged on their door, ringing the bell many times.

As dim lights were lit, I increased the noise, shouting also. In the distance, dogs began a growling chorus, rousing others. After loud enquiries from within as to who I was, the neighbour opened his door the width of a man's thumb.

When I blurted out how my house was deserted, he hissed that it was nothing to do with him and moreover I was frightening his children.

As a last resort, he opened the door fully, stepped out, looked up and down the street, and asked whether any messages had been left in my house. Whereupon, with a firm 'goodnight', he went back inside, bolting the door securely.

I knocked on the doors of several other houses. Each request met the same sleepy response. Nobody knew anything, the matter should be dealt with tomorrow.

As I retreated across the street, an old man hobbled from the shadows, attired in tasselled nightcap and a long gown. It was Luigi, a former wheelwright before rheumatism crippled his hands, with an inquisitive nose longer than a camel's neck.

He loved to spy and could be seen daily at his window. He hoped I would not think him an interfering busybody, which is what he was, but claimed to know something of value.

I ushered him into the reception room where he doffed his cap revealing a bald head. His amazement at our carpets, paintings, tapestries, and furniture was evident though he expressed regret that my expensive clothes were dirtied on one sleeve and down the front.

I poured wine to loosen his tongue.

⚜XV⚜

Luigi had seen the carriage with the Emperor's crest arrive that morning. Did I know a man in another carriage drew up an hour later? Did I know that this man entered the house?

Luigi's method of offering information by means of posing questions was, I suppose, a form of politeness.

The upshot of his tale was that 'the man' went to the carriage bearing luggage, blankets and a cushion or two. After an interim, the Signora emerged with baby and maidservant. The carriage set off in a northerly direction.

At that moment, Luigi had left his own dwelling to take a closer look. In so doing, he encountered Gerardo, our cook, one of his regular drinking companions.

I refilled Luigi's cup when he gazed mournfully into its emptiness. He leaned forward, dropping his voice as if confessing to a priest. The cook had coughed up a tale garnished with bile. The substance of it, filtered through Luigi, shrivelled my heart.

It was said that the Signora always intended to 'elope' with this young man. Known as Antonio, he was greatly admired by the servants.

My face remained, I hope, a mask of indifference.

I poured more wine.

Luigi, becoming absorbed in his tale, added that the servants had been paid off at short notice. Gerardo observed much coinage in the mistress's purse.

Though Luigi's method of telling a tale was discursive, at times confused, by the end his message achieved sufficient clarity. The fragments of his narrative constituted a fable of dire consequence.

After a while he began repeating himself. I ceased listening to his actual words, taking in only the dreadful coherence of the gist of his story.

Every epic eventually ends. Luigi, having downed his drinks, replaced the nightcap on his head as a sign of conclusion. I passed a few coins over and thanked him.

Putting finger to forehead in a parodic salute, he scuttled away. I brooded for a while, drinking cup after cup, sober with fury.

At first light I discovered I was somehow upstairs on my bed, fully dressed, having soiled my clothes, in a house where no woman sang and no baby cried.

XVI

In every town there are men who will do almost anything for coinage. I knew one or two of them. Next day, I went to some of these rascals and put a proposition to them.

It was straightforward – to discover the whereabouts of an absconding wife with her male companion. I did not delve into detail but gave them the bare bones of the situation.

They seemed pleased to get such work. Pursuit of errant lovers was meat and drink to them. They suggested a price, to which I consented.

In Pisan society opinion was divided. Some offered a measure of sympathy, others scoffed. Master John of Palermo sent a letter of condolence lamenting the fickleness of women and the harshness of my fate.

More to the point, Lucia's father showed kindness, expressing regret at what had come to pass. Signor Pugliese assured me he had no prior knowledge of his daughter's intentions, avowing that for him, as for me, the sad event came like a bolt from the blue.

Despite such assurances I was left feeling he knew more than he said. But I was too weary to demand further information, or attempt to force his hand.

Some weeks later the hired ruffians called. They assured me that Antonio had disappeared without trace. Of the whereabouts of Lucia and the child nothing could be verified.

I was displeased with these wisps of nothingness, rumours, fables, fabrications, and bursts of hot air.

When their testimony was disputed they became contentious, showing their true nature.

Fearful for my safety, I was forced to pay the agreed fee and expenses without receiving a moment of comfort or sure knowledge of circumstances.

XVII

I have become reconciled to loneliness. Through accident or folly, every beloved woman of consequence has been lost to me. And now also Lucia, my erstwhile wife, unbearably beautiful in face and form, whom I was so fortunate to have and to hold for a moment. Her remembered face haunts me.

I beg forgiveness for the evil I brought upon her, and pardon any wrongs she inflicted in return.

It was the numbers which offended. Lucia regarded my science as a kind of madness. Such learning is indeed unfathomable to those outside the magic circle.

Moreover she was young and headstrong. A solitary husband, locked in silence for many hours in pursuit of the ineffable, could never have been to her liking.

That she came to hate me for my love of the squares and to believe how, on this account, my mind became unhinged, was in itself somehow logical.

I must allow her that measure of reasoning.

ᴇ꒰ᴇ XVIII ꒱ᴇ

Since the moment she left I have loved her more each day. Her loss is the cross I bear, that I drove her away, and all could have been different.

The world has my books, I have my conscience. I suffer for things done and not done.

I must sleep soon and in that sleep neither guilt, dreams nor logic will wake me. I await the longest night unprepared, unshriven, unforgiven, for I have no stomach to speak with priests.

Of late, severe infirmities afflict me. Ills have crept upon me in abundance since my beloved Lucia departed.

My sight is poor, I hear sounds in my ears like rustling parchment, my bowels are unreliable, pain crushes my chest, knees and ankles ache, my knuckles are enlarged, the fingers puffy, my hands shake.

Physicians are of no help though they take fees for useless medicaments, drawing blood from legs and arms to release bad humours.

Already I am forgetful.

Soon, remembering nothing, I shall be nothing.

Scholars may remember something of my work.

I pray that what I scribbled in the dusty books may not be too quickly forgotten.

Letter from Lucia
to her father Goffredo

From Lucia, To my dear father, Goffredo Pugliese.

A thousand thanks, dear father, for your letters and for your timely avoidance of evil to myself and my precious son by means of your intervention, rescuing me from the madness of poor Leonardo.

It is fortunate you were able to intercede, subverting with bribes those whom, in his jealous wrath, Leonardo Pisano enlisted to find us. As you arranged, I met them at the rendezvous. They seemed decent fellows, drawn into evil ways by poverty and need. They willingly carried back to Leonardo many false messages. By such means I made my escape secure and so am released from bondage.

I am living in Rome in the house which you so generously provided for me. My unhappy marriage was annulled on the evidence you gathered. Your distinguished friends in the Vatican courts helped to expedite the tedious legal processes. My heartfelt gratitude for the monthly stipend you send and the money to purchase necessary things.

I have to tell you that Antonio's scholarship is reaping good dividends, not only in diverse business transactions but also in securing a reputation within the university. He has many students for which he is well rewarded.

Though I have not yet made up my mind, it is possible one day I may consent to marry Antonio. He swears by all that is sacred and true that he fell in love with my beauty at our first meeting. Through this affection his eyes and ears were open when, after secret visits to our house during Leonardo Pisano's absences, I confided in Antonio concerning my husband's dubious sanity.

For reasons of the love he professed, Antonio laid plans to rescue me from despair. Eventually I may grant him his just reward. But for now I remain a kind of widow, betwixt and between, content to see him, but unwilling to enter into a further binding contract.

Antonio, like Leonardo, is a scholar of the numbers. I cannot but think there is an amount of devilry in these mysteries. I shall wait before committing myself to see what transpires. Perhaps Antonio will retain his common sense as well as his avowed love for my person. We shall see. I cannot keep him waiting too long for my answer. He believes that of my own free will I may soon say yes, and yes again. But it will not happen just yet.

I often think of poor Leonardo. Though unbearable in his moods, yet there was good in him. He was devoted to the child. But the numbers and hours of meditation on insoluble problems drove him out of his mind. I understood not a word of his ramblings. His strange passion for me seemed to increase his affliction.

I too am selfish and headstrong. In the end, I did him great wrong for which I pray daily for divine forgiveness. Certainly, I am content enough away from his confines but I will never pardon myself entirely for what passed between us. But when black contrition falls upon me, I think of the manifestations of his disability and the matter is resolved.

I hope to see you all at my residence soon. Luciano is thriving and beautiful. He likes to play in the garden among the flowers and is a happy child.

Greetings and blessings to my beloved mother and dear sweet brother.

Your daughter,

Lucia

Letter from
Master Michael Theodorus
to Master John of Palermo

To Master John of Palermo
from Master Michael Theodorus, in Cairo, Egypt.

Esteemed Master John,

Stung by a noxious insect I am ill with a fever from which my physicians expect no recovery. The heat and smell of this room increase discomfort. From the street there is much noise. But it will not be long before my suffering ceases for ever.

I have bequeathed my belongings to scholars here in Egypt. They have no wealth but are rich in learning.

I have a request, dear Master John. In the haste of departure from Europe, I neglected to commit certain documents to the Imperial Library. They are kept in a writing desk in my house. My servant will give them to you for preservation in the Emperor's Archives. They include diverse philosophical papers and some trivia to be destroyed, according to your judgement.

However, most precious are various letters from Master Leonardo Pisano, great scholar and admired friend, who departed this mortal life only a short time ago.

Within these epistles, Master Leonardo presents the narrative of his early years, his travels, studies, and diverse experiences. Generations to come will enjoy these tales whether they be entirely true or partly false, or the essence of memories seasoned with the spice of imagination.

Such work is rare. Master Leonardo was a genius of the numbers yet his worldly reminiscences will surely also enlighten posterity. To the prudish some confessions may seem excessively detailed. But their true value is as unique as the lost journals of Euclid or Pythagoras – if only we could rescue such treasures from time's oblivion.

I have no more strength. Dear Master John, please collect the papers from my house and deliver them to the Chief Scribe to be preserved as honoured texts in the Imperial Archives.

The Emperor Himself will wish to peruse Master Leonardo's miraculous adventures, tragic though the ending of the tale may be.

Affectionate wishes to your beloved wife, Beatrice, whose beauty inspired us all.

It has been a good life. Pray for me.

Farewell, dear friend.

Yours into eternity,

Michael Theodorus of Antioch

Postscriptum: It may be that Master Leonardo made a further copy of his epistles for he was meticulous in all things.

Letter from Master John of Palermo
to Emperor Frederick II

To My Esteemed Lord, His Imperial Majesty, Emperor Frederick II, from His Humble Servant, Master John of Palermo.

Sire. It is my sad duty to inform His Majesty of the decease of Master Michael Theodorus of Antioch. This followed the passing of Master Leonardo Pisano, some months earlier.

His Majesty may recall when Master Dominick and myself had the privilege to introduce Master Leonardo to Court, and your graciousness in publishing, at great expense to the state coffers, his two dissertations, Liber Abaci and Liber Quadratorum, both dedicated to Your Imperial Highness. As I was his Patron, Master Leonardo frequently enjoyed my hospitality, seeking advice on diverse matters. I believe myself to be as well acquainted with Master Leonardo as any person in Christendom. His passing causes me insupportable grief.

It now appears that Master Leonardo wrote a number of letters to Master Theodorus. In these documents Master Leonardo was most respectful of myself. I have therefore no cause to find fault with such epistles concerning my own reputation. Consequently any action I undertook in regard to these papers was done with good intentions, to ensure that Master Leonardo's reputation remains eternally unsullied by misunderstanding or slander.

Some of the epistles written by Master Leonardo may however be considered grounds to annoy, offend, subvert, deprave, and disgust any Christian who has the misfortune to read them. Among them Master Leonardo admits to crimes and follies of his youth such as complicity in a sailor's death at sea and the murder of a nomad in the deserts of Syria.

Master Leonardo was also subject to lewdness including sinful intercourse with nomad whores, incest with his stepsister, and (oh the abomination!) unnatural desires for a cabin boy as well as similar perversions against a bastard nomad boy (whom he claimed blasphemously to have raised from the dead), in addition to a rampant infatuation with his wife's brother, his pupil.

Added to this catalogue of Master Leonardo's misdemeanours is clear evidence (and his own statement of guilt) concerning the theft of public money belonging to the State from the customs house in Bugia, and his acceptance of bribes to betray his stepsister into marriage with an aristocrat of dubious character.

More recently, the smell of scandal lingered round his marriage with the daughter of a rich merchant. When Master Leonardo sought my counsel with regard to the arrangement of that union, I advised against it. But Master Leonardo, as always, went his own way. This brought about the ruin of his wife and himself.

To ensure that Master Leonardo's attributes are revealed to posterity only through his treatises on mathematical problems, I have forthwith committed these corrupt epistles to the furnace. I regret such cleansing was necessary but can comfort myself that disgrace has been avoided and Master Leonardo's good reputation maintained. It is possible copies of the letters may exist elsewhere. I shall search diligently, for these also must be expunged.

I wish to express my humble gratitude for the preferment bestowed on my person by Your Esteemed Highness, namely the award of a most generous increase in my annual stipend.

Your ever faithful, obedient servant,

John of Palermo

Also by Graham Wade

Joaquín Rodrigo – A Life in Music
Joaquín Rodrigo – Concierto de Aranjuez
A Portrait – Joaquín Rodrigo, His Works, His Life
Distant Sarabandes – The Solo Guitar Music of Joaquín Rodrigo
*A New Look at Andrés Segovia, His Life, His Music,
Volumes 1 & 2* (with Gerard Garno)
Segovia – A Celebration of the Man and His Music
Maestro Segovia
Gina Bachauer – A Pianist's Odyssey
The Art of Julian Bream
John Mills, Concert Artist – A Celebration
Traditions of the Classical Guitar
Your Book of the Guitar
A Concise History of the Classic Guitar
The Classical Guitar – A Complete History
(thirteen essays by Graham Wade)
The Guitarist's Guide to Bach
The Shape of Music
A Concise Guide to Understanding Music

Mother and Other Poems
War Baby and Other Poems
In Whim or Design
Frog and Other Poems
Sea Poems
Wedding and Other Poems
American Suite and Other Poems

Joaquín Rodrigo – A Life in Music
(Travelling to Aranjuez 1901-1939)

My family and I believe that this is the book which needed to be written and that it will generate an enormous interest in both the music and the life of Joaquín Rodrigo. CECILIA RODRIGO,
MARQUESA DE LOS JARDINES DE ARANJUEZ

Every aspect shows the author's sensitivity and meticulous attention to content as well as presentation. There is certainly nothing comparable to this work in Spanish. KATHERINE ZEGARRA,
EDICIONES JOAQUÍN RODRIGO, MADRID

A major achievement and deserving of a wide audience.
WILLIAM YEOMAN, GRAMOPHONE

Author Graham Wade has become the composer's Boswell...Rodrigo's fascinating life story comes shining through...the Rodrigo lover's jackpot.
PHILIP CLARK, BOOK OF THE MONTH, CLASSIC FM MAGAZINE

A substantial contribution to our knowledge of Rodrigo and 20th century music...It is guaranteed an honoured place on the shelf reserved for music biography. COLIN COOPER, CLASSICAL GUITAR

Enter the tireless author, teacher and guitarist, Graham Wade, to tell a story of even more tireless determination to succeed. And the music in all its unfamiliar range is the heart of Wade's mammoth undertaking, the first in English.
ROBERT MAYCOCK, BBC MUSIC

This first biography of Rodrigo in English is further testament to Graham Wade's seemingly inexhaustible energies...a terrific tale...a revelatory read.
ANDREW GREEN, CLASSICAL MUSIC

A New Look at Segovia, His Life, His Music,
Volumes 1 & 2 (with Gerard Garno)

The most remarkable piece of classical guitar scholarship we are ever likely to see. BRENDAN McCORMACK,
INTERNATIONAL GUITAR FESTIVAL OF GREAT BRITAIN

Segovia – A Celebration of the Man and His Music

Graham Wade has spent a generous amount of time putting together this book in praise of 'my first' 90 years. My gratitude corresponds faithfully to his noble intention and the arduous work accomplished...I hope that this lively and affectionate book will be received with the appreciation and success it merits.

ANDRÉS SEGOVIA

Gina Bachauer – A Pianist's Odyssey

I treasure every page of this fascinating biography, a beautiful testimony of love and admiration of both the human being as well as the artist who has left us with so much to enrich our lives.   IRENE, PRINCESS OF GREECE

This book provides an excellent record of a unique life.

SIR EDWARD HEATH

I know of no biography of any pianist - not even the greatest in the world – whose life, both musical and personal, has been chronicled in such illuminating detail. No music lover in the world could fail to enjoy every page of this vivid story.   JOAN CHISSELL

The Art of Julian Bream

Graham Wade is the ideal writer to undertake the task of writing a detailed book about the musical achievements of our most celebrated guitarist...This book is surely indispensable to anyone who values the work of Julian Bream... It comes off successfully, even triumphantly, and will be the definitive book on Julian Bream for a long time to come.   COLIN COOPER,
CLASSICAL GUITAR

This eminently readable and quite fascinating book, superbly and generously illustrated, is most enthusiastically recommended.

ROBERT MATTHEW-WALKER,
INTERNATIONAL RECORD REVIEW

This is a delightful book, for reading or for reference...It will surely be a 'must' for Bream's innumerable fans and for all those interested in the guitar in the twentieth century.   DAVID GRIMES, SOUNDBOARD

Traditions of the Classical Guitar

Graham Wade has shown his love of the guitar from the first page to the last – true love and understanding.   ANDRÉS SEGOVIA

The most important recent publication of the last few years...The first stylistic critique of guitar music from the beginning through all the centuries.
JÜRGEN LIBBERT, NEUE MUSIKZEITSCHRIFT

The Shape of Music

I know of no book like this on the subject of music: and apart from the wealth of information which it contains, it is every bit as absorbing as a work of popular general literature on any subject.   MALCOLM WILLIAMSON,
MASTER OF THE QUEEN'S MUSIC

Mother and Other Poems

Graham Wade's best are his tragic poems, which is rare for most incitements to pity by modern verse-writers are mere sentimentality...His poems have the true pathos of the soul.   KATHLEEN RAINE

www.ingramcontent.com/pod-product-compliance
Lightning Source LLC
Chambersburg PA
CBHW030931020726
47498CB00001B/196